Love Finds You™ in Mackinac Island, Michigan

Love Finds You™ in Mackinac Island Michigan

Melanie Dobson

Summerside Press™
Minneapolis, MN 55378
www.summersidepress.com

Love Finds You in Mackinac Island, Michigan

ISBN 978-1-60936-640-7

Scripture references are from The Holy Bible, King James Version (KJV).

The town depicted in this book is a real place, but all characters are fictional. Any resemblances to actual people or events are purely coincidental.

Cover Design by Koechel Peterson & Associates | www.kpadesign.com
Interior design by Müllerhaus Publishing Group | www.mullerhaus.net
Photos of Mackinac Island provided by Melanie Dobson.

Summerside Press™ is an inspirational publisher offering fresh, irresistible books to uplift the heart and engage the mind.

Printed in USA.

Dedication

To my beautiful Haitian sisters

God has not forgotten you
and neither have we.

THE RESORT ISLAND NESTLED INTO A STRAIT BELOW MICHIGAN'S UPPER Peninsula is known by many names. *Fairy Island. Land of the Giant Turtle.* And my personal favorite—*The island that time forgot.*

From the moment I stepped off the ferry and heard the clip-clopping of horses' hooves along the island's historic Main Street, I was transported back a good hundred years. Pronounced "Mackinaw" like Mackinaw City (but spelled differently so the post office could differentiate between the island and town), Mackinac Island is a place that time did indeed seem to forget.

Even today, Mackinac Island reflects an era when the wealthy and their servants escaped the heat and grime in cities like Chicago and Detroit to enjoy natural spring waters and cool lake breezes. It was an era when women wore beaded gowns and plumed hats and twirled parasols in their gloved hands, when people were just beginning to talk about horseless carriages as they rode in their own horse-drawn carriages to an elaborate ball at the Grand Hotel or to an afternoon tea at what their neighbors would call a "cottage"—a residence that more closely resembled a castle. A nineteenth-century writer once said that the island was so healthy, a person had to leave Mackinac to die.

Mackinac Island hasn't swung far beyond the era of the Victorians, and both residents and visitors alike savor the past. Its diverse history goes back hundreds of years, when Native Americans considered the island the home of their Great Spirit and local tribes gathered there each summer to fish. In the 1700s, lucrative French and American fur companies made their homes and millions of dollars on Mackinac until the British took over during the War of 1812 and held the island for three years before returning it to the United States.

Then, in 1819, the first steamship of tourists arrived.

The main island trade, locals like to say, has evolved over the years from fur (and fishing) to fudge. The tradition of making fudge on Mackinac began after the Civil War, and more than ten thousand pounds are now made on the island each year, with flavors such as chocolate macadamia, rocky road, vanilla pecan, and raspberry truffle.

While almost a million visitors converge on Mackinac for six months of the year, only about five hundred people call the island home during the winter, when the only transportation to the mainland is by small plane or snowmobile ride along the Ice Bridge—a route across the frozen lake marked by discarded Christmas trees.

Horseless carriages are still banned on Mackinac Island, but there are seventy miles of roads and trails to explore by bicycle, carriage, foot, or by renting one of the island's six hundred horses. Mackinac is filled with natural wonder—forested hills, bluffs that climb three hundred feet above the shore, pebbly beaches, towering rock spires, an arched rock perched high above the lake, and hidden caves. The country's second national park was established on half the island in 1875 (Yellowstone was the first). There are more than a hundred varieties of lilacs on the island, and locals say their scent overpowers the smell of horses when summer dawns.

The historic Grand Hotel is just as grand today as it was when visitors came for weeks or even months at a time to hear the hotel's renowned orchestra play on the world's longest summer porch. More than a hundred years later, it remains the world's longest summer porch.

Let's go together, shall we, to explore the beauty and wonder of Mackinac.

The island forgotten by time.

—Melanie Dobson

I have loved the stars too fondly to be fearful of the night.

Galileo Galilei

November 6, 1812

Where are you, Jonah?

Four days I've prayed day and night for your return. Four days I've listened for your whistle outside our windows, for the sound of your footsteps as you walk through the door. But everything has been quiet, terribly so.

The children and I, we haven't left the lighthouse. And we won't, not until I find out what's happened to you. I burn the lamp at night for you, hoping you will see it and return in the darkness.

If only I knew where you went.

If only I knew when you would come home.

Please God.

Please send my husband home.

Chapter One

June 1894

Wind gusted over the bow of the *Manitou* and whistled under the canopy of her deck. Below the deck, a pipe organ entertained those women who wouldn't think of mussing their hair or wrinkling their beaded gowns as the steamer maneuvered through the Straits of Mackinac. The deck was crowded with men smoking cigars and talking about whether their fine country would recover from the utter failure of the economy.

Elena Bissette wasn't talking with the men. She stood against the railing and clung to the organza band that encircled her new hat, trying to keep it from drowning in the choppy waters that marked the juncture of Lakes Michigan and Huron. Strands of light brown hair tangled around her face, and she tried unsuccessfully to secure them behind her ears with her gloved fingers. The breeze tugged at her hair like a child wanting to play, but she couldn't join in. Not until she was alone.

Jillian had put up Elena's hair an hour ago, pinning it neatly into an elegant French twist. Her hair would be a disaster by the time they reached Mackinac Island—and so would her mother, once she saw Elena's hair. When Mama emerged onto the deck, Elena knew exactly what she would say.

Elena Ingrid Bissette. Her mother's fists would ball up against her wide hips. *You're not supposed to be outside in the wind. You're supposed to be in the stateroom until our arrival, waiting with your father and me.*

The admonitions raged louder in Elena's mind, drowning out the roar of the wind and waves.

What if he saw you like this, Elena? What would he do?

Mama would snap her fingers. *He'd move on to the next girl. Just like that. And there will be plenty of young ladies on Mackinac this summer, plenty of pretty girls.*

Tears would follow in perfect dramatic time, just a few of them to inspire the necessary dose of guilt. Then her mother would lean even closer.

Are you trying to ruin what's left of our lives?

Elena laughed in spite of herself. As if tangled hair could ruin the Bissette family name.

She batted the hair out of her eyes, trying to get a view of the island. Elena wasn't trying to ruin anyone's life—her mother was perfectly capable of doing that on her own.

Nor did she care what *he* thought of her, not one bit. In fact, she almost wanted him to see her like this, with disheveled hair and tangled pink ribbons. Then they wouldn't have to waste their time on all the calling and courting. Once he got to know her, she was certain he wouldn't propose.

"I see the hotel," said one of the gentlemen beside her on the crowded deck. He held up his binoculars and pointed at the lump of an island on the port side. Neither he nor any of the men around her seemed the least bit concerned about their hair.

The white columns of the Grand Hotel's wide veranda came into view as it sat perched up on the western bluff. The late morning sun glimmered against the endless rows of windows, beckoning the island's guests through its elegant doors.

Almost every June during Elena's nineteen years, the Bissette family flocked to the island and, ultimately, to the Grand Hotel for its dances, banquets, and elaborate balls. They mingled with other members of the higher society in Chicago and Detroit as well as hundreds of people desperate to climb the ranks.

Her family had once held a high rung on this ladder, but their position had fallen with the collapse of the economy. Invitations to dinners and dances had tapered off in Chicago, and if her mother's plans didn't

succeed, this would be her family's last year of summering on the island. And probably their last year of mingling with Chicago's elite.

A seagull dipped in front of the boat, as if he knew she wanted to play. If only she could grasp onto his wings and fly with him. At the moment, she wasn't particular as to where they would go. Just someplace far away.

The steamer cruised past the hotel and toward the harbor at the southern tip of the island. Elena's long skirts swayed with the wind, rocking as the steamer bumped over the strait. A gentleman edged into the crowd beside her, leaning over the rail with his gray bowler hat in hand.

She felt his eyes upon her, and when she glanced over at the blue laughter in them, her own smile froze. Even in his silence, she knew that Oliver Parker Randolph III was teasing her.

Parker grinned at her and pointed at the island with the hat. "She's a beaut, isn't she?"

Elena closed her eyes to him and the breeze. She'd managed to ignore him through the ship's dinner hour last night and then during the entertainment hour of music and magic afterward. If she pretended he wasn't here now, perhaps he would vanish like the toad in the magician's box.

But Parker didn't go away. She felt him turn toward her instead.

She scrunched her eyes even tighter, wishing again for that magic box.

"You can't ignore me forever, Lanie."

Elena cringed at the name he'd picked for her a decade ago, but she refused to acknowledge him.

Parker tapped her hand on the railing, and she snapped it back. But even as she hid her hand in her skirts, she knew it was useless. No matter how hard she tried, ignoring Parker Randolph would only make him more determined to get her attention.

Her eyes still closed, she spoke to the wind. "You're not supposed to be talking to me."

"Says who?"

"Your mother, and probably your father as well."

"Ah." Parker paused, and for a moment, she thought he had left.

She stole a glance to her left, but he was still there, watching her. "They're being ridiculous."

"It doesn't matter."

He rested his elbows on the railing. "We are going to be friends again this summer, Lanie. Wait and see."

Elena turned her face from Parker and scanned the harbor and village beyond. It had taken her mother mere days to concoct a new plan for the summer, one that no longer involved Parker Randolph or his family. Mama had set her sights on someone much wealthier and more powerful than the Randolphs. Someone with far better connections.

White-winged yachts and sailing boats were moored on both sides of the pier. On the hill above the harbor, a stone wall surrounded the imposing Fort Mackinac. To the right of the fort, settled among the cedar and pine trees of the eastern bluff, was a row of summer cottages.

The word *cottage* usually implied a small bungalow of sorts, but there was nothing small about the cottages on Mackinac Island. Owners took great pride in their palatial cottaged mansions, designing each house a little bigger than the last so theirs would stand out among the others. Some houses had massive white columns that made them look as if they had been imported from the Greek isles. Others were layered with porches and towers and exhibited ornate designs on the eaves. Some were stained dark while others were painted white or yellow. Papa had named their cottage Castle Pines, and she could see its white turret towering above the trees.

The wind eased as they drew closer to the pier. She eyed the dozens of men in blue dress uniforms below them. "Where are the soldiers going?"

Parker turned around, placing his bowler hat on his head. "Now don't you worry, there will be plenty of men left on the island."

"I wasn't worried—"

A gunshot blasted through the sound of wind, and Elena hopped away from the railing. Even after all her summers on Mackinac, she still jumped at the cannon salute that greeted them at the pier.

Parker leaned back on the railing, his elbows resting on the wood.

"You think the British are shooting at us?"

She straightened her hat. Parker knew very well that the British hadn't occupied the island since 1815, when the second war of independence ended. "I don't think any such thing."

He winked at her, and she wanted to push him overboard. He knew the gunshots frightened her, but he also knew as well as she did the importance of minding one's tongue. People in their circle didn't dare show a hint of weakness or insecurity.

As she straightened her skewed hat, Elena checked her silver hatpins to make sure they were still in place. Often she felt like an actress, living each hour on a stage for everyone to see. Every moment of the Bissette script was like a scene from a play, except that there was no final act, no standing ovation. The curtain rarely came down on the theater of her life.

For the next two months, she'd be paraded like a show horse while attending teas and dances and social events. But in the midst of all the socializing, she would escape for a few nights to her own refuge hidden away on the island, a place where she could step off the stage.

The gun blasted two more times.

Parker moved even closer to her. "There's nothing to be nervous about, Lanie."

She nudged her nose a bit higher in the air. "I told you, I'm not worried."

The steamer slowed beside the pier, and the first mate roped a post, pulling the boat close. A bell rang out, and a few of the soldiers waved up at them. Elena waved back, more to ignore the man next to her than anything else.

She almost wished she could stow away on the boat and return to Chicago.

"There you are!"

Elena turned to watch Mama's stately eyes constrict at the sight of Elena's tousled hair around her shoulders. Mama's mouth dropped ever so slightly.

A stranger might not notice the sag in her mother's jaw or the lines forming around her eyes, but Elena prepared herself for the inquisition. Mama saw Parker beside her and reached for Elena's hand, pulling her to her side as if she were rescuing her daughter from a dragon.

Parker tilted his hat. "A good morning to you, Mrs. Bissette."

Mama didn't reply, retreating toward the stairway with her daughter, but Elena heard her father reply with a "good morning" in return. Her chest swelled a bit with pride at her father, at his being kind even when the Randolph family had sought to destroy him and his business. She glanced over her shoulder, and her father flashed a brief smile at her. She grinned back at him.

When they reached the second floor, Mama stopped for a moment in the corridor. Her dark brown hair was covered by the wide brim on her new hat—a design of ivory tulle and mauve ostrich feathers—and her mauve parasol matched the accents on her traveling gown. She set her parasol against a stateroom door and tried to improve the condition of Elena's hair by brushing the loose strands over her ears and back up under her hat before they made their entrance on Mackinac.

Then she pinched Elena's cheeks.

"Mama." Elena groaned, pushing her hands away.

She reached for Elena's cheeks again. "Mr. Darrington might have arrived before us."

Elena took a step back. "If he did, I don't want him to see my mother pinching my face."

Mama studied her for a moment, seeming to contemplate what to do. But before she replied, Elena's father ducked under the staircase to join them in the corridor.

"There's no time to dillydally, ladies," he said. "Our landau is waiting."

Mama's gloves retreated to the folds of her skirt as Papa passed them, one hand on his cane and the other steadying himself against the banister. She glanced at Elena's cheeks one more time, as if she might not be able to resist adding color to them. Elena quickly scooted around her father in a very unladylike manner.

The captain directed them toward the gangplank, and Elena paused to straighten the puffy sleeves on her shoulders and take a long breath before they stepped onto the pier. Her mother looped her arm through Elena's and fixed a composed, staged smile on her face for their walk across the wooden plank. Everyone knew that a good entrance almost guaranteed a successful dance, dinner, or, in this case, entire summer.

Elena picked up her skirts and stepped onto the pier, soldiers and vacationers alike crowding both sides of her. Smells of tobacco and manure and the faint scent of lilac clung to the humid air.

Carriages and hansom cabs lined up at the end of the pier, and in the chaos, someone bumped her mother's arm.

"Good heavens," Mama murmured, clutching her parasol with both hands. "Why are all these people here?"

One of the soldiers lifted his dark blue cap with a wide smile on his lips. "We're going home, ma'am."

"But—" Mama's voice lowered and she turned toward Elena. "Why are they leaving now?"

"They're probably running away from us," Papa replied a little too loudly.

Mama shot a look across the pale pink ribbons on Elena's shoulders to silence him.

Then, in a blink, that placid smile returned to her mother's face. It was an art, really.

A low breeze emanated from the lake and across the crowd, and Elena reached up with her free arm to secure her hat.

"Stop clutching it," Mama whispered, the smile perfectly intact.

Elena didn't let go. "But the wind."

"Jillian pinned it, didn't she?"

"I suppose, but—"

"You look like a laundress carrying a basket on your head."

Elena slowly released the brim of her hat, her hand falling to her side.

"Head up," Mama instructed.

Elena sighed inwardly, even as she nudged her chin a bit higher. Then she smiled as pleasantly as possible into the crowd of strangers.

No one was looking at them, or so it seemed. Though Mama would say that everyone of importance was keenly aware of who was on the pier and what each of the other important people were doing.

As their family stepped through the crowd away from the boat, another swift gust of wind rustled over the pier. It skipped and danced across Elena's face, whispering to her again.

Come. Play.

But she couldn't run with it, nor could she play.

Her eyes focused straight in front of her, her hands at her side. She tried to ignore the wind as she had before. This time it refused her the pleasure. Like a naughty child, it snagged the hat from her head and dangled it above her just beyond her reach.

Mama gasped as the organza ribbons on the hat flapped like a sail, the feathers fluttering and struggling in the wind's grasp. Elena leaped toward her hat, trying to recover it, but the wind taunted her and tossed it toward the water. She pushed through the crowd, scrambling to catch it.

She tried, really tried, to retrieve it, but the hat succumbed to the whims of the wind and slipped over the water, hovering for a moment over the surface. Elena teetered on the heels of her boots at the edge of the pier, watching it bobble for several seconds until a wave crashed over it. Then it disappeared under the water.

Elena's heels teetered again, and she began to slip. Her skirts wrapped around her legs as she slid on the wet planks. Grasping for a hand, any hand, she found one among the crowd and clung to it. As she tried to right herself, she heard her mother's groan rumble across the pier.

So much for a graceful entrance onto the island.

She steadied herself against the arm of her rescuer. Once she stood upright, the soldier slowly released his grasp, and she glanced into the concerned eyes of a man not much older than herself. Her tongue seemed glued to her mouth, so she thanked him with a nod. She tried to smile,

but her lips struggled to respond.

When she turned, her first sight was of Parker smirking. If she'd had her parasol in hand, she would have clocked him.

Papa stood a few steps in front of Parker, trying unsuccessfully to hide his grin as his lips curled up with his mustache. She didn't want to hit her father. Instead, she wished she could run into his thick arms and hide.

Papa winked at her, and she tried to smile again.

The woman next to her father wasn't smiling at all. Flames seemed to erupt in Mama's eyes, and like lava bubbling at the mouth of a volcano, it was only a matter of time before it flowed from her lips.

Instinctively Elena patted her hair, the remaining pins poking her fingers. She twisted and pulled at the strands, trying to tame them, but it was of no use. Her hair was beyond fixing.

Even if every thread of her dignity had been captured by the wind, she could still hold her head high and pretend that her wavy hair was neatly tucked and rolled. Perhaps no one else had noticed her fall.

Mama glared at the young soldier as if he'd tripped Elena. "Riffraff," she muttered.

Elena tried again to whisper her thanks to him, but the words never came.

"Come." Mama grabbed her wrist, escorting her hatless daughter away from her rescuer.

The breeze danced through her hair again, but this time she didn't care.

Chapter Two

The landau rolled through the busy village and began the steep climb up the eastern bluff. Mama's perfectly positioned parasol covered most of Elena's head, so she could neither see outside the open carriage or be seen. The breeze whirled long strands of hair across her face, mocking her. The ostrich feathers in her mother's hat fluttered in the wind, but the hat itself didn't so much as tilt in the breeze.

Elena hadn't meant to let her hat fly away, but there was no use in trying to convince her mother of her innocence. Nor could she remind Mama that she was the one who straightened it before they left the boat and then told Elena not to hold onto it.

Her father tapped his cane on the leather seat beside him, looking across the carriage at Elena. "I never really liked that hat anyway."

The parasol dipped ever so slightly as her mother nodded toward the driver above her shoulder. "Hush, Arthur."

Elena smiled gratefully at her father. When the same hat arrived last week, newly tailored and cushioned with paper, Papa had lavished praise for its beauty and design. She too had liked the soft feathers above the band and the simplicity of the pale pink. The color reminded her of the sun's blush over the lazy mornings on Lake Huron, like a shy maid waiting to greet her beau.

The kingdom Papa had built in Chicago was collapsing around them, the floors cracking under their feet, but oddly enough, he seemed more relaxed than he'd ever been—relieved even. Mama had always been anxious about what others thought, and she was even more anxious this year.

Mama thought the well-being of the entire Bissette family rested on her shoulders and the man she was able to lure into marrying Elena. Some days Elena felt a bit like fish bait, dangling out there on a hook while Mama tried to snag the best catch on her line.

Elena smiled at the image of her mother trying to reel in a man, with both the bait and the fish struggling to be free.

Papa took a cigar from his breast pocket, and as he chewed it, he removed from another pocket the tiny booklet he'd purchased on the Chicago pier. He held up the white-and-red-striped book and opened it to display a row of matches. Plucking one of them, he tried to light it with a quick swipe across the booklet. When he failed, he threw it over the carriage and tried again. This time he lit his cigar with the flame before blowing it out.

The match continued to glow in his fingers. "Marvelous little invention, isn't it?"

Mama rolled her eyes at the stick glowing in Papa's fingers. She had little appreciation for Papa's fascination with the latest innovations. "There's nothing inventive about a match."

"But these are paper." He threw that match over the side of the carriage as well before he slid the booklet back into his jacket. "And I've never had matches that actually fit in my pocket."

"It's still just a match."

Papa was always trying out something new, often to the detriment of his family. Elena enjoyed seeing the latest inventions with her father, but she silently hoped he would use the paper matches outside their cottage. The contraption he'd tried to toast bread with last summer had caught their kitchen on fire.

"Perhaps it was only a few soldiers who saw you fall." Mama twisted the parasol in her hand as if it were a shield warding off the smoke. Her words seemed to offer more reassurance to herself than Elena.

If it had only been a few soldiers watching her fall, the story might remain behind the stone walls of the fort. Or the soldiers would carry the story away with them when they left the harbor, not knowing the name of the girl who'd lost her hat in the wind.

Mama leaned away from the driver, whispering to her husband, "Why were there so many soldiers at the harbor?"

He tapped his cigar on the side of the carriage. "For the entertainment, I suppose."

"Arthur, please."

He took a long draw on his cigar and released the smoke into the breeze. Her mother again fanned it away with her parasol.

"Perhaps they're trying to marry off their daughters too."

Mama glanced up at the carriage driver. "For heaven's sake, Arthur." Her voice was a little too loud. "Don't be so trivial. We're not here to marry off Elena. We're here for the healthy quality of the lake and the air."

"Of course, the quality of the air." Papa winked. Others might come to Mackinac for the pleasant environment, but Mama was most certainly *not* there for her health.

The carriage turned right when it reached the top of the bluff, and the driver stopped for a moment to let the Belgians rest.

Elena leaned her head back on the leather seat. To her mother's dismay, her disastrous slip would probably be the talk of Mackinac Island, and if nothing more exciting happened, the story could linger for days. The vacationers loved to talk, but precious little drama occurred during the summers on Mackinac. Gossip was pulled and stretched like the saltwater taffy at Murdick's, and plenty of young women, along with their mothers, would like nothing better than to keep Elena's story quite alive for the remainder of the season.

Mama mumbled beside her, and Elena knew exactly why. She was praying fervently that *he* wouldn't find out what happened.

Mr. Darrington was scheduled to arrive on the island any day. Elena didn't know much about the man, only the brief tidbits her mother offered. He was the nephew of a woman her mother had met on the mayor's gardening committee. Mrs. Ingram had told Mama all about Mr. Darrington—a wealthy, successful financier from Detroit who had not yet married.

When Mrs. Ingram said that the Darrington family would be summering for at least a few weeks on Mackinac, Mama was positively giddy. In her mind, this Mr. Darrington was the answer to their problems. The prize fish.

"I wonder if Mr. Darrington has arrived." The words came out of Mama's lips as a statement, but Elena knew she was asking a question.

Papa took another draw on his cigar. "I heard he might not be coming after all."

The parasol clanked on the side of the carriage. "What?"

Papa shrugged. "He's a very busy man, I suppose. No time for vacation."

"Mrs. Ingram said he would come."

"A man has the right to change his mind."

Elena couldn't tell her mother so, but she hoped Mr. Darrington would exercise his right to a change of mind. Then she wouldn't have to pretend to be enthralled with him for her family's sake. Of course, when he found out the truth about her family's financial state, he would flee like the society men in Chicago had done.

Now that they were away from the eyes of the townspeople, Mama lowered the parasol. She reached over and patted Elena's hand. "Don't worry, Elena, he'll come."

Elena glanced down at the cliffs that dropped to the lake below and then at the sunlight glistening across the water. Would it be so awful if she prayed that he wouldn't come?

She didn't know this Mr. Darrington, but he was probably like most of the bachelors she knew in Chicago. Those men spent their wealth on horse races and card games and were more interested in indulging themselves than in caring for another. She did want to get married one day, but to a man like her father. Someone successful in his own right. Someone curious and kind and steady during the harder times in life.

Unlike Mama's fascination with everything grand, Elena loved the simpler things around her. The water and the stars, the birds and the splendor of the lilacs on Mackinac... There was beauty all around them, and yet it seemed that most of the people in their circle of acquaintances were too caught up in their own pleasures to appreciate all that God had given them.

She would marry to help secure her family's future, but she prayed that her husband would be a person who could revel in God's beauty with her. Or at least give her the freedom to enjoy it on her own.

The driver clucked his tongue, and the caramel-colored Belgian horses began pulling the carriage again. She closed her eyes and breathed in the sweet smells of Papa's cigar smoke and the cedar trees around them. Perhaps she could lock herself in her bedroom until tonight. While everyone else slept, she would escape into the darkness.

When she opened her eyes, the white turret of Castle Pines rose above arched gables and trees. A deep red paint accented the eaves of the cottage and the three stories of white scalloped shingles. Lattice wove across the base of the house, rising up to a wide veranda that overlooked the lake.

Windows enclosed half the front porch, while the other half was open to the breeze. Purple and yellow flowers cascaded from woven baskets along the open porch, and colorful Japanese lanterns hung above white wicker chairs, rockers, and tables. A hammock hung in the corner of the veranda, though Elena had never seen anyone use it.

The carriage stopped, and the driver helped Mrs. Bissette and Elena to the ground. Her mother hurried up the steps to the front door. Her father took Elena's arm and together they strolled toward the veranda.

"Where's Jillian?" Elena heard Mama's voice demand from inside the house.

She heard Claude reply, his voice as patient as always. He was used to her mother's questioning. "Welcome back to Mackinac, Mrs. Bissette."

"Did Jillian get here before us?"

"She should be coming with the luggage wagons," Claude said. "Perhaps within the next half hour."

Claude was their only servant who remained on the island year-round, caring for the house during the harsh winters. Nell, their Chicago cook, had arrived two days ago to help Claude prepare Castle Pines for the summer.

What would happen to Claude if they had to sell the cottage? Even though he didn't have a family, Mackinac had become his home.

Perhaps he could go back to Chicago with them like Nell did at the end of the season, or the new owners of the cottage could hire him for their staff. At that thought, sadness tweaked Elena's heart. She didn't want Claude to work for anyone else.

Claude greeted them at the door. "Welcome home, Mr. Bissette, Miss Elena."

He took her father's hat and hung it in the front closet. "Nell has prepared tea for you in the drawing room."

The grained floors of their cottage were a yellow Georgia pine, the paneled walls barely visible behind the pictures of horses, mountains, and beaches. Elena stepped toward the pocket doors that enclosed the drawing room, but Mama stopped and motioned toward Elena's hair. Sighing, Elena walked toward the bathroom instead.

Claude bent down and whispered as he passed her, "Your bicycle is behind the house. Same place as last year."

She took a deep breath as her mother disappeared into the drawing room. "You know I adore you."

A mischievous smile lit his tanned face. "The stars were spectacular last night."

She smiled in return.

Claude followed her parents through the doorway of the drawing room, and Elena hurried down the hallway. Inside the bathroom, light sifted through the sheer green curtains that hung over the oval window and shone on the white cast-iron tub. Elena stared at herself in the mirror.

Her eyes were light blue, her skin pale and smooth from the best creams money could buy. She had Mama's slender nose and Papa's light brown hair. Hers was about as unruly as his, as well. She'd always wanted to have golden hair, like Jillian, but her hair was more the color of the pebbles bedded along Mackinac's shore.

A half dozen pins stuck out in angles around her head, with strands of her hair shooting out like a meteor of stars. In the sky the stars were a brilliant sight, but it wasn't so pretty on the top of one's head.

Slowly she tugged out each of the pins, and the rest of her hair tumbled down her back. Waves bounced around her shoulders as she shook her head. Relief filled her as the aching from the pins disappeared.

She heard the *clip-clop* of horses' hooves and then voices. Pulling aside the curtains, she saw ten hired wagons lined up the avenue, the Saratoga trunks stacked in each one filled with gowns for every occasion, parasols, slippers, stockings, capes, wrappers, and suits for Papa. Mama made sure their wardrobes lacked for nothing during their vacation.

"Jillian!" her mother called outside the bathroom door.

Elena sat on the edge of the bathtub, hoping Mama would subdue her anger by the time Jillian walked into the house.

"Elena's hat," she heard her mother say. "It wasn't pinned on."

"Wh–what?" Jillian stammered.

"The moment we stepped off the boat it flew off, as if the pins had vanished into the air."

"But I pinned it on—"

Elena stood up, placing her hand on the doorknob. She understood the fear in Jillian's voice. If she lost this position, Mama would never give Jillian a good reference. And Jillian had no family to return to in Chicago. She needed to work.

Jillian's parents had died when she was young, just like Mama's parents, and she worked as hard as Mama once had. Her mother hadn't said it, and Elena didn't dare ask, but she wondered if Mama saw a bit of herself in Jillian and it frightened her.

Her mother lowered her voice. "I need you to do your job and do it well, or I'll have to send you back to the city."

"Yes, ma'am." Jillian's voice quaked.

"And from now on..."

Elena threw the bathroom door open. "Oh, there you are, Jillian."

Tears welled in Jillian's pretty blue eyes, but Elena didn't acknowledge those. Instead, with a sheepish smile, she held up a handful of pins. "I'm so glad you're here. I'm in desperate need of your help."

Jillian glanced at Mama. Elena didn't care.

"Elena." Her mother's use of her name was a warning, but she didn't stop talking.

"I was fiddling with the pins on the boat." She pointed toward her hair. "I took out a couple without even thinking, and then the wind stole away my brand-new hat on the pier."

"Oh dear," Jillian murmured.

"I'm perfectly angry at myself, but there's nothing I can do about it now." She twisted her hair with her free hand. "Could you please pin it up again for me? Then maybe you can help me find another hat."

Jillian stole another glance at Mama.

Mama waved her hand. "Go."

Jillian didn't hesitate this time, scurrying into the bathroom behind Elena. As Elena locked the door, Jillian collapsed on the stool beside the bathtub, tears flooding her cheeks. Elena turned the faucet on the sink, hoping the sound of running water would drown her words.

Her mother had done her damage. Now Elena had to mop up the mess.

Elena handed Jillian a handkerchief, and she wiped her face. "I know you didn't take out the hairpins," Jillian whispered.

"You pinned it correctly." Elena leaned back against the sink. "It was my fault for being so careless."

Jillian didn't seem to hear her. "I don't want to go back to Chicago."

"You're not going to."

Jillian looked at her as if she were crazy. If Mama decided to terminate Jillian's employment, they both knew there was nothing Elena could do to stop her. She would send her back to the steamy streets of Chicago where the summer air was coated with coal and the river ran red from the slaughter of cattle. All who could afford to travel fled the city during the summer months, taking their servants with them.

"You don't have to stay here with us," Elena said. "There is plenty of work with other families on the island."

Jillian shook her head. "I don't want to work for another family."

"We can still be friends, even if you work someplace else."

"You know that's not true."

Elena turned off the running water. "We could try."

"It doesn't matter who employees me. Your mother wouldn't allow us to be friends."

And she was right, of course. Mama had no idea about the talks she and Jillian had in the privacy of her room or the laughter they'd shared over the three years that Jillian had worked for them. Mama would be horrified if she knew that Elena had confided in their maid, but Jillian was only a year younger than Elena and they had been friends since she was hired to assist Elena's mother's personal maid. When the maid retired, Jillian took over the role for both of the Bissette women.

Jillian leaned back on the stool, and something fell from her pocket. An envelope.

Instead of retrieving it, Jillian stared down at it as if she was scared to touch it.

Elena bent down and swiped the envelope off the floor. Jillian's name was written on the outside.

Elena held out the envelope. "What's this?"

Jillian snatched it from her. "A note from a friend."

Elena tilted her head. "An admirer?"

The tears in Jillian's eyes dried, replaced by a look of panic. "I can't— Just a friend."

Elena watched her face closely. Jillian usually shared her secrets with Elena, and Elena shared most of her secrets with her. She glanced back down at the envelope.

Was Jillian searching for another position already, or had a man garnered her attention? If it was a man, who was writing Jillian?

Jillian sprang from the stool. "I need to pin up your hair."

Elena turned toward the mirror and began twisting the strands together on her own. "It's not necessary."

In the mirror, she watched one of Jillian's eyebrows arch. "Do you want your mother to let me go?"

Elena sighed, the pins still secure in her palm. "Of course not."

Jillian's gaze traveled to the door and then she held out her hand. "We need to do it quickly, then."

Elena fidgeted with the pins. She didn't want Jillian to have to fix her hair. She could do it on her own, couldn't she?

"Elena?" Jillian whispered.

Reluctantly Elena handed over the pins and sat on the stool. Jillian swiftly twirled and tugged on her hair until the pins imprisoned it again, capturing it at the nape of her neck this time. Elena gently patted her finished hair.

"You have a gift, Jillian."

A smile played on her friend's lips. "Your hair looks lovely in any style."

Elena laughed. "Did you see it ten minutes ago?"

"It was still lovely," Jillian stammered. "Just a bit—a bit unusual."

"You're a rotten liar."

Jillian's eyebrows arched again. "You want me to improve my lying?"

"Oh, no. You're one of the few people in my life who actually knows how to speak the truth."

Elena wasn't even certain what truth was anymore. Her mother would say that lying was a sin, yet the pretense of their lives often seemed like lying to Elena. Or maybe it was simply hiding the truth, capturing and molding it like the pins had done with her hair. Over the years Elena had become an expert on truth-hiding as well.

"Is Jillian still in there?" Her mother pounded on the door.

"I'm coming, ma'am." Jillian slipped one more pin into Elena's hair. "For safekeeping."

Jillian rubbed the last of her tears on the handkerchief before she handed it back to Elena.

Elena brushed her hands over her hair again. "I'll keep it out of the wind for the rest of the day."

Jillian's hands went to her hips. "I don't believe you."

"I promise."

"Jillian?" Her mother's voice sounded worried.

Elena whispered as she reached for the doorknob, "She relies on you too much to let you go."

When Elena unlocked the door, her friend rushed past her into the corridor. Elena again sat on the edge of the tub and looked out onto the streets where two servants were unloading the mounds of trunks. It would take days of hard work to unpack, organize, and redecorate their summer nest. Perhaps no one would notice if she locked herself in this bathroom for the rest of the day. With all the frenzy inside the house, they might not notice she was missing.

She tapped her shoes on the tile floor and leaned her head against the plush hand towel hanging on the rack. And she prayed softly that God would give her the strength to not only make it through this day, but to make it through the summer.

"Elena?" Her mother rapped on the door again. "Are you still in there?"

She stood up. "Yes, Mama."

"We need to put away your things."

She sighed as she reached for the door handle. If only she could ignore her mother as her father did with such good humor. Just for once, she wished she had the courage to say no.

"Claude!" Her mother shouted on the other side of the door. "I told you, that crate goes in the kitchen."

Elena sighed and stepped through the door. Servants were scurrying in both directions, hauling trunks and armloads of household items.

Her mother turned Elena's shoulders toward the staircase. "Your trunks are in your room, dear."

One of the women servants almost collided with her, and with a quick apology, the woman rushed around her.

Elena moved toward the staircase and began the climb up to her room.

Only six more hours until nightfall. And then she'd leave this madness behind.

Chapter Three

Most of the passengers on the Detroit and Mackinac Railway slept during the midnight hours of their journey. The train crept through the forest like an animal afraid of the dark—slow yet persistent—until the engine car emerged onto a plain of farmland. Then the train flew across the rails like a sailboat caught in a gale.

Starlight drifted into the private railroad car and settled on the leather satchel in the chair beside Chase Darrington. His arm rested over the bag, one finger flicking the handle up and down. His parents traveled by their steam yacht, but he liked the steady rhythm of steel wheels against rails. The solitude of the night and the slow pace of the D&M was a rare opportunity for a man to use the mind God gave him. Or at least attempt to use it.

He'd almost decided not to join his family on their summer excursion to celebrate Independence Day. In fact, he'd planned to go to Illinois this week to meet someone about an invention displayed at the Chicago's World Fair last year—a wooden tub that washed dishes by cranking a handle. It was one of countless innovations at the fair, one that some of his colleagues scoffed at, but the possibilities intrigued Chase. It would need improvements, of course, but that was what Chase liked to do. Improve things and then invest in their future.

In spite of his family's protests, he'd almost taken the train straight to Chicago, but then Richard, his assistant, had delivered this satchel to him after breakfast. The moment Chase saw the contents, he knew he would be traveling north.

Next week he would go to Chicago.

Chase propped his feet on the plush brown settee and laid his head back on the plump chair. In the early morning hours the train would arrive in Mackinaw City, and after breakfast, they would take a chartered yacht over to Mackinac Island. There would be little sleep for him, though. Perhaps none at all.

His mind raced with possibilities. The world was changing rapidly, and he was trying hard to keep up with the latest inventions. He had no interest in actually doing the inventing himself. He didn't do well at putting together the pieces of a puzzle, but once he saw the bigger picture, he liked nothing better than to usher a new invention into homes and offices across the country. He preferred things grander than dishwashers, but this was the kind of appliance that sold to the masses. The kind that made money. He didn't do it for the money, but the successes were intoxicating.

There had been plenty of failures too, in the ten years of working with his father. An electric iron that sporadically caught itself on fire. The bicycle pedal that locked to the rider's shoe, more often than not refusing to release the rider from its clutches. The fruit-flavored chewing gum that sent hundreds of people running to their doctors.

But the failures didn't stop him from seeking out new things.

In the dim light, Chase stood and walked toward the small kitchen at the side of the railroad car. He retrieved a bottle of apple brandy from the stocked cupboard and poured some into a glass. As he sat down, he swirled the amber liquid around in the cup. He'd sent their steward away to retire in a sliver of their private quarters a half hour ago, wanting to be alone. Sarah and her maid had gone to bed an hour ago in the larger stateroom.

He planned to sleep right here.

Pullman had built this palatial car, but the Darrington family had made it their own. The woodwork was polished mahogany, and the drawing room housed a settee, two chairs, and a writing table along with the kitchen. Sarah had ordered lace curtains for all the windows and secured books behind a wooden railing on shelves to make a library.

Chase took a sip of the brandy. He wasn't particularly thirsty, but perhaps the drink would calm his racing mind. He set the drink on a small table. The drink swayed back and forth in his glass with the steady movement of the train, but it didn't spill.

Propping his feet back up on the settee, he reached out and fiddled with the handle of the bag again. If he actually got tired, he'd sprawl out on the settee, but even with the brandy, he doubted sleep would steal him away anytime soon.

Gaslight filled the room, flushing the subtle light from the stars, and he turned around to see Sarah standing in the doorway of her stateroom. Embroidered flowers covered the burgundy wrapper over her nightgown, and her hair was braided down her back.

"Are you still coddling that thing?" she asked. His sister was almost twenty-eight, but with her hair down, she looked more like she was twelve.

He grinned. "Don't you look smashing?"

She stuck out her tongue, a particularly bad habit of hers since she was about four years old. It manifested itself whenever he pestered her. She left the door cracked open, the narrow light trailing her as she crossed the room. "If you'd devote as much attention to one woman as you've done to that ridiculous bag, you'd be married by now."

He grinned. "I'm not looking to marry anytime soon."

She stood beside his chair, nodding at the satchel. "What's so important in there?"

He smiled at her as he clutched the handle. He wouldn't put it past her to pounce. "You know I can't tell you."

She sighed, clearly exasperated. "You're hopeless, Chester."

In her eyes perhaps he was hopeless, but hope was what drove him. Hope and speculation for what lay ahead.

She pointed at the chair beside him. "Are you going to let me sit down?"

He didn't move the satchel, but he removed his feet from the settee across from him.

She shook her head before she sat. "You should get some sleep tonight."

He picked up the brandy and twirled it again. "I was trying to."

"Edward thinks you're working too hard."

"*Edward* thinks I'm working too hard?" He hadn't meant for his laugh to sound so sardonic, but his brother-in-law had developed a certain immunity to work in his middle years, preferring the rush of horse racing and high-stakes poker to the more intellectual investment work of stocks, bonds, and financing new projects that could revolutionize their world. Their father refused to put any of the Darrington money into Edward's schemes.

Chase took another sip of his drink. They were all chasing the wind, he supposed, but the investments of S. P. Darrington & Company were based on both speculation and fact. Edward's form of investing was based on extremely bad guesswork.

Sarah tucked her feet under her wrapper. "Edward says you should stop and enjoy all that you've worked for."

Chase took a long sip of the brandy. "There's no comparing my work habits with Edward's."

"He works plenty. He just knows how to play too." She fingered the hem on her wrapper. "Play is good for the body and the soul."

"The soul?" He scanned the small library of books beyond the chairs until he found the large black book among them. "Where do you find that in the Good Book?"

She waved her hand at his comment. "Even God rested on the seventh day."

He patted the bag. "But I'm pretty sure He worked hard during the other six."

She glared at the satchel like it was her archenemy. "All I'm asking is that you attend several of the parties with me. Pretend, at least, that you're interested in the young ladies."

He grinned. "I don't have to pretend. I have a great appreciation for women."

She grabbed a cushion from the couch and threw it at him. "One of these days, someone is going to make you care."

"I do care, Sarah. Just not about the things you care about." He shifted in his chair. "How is my being on Mackinac going to benefit you?"

She hesitated. "Edward needs to improve his connections a bit."

And probably his reputation, Chase thought, but he didn't say it. It wasn't Sarah's fault that her husband was a louse.

"And I want you to meet a dear friend of mine."

One of his eyebrows slid up. "A married friend?"

Sarah gave a little roll of her eyes, a habit she seemed to reserve solely for him. "Her name is Gracie Frederick. She is from Philadelphia."

"Why is she vacationing in Michigan?"

"Her parents have a home on Mackinac."

"And you think I need a new friend?"

"You don't need another friend, Chester. You need a good woman in your life."

Sarah knew he hated it when she called him Chester, but he still laughed at her words. "Between you and Mother, I have enough good women in my life."

She crossed her arms and spoke slowly, as if she wasn't sure he could understand. "You need a wife."

He shook his head. "I'm not looking to marry Gracie or any other woman on the island."

Sarah sighed. "I'm not saying you should marry *her*, necessarily—just someone like her."

"I'm glad we've worked that out."

His sister leaned forward. "Gracie's father owns the biggest lumber-yard in Philadelphia, and Edward wants to partner with him. You know how to play up the charm without the slightest hint of a promise."

"Is this Miss Frederick homely?"

"Of course not!"

"Then why does she need you to find her a husband?"

Sarah huffed. "She doesn't need me, nor does she need a husband. I'm only asking you to attempt to find her interesting."

"And if I don't?"

"Then pretend."

He patted the bag again, sighing. "I'm not spending my few days on the island sacrificing for Edward."

She stood up, a smile playing on her lips. "I don't believe you'll consider time with Gracie to be a sacrifice."

Sarah walked to her stateroom, and the door closed with a soft *thud*. Instead of sleeping, Chase leaned back in his chair, listened to the rhythm of the wheels, and watched the stars glow in the night sky.

Miss Frederick, he was certain, would be like the rest of the debutantes who crested the powerful ring of Detroit's society. Their families married them off to build prestige or power, and the women themselves were willing pawns in the grand scheme of these alliances. He was busy enough, building alliances in their businesses. He didn't want to come home every night to an alliance as well.

He had a deep appreciation of all their hours of toil before a social event, but no matter how beautiful the woman, he didn't plan to marry for power or prestige. In fact, he didn't know if he would ever marry.

He patted the satchel again.

Only two women had captured his attention in his twenty six years of life, and both those encounters had been brief. One was a striking woman he'd met at a dinner in New York City. He'd called at her home several times and thought her interest in his investments charming until he discovered that she was the granddaughter of a man who'd been pursuing the financing of S. P. Darrington & Company for three years. She'd known who he was the entire time, feigning interest in him so he would invest in her family's work.

The second woman, he'd met at a gallery in London. They'd dined together several nights, laughed together, and discovered their mutual love of art. Then he discovered that not only did she know who he was, but she'd followed him to London. And she didn't have the least bit of appreciation for art.

It seemed impossible to meet a woman he could trust, but if he ever married, it would have to be to a woman who loved him for more than his family's money. A woman who knew how to harbor his secrets...and he would harbor hers.

* * * * *

Elena rocked back on one of the veranda chairs as the breeze rustled the curtains around the open windows and settled over the blanket she'd tucked over her walking dress. Her parents had retired a good half hour ago, and when they did, everything within her wanted to flee the house. She couldn't go though, not quite yet. Her mother always came down the steps to check on her one last time.

The tiny crescent of a moon crept over the dark horizon, and the waves below glistened like icy cakes of snow. Shoots of light sprayed across the night, and the beauty of it all reminded her of the powerful scene in the Scriptures where darkness collided with light for the very first time.

The breeze chilled her face when she closed her eyes, the light blazing across her mind as she imagined it had so long ago.

She'd memorized the poignant words in Genesis years ago, about the void God created—a void called earth—and the darkness that rested on the face of the deep. And then, like the soft breeze that rustled the curtains, the Spirit of God moved across the water, and with a thundering voice that commanded the universe to obey, He said, "Let there be light."

After the light flooded out of the darkness, God said it was good.

Goose bumps bubbled on her arms and she rubbed them. What would it have been like to be trapped in that murky blackness and then to feel the rustle of God's Spirit as He moved across the waters, to hear the roar of God's voice when He commanded there to be light?

Perhaps that first spark of light flickered on one of God's fingers like the tip of a match and then, in a blaze of His glory, swallowed up the darkness. In that moment, when darkness was confined, light ruled the earth.

Footsteps interrupted her thoughts, and she held her breath. Perhaps if she kept very still, the darkness would hide her tonight.

She could feel her mother's presence behind her, but she didn't turn.

"It's getting late, Elena."

"I know, Mama." She opened her eyes. "I just wanted to watch the stars a bit longer."

Her mother stepped beside her. "Mrs. Frederick said that Mr. Darrington might arrive tomorrow."

Elena sighed. "I thought he wasn't coming."

"She said he wanted to meet Gracie." Mama smiled. "But that's only because he hasn't met you."

Elena tucked her feet under her skirts. "I'm fairly certain that this Mr. Darrington won't care if I watch the stars."

Mama tapped her fingers on the arm of the chair. "He might not care about the stars, but he will notice the dark circles under your eyes if you don't get some sleep."

She could lie and say she wasn't the least bit tired, but that wasn't true. The day had exhausted her. "Mr. Darrington is not going to be interested in me."

Her mother crossed her arms. "Now why would you say a silly thing like that?"

"Because he'll want to marry for connections as well as for money."

Mama huffed. "He has plenty of money."

"I'm only trying to say—"

"Your father is still quite connected," Mama interrupted. "And he'll recover the factory—and his other investments—in the fall."

The confidence in her voice faltered. They both knew their family connections were dwindling as fast as their investments and bank account. The railroad her father invested in had gone bankrupt, his real estate holdings were practically worthless at the moment, and the factory to make farming equipment that had been his—as well as his father's—livelihood for almost fifty years had shut its doors.

Elena tried a different tactic. "I'm sure Gracie Frederick isn't the only one with her sights set on Mr. Darrington."

Mama sat down on the rocker next to her. "You're just as pretty as the lot of them, Elena, and smarter too. If you'd try a little, you can get his attention."

Elena knew she wasn't as pretty as most of the girls on the island, at least not in a pampered way, but even if she could capture Mr. Darrington's attention, she didn't want to compete with the other girls. Nor did she want this Mr. Darrington or any other man looking to acquire her like an investment or merchandise. She just wanted to be left alone.

Mama stretched out her hand, waving her back into the house. "Come."

Elena draped the blanket over her shoulders and followed her mother to the stairs. The wide staircase led them up to a balcony with tall bookshelves and overstuffed chairs. Down the narrow hallway, her room was across from her mother's room, and her mother kissed her cheek before she opened Elena's door.

"You need to rest."

"Yes, Mama." Elena slid inside and shut the door. And waited. Her mother should go to sleep now that Elena was safely tucked away in her room.

She turned on the gaslight. A poster bed stood against the wall to her right with a giant blue-and-white canopy draped over the sides. A bay window looked over the dark gardens and the lake beyond, and along the window ledge were glass bowls filled with seashells and shiny rocks. On the wall to her left, blue-and-white curtains matched the pattern on her couch. Paneled walls behind the couch and dressing table were decorated with colorful watercolors of island scenes, sketches of her family, and pithy needlepoint sayings like Lewis Carroll's famous quote, "If you don't know where you are going, any road will get you there."

Her nightdress was draped over the coverlet on her bed, but instead of changing into it, Elena felt under her pillows and pulled out the calico work dress that Jillian had discarded three years ago. She threw her blanket over a chair, exchanged her walking dress for the baggy one, and braided her long hair. She left her cotton stockings on her legs and her corset in her armoire.

Lifting a stack of pillows from the davenport, Elena stuffed them under the sheets of her bed. If her mother came to check on her again, she wouldn't dare wake her from her beauty sleep.

She reached for her riding jacket and began tiptoeing toward the doorway, but before she touched the knob, someone knocked on the other side. When the door began to open, she dove back toward her bed, balling her nightdress in her arm. Pillows scattered across the Persian rug as she threw the coverlet over her work dress.

Mama stepped into the room, a candle in her hand. She eyed the pillows at her feet. "I thought I heard something."

Elena yanked the cover over her chest, hiding the old dress underneath. "I was rearranging a few things."

"Now you're going to sleep, aren't you?"

Elena fidgeted with a string on the coverlet. "Yes, Mama."

Her mother hesitated. "I'll have Jillian make you some chamomile."

"It's not necessary."

Mama stepped back and rang a bell.

It would take a good twenty minutes to heat the water and steep the leaves.

Elena's gaze wandered wistfully to the window and the moonlight outside. There would be no escaping Castle Pines, at least not tonight.

Chapter Four

"Did you hear about Hilga Brunet?"

Mrs. Grunier leaned toward the four other women gathered at the table, and three of them huddled close to her as if they couldn't trust the columns on the Gruniers' wide portico with their gossip. Elena leaned back in the wicker chair, pretending she didn't care to hear about Hilga, but in reality, she wanted to find out what had happened to one of the few young women who'd befriended her on Mackinac last year.

Trudy Grunier, Mrs. Grunier's seventeen-year-old daughter, spoke first, just loud enough for Elena to hear. "They already know, Mother."

Mrs. Frederick's commanding voice dipped to a whisper, like she hadn't heard Trudy. "What happened?"

Mrs. Grunier took a sip of her English tea, seeming to relish the moment. "After Hilga was caught last summer—"

Mama's hand flew to her bodice. "I'd almost forgotten."

Elena straightened her skirts on the wicker chair, resisting the urge to correct her mother. None of them had forgotten what happened to Hilga Brunet last year.

Mrs. Grunier's voice dropped even lower. "I heard she had her confinement in Indianapolis."

"Dear me," Mama exclaimed, her fingers at her throat. "I hope she is all right."

Mrs. Grunier took another sip of tea. "She returned to her parents' home in Cleveland this spring."

The words settled over the four ladies. No one dared to ask about the baby or its father.

Hilga had been one of the most beautiful debutantes on Mackinac. On a tour around the island last summer, she had met a dashing soldier named Santino. On the night she snuck away to meet him, several young vacationers were building a bonfire on the beach. They discovered Hilga and her lover together, and the news of Hilga's indiscretion whipped through the top echelons of society like a tornado. It yanked the roof off the Brunet family's reputation and destroyed their good name.

Elena eyed her mother as the women continued whispering as if that would keep the secret locked away. Mama pretended to be horrified for poor Hilga and her family, but Elena was very aware of what she thought, both then and now. She wasn't particularly concerned for Hilga's well-being—only that there was one less debutante to compete for the more distinguished island men.

"Will Hilga be returning to Mackinac this summer?" Elena asked.

"Most certainly not." Mrs. Grunier looked at Trudy as if her daughter might be tarnished by someone like Hilga vacationing on the island. "I heard they would be summering in Saugatuck."

"Dear me," Mama repeated, apparently afraid for the young people in Saugatuck.

"Did you hear that they are closing Fort Mackinac?" Mrs. Frederick asked.

Mrs. Grunier nodded. "My husband told me a few weeks ago."

Elena watched Mama's smile dim.

"Having those soldiers leave—" Mrs. Grunier glanced at Trudy again. "It will help to keep our daughters safe."

"I thought the fort was built to keep us safe," Elena ventured.

Mama hushed her with a glance.

Elena reached for a flower-shaped cookie decorated with pink-and-yellow flourishes. She knew she wasn't supposed to contradict the ladies during these luncheons, but sometimes she couldn't help herself.

Trudy nibbled a cookie next to her, and Elena wondered if she was bored as well. There was so much on the island to see, and yet here they sat at a tea party instead, talking about the mistakes of everyone else like they were above any sort of indiscretion.

"Why are they closing down the fort?" Mama asked. Apparently her curiosity for information overcame her embarrassment regarding her lack of knowledge.

"We haven't needed the fort since that war with the British, back in 18-something," Mrs. Frederick replied.

"Eighteen twelve," Elena murmured.

"If they close the fort, then all the soldiers will leave," her mother replied.

"Not if, Deborah," Mrs. Frederick said, "when. All the soldiers should be gone by summer's end, maybe even before."

Mama's hand went to her chest again. "Oh dear."

There were never enough men for all the unmarried women who swarmed the island each summer. The unmarried officers and seventy or so enlisted men offered a distraction for the women who weren't courting a bachelor from Chicago or Detroit. The officers were invited to the dinner parties and dances. The enlisted men secretly entertained young women like Hilga in other places around the island.

Even as Mama reached for her teacup again, Elena watched her lips move quietly. Heat climbed up Elena's cheeks at the thought of what her mother was doing. Counting, without a doubt, the number of bachelors vacationing on the island this summer.

"Where is Gracie this afternoon?" Mrs. Grunier inquired of the woman next to her.

"She's resting," Mrs. Frederick replied, dabbing her thick lips with a cloth napkin. "We're expecting company tonight."

"Oh—" Elena watched her mother take a controlled sip of her tea before she spoke again. "What sort of company?"

"Mr. Darrington and his sister are dining with us."

Mama lowered her teacup. "I didn't realize he had arrived yet."

Mrs. Frederick nodded. "He is supposed to be on his way today."

Mrs. Grunier leaned toward the table again. "I thought Mr. Darrington might not be coming after all."

"Oh, he's definitely coming."

Elena groaned inwardly. She'd been hoping he would change his mind.

Trudy scooted closer to the table. "What type of work does this Mr. Darrington do?"

"He works for his father's investment firm," Mrs. Frederick replied with much authority. "He's a financier...and an inventor."

"I heard he invented a book of paper matches," Mrs. Grunier said.

"How fascinating," Mama replied. Elena closed her eyes so they wouldn't roll at her mother's sudden interest in matches.

Mrs. Frederick's pinky finger dangled in the air as she lifted her cup in a salute of sorts. "I hear he is a very fascinating man."

"He certainly is an elusive one," Mrs. Grunier replied. "My cousin has invited him to their home in Detroit on three separate occasions to meet her daughter. Each time, he declined due to his business affairs."

Mrs. Frederick's eyes sparkled. "I will tell you all about him."

"I do hope you intend to share the man's company, Elizabeth." Mrs. Grunier sipped her tea. "There are plenty of young people on the island who would benefit from getting to know an innovator like him."

Elena fidgeted in her chair as she fought a yawn. This kind of endless discourse exhilarated her mother, but it exhausted her. And it had only just begun. They would sit on this portico, shaded from the sun, siphoning every morsel of news from their acquaintances, and then they would move on to the next tea party or luncheon tomorrow to spread it.

Thankfully, no one had mentioned her incident on the pier yesterday. Perhaps none of the summer residents had seen the fall.

Several houses down from the Gruniers' house sat Castle Pines. Behind their house, at the top of the hill, grew a huge hydrangea bush. If Claude had kept his word, a bicycle awaited her behind it. Tonight she wouldn't let anyone stop her from leaving the house.

"There is no reason for me to entertain Mr. Darrington and his sister exclusively," Mrs. Frederick replied. "I'm just accommodating his request to meet Gracie."

Mrs. Grunier folded her hands. "Surely he will come to the dance on Thursday night."

"I'm certain he will," Mrs. Frederick said. Even though she didn't say it, Elena knew she was hoping that he would attend with Gracie on his arm.

* * * * *

The moment the Bissette family sat down at the dinner table, Mama exclaimed, "Why didn't you tell me they were closing down the fort?"

Papa picked up his fork. "I hope you had a pleasant day as well, Deborah."

Elena toyed with the goblet of mixed fruit before her. Mama prided herself on knowing everything that happened on the island along with every notable fact about the wealthy people who visited it. Papa prided himself on withholding the juicier tidbits from her.

Papa took a bite of fruit. "I didn't think you wanted to know about the island *riffraff*."

Mama made an unladylike sound in response, and Elena glanced toward the kitchen door. Claude was waiting for them to finish the course so he could serve whatever Nell made next. He was doing a good job of at least pretending to ignore the conversation. They all had to be actors in some way, Elena supposed, no matter which rung they'd secured on society's ladder.

"It's your responsibility to keep me apprised of the news on the island." She glanced over at Elena. "We don't want to be made out as fools."

A cough escaped Papa's lips. He held his napkin over his mouth and pounded on his chest.

"Stop grinning," her mother demanded. Elena swallowed her smile, but she was still smiling on the inside.

"Even Martha Grunier knew about the fort's closing."

When he stopped coughing, Papa took a sip of wine. "The Gruniers have been here for a good week now. She should know about the fort."

Mama lowered her voice. "You both may think me a fool, but I am the only one in this family who is trying to secure our future. In order to do that, I need to know what is happening on the island."

"But you do know what is happening," he replied.

She pointed at Elena's goblet. "Eat your fruit, dear."

Elena picked up the chilled fork and pushed the sugary peach slice around before she pierced it, but she didn't take a bite.

"Did the Darrington family arrive yet?" Mama asked.

He took another sip. "I believe so."

"And Mr. Darrington?"

Papa's eyes twinkled. "I saw him arrive at the Grand this morning."

Elena squirmed in her chair. She'd been hoping the man would still change his mind and stay in Detroit for the summer.

Mama's fork clanged on her goblet. "You need to tell us these things, Arthur."

"I believe I just told you."

"But if I hadn't asked—" She sighed. "You wouldn't have mentioned it."

He ate another piece of fruit.

Mama's gaze was still upon him, as if she was trying to untangle something he had said. "Why were you at the Grand?"

"I had a lunch meeting with Oliver Randolph."

Her eyes narrowed. "Oliver already burned the bridge between you and him."

"Bridges can be mended."

"Perhaps," Mama replied. "But not all bridges *should* be mended."

He nodded toward Elena. "Oliver's son asked if he could escort our beautiful daughter to the dance on Thursday night."

Her mother's hands balled on the table. "Most certainly not."

"I hope you don't mind, Elena," he said. "I told Parker you could go."

"Oh, Papa," she groaned.

His face suddenly looked older than his forty-eight years. "I will send your regrets, if you'd like."

Claude removed Elena's goblet to make room for the main course. Could Elena spend a whole evening in Parker's company after all his parents had done to disparage her family? Papa's earnest eyes were on her as he waited for her answer. And Mama awaited her answer as well, wanting her to decline spending the evening with a family she'd grown to despise. Elena hated being in the middle, caught like a snared rabbit between the two people she loved.

She turned her head toward her mother. "Perhaps I should go with Parker."

"Most certainly not!"

Elena continued. "That way Mr. Darrington won't think I'm attending the dance solely to meet him, like so many of the other girls."

Mama considered her words. "But you don't want to appear intent on marrying Parker."

"Nor do I want to appear intent on marrying this Mr. Darrington."

Mama thought for a moment. Elena knew that as long as her mother thought she had developed the plan herself, she would implement it with vigor. "I suppose there is wisdom in accompanying another suitor for the evening. So you don't frighten Mr. Darrington if he's not yet ready for matrimony."

Papa nodded his head. "A most wise choice."

Elena ate a few bites of her chicken cordon bleu. She would need the strength for later tonight, when her parents finally went to bed.

Claude assured her that the bicycle was still waiting for her outside, hidden at the top of the stone terrace.

Nothing would stop her tonight.

Chapter Five

The Darrington family suite overlooked the sun-glazed waters of Lake Michigan. The Grand Hotel wasn't nearly as long as the exaggerated picture displayed in the advertisements, but it was still quite large. Fifty or so columns stretched across the veranda, and inside was an ornately decorated lobby and dining room and a ballroom that Sarah said hosted the season's most important events on the island.

When Chase arrived at the hotel with Sarah and her maid, a board on the lobby's wall listed the activities for the afternoon and evening. A concert on the porch. Lawn tennis lessons. A dog race. He'd laughed. Who had time to watch dogs race?

The island seemed to be as charming as his sister had promised, but if he were forced to attend the list of leisure activities, it would be the death of him.

Once in his room, Chase carefully placed his satchel on the burgundy bedspread. The bed itself looked like a giant sleigh with its curved headboard and footboard.

He flung his jacket beside the satchel. For the remainder of the day, he sat at the desk, writing letters and reading through the stacks of papers Richard had sent with him.

Someone knocked on the door, and when he opened it, Sarah's dark green skirt brushed across the floor as she hurried inside. Ringlets of auburn hair were piled on her head like sugar ornaments on a Christmas tree, and they bounced as she glanced around the room and then focused back on him. "Why aren't you dressed yet?"

He looked down at his trousers and the suspenders over his white shirt. "I believe I am dressed."

"For dinner," she groaned. "At the Fredericks' home."

"Ah, the residence of the homely Miss Gracie."

"She's comely, Chester, not homely." She put her hands on her hips. "I told you we were going tonight."

He glanced at the clock hanging beside the wide window. "You said we were leaving at five."

"It's a quarter till."

He waved his hand. "There's plenty of time to dress."

She glanced at his attire. "I'm taking those clothes to the steward to burn when you change."

He looked down again at his trousers and shirt. They looked perfectly fine to him. "What's wrong with these?"

"Your trousers are practically threadbare, and your shirt—" She pointed at a spot on it. "What is that, an ink stain?"

"Probably."

Her eyes grew wider. "And it's missing a button."

"You can sew on a button, can't you?"

She folded her arms over her chest. "I'm not sewing on a button!"

"These clothes are perfectly comfortable and entirely wearable."

"For a pauper," she mumbled.

"Perhaps I will wear them to dinner."

"Hurry, Chester." She eyed the worn satchel on the bed. "And don't bring that ugly bag with you."

He smiled. "I most certainly am bringing it."

"Chester Darrington—"

He gave a mock sigh, looking back at the satchel. "I suppose I can send my regrets."

"You are more like a child than an adult," she huffed. "A disobedient child at that."

He sat down on a chair. "I truly don't mind staying in my room."

"Oh, bring your bag," she said, exasperated with him. "But hurry. The carriage is supposed to arrive in ten minutes."

He laughed to himself as Sarah rushed out of the room. He didn't mind her hedging him into a social outing or two, even if she wanted to find him a mate suitable to her standards, but he was in no rush to attend this dinner.

At twenty minutes after five, their carriage pulled up in front of an imposing stone mansion hidden back in the trees on Mackinac's western bluff. The iron arch, long avenue, and sloping lawn were built to impress visitors, but structures never impressed Chase, not like a grand idea did. It would be a very long evening if the Fredericks were the kind of people who tried to impress their guests by the size of their house.

His sister waved a hand in front of his face. "Please be nice, Chester."

"Of course I will be nice."

"And please don't spend all evening boring the Frederick family about some new invention."

He grinned. "I can't make any promises."

Edward tapped his walking stick on the floor of the carriage, though his head was turned to the window. "Don't be a cod, Darrington."

Chase looked at his brother-in-law across the enclosed carriage; Edward avoided his gaze. Some women might think Edward's dark, curly hair and trimmed mustache attractive, but there wasn't much substance under his neat facade. Sarah and her husband looked out opposite windows, the inches between them more like a fissure.

Edward first called on Sarah six years ago, and even then Chase had wondered what his sister saw in him. Sarah had found him charming and dashing, and at the time, the Powell family was a rung or two higher on the ever-changing ladder of Detroit's society. None of them realized at the time that the Powells were clutching to maintain their status. Two years later, the ladder tipped when the senior Powell squandered the last of the family's fortune. Edward's father ended his life with a single gunshot, and his mother moved to New York City with her new husband.

Even before they knew about the Powell family's shaky financial status, no one in the Darrington family encouraged the marriage. Perhaps that in small part sparked Sarah to continue the relationship. She was a deliberate social climber from her youth, while their parents inadvertently climbed the ladder without trying.

Chase hadn't been privy to the conversations behind closed doors during Edward's days of calling—he referred to them as the *End Days*—but his mother hadn't welcomed Edward as warmly as she had Sarah's other suitors. Edward married Sarah for the Darrington family money and was sorely disappointed when he realized that his father-in-law wouldn't be investing in his new son-in-law's ideas. So, much to Sarah's chagrin, Edward began investing in his own schemes. She tried her best to keep them honest.

Women still swooned over Edward as if he'd never married, and though she hid her irritation well, Chase often saw the spark of jealousy in his sister's eyes. Sometimes he wondered how she put up with his unfaithful attention, along with the women who encouraged his roaming eyes.

Edward tapped the stick again, turning his head back toward Chase. "The hotel is hosting their first dog race tonight."

He tried to swallow his smirk. "A worthy venture, I'm sure."

Edward watched him like he was trying to determine whether Chase was being genuine. Chase didn't offer him the pleasure of a smile.

"I don't suppose you want to go with me?"

Chase rested his arm on the satchel. "I've got other things to do after dinner."

Sarah glanced at the satchel and then back at him. "Are you certain you'll be on your best behavior tonight?"

Chase straightened his waistcoat. "It all depends what you mean by best behavior."

Sarah sighed. "You're impossible."

"Behavior is relative."

"If you can't be nice," she said as she crossed her arms, "perhaps it is better for you not to talk at all."

"Then I would be perceived as a bore."

"Better a bore than a fool." His brother-in-law didn't even have the courtesy to mumble.

The carriage crawled to a stop, and the driver opened the door. Chase helped his sister and her yards of dress descend the narrow steps. Then he reached for his satchel and escorted Sarah into the house, since Edward was too busy admiring the gray stone stables nearby.

Mrs. Frederick met them in a drawing room heavily decorated with Oriental rugs, sculptures, and paintings. She eyed his bag as they exchanged pleasantries, but she was polite enough not to ask about it.

Gracie Frederick breezed into the room like a warm summer wind. She was beautiful, to be certain, like one of the room's valuable sculptures or paintings, and as any observer of good art, Chase appreciated her fine silk dress and hair as black as night.

After her mother introduced them, Gracie tilted her head, studying him as well, before she offered him her hand.

"You look lovely, Miss Frederick."

She smiled at him as she shook his hand, but she didn't blush like some women would at the compliment. "I hope you had a pleasant journey to the island."

"Quite pleasant."

She eyed the satchel in his hand. "Did you bring entertainment for us?"

He admired her for not ignoring his bag like the others. "It is a personal belonging."

Sarah made a groaning noise. "He carries the silly thing everywhere with him, but he won't give anyone a hint as to what is inside."

"Well, now I'm curious, Mr. Darrington." Gracie's fingers brushed over the leather. "What could possibly be so valuable as to not leave your hands?"

"Ah," he said, still smiling. "It's a secret."

"Ooh, I simply love secrets." She clapped her hands. "I shall have to guess." She thought for a moment. "Is it some sort of exotic animal? Perhaps it's a snake or a lizard."

Sarah's eyes narrowed. "I should hope not."

"Or maybe you are carrying some sort of secret papers for the government. I've heard they have spies all over."

He shrugged. "You never know..."

Gracie arched her fingers together. "But I suppose it's not government work at all. I would guess it's some sort of new invention, and I am intrigued, Mr. Darrington. What could possibly be so important that you wouldn't let it out of your hands?"

"Something that could change the world." He clutched the handle a bit tighter. He would smile and attempt to be charming for Sarah's sake, but no amount of charm or coercion would force him to confide in this woman.

Edward stepped up. "Chester doesn't appreciate the company around him like he should."

Gracie shifted her smile to Edward. "Most men won't admit to enjoying the company of ladies."

Edward gave a slight nod. "There are few men who wouldn't enjoy your company, Miss Frederick."

Chase stepped toward Edward, flashing Gracie a smile of apology. "I believe my brother-in-law must have left his mind and his manners back at the hotel."

Edward glared at him. "I was only complimenting Miss Frederick."

"He meant, of course, that most men would enjoy the presence of each of the fine ladies in our midst."

Edward's silence seemed to echo around the room.

Sarah cleared her throat. "Do I smell lamb?"

"With a mint sauce," Gracie said, reaching for Sarah's arm to escort her into the dining room.

Gracie's father and two younger brothers—Peter and Matthew—were waiting for them in the dining room. Candlelight glowed on the long table, and Chase sat down on a dark-red-and-gold upholstered chair. Oil paintings hung on the wide panels around the room, and two uniformed servants stood waiting by a door he assumed went into the kitchen.

The first course, Mrs. Frederick announced, was a wild mushroom pastry, but when he took his first bite, he thought it tasted more like leather than mushrooms. He put his fork down and turned to the boy next to him.

"Do you like to ride horses?"

Peter nodded.

Instead of eating their pastry, they talked about the hundreds of horses on the island.

"It won't be long before we don't need horses to transport us," Chase said.

Edward shook his head across the table. "That's nonsense."

"Have you seen a horseless carriage?" the older brother, Matthew, asked.

"I actually rode in one last summer."

Matthew's eyes grew wide at the revelation, and Chase smiled at him—he'd had the exact same reaction after the ride.

"What was it like?" Matthew asked.

How could he describe the exhilaration to the lad? The wind rushing through his hair as he bumped along the road in the gas-powered vehicle, moving faster than a carriage and with more control.

"Oh, Mr. Darrington doesn't want to talk about horseless carriages," Gracie scolded her brother. And in that moment, his mind flashed back to Sarah's reprimanding him for his dull conversation when they were children.

Chase winked at the boy. "Actually, I love talking about them."

Gracie's fork lowered to her plate. He didn't care if she was offended at his subtle rebuke, nor did he care whether Sarah was angry with him. The world was changing quickly, and Matthew needed to embrace the latest in technology if he was going to succeed one day in the business world.

"What was the weather like when you left Detroit?" Mrs. Frederick asked.

"Terribly hot," Sarah complained. "And it's not yet July."

He leaned his head down to the boy. "Perhaps we can discuss it later, if you'd like."

Matthew grinned. "I'd like that very much."

"There is nothing like the cool weather on Mackinac." Their hostess took a sip of water. "How long will you be staying on the island, Mr. Darrington?"

He caught Sarah's gaze across the table. "I have a meeting in Chicago the middle of next week."

Mrs. Frederick slipped her hands into her lap to allow the servant to take her crumb-filled plate. "So you'll be attending the dance on Thursday night?"

Another servant set a tiny bowl of soup in front of him.

"Which dance is that?"

"At the Grand Hotel," Gracie explained. "They have a dance every Thursday night."

He glanced at Sarah again, who had her eyes on her soup. Even if his sister continued to annoy him, he still loved her. He couldn't live his life for her and her snake of a husband, but he could attend a dance for her.

He smiled again. "Now how could I miss that?"

Sarah glanced up with him, her face relieved.

"Next week is the Independence Day ball," Gracie continued. "That's the biggest event of the season."

Edward dipped his spoon into his soup. "I hear the lumber business is good in Chicago."

Mr. Frederick wiped his mustache with his napkin. "It's been very good to us."

Edward sipped his soup, speaking low. "I recently came into the ownership of five hundred acres of property in southern Michigan. Prime land for lumbering."

Mr. Frederick watched him. "Who sold you this land?"

"I acquired it...from a friend."

Chase watched Sarah cringe at Edward's explanation and then focus intently on her soup. Had his brother-in-law "acquired" his new property at a horse race, or did he win it in a gambling hall back in Chicago?

Mr. Frederick leaned toward Edward. "What sort of timber is on it?"

"Mostly cedar and oak. The land's worth almost eight hundred thousand dollars."

Mr. Frederick arranged his napkin in his lap. "I've got plenty of land for timbering."

"But this land is—"

"Oh, Edward," Sarah interrupted, "it's so distasteful to talk about business at the dinner table."

Silence pervaded the dining room, and Chase wished Sarah hadn't interrupted her husband. He was curious to hear how Edward would attempt to sell Mr. Frederick this property, land he'd never seen before.

Chase ate a spoonful of the soup, a salty broth with no vegetables or meat. Even with five courses, he wondered if he would leave the Frederick home hungry.

"It's flavored with fennel," Mrs. Frederick explained.

Sarah lifted her spoon again. "Most delightful."

Chase finished his soup in four spoonfuls and glanced around at his companions. What else were they going to talk about if they didn't discuss innovation or business? This was the exact reason he avoided these types of social functions in Detroit. They were duller than dishwater.

"It might rain this weekend," Mr. Frederick offered.

The women all nodded.

Chase stifled a yawn under his napkin as the soup bowls were whisked back to the kitchen and replaced by a salad made of spinach, strawberries, and pecans. If they didn't find a more exhilarating topic for conversation, he might have to crawl under the table and nap.

"Did you hear what happened to the poor Bissette family when they arrived on the island?" Gracie volunteered.

Sarah nudged a piece of lettuce with her fork. "What happened?"

"Oh, it was just dreadful," Gracie replied, seemingly too horrified to say another word. Her mother sprang to her rescue.

"Do you know the Bissettes of Chicago?" Mrs. Frederick asked. "Mr. Bissette owns the largest factory for farming equipment in our country."

"Owned it," Mr. Frederick corrected her.

"Of course, silly me, he *owned* it. The Bissettes have had a difficult year."

"I've heard the name," Sarah said.

Chase had never heard of the Bissette family, but he didn't often mingle with the same people as his sister. Even if Sarah hadn't heard their name, she probably didn't want to admit it.

"They are already on the verge of losing everything in their financial affairs," Mrs. Frederick explained. "And then when they arrived at the boat dock—"

Sarah curbed her voice into a moderate tone of interest. "What happened?"

"When they arrived—their daughter's hat sailed off in the wind."

"Tragic," Chase murmured.

"That's not the half of it." Mrs. Frederick leaned closer. "Miss Bissette ran across the pier, trying to rescue it."

Sarah gasped. "No—"

Dumbfounded, Chase looked at the adults around the table. They wouldn't talk about the latest in technology, but they would discuss with great interest a woman chasing her hat. Everyone except the boys seemed to be interested in this poor woman's plight. It boggled the mind.

Sarah pushed herself back in her seat, wiping her mouth with her napkin.

"And not only that"—Mrs. Frederick dropped her voice to a whisper—"she slipped and fell."

Mrs. Frederick paused as if to let the devastation of this information sink in. "One of the soldiers had to rescue her."

"Was she all right?" Chase asked as he lifted a bite of salad.

"Oh, most definitely. Her mother is a dear friend of mine, and I saw her and her daughter just this afternoon. No worse for the wear."

Chase glanced around the table, feeling a bit sorry for the woman Mrs. Frederick claimed as a friend.

"Of course—" Mrs. Frederick continued.

Gracie leaned forward. "What is it, Mama?"

Mrs. Frederick stared at Chase so intently that he actually squirmed like a schoolboy in his chair. "I hear Miss Bissette has her sights set on marrying you, to help her family's state."

Chase choked on his food.

"Good heavens," Sarah gasped. "How—how primitive."

Gracie folded her hands. "You can't fault Miss Bissette for wanting to marry a quality man."

"Quality has nothing to do with it," Edward muttered from across the table.

Gracie smiled. "Well, you can't blame her for wanting to marry an established man."

"Or a wealthy one," Edward added, bitterness weighing his tone.

Chase shifted his chair. He'd wanted to talk about something interesting, but his marrying anyone, for any reason, was not something he wanted to discuss over dinner with his family, let alone with strangers.

"Perhaps Matthew and I can talk about flying machines over dessert," he said.

The boy grinned.

"There is a concert tonight at the Grand," Mrs. Frederick said, glancing at her daughter and then back at Chase. "Will you be attending?"

His foot tapped the satchel on the floor as he looked at Sarah. If he had to spend the evening listening to comments about the weather or eligible women to marry, he might catch the first boat out in the morning. Then his parents would be upset with him as well.

"Oh, I would love to attend." He smiled again. "But I was planning to join Edward this evening."

Edward's head jerked up. "You were?"

"I couldn't possibly miss the first annual dog race."

"Dog race?" Mrs. Frederick sounded a bit disturbed.

"The manager at the Grand is hosting it," Edward explained.

"Well, I suppose, if it is at the hotel..." Her voice trailed off. "But you will be attending the dance tomorrow night."

Sarah leaned forward. "He wouldn't miss it."

He glanced at the smile frozen on his sister's face. "Of course not."

The servant replaced his salad plate with a stuffed Cornish hen.

"Very good," their hostess said before she picked up her fork.

Chase began eating his main course as if his life depended on it. The sooner he left for the dog race, the happier he would be.

Chapter Six

Chase had never attended a dog race before, but he was quite certain this one wasn't going as planned. A crowd of men had gathered on the wide lawn behind the hotel for the publicized race, but it had turned into a dog *chase* instead of a race, and a bumbling one at that.

The hotel employees had lined up a dozen dogs to race, goading them to the starting line with fresh meat. But instead of sprinting toward the finish line, three of the dogs were scratching themselves near the start. Others had taken off toward the woods with their cuts of meat. Frantic hotel workers ran after them, trying to retrieve the dogs before they fled back to their homes in the village. Only five of the dogs remained on the middle lawn, and not a one of them seemed interested in a race. If Edward hadn't wagered on the outcome, Chase was certain even his brother-in-law would be laughing at the fiasco.

A cloud of cigar smoke hovered over Chase, twilight settling over the lake in front of him. Torches were lit in preparation for nightfall, but he doubted that the assembly of men would be here much longer even if they preferred the amusement afforded by the dogs over a concert.

One of the dogs, a white mutt with black spots, sat down beside Chase and looked up at him as if Chase could rescue him from the absurdity of humankind. He petted the dog's head until a hotel employee arrived with a length of rope in his hands.

The employee tied a lasso of sorts around the dog's neck and tried to pull him away, but Chase stopped him. "This dog is done racing."

The employee shook his head, tugging on the dog again. "They're gonna race them to shore."

Chase reached down and released the animal from the rope. "Not this one."

The employee studied the plain trousers that Chase had changed back into and the shirt that Sarah wanted him to burn. Then he looked at the dog, as if he were uncertain whether to argue with one hotel guest for the sake of entertaining the others.

"Mr. Darrington?"

Chase looked up at the hotel manager, a dapper man with a waxed mustache that curled up at the ends. When he and the Powells arrived at the hotel, the manager had assured them that he was available if they needed anything. Perhaps now was the time to collect on his offer.

The manager looked down at the animal. "Did you find a new friend?"

Chase petted the dog again. "I believe I did."

The manager glanced back up at his employee. "Did you have a question for Mr. Darrington?"

The employee backed away. "No, sir. I was just collecting the dogs."

The man pointed at the dog beside Chase. "I believe this one is just fine where he is."

"Yes, sir."

The manager surveyed the chaos around him and then turned back to Chase. "This race isn't exactly going as we expected."

"If you wanted to entertain the gentlemen, you're doing a fine job."

The manager laughed. "I suppose we are."

The man hurried toward the water, trying to organize his employees as they coaxed the other dogs into a boat and paddled them out onto the lake. Someone shot a pistol into the air, and the employees dumped the dogs over the side of the boat. The creatures swam frantically toward shore until a brown mutt emerged on the grassy hill, the winner of the race. Several of the men cheered.

Instead of celebrating his win, the lead dog sprinted right, toward the village, and the other dogs followed. This time no one bothered stopping them. The dog beside Chase nudged his hand one last time and then joined his comrades in their new race away from the crazy men.

This, Chase speculated, would be the first and last dog race at the Grand.

As the men around him cheered, Chase glanced back at the flickering lights of the carriages as they moved up and down the hill.

"I'm going to take my leave," he told Edward. "Perhaps I'll follow those dogs into town."

His brother-in-law nodded but didn't reply, his focus obviously on the results of the wagering. Chase marveled how even the most inane races could capture a gambler.

Chase didn't look back at the shore. As darkness settled around him, he strolled up the hill, past the line of carriages that stretched the length of the hotel porch. On the other side of the building was a carriage barn available for use by the guests. Inside were a dozen drivers and liverymen.

One of the men eyed Chase's clothes and the worn satchel in his hands.

"I'm a guest of the hotel," he tried to explain.

His eyes narrowed slightly, questioning Chase in his silence.

He sighed. "The name is Chester Darrington."

The man stood straighter. "Would you like an open or enclosed carriage, sir?"

"An open one, please."

"Of course," he said before rushing forward to open the door on one of the carriages. A lantern hung on each side of the driver's seat.

He motioned to one of the men waiting on the side. The man's dark skin was wrinkled with age, his graying beard drooping to his collar, but his eyes sparkled in the lantern light. "Henry's one of our best drivers."

"It's a pleasure to meet you," Chase said as he pushed his satchel across the plush seat and climbed inside.

Henry fed each of his horses a carrot before he climbed up onto the driver's seat, taking the reins for two Standardbreds in his hands. "Where would you like to go?"

"I'm not quite sure."

"Well, now." Henry put his arm over the seat and looked back at him. "Most people around here know exactly where they're going, and they're in quite a hurry to get there."

"I want to go someplace high," Chase explained. "And as far away as possible from the village lights."

"I suppose that would be up to the site of the old fort, in the center of the island." Henry clicked his tongue and the horses moved forward, out of the barn. "The fort burned down a long time ago."

"That sounds like the perfect location."

"Step!" Henry commanded as he directed the horses left, lumbering farther up the hill. Then he glanced over his shoulder again. "I don't think I've ever driven up to Fort Holmes at night."

"It's a grand adventure for both of us, then."

"Indeed."

The minutes passed slowly as Chase's heart beat faster. When his assistant had given him the satchel, he'd told Chase about the incredible power of this invention, but Chase needed someplace dark to test it. Someplace remote. Tonight he would finally see if it was as grand as Richard proclaimed.

Chase leaned back on the seat. "I thought Fort Mackinac was the only fort on the island."

"It's the only active fort now." Henry paused. "Fort Holmes was active for just a few years. Run by the British."

"The British?"

Henry glanced back at him. "You haven't heard the story of the British taking over our little island?"

Chase shook his head.

They turned right at the top of the hill, the hotel lights fading away behind the trees as Henry began to tell the story. "Heads of fur traders used to come here to trade, back in the last century. Whoever controlled our island was master of the Great Lakes...at least the upper portion. Both sides wanted Mackinac when we fought with the British again in 1812."

Chase couldn't see much around them, with the light from the carriage lantern fading into the darkness, but he could smell the scent of lilac bushes mixed with the odor of the horses harnessed in front of them. "We must have won the island."

"Eventually, but it took awhile. When President Madison first declared the second war on the Kingdom of Great Britain and Ireland, no one bothered to tell the commanding officer at Fort Mackinac that we were at war again. Unfortunately for us, the British telegraphed their men over on St. Joseph Island, and they rustled together an army of natives and voyagers to fight with them. The new army rowed right over to Mackinac, and the soldiers here were in so much shock that the British took control of the fort without so much as a gunshot."

"No one was hurt?" Chase asked.

"Not that time around. The Americans surrendered, and the British built a blockhouse and stockade at a higher point on the island to protect the larger fort and called it Fort George. Legend has it that it burned down twice on their watch." Henry sniffed. "Seems to me, someone was trying to tell them something."

Chase leaned forward. "How long did the British occupy the island?"

"For three years. An American army invaded the island in 1814 in an attempt to take it back, but they were sorely defeated. When the Americans finally got the island back, they renamed the fort for Major Holmes since he was killed in that battle. There isn't much left up there anymore."

Perfect. All Chase needed was solitude, darkness, and a cloudless sky.

Henry stopped the carriage by a hillside. "You'll have to climb from here."

Chase grabbed the satchel and hopped out of the carriage. "How far up?"

"A couple hundred feet, if you stay on the path." The driver handed him one of the lanterns. "Don't rush for my sake. I'll enjoy the night and maybe even take a little nap while you're gone."

Chase took the lantern and clutched the satchel in his other hand.

The hike was a strenuous but quiet climb through the forest, far from the chaos of the dog races and hotel music. Chase breathed a bit harder with every step up the steep hill, but he didn't stop. He'd come to the island to test out this new invention, and he wouldn't return to the hotel until he had tried it.

Trees circled the site of the old fort, and he climbed a small hill where the blockade probably stood at one time. A few piles of limestone were all that was left of the buildings. In the distance he could see the glow of the village, but it would have to do.

The wind whisked over the trees and rustled his jacket. He wished he could be even higher, far above the trees and away from the lights, but this would suffice for tonight.

He opened the satchel, and the copper barrel glistened in the lantern light. He lifted the cylinder carefully out of the linen that cushioned it. A man by the name of Nelson Reese had spent his entire inheritance to develop this telescope. Chase would do everything in his power to keep it safe.

Many of his colleagues were investing in the giant refracting telescopes to be housed in domes for scientific use. It was a wise investment, Chase believed, to put money into the study of astronomy, but he wanted to invest in a telescope that wasn't used by science. He wanted to sell a telescope to people of all incomes who wanted to view the wonders of the universe from their front porch.

To his knowledge, no one except a scientist inside a dome had ever used such a powerful telescope as the one in his hands. The only difference was, the scientist had to wait for the right weather conditions to watch the stars from the observatory. Reese's telescope collapsed to eight inches, so instead of waiting for the right weather conditions, one could easily transport it to where they could be found.

Chase set the lantern behind a tree to keep the flame burning without being distracted by its light. Above him, the entire galaxy seemed to serenade him like a majestic choir above the earth. He wished he could see the full moon as well, but tonight it was scaled back to a sliver. In a week or two, he would be able to see it in its fullness.

He took a tripod from his satchel and secured it on the grass. Then he removed the lens cap of the telescope and pushed out the three draws, extending it to twenty-four inches, before he secured it on the tripod and slid away the covering that protected the eyecup.

Dipping his head back, he looked through the telescope for the first time, and his heart leaped. The stars appeared almost life-size, and he could see dozens more of them through the telescope than with his naked eye. He knew this portable telescope was only a link to what was to come, but it was an important link. Photographers like Andrew Common and John Draper had taken beautiful pictures of the heavens, but he had never seen anything as spectacular as this.

A breeze rippled over the hill as he watched the stars. In time, students and scientists alike would learn more about the stars and planets. They would find out if there was life in the skies beyond the earth. If the men and women in Matthew Frederick's generation persisted, perhaps they would even develop some sort of flying machine that would take them high into the worlds above them. The possibilities were endless if one only escaped the frivolous distractions of life and imagined what could be.

Chase didn't know how long he stood on the hill, gazing at the lights stretched out above him, but he was mesmerized by the power of the instrument in his hands. He would wait a few days or even weeks longer, if he must, to test out the telescope when the moon returned to its fullness, to see what only a few scientists had been able to see and perhaps even more. If he and Richard could find a way to make many more of these, if they could distribute them to the masses around their country and Europe, he was almost certain they would sell.

Who wouldn't want to see the wonders of God's creation?

November 21, 1812

The wind blows harder now. I am trying to keep the lantern lit for the passing ships, but it won't be long before ice covers the strait. Then no one will pass this way until spring.

Oh, Jonah, where are you? Why do you not come home?

I can't stop my mind from wondering what might have happened if Thomas and I hadn't gone to fetch water that morning. What if we hadn't stopped to collect butternuts to roast? What if we had hurried home instead of lingering to enjoy autumn's bounty?

When we finally opened the front door, excited to show you our find, you weren't here. Only Molly was in the lighthouse, asleep in the crib you made for her.

If it weren't urgent, you never would have left Molly on her own. You would have taken her with you, wherever you went.

Why didn't you leave me a letter? Why didn't you ring the bell to call me home? If you needed help, I would have come running to you.

I never should have stayed out for so long.

Chapter Seven

With her boots clutched in one hand, Elena cracked open her bedroom door with the other. Across the dark corridor, she looked at the hallway door that separated her from her mother's room, searching for the thread of light that often escaped underneath. It was dark.

Perhaps Mama had finally gone to sleep.

She padded down the back staircase in her stockings, past her father's room at the end of the hallway, and sat on the back step of their cottage. Quickly she laced her boots and then grabbed the dark lantern Claude left for her on a post. Hurrying down the steps, she rushed into the backyard before anyone, including Claude, saw or heard her. Claude might hide the bike for her at the far edge of their yard, but she never wanted to implicate him in her excursions. If Mama found out that he helped her—

Behind their cottage, a cobblestone pathway wound between Mama's prized flower and vegetable gardens. Starlight turned the budding irises a steely gray color and washed silver across her path, glittering in the reflecting pool. Her heart leaped at the beauty of it and she moved even faster, trying to be quiet and yet feeling the urgency of her escape.

At the end of the path, a stone terrace led up into the trees, and she climbed it with ease. The bicycle was exactly where Claude had said he left it, hidden behind a hydrangea bush on the top terrace. She brushed the leaves and dirt off the bicycle and then looped the lantern over one of the handles.

Spindly arms of pine trees swayed above her and shadows danced around her feet as she unlatched the gate at the back of their property and pushed the bicycle toward the alley that wove behind the cottages.

A dog barked, and she stopped for a moment, holding her breath. Someone yelled at the dog but no one called out to her, so she hurried forward before the dog began barking again.

The inland roads along the east side of the island were a mix of rugged wetlands and treed knolls. Sometimes carriages brought tourists during the day, but most Mackinac visitors never ventured far into the forest. And the carriage drivers never navigated the island's back roads at night.

Every once in a while she saw a soldier walking away from the fort, sometimes dressed in his uniform and other times in more casual attire. And sometimes a soldier would be accompanied by a young lady. The few times she'd seen the latter, she'd looked the other way without a word, assuming neither he nor his escort wanted her to see them either.

She put her leg over her bicycle, knotting her dress so it wouldn't get caught in the spokes, and carefully pedaled up the narrow lane. Once she reached the last cottage on the eastern bluff, the road widened and she pedaled harder, every rotation taking her farther away from Castle Pines.

Her hair fluttered in the breeze. She was free of hats and pins, free of her bustle and corset and her mother's critical eye. For a few hours, under the cloak of darkness, she was free to be who God made her to be.

The morning hours would be hard, no doubt, but it wasn't like she had to be someplace after breakfast. And if this Mr. Darrington happened to see her tomorrow, perhaps the circles under her eyes would scare him away.

Elena shook her head, chastising herself for the thought of trying to scare away Mr. Darrington. It was her job to woo the man, not frighten him, but the unpleasant scheme of marrying a man for his money and status warred against her desire to do what was expected of her. One day she would have to marry for her family's sake, whether it was to the mysterious Mr. Darrington or another man like him. With her father's business affairs in ruin, she would have to bear the load of helping the entire family...but she hoped it would still be a few years before it became imperative.

At one time in her life, she'd hoped she would marry for love. It was an impossible dream; she knew that now...but in the quietness of the night, she still liked to pretend. One day, she would marry the man her parents chose for her, but until she did, she would enjoy these moments of freedom whenever she could.

Her legs burned as she climbed the inland hills behind her house. The rare times she biked in Chicago were on straight, smooth paths. It had been almost a year since she'd pedaled along these roads, but in spite of the aching in her thighs and calves, she was determined to reach the top.

After biking for ten minutes, the road leveled and she pedaled around a wide curve before turning off the lane onto a smaller trail marked by a faded ribbon. The hanging branches made it impossible to continue any farther on her bicycle, so she set it against a gray rock and slid the lantern off the handle. Then she dug into her pocket for one of her father's new matches.

She eyed it for a moment in the starlight. Had Mr. Darrington truly invented this booklet? She didn't want to be impressed, but she couldn't seem to help herself.

Her fingers shook as she ripped one of Mr. Darrington's matches off the booklet. Funny, she hadn't even realized her hands were trembling until now.

She hated running away from her parents' home like a fugitive, hated knowing how much it would anger her mother and disappoint her father if they found out, but she had to get away on her own, even if only for a few hours. In Chicago, she could only run as far as the gazebo in their backyard, but here—here she could run into the forest, high above Lake Michigan's shore.

It took several attempts, but finally she managed to light a match without the wind blowing it out. Her lantern light illuminated the branches of the beech trees, tall grasses, and moss-covered rocks scattered in the forest. Ahead of her was a high bluff, and she hurried toward it. Her breaths came harder the farther she climbed, but she didn't slow her pace, nor would she slow it until she reached the top.

At the peak of the bluff, she stopped and leaned back. There in front of her, in all its glory, rose the beautiful stone tower that once lit Mackinac's shore. Her refuge for the past six years.

A tear slid down her cheek and she felt completely silly, crying at the sight of a lighthouse, but she'd been so worried it had been destroyed over the winter. If it was gone—she hadn't known what she would do without it. This was her sanctuary. Her safe haven in the storms. No one could destroy her peace and solitude here. Not even Mr. Darrington.

The wind blew up from the lake, rustling the trees. Her hair tangled around her head and a giggle bubbled on her lips. She tried to suppress her laughter at first, but then she remembered that no one could hear her, no one was out here for her to impress or fear.

The same wind that had taunted her on the pier delighted her now, as if it had been waiting for her to play.

She laughed into the wind. And she twirled once before she moved toward the door of the lighthouse.

He was here; she could feel Him. Not a man like her mother was seeking for her, but the God of the heavens and the earth. The mighty Creator. God was in the midst of the rugged beauty of the trees, in the light of the stars and the lapping of the waves. He was in the intricate designs on each leaf and in the clefts of the rocks. She could almost hear the faint sound of creation singing His praises.

The path to the doorway was overgrown with brush and branches, and she pushed them away from her face. It didn't look like anyone had visited the place since she'd been here last year, and she was grateful for that. As far as she knew, she was the only one who had come in the past six years.

Claude had helped her to find this place back when she was just starting her teen years. She'd confided in him that she wished she had a tree house like some of the other children, a place to escape, and he told her he knew of a place much better than a tree house. He'd brought her here one day, marking the trail with the same ribbon that was now battered by the rain and bleached by the sun.

She'd once told Parker Randolph about the abandoned lighthouse, but he didn't seem the least bit interested in her find. She often wondered if anyone else except Claude cared or even remembered that it was here.

The heavy door creaked when she opened it, and she hesitated at the frame, listening for little feet scurrying across the floor. The people on Mackinac might not remember the lighthouse, but plenty of critters called it their home. When the sounds from the mice quieted, she stepped inside. They always stayed hidden during her visits.

At the base of the lighthouse was a small house where the keeper of the light once lived. Old furniture covered in dust and grime stood in the three rooms—a parlor, a bedroom, and a kitchen. The hearth of the kitchen fireplace was filled with twigs and leaves. Mice had destroyed the few books and quilts left in the bedroom.

The room closest to the door was the parlor. She stepped into it and smiled as she opened the roll top of the writing desk. Inside was the sketchbook she'd smuggled from Chicago two years ago, hiding it in her luggage. And a small set of pencils, wrapped in cloth. She couldn't leave it at the cottage, but it was safe here.

She tucked the pad and pencils under her arm and began to climb the fifty-four steps up the tower. Her lantern light glowed on the rock walls cracked by years of age and neglect, and she wondered if the lighthouse had been as lonely for her company over the winter months as she had been for it.

One of the glass panels had broken at the top and shattered around the floor. Fresh air stole through the crack, and she breathed deeply. Others might find God in a church building, but this was her sanctuary. Her tabernacle. No one was watching her as she prayed and worshipped here. No one was criticizing her gown or her hair or whispering what they thought she should wear to services. As she looked out at the branches dancing in the wind, no one told her to bow her head.

At one time, the lighthouse would have shone its light out to steamers and boats traveling through the strait, but now the view was obliterated by the trees. Or at least she thought it was. She'd never actually been here during the day.

The old lighthouse lantern was behind her, the same one that used to warn ships of these bluffs before the war with the British. Outside the windows was a narrow platform the lightkeeper probably used to clean the windows or watch the waters below.

She stepped onto the platform and blew out her lantern.

Stars twinkled by the thousands, glittering and shimmering like diamonds encrusted in the wall of a dark mine. The chalky glow of the Milky Way blazed across the expanse of the sky.

With her eyes wide open, Elena worshipped her Savior.

A sliver of the moon was cradled in the sky, and she squinted at it.

Were there lakes on its surface? Mountains and forests? She often wondered what was out there beyond their planet, beyond the world they had created for themselves, in the universe that God had created for them. She'd never know what was on those planets, at least not in this life, but she could imagine the world up there. A world, perhaps, where people were free to make their own choices.

Where they were free to marry for love instead of for money or position.

She envied a woman like Jillian, who could marry someone she loved. But even if Elena didn't love her husband, she prayed she would marry a man who understood her desire to worship God in her own way, in a place like this. God knew her heart and the desires harbored within. In the starlight, on her lighthouse, she prayed the impossible prayer. She didn't pray for love or security or even for the freedom that she longed for, but she prayed that somewhere out there was a man who dwelled alongside their Savior, a man whom her mother would approve for her to marry.

The minutes passed, perhaps an hour, as Elena prayed and listened. Then she relit her lantern and began sketching the back of a woman in a plain dress whose hair flowed loose in the breeze. Her feet were bare, and she stood tall on the sandy beach as if she were searching for something on the lake.

When the drawing was complete, she reluctantly climbed down the stairs and hid her sketchbook in the desk. She didn't want to leave, but it would be dawn in the next three or so hours. If she didn't get home before

the household staff began to wake, someone might stumble upon her and her secret.

She closed the door to the lighthouse and hiked back to her bicycle to begin her ride home. She was humming to herself, pedaling against the breeze, when she heard the *clip-clop* of horses. She veered off the road and hid behind the trees, the hem of her dress tearing on a tree limb. The air smelled of fragrant wild roses, and as she ducked into the thicket, thorns scraped her cheek.

She watched quietly, assuming a couple had snuck away from the village, until the carriage crept slowly by her. By the carriage's lantern light, she could see the driver and one lone rider in the back. A man.

She watched the carriage until it rounded the next bend.

Who else was out exploring the island so late in the night?

Chapter Eight

Something pounded against Elena's head…or, at least, that's what it felt like. She rolled over on her bed, pulling the pillow over her head, but the feathers did nothing to stop the hammering.

"Elena," her mother called from the hallway, "unlock this door right away."

Elena opened her eyes, peeking out from under the pillow, and then squeezed them shut again. The bright light hurt her head almost as much as the noise.

"Claude!" Mama yelled.

Elena groaned into her pillow. She'd locked her door a few hours ago for one reason—so that no one would disturb her until long after breakfast. Her legs ached from the bike ride and her mind was still fuzzy, but the midnight hours at the lighthouse would be worth every pain today. There was hope for her as long as she had a place to escape to, a place where she could dwell in solitude with God.

Something rustled in the hallway and her doorknob rattled. Claude had probably retrieved the key.

She sighed and rolled over. They were supposed to be on vacation, away from the hustle of their life in Chicago. Surely she could sleep for a few extra hours in the morning.

"I'm awake!" she shouted toward the door even as she clung to the remnants of peace that had flooded her soul. The peace dissipated the moment her door slammed against the wall.

Mama whooshed into her bedroom. "Why did you lock the door?"

Her eyes were still closed. "Because I was hoping to get some extra rest."

"You and your father have gotten plenty of sleep this morning. It's already half past nine."

"It was a long trip, Mama."

"And that's why I've let you both sleep so late this morning." She pushed open the curtains. "But you have to get up now."

"Did something happen?"

"Martha Grunier just sent me a message." Elena cracked open her eyes and saw the envelope in her mother's hand. "She heard that Mr. Darrington and his sister might be making calls today."

Elena rolled over again.

"Elena." Mama nudged her. "He could arrive at any moment."

"He wouldn't be calling until this afternoon."

"You don't know for certain. They may do things differently in Detroit."

Her mother bustled around the foot of the bed and sat beside Elena. A look of horror crossed her face.

"What happened to you?" she exclaimed.

Elena looked up. "What do you mean?"

"Your face—it's all blotched."

Elena put her fingers up to her cheeks. She remembered getting scraped when she hid from the carriage.

"And your eyes—" Mama continued. "It looks like you've been up all night."

Elena smiled to herself. Not quite all night.

"Are you sick?" Mama asked, desperation lacing her voice.

"I feel perfectly fine. Perhaps the blotches are from the fruit last night."

Mama wrung her hands. "I hope you're not getting ill."

"I'm not."

"The dance is tomorrow night!"

"I'm sure I will be fine by then."

"If Mr. Darrington and his sister stop by today—" Mama brushed her hands together. "We can tell him you're ill."

Elena inched up on her pillow. "But I'm not ill."

"You're right." Mama stood up, pacing the floor. "We can't tell him you're sick. It might frighten him away."

"You could tell him I'm sleeping—"

Mama shook her head. "We definitely can't tell him that."

Elena put the pillow over her face again, her voice muffled. "But I am sleeping."

Mama snagged the pillow and tossed it onto the window seat. "If he calls today, you'll need to smile and pretend there is nothing wrong with you."

"There isn't anything wrong with me."

"Jillian!" her mother shouted. "Go fetch the almond oil."

She heard Jillian's voice on the other side of the door. "Yes, ma'am."

"And powder."

Jillian was already gone, so her mother rushed out of the room.

When Jillian returned, she handed Elena the tin of creamed almond oil, and Elena began rubbing it on her scrapes. She and Mama would sit around the house doing needlework or reading, just in case Mr. Darrington and his sister appeared. Or she could play the piano. She would like to draw, but Mama thought it quite unladylike to do so.

The day seemed daunting to her.

"What's wrong?" Jillian whispered.

"It seems as if my summer is going to be dictated by the whims of a man I've never met."

Jillian smiled sadly. "At least you're able to marry."

Elena saw the longing in her friend's eyes. It had never occurred to her that even though Jillian had the freedom to marry whom she chose, she might not be able to do so, not if her husband couldn't support them. She wouldn't be able to retain her position as a maid if she married.

"This Mr. Darrington has made no attempts to court me."

"But he will, once he sees you."

Her father shuffled into the room with his cane, a cigar teetering between his lips. "Don't you look pretty?"

"You need some more sleep, Papa."

He yawned as he fumbled with his pockets. "I seem to have misplaced my new pocket matches. Have you seen them?"

Elena looked back at the mirror. "Someone might have borrowed them."

"Ah." Papa stepped back toward the door. "Then could you kindly ask this person to return them to my jacket pocket so I can enjoy my cigar?"

Elena giggled. "Yes, sir."

Mama hurried back into the room with the powder in one hand and a light moss-colored gown hung over her arms. "This dress will be perfect for today."

Elena shook her head. "He's not going to come."

"Oh yes he will," she replied. "And we will be ready when he does."

*****

Intrigued. Chase scribbled the word on a piece of paper inside the hotel lobby, but even though it was cryptic, it still made him uneasy to send. He didn't want anyone to guess at what had interested him. *Decision soon.*

The telegraph operator rapped his fingers on the note. "I'll send it right away."

Chase glanced up at the clock. Richard should have the telegram within the next two hours, and he would be thrilled. Ever since Nelson Reese approached Richard, Richard had insisted that Chase try it for himself. Chase wasn't sure he could believe that such a powerful hand telescope existed until he'd tried it last night. Now he didn't want to move too slowly, nor did he want to make a rash decision.

Hopefully, the telegram would keep both Richard and Nelson at bay until Chase made a final decision. It was a constant battle for him, balancing the enthusiasm for a new invention with the patience to make a wise investment.

The operator handed Chase two telegrams from the morning, and he sighed when he read the first one. His meeting in Chicago was postponed until the following Friday.

"There you are," Sarah called, and he turned toward her. Her smile was strained, perhaps because of her late night socializing in the hotel. "It's supposed to be terribly warm today."

"Funny thing about summer—"

"We're all going on a picnic, to Bois Blanc Island across the strait."

Chase's eyebrow slid up. "Who is included in the 'we'?"

"Me, Edward, Parker Randolph, and a few other young people from the hotel." She flicked something off her sleeve. "And Gracie Frederick, of course."

"Of course." He glanced down at the second telegram. It was from a business associate in Cleveland. "Have you heard from Father and Mother?"

She nodded. "They're supposed to arrive on Saturday."

His gaze wandered across the wide lobby to the sunshine streaming through the windows. Sarah liked to surround herself with influential people, but having many acquaintances didn't mean she had many friends. She considered the women who flirted with her husband to be enemies, and she seemed to be suspicious of those who didn't.

He could bow out of the picnic, but there was nothing else pressing for him to do this morning. It wouldn't hurt, he supposed, to take a few hours of leisure to spend with Sarah and her little party. Perhaps it would be good for him.

Sarah looked on the floor around him. "Where's your bag?"

"Resting in the room's safe."

She glanced around the lobby as if she were trying to see who else was nearby. "I hope you'll join us for some rest as well."

* * * * *

An hour later, three carriages rolled away from the hotel containing seven ladies in colorful straw hats, four men, Gracie's personal maid, and enough supplies to outfit a weeklong excursion to the beach. The open carriages rang with laughter as they plodded toward the northeastern side of the island.

In the first carriage, Chase sat beside Gracie, and one of her friends sat on her other side. Edward, Sarah, and Parker Randolph sat on the bench behind them.

As the ladies traded news from cities along the Great Lakes, Chase watched the bluffs above them. Trees were lined like a formidable army up the steep hill, and he wondered if it was possible to climb. The old fort last night had been a good place to try the telescope, but perhaps he could try it out on a cliff as well, away from the trees.

Gracie laughed. "What do you think, Mr. Darrington?"

He started at the sound of his name and cleared his throat. "About what?"

Gracie's friend giggled, but Gracie kept her own smile intact as she fanned her face. "About fashionable women trading their dresses for bloomers."

He flashed her a smile. "Personally, I think fashionable ladies should trade their bloomers for bathing costumes."

She clapped her hands. "Oh, you are perfectly awful."

"I think women should be able to wear what they like," Edward said from the backseat.

Gracie looked over her shoulder. "Even bloomers?"

"Why not?"

She turned back to Chase. "I would think that Mr. Darrington here, with all his inventions, would be especially interested in the fashion trends."

"My investments usually last more than a season."

"Perhaps you should be more modern in your interests, like your brother."

Chase cleared his throat. "Actually, he's my brother-in-law."

Edward clapped him on the shoulder. "But we're just like brothers,

aren't we?"

Chase almost choked on his retort. Edward might try to impress Gracie and her friend with his interest in fashion, but he was about as interested in fashion trends as he was in being Chase's brother.

As the women chattered about the latest in gowns, Chase tilted his head again, searching for a place along the high bluff to test the telescope. Someplace where he could capture the stars over the expanse of the lake.

He heard the women's laughter, but to him, it was like the sound of the horses' hooves drumming a rhythm on the street, a steady clamor that helped him to think.

If the telescope could capture the contours of the moon, and if he and Richard could produce thousands of them at a reasonable cost, he could sell them to men and women like those on this excursion—people who were constantly searching for something new. And people who could afford it. If they were willing to buy Nelson's telescope, it could change their entire perspective on the universe.

But what if astronomy didn't interest them? It was possible that it would be like the bread toaster he'd tried to sell. No one wanted to buy it.

He looked back at Gracie. "Have you ever seen the stars before?"

She blinked. "Is this some sort of joke?"

"Of course you've seen the stars." Chase laughed at himself. "But have you seen them up close, through a telescope?"

The ribbons on her wide hat ruffled with the shake of her head. "I've never known anyone who had a telescope."

"But if you had—if you could go to an observatory—would you want to see the moon and stars?"

She brushed one of the ribbons back over her hat. "Are you planning to build an observatory, Mr. Darrington?"

The woman beside her giggled again. He couldn't tell her, but he didn't have to build an observatory. He could bring the observatory with him wherever he went.

It was no use being evasive with this woman, and he didn't dare tell her about the telescope. He was certain she couldn't keep the secret. "I'm intrigued by the stars."

"I suppose they are interesting," she said, but there was no enthusiasm in her voice, not like when he and Richard talked about the stars. And he wanted both men and women to enjoy the telescope.

But just because Gracie wasn't interested in the galaxy didn't mean that other women weren't interested in it. Sometimes he invested for the good of science, and the good of their country's future, instead of for the money. But people would still have to be interested in learning about their universe to buy this.

"I know someone who loves the stars," Parker Randolph said.

Chase turned. "Who?"

The carriage stopped, and instead of answering, Parker opened the door and climbed down to help the ladies.

Four rowboats waited for them along Mackinac's pebbly shore, and the carriage drivers piled picnic baskets, blankets, and an assortment of other paraphernalia into the back of the boats for them. Chase sat in the center of one of the boats to paddle, and Gracie, along with her maid and another lady, joined him. Parker, Sarah, and Edward rode in the boat next to them, Edward extending the rowing privileges to Parker before their party crossed the channel to Bois Blanc.

The island wasn't as tall in the middle as Mackinac, sprawling across the horizon instead. The only living things on the island, Parker told them, were birds and some small animals.

Clear blue water swept gently over the sandy shore as they beached the rowboats, and after the ladies stepped out, Chase pulled his boat onto the sand. Parker took a shovel from the stack of supplies, and Chase helped him bury two watermelons to cool them while Gracie's maid, a stout woman named Fanny, spread out one of the blankets. Then Fanny hung a curtain in the trees and the women took turns changing into their shorter bathing costumes to enjoy the beach.

It took the women a full half hour to change into their costumes, and

Chase had begun to wonder if they would spend their beach day hiding behind the curtain. When Gracie finally finished, she sent Fanny off to find a pillow and then sat on the blanket next to Chase, sprawling her long stocking-covered legs in front of her and pulling her wide-brimmed hat down on her forehead. Chase kept his eyes on the lake. Mackinac Island lay across the channel from them, and he watched as several gulls dipped down, their wings clipping the water.

"Isn't it lovely?" Gracie asked.

"I suppose it is," he replied.

She crossed her feet. "I could stay out here forever."

Chase eyed her, wondering if she was being genuine. "You'd be bored in no time."

Fanny arranged several more pillows behind Gracie's back, and she settled into them.

"Perhaps in a day or two, but not if I could hear the music from across the water." She looked at Chase. "You would go crazy over here, wouldn't you? No horseless carriages or flying machines."

"I prefer the city whenever possible."

Parker sat on the other side of Gracie, brushing sand off his trousers. "Which do you prefer most in the city—the smoke or the stench?"

Chase leaned back on his elbows. "Definitely the smoke."

"Chester does not like the smoke," Sarah replied as she sat on the blanket beside him. "He likes all the people running around, working like mad."

"I like progress," he said with a shrug. "Things are always changing and growing in Detroit."

Gracie fanned her face again. "Everyone needs a break from the city."

He had no qualms about relaxation—everyone needed to vacate at times—but he had a certain disdain for people who claimed to escape from work when they rarely lifted a finger either in the city or on an island. In reality, it was hard work for him to attend operas, balls, and dinners for purely social reasons. If he stayed on an island like this for months at a time, his parents would have to lock him up in an asylum.

He looked across at Mackinac, at its hump rising in the middle. "It looks like a turtle."

"That's why the Indians named it Michilimackinac," Parker said. "Home of the great turtle."

"Were there a lot of Indians on the island?"

"Indians, fur traders, and fisherman."

He could almost see the island busy with people selling, buying, and exporting their wares. He probably would have enjoyed it more back then, when it was teeming with trade.

He scanned the bluffs again, looking for some sort of outcropping to try Richard's telescope. In the midst of the trees, he saw something shimmer in the sunlight. He stopped scanning, squinting at the glare, but couldn't make out what was reflecting the sun.

He pointed at the beached rowboats. "Did anyone happen to pack a pair of binoculars in that stash?"

Sarah glanced at the mound of stuff. "I believe we did."

He started to push himself up, but Gracie stopped him. Her eyes were still on him when she spoke. "Fanny, go get Mr. Darrington the binoculars."

"Yes, ma'am."

"I can get them—" he insisted, but Gracie reached for his arm. He hated being trapped like this, between doing what he knew to be right and what he knew to be polite. It would be rude to undermine Gracie, but he hadn't asked either her or Fanny to retrieve the binoculars. He didn't want to insult Fanny either, or perhaps get her into trouble when she returned.

She returned quickly, depositing the binoculars into his hands. "Here you are, sir."

"You're a gem, Fanny."

"I wouldn't have guessed you to be a bird-watcher." Gracie sounded agitated, probably because Fanny had managed to steal a moment of his attention.

"I have a deep appreciation for all God's creation," he said as he scanned the women's faces. Gracie's friend giggled again, but when he lowered the binoculars, Gracie was frowning.

Chase turned to the bluffs in front of them and scrutinized them through the binoculars, searching for the source of the reflection. And then he saw it. Some sort of tower on the hill right across from them, its dark roof blending into the trees.

Gracie inched closer to him. "What else intrigues you, Mr. Darrington?"

He put down the binoculars. "Right now, I'm very intrigued by those watermelons hidden in the sand."

When Parker returned with one, Gracie instructed Fanny to cut it for them on the portable table they'd stowed on the boat.

"Has your father said anything to you about the Michigan land we discussed?" Edward asked Gracie.

"I don't talk to my father about business."

"You should," Edward said with a smile. "A smart woman like you—"

"Edward," Sarah interrupted, her voice strained, "could you help us cut the watermelon?"

Chase wanted to pummel his brother-in-law, but he stood instead, inviting Parker to join him at the water's edge as Edward moved slowly away from Gracie to assist his wife.

Chase handed Parker the binoculars and pointed at the island. "Any idea what that is?"

Parker looked through the lenses. "All I see is a forest."

Chase nudged the binoculars in Parker's hands to the left until they were focused on the tower.

Parker paused. "That must be the old lighthouse."

Chase took the binoculars from Parker and looked through them again. He'd read about lighthouses along the Atlantic Coast, but he'd never actually seen one. "How do you get to it?"

Parker plucked a long piece of sea grass out of an outcropping of rocks and chewed on the end. "I have no idea, but you can't get to it from the road that circles the island. There are no trails up to those bluffs."

"Perhaps one could climb it without a trail."

Parker laughed. "If one wanted to lose one's life."

"How did you find out about it?"

"I—someone told me about it once. It was built many moons ago to keep boats from making an unexpected landing on the island in the fog."

"Is this the same person who loves the stars?"

"The watermelon's ready," Sarah called.

Chase looked back at the lighthouse. People on Mackinac seemed to stay on the south coast of the island, near the village. "Does anyone use it now?"

"Only the island ghosts." Parker grinned. "I'm told they aren't fond of strangers."

Chapter Nine

Elena heard soft laughter outside the open window. It was such a rare sound, even when they had company in their home, that she closed her book and listened. It sounded like Jillian's laugh.

The laughter ended, and she heard a man's voice below.

Setting her book on the chair, she tried to push herself up on the leather arms. Under her mother's close watch, Jillian had pulled the steel bands of her corset so tightly that she could barely walk. She wasn't sure how she was supposed to dance as well.

On her third attempt to stand, Elena rose and moved toward the window of the small library. The laughter seemed to be coming from the porch that wrapped around the side of their house, but she couldn't see under the roof.

She brushed her fingers over the red silk that flared from her waist to the floor. Her gown had capped sleeves made of black lace to match the lace around her neck and the hem of the skirt. Her face was powdered with talcum to hide the faint redness from her scratches, and a gold locket in the shape of a heart rested at the base of her throat. Her father had given it to her when she turned eighteen, and she preferred its simple beauty to the diamonds and pearls that many of the women wore.

Jillian laughed again, and there was freedom in her laughter, a sense of letting go of oneself and enjoying the company of another. Elena took a shallow breath. Unlike Jillian, she wouldn't be doing much laughing tonight, not with this corset chained around her ribs.

Her stomach ached as well as her ribs. She didn't want to fail her parents tonight—especially her father—but she didn't know how to wrangle a man into marriage. It seemed that Gracie Frederick had captured Mr. Darrington's attention, and she wasn't entirely sure whether to be glad or upset at this news.

What if Mr. Darrington ignored her, or even worse, what if she despised him? She didn't have to like him entirely, she supposed, but she prayed that he would be tolerable.

Laughter rang out again, this time from a man, and Elena sighed. What would happen if she did marry him and couldn't find a refuge in Detroit? She would suffocate for certain.

Claude knocked on the open door to her father's library, and she called for him to come inside.

"You look stunning, Miss Elena."

She blushed. "Thank you."

"The Randolphs are here to accompany you."

Was Parker the one instigating the laughter with Jillian? It didn't surprise her that he would be the instigator—laughter seemed to follow him wherever he went—but why was he alone with Jillian?

Both her parents were waiting for her downstairs. An hour ago, Elena had promised her mother that she would in no way act like the Randolphs had wounded or even offended their family. Or that the Bissette family had been shunned from many of Chicago's society events.

She'd assured Mama that she would be fine. She would pretend with the best of them.

Her parents kissed her cheeks.

"Would you like to join us in our carriage?" Parker asked her mother.

"It's kind of you to offer," Mama replied with a remarkable amount of grace, "but we will be following soon."

Papa smiled. "We can't stay out as late as the younger people, you know."

"I believe you both could stay out as late as you wanted," Parker replied. Even her mother managed a small smile.

Parker held out his arm, and Elena took it. "You look lovely as always, Lanie."

She tugged on his elbow as they walked down the front steps. "Stop calling me that."

He patted her arm, looking at her with mock surprise. "Lovely?"

"You know what I mean."

"Good evening, Elena," Mrs. Randolph said as she climbed into the carriage. Mr. Randolph nodded to her as well.

At one time, before the pressure of matrimony wedged a gulf between them, she and Parker had been good friends. She well remembered that summer, two years ago, when they'd snubbed their parents' attempt at formal matchmaking for a day and snuck away to ride bicycles around the island. When her mother found out, she reprimanded Elena for her indiscretion and ordered up an appropriate chaperone and four notable acquaintances for a dull carriage ride. Parker had made ridiculous faces at her the entire time.

Last year Parker had spent most of their summer months in a half-hearted pursuit of her, trying to turn their childhood friendship into some sort of romance. Elena's mother had spent those same months trying to convince Elena not to run so fast. Playing hard to get was good and fine, her mother informed her, but Parker needed to catch her every once in a while or the chase would get old. Elena was fine with the chase getting old. Her mother was not.

Even as Parker pursued her, she suspected the only reason he did so was at his mother's insistence. They were both the only children in their prominent families, and at the time, a marriage between the families seemed ideal for both social and financial reasons.

The Bissettes owned, among other things, one of the largest factories in Chicago. Mr. Randolph had partnered with Elena's father for three decades to make farming equipment, and it had made them both wealthy men. But after the economy crashed last year, the senior Randolph managed to manipulate the legal system and pull out of their partnership. Her father was left to pick up the pieces of the failing business that might have been salvaged if Mr. Randolph had honored their agreement.

Her father tried to keep most of the details of their financial affairs from her and Mama, but she heard the whisperings of others. Her mother was convinced that their future was bleak if Elena didn't marry well.

Neither the Bissette nor the Randolph parents were interested in a match between their children any longer. They didn't even seem to want to be friends. The Randolphs hadn't invited the Bissettes to the Easter gala at their home, an annual event that every upstanding member of society attended. To not be invited was the ultimate snub. And at the McCormicks' spring luncheon, Elena's mother and Mrs. Randolph had refused to sit by one another. Elena had been mortified when her mother moved to an open table on the far side of the room.

Over the spring, Mama had concocted a new plan for Elena's future, one that no longer involved Parker Randolph or his family.

Mrs. Randolph examined her face in the twilight. "We haven't seen you in a long time."

Elena kept her face as stoic as possible. She refused to be intimidated.

"It has been a busy season for our family," she said. Ambiguity was always the best choice when one couldn't tell the truth. "We have been quite preoccupied."

"So I have heard." Mrs. Randolph tapped her fingers on the dark blue folds of her skirt. "We have been as well."

"So many important things to do back in Chicago." The sarcasm weighed heavy on Parker's lips. "At least we get to see you and your family now."

"A delight indeed," Mrs. Randolph replied with a slight nod.

The delight seemed to fade as they drew near the facade of the Grand Hotel, which glowed with light from their generator. Music drifted down the wide lane and into the village below. The sky was cloudy this evening, and that gave her some conciliation. If she had to be inside all evening, at least the stars were hidden as well.

Parker escorted Elena and Mrs. Randolph up the red-carpeted steps. Elena took as deep a breath as she could manage. It had been a few months since she had been to an event like this, but she'd climbed the steps of the Grand Hotel many times before. There was nothing to be intimidated by, not the imposing entrance or the lofty guests or even the venerable Mr. Darrington.

A chandelier shimmered above the crowded ballroom as they stepped inside, and people lined the ornate balcony, watching the dozens of dancers below.

"There's Sarah Powell." Mrs. Randolph pointed to a beautiful woman wearing a golden dress and a jeweled hair piece that glittered in the light. She looked as though she'd fallen from the night sky. "She's the only daughter in the Darrington family."

"And there's her brother," Parker murmured.

There was a man standing on either side of Mrs. Powell. Elena couldn't see the face of the man on the far side of her, but the man closest to them had curly black hair and sharp, defined features—almost as if his face had been chiseled out of stone. He was a few inches taller than Sarah, and when he turned, he caught Elena's gaze and bowed his head toward her. Elena could feel a blush swimming up her cheeks, and she hoped he would think the heat of the room was warming her skin.

The man glanced back and forth between her and Parker, and then he stared at her with open admiration. She looked away.

At least it hadn't taken long for her to get Mr. Darrington's attention. Her mother would be pleased.

The orchestra began a new song and the guests began a fast Viennese waltz across the shiny floor.

Parker offered his arm. "Shall we dance?"

"I—I don't know."

"That's why we're here, Lanie. To dance."

She didn't protest, but dancing was only a means to an end for her. She was here to meet Mr. Darrington.

Parker didn't ask again. Instead, he whisked her onto the dance floor and she followed his lead, her posture perfect more in an attempt to breathe than impress any man. She tried to scan the crowd as Parker rotated her, but she was moving too quickly to recognize faces.

Where had Mr. Darrington gone, and if she found him, would he be interested in spending time with her? What would happen to her family if he wasn't?

When the dance ended, she pulled Parker off the floor. "I need to catch my breath."

He grinned. "Did I steal it?"

"Your dancing did."

He took her hand and led her toward a long white-clothed table decorated with displays of fresh flowers and vines. Woven through the flowers were platters of shrimp, oysters on the half shell, iced salmon, cheese, bread, and pastries powdered with sugar and surrounded by fresh cherries and blueberries.

"I'm told they're serving some sort of icy raspberry concoction for punch."

"That sounds wonderful."

When he left to retrieve the punch, she waited by a column and listened to the laughter around her. Did other people actually enjoy evenings like this, or were they all putting on a show, to be seen in their successes by the people they deemed important?

She heard a woman's voice behind her, talking loudly to compete with the roar of the music. "Did you hear what happened to Elena Bissette?"

Elena didn't turn, but she knew who was talking about her: Gracie Frederick. The debutante was always nice to the people around her, but she could be as venomous as a cobra when her prey was away. Two years ago, Gracie's favorite suitor for the summer had turned his attention to Elena. Elena hadn't been the least bit interested in the man, but ever since, Gracie had done everything in her power to damage Elena's reputation.

The orchestra stopped playing, but Gracie didn't appear to realize it. Her next words echoed across the room. "Elena went sprawling across the pier."

People turned toward Gracie, many of them stopping to look at Elena before their gazes swept the floor.

In that moment, Elena wished the dance floor would open up and swallow her. Or that the magician back on the *Manitou* would snap his fingers and make her disappear. Someone had reported her fall back to the circuit, and they were gladly passing it along.

She sighed. There were no secrets on Mackinac.

She heard the snickering as Gracie relayed the facts of the story about the wayward hat. Then the exaggerations began.

"She knocked two or three people down when she fell," Gracie said. "Then she lay there for a minute or so, her skirts up to her chest."

Someone gasped. "No—"

She could confront Gracie about her inaccuracies, but it wouldn't do any good. People cared more about a good story than the truth, and as they pushed the story along, they'd probably enjoy talking about Elena's anguish alongside of it.

A good actress never let the reviews bother her anyway.

"The Bissettes always summer here," another woman replied.

Gracie lowered her voice, and Elena inched closer.

"Yes, but this year, I heard they're on the verge of bankruptcy," she confided.

"Bankruptcy?"

"Her father lost nearly everything last year. Bad investments, I'm told."

Elena's hands began to tremble inside her gloves, and a wave of heat climbed to her face. How dare Gracie talk about her father's loss with so much glee?

"My father says he is a terrible manager of money."

Elena's hands shook harder, and she took as deep a breath as possible, trying to calm herself. She could pretend not to care what Gracie said about her accident on the pier, but she wasn't going to let this woman insult her father.

She smoothed her hands over her gown and stepped forward into the circle with as pleasant a smile as she could manage. "Hello, Gracie."

Gracie's smug smile collapsed.

"Elena—" she stuttered.

"If you're going to talk about my family, you should probably get the facts straight."

Gracie's voice returned. "I didn't realize you were going to be here tonight."

"Of course not. If you'd known, you would have chosen another topic to entertain your audience."

"I'm only telling the story that Minnie Falstand told me."

"I don't recall seeing Minnie at the pier."

"It doesn't matter that much, I suppose."

Elena swallowed hard, trying to shape her next words. "If you're so interested in my fall, please talk about it all you'd like, but you don't know a thing about my father or his financial state."

Gracie's chin lifted a notch. "My father knows all about it."

Elena mustered the perfect smile for the small circle of people dressed in their fashionable clothes and balancing their glasses of wine or mineral water in their hands. "I seem to remember a little incident last year at Skull Cave.... Let's see, who was it that got stuck—?"

Gracie stopped her. "There is no need to repeat gossip."

"Your story isn't gossip?"

"Not the part about the pier. Minnie said she knew for certain what happened."

"I slipped, I fell, and I got right back up again," Elena said. "It wasn't nearly as entertaining as you and Minnie seem to think."

The impeccably dressed man who had been admiring her earlier stepped forward. Mr. Darrington, she assumed. "It's those ridiculously long dresses you ladies wear," he said. "I'm surprised the lot of you don't trip every time you go out."

Gracie blinked. "You prefer shorter dresses along with bloomers?"

"Most certainly."

"Elena Bissette, have you met Edward—" Gracie was interrupted by another blast of the trumpets. "Oh, bother."

Edward stayed beside her as the others fled toward the dance floor. She didn't care if he heard about her fall, but she hoped he hadn't heard about her family's financial state. If he knew the truth, he might never consider the union of their families.

Edward nodded down at her, but instead of pleasure in his eyes, she saw arrogance. His tailored black tuxedo with tails was certainly one of a gentleman's, like Lottie Ingram described, but he wasn't nearly as handsome as his aunt implied. Nor did he have Parker's genuine smile or the confident smile her father liked to flash to make her think everything was all right.

Edward might be considered handsome, but there was something behind the facade that disturbed her. It was as if he expected Elena to enjoy the pleasure of his company without his attempting to enjoy hers. But if this was the man who could rescue their family's state, she would be polite enough. The way he looked at her—it didn't seem like it would be too difficult to hook him.

The man saluted her with his drink. "Well done on the retort."

Her face felt warm again. "Someone had to set the story straight."

He emptied his glass and motioned for one of the waiters to take it. For a moment she thought she'd lost him, but he returned his attention to her. "I trust you've had a good summer so far."

She nodded. "With the exception of my fall."

His laugh was dry, and as he stepped even closer to her, she could smell the bourbon and tobacco on his breath. The plight of her entrance on Mackinac didn't seem to discourage him, nor did the news of her father's impending bankruptcy—if he knew about the bankruptcy.

She glanced over his shoulder, searching the room. Had her parents arrived yet? Her mother would be most pleased that she'd already received a proper introduction to Mr. Darrington. Once her mother saw that Elena had made his acquaintance, she would dance again with Parker.

Mr. Darrington asked questions about her and her family, but the more he probed, the more her sense of comfort faded. Even though they stood in the midst of several hundred people, she felt as if she might need to run. The way he looked at her made her cringe, licking his bottom lip as if he were hungry.

She wanted him to find her attractive, for her parents' sake, but she didn't like the feeling that she was an item to be chosen from a menu. No matter how hungry the man was.

Parker slid to her side, clutching a glass of red punch. "I'm sorry it took so long. I—"

His sentence dropped off as he eyed Mr. Darrington standing next to her.

"Parker Randolph," she said, "I would like you to meet Mr. Edward Darrington."

Instead of greeting Parker, Mr. Darrington appeared to be surprised at her words.

Had she been wrong to introduce the two men? Sometimes it was difficult to know who was avoiding who, like her mother and Mrs. Randolph. Mr. Darrington cleared his throat.

"My friends call me Edward," he finally replied, speaking more to her than to Parker.

Parker held out the punch glass for her. "Edward and I picnicked together yesterday."

"Picnicked?"

Parker nodded. "Over on Bois Blanc. It was only a small group of us. Edward and his brother-in-law and his w—"

Edward interrupted him. "Would you like to dance?"

"No, thank you," Parker quipped. "My feet are killing me."

Elena almost laughed at the surprise on Edward's face.

His eyes narrowed. "I wasn't speaking to you."

Over Parker's shoulder, Elena met the eyes of Edward's beautiful sister, but Sarah Powell wasn't smiling. In fact, it looked like she'd swallowed a cherry pit.

Elena looked back at Edward.

Parker took the punch glass from her hand before she took a sip. "Elena and I were about to dance."

Worry creased her forehead as she glanced back and forth between them. Either Parker was jealous, or he thought there was something wrong with Mr. Darrington.

Edward reached for her hand. "Surely you can spare her for one waltz."

She looked down at her glove encompassed firmly in Edward's fingers, and the urge to run overwhelmed her. No matter what her mother said, no matter how badly her father's business was faring, she didn't think she could marry this man.

"I was actually on my way to the powder room," she said, trying to keep her voice light. Though she refused to wince, her fingers actually hurt in Edward's grasp. She couldn't imagine being married to a man who treated her like a possession instead of a person. Someone who demanded she succumb to him instead of respecting her will and intellect.

"I will take the next dance, then," he insisted.

Sarah Powell glided up beside her, her golden dress trailing down her slender figure. Elena smiled at her, but she didn't seem to notice. Her eyes were on Edward instead. "Dancing is a fine idea."

"I was just telling your brother—" Elena started.

Sarah looked at her, and Elena saw anger in her eyes. "Who are you?"

"I'm Elena Bissette." She shook her hand from Edward's grasp and held it out for Sarah. The woman just looked at it.

"You're the woman who fell on the pier."

She sighed. "Unfortunately."

"My name is Mrs. Sarah Powell." She nodded at the man beside her. "Edward's wife."

"Wife?" Her voice squeaked the word even as her mind spun. How could this man be married? The married men were usually cordial, but they would never clutch her hand, not like Edward had, nor devour her with their gazes.

"I'm sorry. I didn't know—" She looked at Edward, but he didn't seem embarrassed in the least. Parker, on the other hand, was studying his glass quite intently.

Sarah took her husband's arm and pulled him away, as if Elena had been trying to entrap him. With a sickening feeling, Elena realized that was exactly what she had been trying to do. But she hadn't realized she was trying to trap the wrong person.

She cringed again when Edward turned back to her, nodding his head. She looked away.

Parker set her glass on a tray filled with chinaware. "Do you still need to go to the powder room?"

She faced him, frustration burning inside her. "Why didn't you tell me he was married?"

He shrugged. "I figured you knew."

The way he said it, Elena wondered whether it was a pastime of Mr. Powell's to attempt to charm unmarried women. Her mother was so concerned about the soldiers at the fort, but there were snakes living among them, as well. His poor wife.

"I most certainly did not know. If I had—" She took as deep a breath as she could muster. "You know I wouldn't entertain a married man like that."

Parker took her hand lightly and led her to the dance floor. As she whirled in his arms, she scanned the floor again.

If this Edward wasn't the elusive Mr. Darrington—

Then where had Sarah Powell's brother gone?

December 5, 1812

It's been a month now and still you don't return.

I want to leave the lighthouse. I want to look everywhere for you, but I can't leave with Thomas and Molly.

If I lost one of them…dear God, I don't know what I would do if I lost one of our children too.

Some nights I feel like I'm going crazy, not knowing where you went. In those terrible moments, when my mind goes wild, I imagine horrible things.

An animal attacking you.

A stranger coming to hurt you. Or a friend.

But there are no wild animals on Mackinac Island. Not even a poisonous snake.

And who would want to hurt you?

Did you fall someplace, in one of the island's caves or crevices? Or did you drown in the lake?

But that makes no sense to me. You would never leave Molly to go down to the lake.

The wonderings tangle in my mind like a vine choking the life out of a tree.

Perhaps I have already gone crazy.

I keep thinking you will come back to me at any moment, but you do not.

Chapter Ten

The orchestra played at the other end of the long ballroom, partners whisking each other around the dance floor as if they were trapped in a whirlpool. Chase was in a corner of the ballroom talking with two businessmen from Chicago—a Mr. Lloyd Grunier and Mr. Arthur Bissette.

Mrs. Frederick had warned him about the intentions of Arthur's daughter, but this man seemed to be a fine enough fellow. He never mentioned his daughter once in their conversation. Either Mrs. Frederick was exaggerating, or Arthur wasn't trying to marry off his daughter as readily as Mrs. Frederick implied.

Either way, he enjoyed the conversation of both gentlemen. He'd only spent four days at the World's Columbian Exposition last fall, but these men had spent weeks looking at all manner of inventions—electric drills, incandescent lights, elevators, a cotton gin, a new sweetener called saccharin, and more.

The number of innovations might have been overwhelming to some visitors, but it was exhilarating to him. His favorite during the Chicago visit was the movable sidewalk on the pier, but he had invested in more affordable items that the common household could use—the eggbeaters, washing machines, frying pans, and flour sifters that helped women and their servants to be more efficient with their work so they could enjoy other new inventions, like the phonograph or praxinoscope to watch moving pictures.

Mr. Bissette took his cigar out of his mouth, and the new smoke joined the cloud that hovered above them. "What are you considering right now?"

Chase smiled. "I'm never working on just one thing."

Mr. Bissette glanced at Mr. Grunier. "I suppose we'll have to hire a detective to find out."

"You can try," Chase joked, "but it would have to be a pretty good detective."

Mr. Grunier's jovial smile widened. "All we're asking for is a bit of a preview."

"Ahh, a hint." Chase leaned closer. "I'll tell you all about it…after the patent comes through."

The men chuckled.

Mr. Grunier took a sip of wine. "Do you like our little island?"

"I'm enjoying—" he began, but what was he supposed to tell the man? He couldn't tell him about the stars, nor could he tell him how amused he was with the island people. "I've enjoyed exploring it."

Sarah stepped up beside Chase, nodding at the other men as she took his arm. "Aren't you gentlemen going to dance with your wives?"

They shrugged, looking sheepish, but neither one of them moved. It seemed they were as anxious to dance as he was.

"Gracie has been asking about you," Sarah whispered.

"Please tell her that I'm doing incredibly well this evening."

"Just dance with her once, so she knows you're still interested in courting her."

He nodded at the men. "I'll return in a moment."

They smiled at him, part in understanding and part in pity.

He directed Sarah toward the door. "I'm not interested in courting her."

"Her father is—"

He smiled. "An expert on all things related to the weather."

"He is more than that."

Chase brushed off his sleeves. "He spent our entire evening avoiding any sort of decent discussion."

"Mr. Frederick was being polite for the women. Unlike other people—"

"Edward ruined his opportunity to do business with the man, and now he is trying flattery on the daughter."

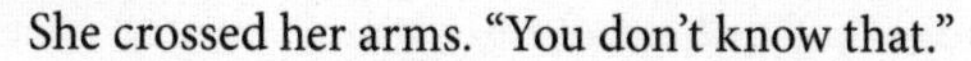

She crossed her arms. “You don’t know that.”

“All that discussion about a treed property that he’s never even seen… Mr. Frederick isn’t stupid.”

“The property is treed.”

“How do you know?”

Sarah didn’t answer the question.

He loved his sister, but he wouldn’t marry or even court a woman because of Edward’s business prospects. It hadn’t worked when Sarah married Edward, and it wouldn’t work if Chase married Gracie Frederick, either. It didn’t take a brilliant businessman to figure out that Edward was as dangerous as dynamite when it came to finances. Investments were blown to smithereens at his touch.

Sarah’s gaze trailed over his shoulder, and she fluttered her fingers at someone. He turned and groaned when he saw Gracie crossing the crowded room.

Sarah smiled pleasantly as the woman approached. “We were just talking about you.”

Feathers adorned Gracie’s hair, and her bodice dipped so low that he wondered for a moment where it ended. He struggled to keep his eyes on her face.

She smiled at him as if she was enjoying his battle to control his eyes. Sometimes he wondered what was wrong with women. They enjoyed tempting and teasing their male counterparts and then were angry when a man succumbed to appreciating the temptation.

She opened her fan and breezed it across her face. “I hope it was a good conversation.”

“Of course,” Sarah insisted.

A trumpet blasted behind him, followed by an assortment of instruments, and couples swarmed onto the floor to dance the polka.

Sarah leaned closer to Gracie. “Did I tell you that my brother loves to dance?”

Gracie tilted her head. “Your talents continue to amaze me, Mr. Darrington.”

He had no good choice but to hold out his arm. "It would be my pleasure."

She took it, and he led her to the floor. His steps felt awkward, but he managed to avoid her toes.

"You are a fine dancer," she said.

He shook his head. "Lying doesn't become you, Miss Frederick."

"I'm not lying."

But they both knew that she was. It was everything he could to do to keep his arms up as he counted the beats in his head.

When the song ended, he gave a slight nod of his head. "And now I must bid you adieu."

She clung to his arm. "Whatever for?"

"I have some business I must attend to."

She tilted her head, smiling at him in a way that made him want to run. "Business can always wait."

He shook his head. "Tonight it is urgent. Business before pleasure, as they say."

She released his arm. "Who would say something so ridiculous?"

"Good night, Miss Frederick," he said, turning on his heel and marching straight toward the veranda. He didn't check to see whether she was following, but when he stepped onto the patio, he was alone.

With the hotel's electric lights behind him, he couldn't tell if the clouds were gone this evening, but even if he couldn't see the sky, he wanted to find the lighthouse. Tonight.

He slipped back into the hotel, taking a door into the lobby instead of the ballroom. Hurrying upstairs, he unlocked the safe and retrieved his satchel.

Henry was at the carriage house, and when he saw Chase's satchel, he smiled. "You want me to take you back up to the fort?"

He shook his head. "Not tonight. But I wonder if you could take me someplace else."

"Where's that?"

"To the old lighthouse on the eastern bluff."

"There's no lighthouse on the island."

"It's supposed to be hidden behind the trees."

Henry pulled on his beard. "Well now, I can't say I've ever driven that far from the village at night."

"If you could just get me close, I'll look for it."

It took fewer than twenty minutes for the carriage to cross the interior of the island. Henry stopped where Chase directed, even though it was only a guess. Chase took the lantern that Henry handed to him and began to walk along the road, looking for some sort of trail through the forest. As far as he could tell, everything was overgrown.

He hiked north, searching the trees with his lantern, but there didn't seem to be any path. He stopped by a rock, looking back through the trees with the ray of light. The weeds seemed a bit lower at one point, as if someone had tracked through them recently. He stepped closer and saw a ribbon tied around a branch. The color was faded and bleached by the sun, the ends raveled, but he hoped it was some sort of marker.

Walking up a hill, he searched the trees until he spotted the walls of a gray stone house above him. And the tower.

He moved quickly now until he reached the doorway of the house partially hidden in the overgrowth. If the tower was still intact, perhaps he could see the stars from there.

A thick blanket of dust covered the floor and the furniture on the first floor, and in the dust, Chase saw footprints. He knelt down to examine them. They were much too small to be a man's.

Perhaps the place *was* haunted.

He laughed at himself. A ghost wouldn't leave footprints.

He followed the prints across the room to a writing desk. Rolling the top back, he found some sort of tablet inside. He picked it up and opened it.

On the first page was a pencil sketch, beautifully drawn. It was a picture of a woman looking out at the water, her long hair blowing in the wind.

On the next page was a woman walking on the beach alone. Her long hair was loose again, trailing behind her. Above both women were dozens of stars.

He flipped the pages and saw more drawings of stars and several of the lighthouse. And multiple pictures of the same woman—sitting on a rock, riding a bicycle, running through the water with the hem of her gown bustled in her hands.... Whoever had drawn these captured both longing and beauty on paper, but the artist hadn't signed her name—and he was fairly certain the artist was a woman.

He put the sketches back inside the desk.

What manner of woman would come to a lighthouse to draw?

An intriguing woman.

He climbed the steps to the tower, being careful to duck when he got close to the top. The clouds hid the stars tonight, but there was no glare from the village lights like there had been at Fort Holmes.

When the clouds went away, the view would be nothing short of spectacular.

* * * * *

Mama waited to bring her a tray of coffee and toast until the sun had been up for several hours. Elena propped herself up on her pillow and thanked her for the food. Parker and his driver had brought her home around three in the morning, long after her parents were in bed.

Mama was already dressed for the day, but she looked like she might need another cup of coffee. "Did you find Mr. Darrington?"

Elena leaned back against her pillows, a china cup with black coffee cradled in her hands. Warm air blew through the open window. "I tried."

"I spent the evening searching for him, hoping for an introduction," Mama said. "Martha Grunier pointed out Sarah Powell to me, but not her brother."

Elena set her cup back on the tray and rubbed her sore feet. She'd looked for Mr. Darrington for the remainder of the dance as well, worried about meeting him and yet intrigued by how elusive he'd managed to be.

"I met Edward Powell," she said, watching her mother's face for her reaction.

Mama's eyes narrowed. "Mr. Powell has a very poor reputation."

"I guessed as much."

Mama scooted her chair closer, her voice urgent. "You must stay away from him."

Elena nodded. Even with his wife beside him, Edward continued to flirt with other women during the night, not seeming to care in the least about his wife's reputation or feelings. Some people in their circle might be okay with his indiscretions, but the Bissette family was not.

"Does Mr. Darrington have a poor reputation as well?" Her voice trembled.

Mama shook her head. "I would never ask you to marry someone like Mr. Powell."

She studied her mother's face again, and she believed her. Even though Mama was desperate for Elena to marry a wealthy man, she wouldn't urge Elena to marry someone who would mistreat her. Her future husband would have a reputation for being honorable, but even her mother couldn't guarantee that he would be faithful to her.

"Apparently Mr. Darrington took Gracie on a picnic yesterday." Her mother sighed. "Elizabeth Frederick promised she'd share the man's company."

"You can't be upset with her for trying to marry off her daughter too."

"You are just as pretty as Gracie Frederick." Mama examined her face. "Maybe more so."

"I'm sure there are plenty of pretty women in Detroit as well, and yet Mr. Darrington has chosen not to marry."

Her mother's fingers curled around the arms of the chair. "We have to figure out what this Mr. Darrington is looking for in a wife."

Elena sighed. What if he wanted the perfect hostess or a stern manager of the servants in his household? Things she was not.

She picked up her coffee again. After a night on Mackinac's social stage, she was exhausted, but it was one thing to perform during an event like the ball. It was quite another to have to pretend in one's home.

She didn't want to spend the rest of her life trying to perform for her husband. It wasn't fair to deceive any man into thinking she was someone else.

"The future Mrs. Darrington will have to be charming, for certain, and perhaps inquisitive like he is," her mother said.

"I don't know the first thing about inventing."

Her mother sat back. "Or perhaps he doesn't want a wife to be so inquisitive. Maybe he would want someone to support his work rather than partner with him in it."

Elena sighed again.

Her mother patted her hands. "You'll make an excellent wife to him either way."

She wanted to bring honor to her husband's name and not embarrass him. And she prayed she wouldn't marry a man like Edward Powell, whose eyes wandered.

Her father peeked around the door. "Is my little girl awake?"

She saluted him with her cup of coffee. "I'm not a little girl."

He stepped into her room. "You were quite the belle last night."

"Those dances are exhausting."

"They're supposed to be exhilarating," Mama said.

Papa sat on the side of her bed, his cane resting beside him. "Did you enjoy your time with Parker?"

She nodded.

Mama smoothed her hand over the bedcovers. "We were lamenting the fact that Mr. Darrington didn't make an appearance last night."

"Mr. Darrington?" She saw the twinkle in her father's eyes. "He was there."

Mama swiveled in her chair. "He was?"

"A fine gentleman, I must say."

Mama brushed her hands over her skirt. "You met him?"

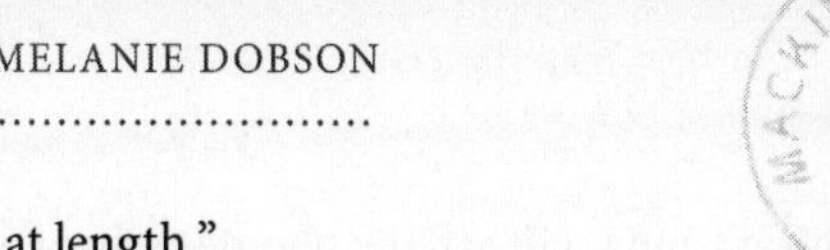

"Of course. We talked at length."

"Arthur!" she exclaimed. "Why didn't you introduce me...and Elena?"

"Well...Elena seemed busy dancing, and Mr. Darrington was equally as busy avoiding the dance floor."

Elena watched Mama's face, which was teetering between whether she should reprimand her husband for not introducing them or forgive him quickly so she could get the information she desired. Apparently she chose the second route.

"What was he like?" she asked, her voice as sweet as the fudge they sold down on Main Street.

Elena leaned forward, waiting for Papa's answer. She didn't want to be intrigued, but she couldn't help herself.

"Mr. Darrington was a sordid man who kept picking his teeth and talking so much that the hotel manager had to evict him from the ball."

"Papa—"

"And you should have seen those teeth. They were gigantic."

Elena giggled. "I can't marry a man with big teeth."

He tapped the covers, his face as serious as his voice. "Absolutely not."

"Oh, Arthur," her mother sighed. "What was he really like?"

He moved to a chair, crossing his legs quite leisurely. Apparently he was in no rush to tell his story. "I suppose he was as intelligent as most men. And a friendly sort."

Her mother glanced at her. "Was he handsome?"

"If you like big teeth." Papa laughed at Mama's loud groan. "I have no idea what handsome looks like."

"Was he tall?" Mama asked.

"He stood an inch or two above me."

"You're tall, Arthur."

Papa puffed out his chest. "Do you consider me handsome as well?"

Mama rolled her eyes. "What color was his hair?"

"A brown color, I suppose."

"A honey brown or a mousy brown?"

"Next time I will ask the photographer to take his picture."

Elena met her father's gaze. "Did he smile, Papa?"

"That he did. And quite often."

She was relieved to hear it. She couldn't stand the thought of marrying a man like Edward Powell, who didn't smile.

Mama clapped her hands together. "You must invite Mr. Darrington over for dinner this week."

Elena looked at her father, and he patted her hand. "I just might do that."

"Right away."

"Now, Deborah, we don't want to rush him."

Elena's gaze wandered to the window. "Can I do something outside today?"

Mama shook her head. "Mr. Darrington might call."

"Perhaps we can take a horse ride this afternoon," Papa offered.

"Elena can't be off riding when Mr. Darrington comes."

She sank back against her pillows. "He's not going to come visit me."

"Maybe he will visit your father."

That's just what she needed. A suitor more intrigued with her father than with her.

She heard the bell ring for their front door.

Mama hopped out of her chair. "Who do you suppose that is?"

Elena looked at the clock. It was a quarter after ten. Mr. Darrington wouldn't be calling. Or, at least, she hoped he wouldn't be.

"It's probably the ice delivery," Papa offered, but her mother didn't reply.

Footsteps traveled down the hallway, and then Jillian stepped into her room. "Miss Elena has an invitation," she said as she held out the envelope in her hands. "The messenger is waiting for her reply."

Her mother rushed to the door, taking the note, and then slid her thumb under the wax seal to open it. After she read the note, she tossed it onto the bed.

"Parker Randolph has invited you on a carriage ride around the island this morning."

Elena watched Jillian's face, and her friend looked like she was about to cry.

Elena picked up the invitation and skimmed the words. "He is inviting me along with several others."

"You'll have to tell him you can't go," her mother said.

Her gaze traveled back to the window, to the lake beyond. At least she could get some fresh air today. "Why not?"

"Because Mr. Darrington might call."

She turned her head. "Papa?"

He cleared his throat. "Actually, your mother is correct."

"She is?"

"Mr. Darrington might call." He paused. "But last night he told me that he especially enjoys exploring outside the village. With this kind of weather, you might have better luck in seeing him on a carriage ride than staying here."

Mama's eyes sparked. "Are you certain?"

He nodded. "He might even join Parker's party today."

Mama clapped her hands. "Like he did for the picnic with Gracie Frederick."

"That's a splendid thought, Deborah."

Mama pointed toward the envelope. "What time will they leave?"

Elena glanced at the invitation. "He said he could arrive here at eleven."

"We must hurry, then." Her mother looked toward Jillian. "Tell the messenger that Elena will be ready at eleven fifteen."

Jillian nodded, but Elena could still see a trace of sadness in her eyes.

"Mama," Elena said slowly, "might Jillian join me this morning?"

Her mother eyed the maid and then looked back at her. "Jillian is needed here."

"With all that happened on the pier," she started, "I just thought—

if something happened to my hair again...," she said slowly. "Jillian would be there to help me fix it."

A gust of wind blew through the window as if to remind them of the dangers.

Her mother cocked her head, searching Elena's face for her motive. Elena smiled in return. She just might need Jillian.

"There might not be room in the carriage," her mother said.

"I'm sure Parker would make room. I heard Gracie Frederick always brings her personal maid with her on outings."

Her mother considered this news for a moment. "Tell the messenger that Miss Elena and her companion will be joining Mr. Randolph." She eyed the clock again. "At eleven thirty."

Chapter Eleven

A team of horses pulled their spirited party of eight—including one hired photographer—toward Arch Rock, a limestone bridge that hung a hundred and fifty feet above the water. Except for the photographer, no one else in the party owned a camera, but they all loved to have their pictures taken. On outings like these, often a photographer and his equipment accompanied them.

The women laughed gaily around Elena as they rode through the forest on the island's interior roads. She couldn't understand what the ladies thought was so funny, but she was grateful to be out of the house. Her mother would be disappointed when she returned. Mr. Darrington was not among the party that Parker had gathered for the excursion. She'd been relieved when she realized that Mr. Powell—she would never think of him as Edward again—was not among them either.

"Did you enjoy the dance last night?" Trudy Grunier asked her.

She resisted the urge to yawn. "I suppose."

"Did you see that atrocious hat on Minnie Falstand?"

"I can't say I noticed," she said, though she couldn't help but see the extravagant concoction of orange-and-yellow on the young woman's head.

Trudy laughed. "She looked like a street lamp."

Elena glanced over at Jillian, but her friend wasn't looking at her. Her eyes were on Parker as he told a story about his visit to Boston. Had she met Parker on the steamer, or had they known each another before? And did Parker feel for Jillian what she apparently felt for him?

Plenty of wealthy men showed interest in their servants, but not in public settings. That was behind closed doors, after one stepped out of the limelight. She never wanted Jillian to live in a place where a man like Edward Powell might knock on her bedroom door.

"Do you think the rain will spoil our day?" Trudy asked.

Elena eyed the clouds piling up above them. She didn't care much about the day, but she didn't want it to rain tonight.

The carriage stopped near the arch, and Parker hopped out to help the ladies down. His grasp, Elena noticed, lasted a bit longer when he was helping Jillian. Perhaps he did care about her.

"Come along, Elena," Trudy directed.

Jillian stayed by the carriage.

Parker stopped and turned around. "You don't want to miss the view of the water, Miss Bernard."

Jillian looked at him. "I can't come."

He turned toward Elena. "Lanie, could you please instruct your lovely friend to join the rest of our party?"

Elena smiled. The feelings were indeed mutual, and she loved Parker for it. Not only had he shown Jillian respect by addressing her as Miss Bernard, but he'd called her Elena's friend instead of maid.

"Please come with us." She waved. "It's a beautiful sight."

Jillian reluctantly stepped forward, eyeing them both for a moment before her gaze turned to the exquisite view in front of them. The stone bridge was arched fifty feet across the cliffs, with the turquoise water sparkling below. Elena couldn't imagine a single place under the stars as beautiful as this.

"Everyone get together," Parker directed, "so we can take a photograph."

Elena climbed carefully out onto the rocky bridge with the others. A strong gust of wind could blow them all over the edge, but the wind seemed to have taken a vacation for the moment as well. Parker joked as they lined up on the natural bridge. Jillian didn't join the rest of them at first, but Elena watched as he coaxed her onto the narrow slip of rocks.

When they were all in place, the photographer instructed them to hold their breath and silently count to fifteen. After the serious picture for their parents, they took a silly picture with each of them gazing off in a different direction. The others didn't know it, of course, but Elena posed looking north of the rock, toward her secret place.

When they finished the last picture, Parker directed them back off the rock. As they descended toward the carriage, she heard something rustle in the trees. Two men emerged onto the grassy area, suspenders strung over their plain shirts and work shoes sticking out from under their trousers. The lankier man held a bundle of poles in his hand, the sides of his handsome face flanked by sideburns. His companion held a wooden box.

"All right, ladies," Parker called to them, his voice more urgent, "time to get into the carriage."

He held out his hand and helped first Jillian and then Elena into the carriage, but Trudy lingered by the door.

"There's no reason to rush," Trudy said, eyeing the men.

Parker nudged her elbow toward the carriage. "I, for one, am starting to get hungry."

Trudy shooed him with her fan. "You're not going to starve."

Elena glanced over as the men hiked by them, apparently headed to the water below Arch Rock. Neither of them even looked at Trudy, and she seemed quite disconcerted by their inattention. One of them men turned back, and Elena felt a blush climb up her cheeks. It was the soldier from the pier, dressed in plainclothes.

Parker sighed. "We might just have to leave you, Tru—"

"Wait a minute." Elena scrambled over the legs of those already seated.

"Where are you going?" Parker asked.

She climbed down the steps, glancing back at Jillian. Her friend looked just as concerned.

"I'll be right back," she said simply and rushed toward the soldiers. Trudy sighed loudly behind her.

"Just a moment, please!" she called out to the men.

They turned slowly. The taller one looked at her with appreciation, but his companion's eyes grew wide as he seemed to recognize her.

"You were at the pier," she said. "I thought you were leaving on the steamer."

"No, ma'am." He shook his head. "I was saying good-bye to a friend."

"I didn't get to thank you." She thought he might be in his early twenties, though it was hard to tell.

He looked at his toes. "You don't need to thank me."

"If you hadn't caught me, I would have fallen into the water."

He scratched his foot uncomfortably in the dirt.

"I'm sorry my mother was rude to you. She had no right to be unkind."

He met her gaze. "Any good mother would have been scared."

Scared?

She blinked as she slowly processed his words.

Had her fall frightened her mother? If she had gone over the dock in her heavy skirts, it would have been difficult for even the best swimmer to rescue her. Had Mama been worried about her drowning even more than her fall?

She looked at the poles in his hand. "What are you carrying?"

He held it up. "A fishing pole."

"It's in pieces," she said and then felt silly. Of course he knew it was in pieces.

Trudy joined her side. "Are you going to try to fish with that?"

He lifted his chin a notch. "I've already fished with it."

"But how?" Elena asked.

He clicked the three poles together to make one long fishing rod.

"Impressive," Trudy said.

The second soldier elbowed his friend. "Lieutenant Hull made it."

"Are you coming?" Parker called from the carriage.

She thanked the lieutenant one last time. If he hadn't grabbed for her hand on the pier…she didn't want to think what might have happened.

*****

As Chase walked down Main Street, he bought a German sausage wrapped in brown paper and a bottle of Coca-Cola from a street vendor. Sipping the icy drink, he passed by the post office, the opera house, a theatre featuring *Edison's Kinetoscope* with the accompaniment of a piano player, and plenty of hotels for those who couldn't afford to stay at the Grand. The sidewalk was crowded with tourists stopping to get fudge or have their picture taken in the photography studio, and he enjoyed the anonymity of losing himself amongst them.

His sister was livid this morning, angry at Elena Bissette for trying to seduce her husband last night. For the life of him, Chase couldn't understand why any woman would want to seduce Edward. If this Miss Bissette was the gold digger Miss Frederick implied, she must think that Edward was wealthy. Or she was trying to charm him into spending the little money he still had on her. At least this Miss Bissette was no longer intent on marrying him.

Even as Sarah ranted this morning, Chase felt sorry for his sister. He had no doubt that this woman had flirted with Edward, but if Edward wouldn't encourage these advances, women would stop pursuing him as well.

He'd left his sister beginning her preparations for the masquerade party at the governor's mansion tonight. He had no idea where Edward had gone. Chase's pressing business was done for the day, so he'd walked through the small art gallery at the hotel for a half hour before coming down to the village. The paintings only made him wonder anew about the artist at the lighthouse. He had just a few days left on the island, but he hoped he might meet the woman before he headed to Chicago for his meeting.

Tonight he would attend the masquerade party with Sarah and Edward. It was one invitation he wouldn't try to wiggle out of, even if he had to dress in costume. He'd only met Governor Rich once before, but he was impressed with all he'd read about the man's integrity. At least the governor was trying to recover the state's economy after the panic last year.

Chase wandered the village streets, eating his sausage and watching the wagons haul crates and mammoth trunks up to the summer cottages. It intrigued him to see how things operated—in this case the organization of a town that existed primarily for its tourists. He would have liked the place a lot better when they were trading fur or the fisherman were hauling in their catch for the day to sell instead of pandering to the summer guests.

As he strolled toward the edge of town, he heard a bark. A dog slid under a gate and sprinted toward him. It was the mutt from the races. He looked more brown than white today, with mud splotching his coat alongside the black spots.

"Hello there," Chase said as he continued walking.

The dog followed him.

Chase waved his hand back at the house. "You'd better go home."

When he took another step, the dog stayed at his side, his tongue wagging as he watched the sausage in Chase's hands.

Chase sighed. Everyone—even this dog—wanted something from him.

He took one last bite of the sausage and then fed the rest to the dog. He thought the dog would run away once the food was gone, but he continued to follow him.

Chase and the dog rounded the corner of the island, slipping away from the village. Somewhere ahead of him, hidden up in the bluffs, was the lighthouse. With the busyness of the village far behind him, all he could hear was the ripple of water on the shoreline. There were rocks to his right and the tall bluffs on his left. He would turn back in a bit, but he could think clearer out here than he could at the hotel.

In front of him were two soldiers out on a dock, fishing. Chase wandered up behind the men and stopped to watch.

"Sit," he commanded the dog, and the animal obeyed. Together they spent the next fifteen minutes watching the fishermen cast their lines and reel in their catch. When the soldiers finished, they didn't put the fishing poles over their shoulders. Instead, they pulled their bamboo poles apart into three pieces and bundled them in their hands.

Mesmerized, Chase stepped forward and spoke to the younger man. "You just—you folded up your fishing rod."

"I did."

"I've never seen anything like that before."

The young soldier held up the three pieces of his rod. "It makes it easier to carry."

"Did you make that?"

"It wasn't hard," he said with a shrug. "I just put these joints in here and strung the line through the bamboo."

Sometimes it was the simplest of ideas that made the most money.

Chase leaned closer, lowering his voice, though no one was around to hear. "Did you get a patent for it?"

He shrugged. "Why would I need a patent?"

A white carriage stopped behind them, and Chase turned to see Edward watching him. The man's timing couldn't be much worse.

He turned back to the soldier. "What is your name?"

"Silas." He reached for the string of whitefish with his free hand, and they glistened silver in the sunlight. "Silas Hull."

"Could you meet me in the lobby at the Grand Hotel? Tomorrow?"

He shook his head. "I'm on duty tomorrow, up at the fort."

"Then perhaps Monday?"

Silas shook his head again. "I could be there on Tuesday morning, say, around eleven."

Edward stepped up beside him, clutching Chase's shoulders as if he needed an anchor. His words slurred when he spoke. "Sarah—she's worried about you."

Chase glanced over at the two soldiers, embarrassed by his brother-in-law's display. The men were compiling the contents of their tackle boxes. Chase unwrapped himself from Edward's arm and let it drop. "How much have you had to drink?"

"Not enough." Edward laughed. "Sarah doesn't think you got yourself one of those costumes for tonight yet."

"She's right."

Edward looked down at the dog and then back at the soldiers. His eyes focused on the short poles in Silas Hull's hand, and Chase's stomach dropped. Would his brother-in-law beat him to this investment?

"What's that ridi—" He paused, trying to form the word. "Ridi—"

"Ridiculous?" Silas offered.

He nodded. "What's that ridiculous thing?"

Silas sighed. "It's a fishing pole."

"Not that." Edward's hand shook when he pointed to Chase's side. "That."

When the dog growled at Edward, Chase laughed. "He's one of the participants from the dog race."

"Well, he looks pathetic."

"I could say the same—" Chase stopped himself. There might be nothing ridiculous about the dog, but it was ridiculous to fight with a drunken man.

The dog growled again, and Edward backed toward the carriage. At least the animal was a good judge of character.

"It's time to go," Edward said as he climbed back into the carriage.

Chase looked back at the poles and then met Silas's eye. "Don't forget. Tuesday morning."

Silas nodded.

Chase petted the dog again and climbed into the carriage. When he turned around, the soldiers were gone but the dog was still sitting there, watching him. He wished he could spend the afternoon with the dog instead of Edward.

December 21, 1812

The nights seem to last forever. There is no more oil to light the lantern, no way to obtain any more, but there is enough food to last us through the winter, enough wood to warm our house.

It is almost as if Jonah knew he would be going away.

I can no longer write these words to my husband, but I must write for myself. And for our children. Every day, I think back to those moments that Jonah disappeared. It seems so long ago now, but my mind still sifts through our last hours together that morning. He might have seemed nervous that day. Or was he scared?

In my hurry to fetch water, I never tried to console him or even inquire about his feelings. Everyone who visited us seemed scared at the time, not knowing what the British would do now that they occupied our island.

We haven't had any visitors since Jonah left, nor have we gone to church or even to the market.

I don't know if everyone else is afraid, for I am now too scared to leave the house. Scared that I will miss Jonah if he returns. Scared that someone will remember that the children and I are still here and take us away as well.

Chapter Twelve

Mama stood over Jillian, instructing her how to clip and curl Elena's hair. Elena stared into the mirror of her dressing room as the women hovered over her. Twenty minutes ago she'd declared her hair finished, yet Mama insisted that Jillian continue to curl the strands over and over again around the pearl clip that held back her hair. Her scratches were almost gone, the remaining lines covered with powder, but it didn't matter. She was wearing a mask tonight.

She squirmed in her chair. "I'm about to fall over."

Mama patted her shoulder. "You're doing just fine."

The clock chimed from across the small room. "The party starts in a half hour," she pleaded. Anything to get her out of this chair.

"We don't want to arrive too early, nor do you want to look like you've been tromping around the island all afternoon."

The invitation to attend a masquerade with the governor had arrived while Elena was away on the carriage ride. Her mother hadn't expected invitations to events like this over the summer, and she was thrilled about another opportunity to meet Mr. Darrington, since the man had managed to elude them last night.

The remainder of Elena's afternoon had been spent in a flurry, airing out her costume dress for the dinner and then the endless rearranging of her hair and powdering of her face.

"Tuck another feather right in here," Mama directed, pointing at the two feathers already secured in the pearl clip. "Then we'll finish my hair."

She rushed out of the room.

Jillian added the feather and then carefully curled the strands around the clip one more time. When Elena tilted her head, the curls bounced.

"You're an artist," Elena said.

Jillian kept her eyes on her hands as she continued to work, but Elena saw the hint of a smile. No matter what Mama threatened, she'd never let Jillian go. A personal maid who could arrange hair in the latest fashions was in high demand.

"Mr. Darrington won't be able to take his eyes off you," Jillian whispered.

"He won't be able to see my face."

Jillian winked at her. "He won't need to."

"I wish you were going with me, to see Parker."

"Hush," Jillian said with a nervous glance toward the door. "No one can find out."

"How long have you two been—communicating?"

"Since October, when he came to the benefit at your house."

"But he hasn't been back since then."

Jillian smiled. "Nell's son is Mr. Randolph's steward."

"So you've been writing?"

Jillian shrugged.

Elena reached for the heart locket, and Jillian clipped it on. The necklace would be hidden under her cape, but she still liked to wear it whenever she went out.

She met Jillian's gaze in the mirror. "Has he said he loves you?"

"Of course not."

"Well, he does. I can tell."

"But you and Parker—" Jillian began.

"Are just like brother and sister. We always have been, in spite of our parents wanting us to marry."

Jillian shook her head. "We could never marry."

"You don't know that."

"I do know and so does Parker, but he wants to enjoy this season... and so do I."

If only Elena could figure out a way for Jillian and Parker to be happy together.

* * * * *

Jillian handed Elena the papier-mâché mask of a cat before she stepped into the carriage. Sequins glittered on the yellow cape that enveloped her gown, and she felt a bit like a princess. The costume reminded her of the spring she spent three years ago in Italy with her parents, walking along the canals in Venice and visiting the halls of art museums in Florence and Rome. And going to a Venetian ball.

The governor's cottage was high on a bluff, overlooking the harbor. Stepping outside the carriage, Elena breathed in the scent of lilacs that bordered the walkway. There was a long row of carriages behind her parents' carriage, waiting for their guests.

"Put your mask on," Mama instructed as she adjusted her own red-and-gold mask. Jillian had woven red-and-gold plumes into her pompadour.

Elena strung the ribbons of her mask behind her head and tied it. She didn't need a mask to pretend to be someone else, though. She'd become plenty good at pretending on her own.

Masqueraded in a white mask, black tricorne, and flowing cloak, Papa escorted her toward the door. Mama followed close behind.

"Tonight's the night for you to meet Mr. Darrington," Mama whispered as they walked toward the imposing front door. "I can feel it."

"He might not come."

"He'll be here," she insisted.

A bronze chandelier hung from the towering ceiling in the entryway of the mansion. The ebony staircase split into two on the second floor and wound around the top of the room. Governor Rich greeted them with a well-practiced smile, and Elena lowered her mask, shaking the man's hand gracefully and yet with perfect control as they'd taught her to do at the Lawnton School for Girls in Chicago.

His smile widened when he shook her father's hand. Then he motioned for Mr. Bissette to follow him. "There is someone I'd like you to meet."

She watched Papa walk away with the governor and then stepped forward beside Mama into a ballroom with a banquet board that stretched the length of the ballroom in preparation for dinner. A dozen windows looked out over the village and the lake, and people were pressed together near the windows.

Mrs. Grunier rushed up to them, her lips trembling. "Mr. Darrington is already here."

Her mother stopped, glancing at the small crowd. "Where is he?"

Mrs. Grunier pointed toward another room. "Last time I saw him, he was talking with Trudy in one of the drawing rooms." Her smile widened. "He was enjoying her company."

Elena managed a smile in return. Poor Mr. Darrington. There didn't seem to be a mother on the island who wasn't trying to marry off her daughter to him.

"Elizabeth swears that he's practically offered his hand to Gracie, but I don't know how that's possible, so soon after meeting."

Mama nudged her forward, toward the drawing room. "What is Mr. Darrington dressed like?"

Mrs. Grunier hesitated, as if she wasn't sure if she should divulge this information. "A phantom."

"Perhaps you would be able to secure an introduction for us," her mother suggested. "Since Elena and Trudy are such dear friends."

"I suppose I could," Mrs. Grunier said, a bit reluctantly.

"Then we will all have the pleasure of making his acquaintance."

Elena nodded to Mrs. Grunier and followed her mother to the next room. People were crammed into the large drawing room, shoulder to shoulder, and sipping the finest of colorful drinks to accompany their attire.

Mama grasped for Elena's hand, and they carefully navigated their way through the room. Her mother scanned the crowd, but Elena focused her gaze straight ahead so no one could accuse her of searching for Mr. Darrington.

"Do you see Mrs. Powell?" Mama whispered.

Elena glanced to her side, surveying the room of mysterious masks and costumes, and then shook her head.

She knew that her mother was starting to feel desperate with so many debutantes already making Mr. Darrington's acquaintance. If he truly enjoyed Gracie's or even Trudy's company, Elena almost hoped he would marry one of them.

Then she scolded herself for her thought.

Mrs. Frederick stopped them as they entered the library, telling them in detail about the picnic Gracie and Mr. Darrington had attended. The man was indeed quite smitten with her daughter, Mrs. Frederick confirmed.

Elena retied the strings on her cape. It seemed to be quite the epidemic—Mr. Darrington enjoying the company of unmarried women across the island.

"Have you met him yet?" Mrs. Frederick asked, her eyes on Elena.

"Mr. Darrington will be joining us soon for dinner at our home." Her mother fanned her face leisurely. Elena knew she didn't dare allow the Fredericks to find out that she hadn't yet secured an introduction to Mr. Darrington, not when Gracie Frederick was their toughest competitor. "He and my husband have become business acquaintances."

"I didn't realize—" The surprise in Mrs. Frederick's tone was apparent.

"A lot of people enjoy my father's company," Elena interjected. Even if their money was almost gone, her father hadn't changed one bit.

"I didn't mean any offense," Mrs. Fredrick said.

"Of course you didn't," Mama replied, squeezing Elena's hand lightly.

She had most certainly meant to be offensive. Why didn't her mother stand up to the woman?

"I'm certain you will enjoy Mr. Darrington's company as much as we have."

A bell chimed, calling them to dinner.

Her mother found the cards with the Bissette names on them in the dining room, above each setting with its china plates, wine glasses, and eight pieces of polished silverware. Elena smiled when she read the place card next to hers. Parker Randolph.

The governor had seated the Randolph family with them.

Parker sauntered up to the table wearing a joker's mask designed with silver foil and a purple joker's hat with dangling silver bells that chimed when he turned toward her.

He lifted his mask. "How are you, Lanie?"

She inched her chin up. "Quite fine, thank you."

He looked around the room. "There don't seem to be any soldiers here for you to chase after."

"Be quiet." She shot a nervous glance at her mother. Her mother would be appalled if she found out that Elena had stopped to talk with Lieutenant Hull and his friend.

Parker grinned again. "Or perhaps you are fishing for a bigger catch tonight."

"I'm not fishing for anyone."

"Every debutante in this room seems to be focused on hooking poor Chester Darrington."

Chester.

She'd wondered about his first name. It was dignified, she supposed, if a bit stuffy. He was certainly aloof enough to rise to such a name.

"You can stop looking for him," Parker said.

"I'm not looking for him."

"I just saw him surrounded by a consortium of young ladies on the veranda."

Her mother turned. "Are you talking about Mr. Darrington?"

"I am."

"Then come along, Elena," Mama said.

"Don't worry, Lanie." Parker laughed. "I'm sure this fish will bite."

Elena trailed her mother through a series of small rooms until they reached a large drawing room outside the veranda.

"Wait here," her mother whispered. "I'll find him."

With the mask hiding her face, Elena waited near the doorway as the voices around her blended together. The glass doors along the drawing room were open, and as the sun set on the horizon, Elena could see the lights of the boats twinkling below them. The stars would be coming out tonight on a stage of their own, to perform for her and for those who paused their busy lives to watch the performance.

Stepping outside, she moved down into the maze of sculpted hedges and manicured gardens, joining people standing in pairs and enjoying the warm evening. There was a fountain and a small gazebo, and torches were lit along the pathways.

Then she saw a man dressed in a black cape and mask painted with green-and-black diamonds, looking down at the harbor below. She stood frozen by the hedge, yet she was curious to know if this was Mr. Darrington. And if it was, where had all his admirers gone?

Someone walked toward them and Elena turned away, looking at the rosebushes in the garden. Then she heard Mrs. Grunier's voice. "I was hoping to find you," she said. "I'd like to introduce you to a friend of Trudy's. Miss Elena Bissette."

Elena took another breath. It was finally time to meet this man.

Mr. Darrington spoke, his voice muffled by his mask—but his words were still clear to her. "I'm afraid Miss Bissette's reputation precedes her."

Afraid? Did he think she'd acted improperly with his brother-in-law?

Elena leaned back on a post, wanting to run and yet worried they might hear her if she left. She put her hand on her warm head. She couldn't allow herself to faint.

"I don't understand," Mrs. Grunier replied. "There is nothing unusual about Miss Bissette's reputation."

"I do not care to indulge in gossip."

"I am not asking you to," the woman said. "Miss Bissette has never been anything but kind to our family."

In that moment, Elena wanted to hug her.

"I'm still afraid I must decline," the man replied.

A steward stepped onto the porch and called out that dinner was ready.

Tears filled her eyes as she moved away from Mr. Darrington, and she blinked them back. Her mother wanted her to marry a man who had no interest in even meeting her, a man who thought her reputation to be a poor one.

If she were fishing, this was one man she'd never want to catch.

* * * * *

Chase snuck out of the party immediately after dessert. He left his costume in a pile on the floor of his hotel room, changing into his old clothes. Then he grabbed the satchel to trek the mile or so across the island under the cloak of night. Henry was still at the governor's mansion, waiting to drive Sarah and Edward home from the party, and he didn't want to hire another driver to take him on this journey.

Above the trees, he could see the sliver of the moon. It would be too early to see what was on its surface, but the lighthouse—and the artist—drew him back. He wanted to go one more time before his parents arrived in the morning. He was leaving the island on Thursday.

His pulse raced as he approached the lighthouse again. There was something special about this place. Perhaps it was that no one else on the island—with the exception of the artist—seemed to know about it. Or it could be the contrast of its quietness so close to a busy village.

He ducked under the doorway, but before he walked up the stairs, he rolled back the top on the desk. The sketchbook was still there, and he opened it and scanned the pages with his lantern light. Nothing new had been added since his visit two days ago. And he felt an odd sense of disappointment that she hadn't been here.

It might have been weeks or months since the artist was here last.

She might have even left the island by now.

But if she had gone, then whose footprints had he seen in the dust?

He picked up the sketchbook and climbed the steps so he could look at them one more time before he went to Chicago.

The canvas of the sky over the lighthouse was a masterpiece. The clouds were gone, replaced by a host of stars and the sliver of a moon cradled in the sky. He took out the telescope and removed the tripod. With his foot, he tested the balcony that surrounded the lighthouse. It held steady. He stepped onto it, tentatively at first. It swayed a bit but held.

Almost three hundred years ago, Galileo was the first to see the moon with a telescope, but outside an observatory, there was nothing as powerful today as the telescope in his hands. Richard said he could see the contours of the moon.

Scientists knew of eight planets in their solar system along with twenty moons. Some day, if the public demanded it, perhaps they would have a telescope that could see beyond the one moon, but he would be satisfied if he could explore the one with his eyes.

He set the telescope on the tripod and pressed the cup to his eye. Without the city lights, he could see the reds and blues in the stars.

Even if Gracie and her friends weren't interested, there would be people who wanted to see the stars and the moon.

Something scuffed below him. He glanced over the railing but didn't see anything. There were no deer or coyote on the island. Perhaps it was a possum or raccoon.

He listened for a moment, but the sound was gone.

His eye back on the telescope, he marveled again at the expanse of the sky until he heard a loud *clang*. This time it was from inside the lighthouse.

Had the artist come back?

Stepping back into the dome, he picked up her sketchbook in the darkness. If so, he was looking forward to meeting her.

Chapter Thirteen

Elena stared at the open desk from the doorway. She always shut it when she left so the mice wouldn't chew her sketches into small pieces for their nests. Mice couldn't open a desktop…could they?

The door clanged behind her, and she jumped.

When she moved back toward the desk, she leaned down and looked for her sketchbook. It was gone.

Her lantern in her hand, she searched under the desk and on the shelves nearby. In the six years that she'd visited the lighthouse, she'd never seen another person here. But someone must have come and taken her sketches.

She collapsed on the stone wall behind her. The sketches were more than just pictures. They were the secrets of her heart drawn in pencil.

Why would someone steal her secrets?

She stepped away from the desk, rubbing the goose bumps on her arms. If only she could trust herself to think straight…

But it was long after midnight, and she was exhausted after the masquerade party, after hearing Mr. Darrington disparage her reputation and then avoid meeting her.

She sat down in a chair beside the desk.

Her family needed her to marry, but it would never happen if she couldn't even get a man like this Mr. Darrington to meet her.

Her mother was frustrated, and Elena wondered if the news of their financial ruin had reached Mr. Darrington's ears. Perhaps that was the real reason why he didn't want to meet her.

In that case, she didn't want to meet him either.

If only her mother wasn't so intent on securing a partnership between them. Neither of them could force this man to propose to her.

When her family arrived home tonight, her mother had gone straight to her bedroom. Elena was tired as well, but the stars seemed to call to her as they rode home from the ball. More than anything, she wanted to escape to her safe place and fill herself with the beauty of God's creation while she created along with Him.

At the moment, her safe place didn't feel quite so safe.

She rushed to the bedroom and opened the trunk, pushing through the old clothes until she found the diary she'd discovered so long ago. At least the story of the lighthouse was still here.

Her thoughts wandered back to the desk.

She didn't know if she would be able to obtain another sketchbook on the island, at least not secretly, to bring here. It didn't make any sense for someone to take it. Her work wouldn't be valuable to anyone else, but she felt closest to the Creator when she created. Now the sketchbook, her own creations, were gone.

But He was still here, even if she couldn't draw. He was in the stars and the light and the lapping water below. Perhaps she didn't need her sketchbook to experience Him and His presence.

Picking up her lantern, she began to climb the steps. With or without her pencils and paper, she needed to be close to Him tonight.

* * * * *

A surge of lantern light illuminated the tower, blinding Chase. He shielded his eyes against it.

"Who are you?" a woman demanded.

He peeked between his fingers to see the woman, but all he saw was her shadow. "Would you be so kind as to lower your lantern?"

Instead she lifted it higher. "As soon as you tell me who you are."

He smiled. Most women would be terrified, finding an unknown man alone in the forest, but this lady acted as though she owned the lighthouse. Perhaps she did.

"A gentleman," he replied.

The light still shone in his eyes. "Anyone can say he's a gentleman."

"If you put any stock in promises, I vow to you that I will remain a gentleman." He blinked again. "If you lower your light."

"And if I don't?"

"I've told you I'm a gentleman," he said. "But who are you?"

She took a step toward him. "Someone who wants her sketches back."

He folded his arms, smiling. "You're the artist."

"I—I wouldn't call myself an artist."

He leaned back against the window as his eyes started to adjust to the light, but he could still only see the outline of a woman.

"You have a good eye for art," he said. "And a good hand."

She lowered her lantern several inches. "How would you know?"

He shrugged. "Good art makes the beholder feel something. Come alive, in a sense. Your pictures are filled with emotion."

As his eyes focused, he saw the almond-colored hair on the young woman in front of him. It was swept back in a long braid instead of hidden under a hat like most of the women in his circle. He doubted that she was yet twenty, and she was quite attractive at that. She wore a calico work dress with a big gash across the hem and a simple gold locket around her neck in the shape of a heart. He was suddenly very glad he hadn't let Sarah burn his old trousers and ink-stained shirt.

Perhaps she was a maid to one of Mackinac's families—her confidence and speech were certainly influenced well. Or maybe she was educated, working as a governess to a family who couldn't pay her well.

Women like Gracie Frederick would be appalled at the sight of this woman's old dress, not to mention his own worn clothes. The very thought made him smile. It was easy to feign an aura of attractiveness when one had a thousand dollars and a magician in Paris who mastered in illusions.

A certain confidence and even beauty emanated from this woman in spite of her attire.

Yes, she was quite beautiful.

"Why are you smiling?" she demanded.

"Was I smiling?"

"If you are mocking me, Mr.—"

"I can assure you, there is only pleasure in my smile."

Instead of returning the sentiment, she held out her hand. "I'd like my sketches back."

"What sketches?"

Her eyes narrowed. "I don't appreciate your playing games with me. I know you have my book."

"The word *sketches* sounds so elementary." He tapped his fingers on the railing. "I don't know much about sketching, but I found some beautiful artwork in a book downstairs."

She hesitated, the accusations in her voice softening. "Do you still have it?"

"Certainly," he said, retrieving the book from his satchel with his free hand. When he handed it to her, she clutched it to her chest.

"Thank you," she said, and then her eyes traveled to his side. "What are you carrying?"

He tightened his grip on the copper in his fingers, thinking quickly about how to answer. He should make up a story about the instrument, saying it was some sort of eyepiece or compass. Or some sort of weather instrument, even. Perhaps she wouldn't know the difference.

And yet, he had seen a glimpse into the heart of this woman through her drawings. He might be crazy, but he felt like he could trust her with this secret. At least, he wanted to trust her. He didn't have to tell her about the importance of its power or that he planned to invest in it. Only that he could see the stars like the astronomers did in observatories.

He held up his hand. "It's a telescope."

Her gaze remained on the instrument, studying it. "What can you see with it?"

He could hear the glimmer of excitement in her tone even as she tried to keep her voice calm.

"I'm told you can see the ridges on the moon and what looks like a giant lake or ocean."

She tipped her head, studying him now instead of the instrument, as though she wasn't certain she should believe him.

"Are you telling me the truth?"

"I've been accused of many things in my life, but I can't remember anyone ever calling me a liar."

"Can I—" She pointed at the telescope. "Can I look through it?"

He shifted the instrument to his other hand. He didn't want anyone else to use it, not until he and Richard secured the deal with Nelson. Especially not a woman he didn't know. She could be the daughter of a competitor—or the wife of one.

"Do you live on the island?"

She cocked her head again. "Does it matter?"

"I'd like to know who you are."

She pulled her lantern closer to her. "I'm a wanderer."

Her wide eyes watched him, waiting for his response. He supposed, if he were honest, he was a bit of a wanderer too.

"And I love looking at the stars."

"Well, we have that in common, at least." If she was telling the truth.

He didn't want to travel down the road of paranoia like many of his investor friends had, yet it seemed strange for her to show up right after him and ask to use his telescope.

"What is it about the stars that you love so much?" he asked.

Her gaze traveled to the window. "The reminder that God loves beauty and He displays it for us every night." She took a long breath. "So many people spend their evenings under a roof, never even looking up at the masterpiece He's created. Yet He doesn't hide the stars for long.

They continue to blink at us, even when we aren't looking."

She looked back at him. "It reminds me that God is always there, beckoning us with His light and the cry of our heart, but too often we're too busy to stop and watch for him."

Chase stared at the girl. Who talked about God like this? His parents sometimes did, but none of the men or women he met at the society functions ever did. Even the church people he knew weren't this enthusiastic about God or His creation.

She looked back at the telescope.

He supposed he could deny her the use of it, but doing that would only raise her suspicions. Truth be told, he wanted to know what a lover of the stars thought about Nelson's invention.

"Can you keep a secret?" he asked.

She eyed him carefully. "It depends."

"I can't allow you to look at this unless you promise to keep it a secret."

She looked down at the telescope again. "I won't tell a soul."

He watched her for a moment longer. Trusting her was a risk, almost like Edward and his gambling, but he wanted to trust her.

"You'll have to turn off your light."

She didn't hesitate. She turned the knob to stop the kerosene, and the light faded away. Then she set the lantern down and her drawings alongside it.

He motioned for her to step out onto the balcony. She didn't test the floor as he had done, seemingly confident that it would hold for her. They stepped outside together, his eyes adjusting again to the night.

The woman close to his side smelled of jasmine and rosewater, and he shook his head, trying not to get intoxicated by the scent. He would enjoy their time together, perched above the trees, but it was nothing else.

"You can't see much on the moon tonight."

"I want to see the stars."

When he locked the telescope onto the tripod, she leaned toward it. Her shoulder brushed his arm, and he flinched from the surge that shot across his skin.

He was being ridiculous. He had danced closer to many a woman, holding their hands and shoulders as he guided them across the floor. But not one of them made him tremble like this woman beside him. Tonight he would have to pretend it was a dance. In the morning, she would be gone.

"Get closer to the eyepiece," he instructed as he held the telescope for her, being careful not to touch her skin again.

She was silent for a moment, and fear clenched him. If this beautiful woman, a self-proclaimed lover of the stars, hated the telescope, he would never garner the word of mouth he needed to distribute it. He needed both men and women to tell their friends about the extraordinary power of this instrument. And about the mysteries it revealed.

"Amazing," she whispered as she swiveled the instrument across the night sky.

He smiled in the darkness. It was exactly what he'd hoped she would say.

"It's spectacular, isn't it?"

She looked at him in the starlight, quoting words from Scripture: "'God made two great lights; the greater light to rule the day, and the lesser light to rule the night.'"

"He did a mighty fine job, didn't He?"

She bent to the telescope again, and the minutes passed slowly as she savored the sky. "I can see dark blue patches with the red on Mars. I read once that there might be life on that planet."

"Do you see Saturn?" he asked. "It has the wide ring around it."

She took a deep breath. "I never imagined seeing the planets like this."

He pointed out the constellations—Orion, Gemini, Cassiopeia—and she studied each one.

"Did you make this?" she asked as she finally straightened.

"No," he paused. "A friend did."

"Tell your friend it's extraordinary."

Chase nodded. "He would thank you."

"Sometimes I wonder—" She looked back up at the skies. "Do you think anyone does live up there?"

"I don't know."

"Perhaps they are looking down at us, wondering about the earth." She took a deep breath. "Out there are supposed to be galaxies beyond ours. And maybe even thousands of stars and planets that we can't see without a telescope."

"Have you seen Isaac Roberts's photographs?" he asked.

She glanced back at him, and for the first time, she smiled. "I have. The one of the spiral nebula is my favorite sight in all the heavens."

"Your favorite?"

She shrugged, so slight that he might have missed it if he weren't studying her. "I understand her, that's all."

It was a strange thing to say, but he didn't press her. There was a hint of wildness in her eyes, like an untamed horse poised to flee.

"They call it the Great Nebula of Andromeda," she said.

He glanced back out at the stars. "I wonder what *Andromeda* means."

"I've been here far too long." She stepped back into the dome. "It's late."

He pulled out his pocket watch. It was half past two. "I believe it was already late when you arrived."

"Do you live at the fort?" she asked.

He hesitated. If she found out who he was—it might break the magic. "I'm living near it, for now."

"I heard everyone is leaving."

"I'm not leaving until next week."

"Do you know a Lieutenant Hull?"

His eyes widened. "I do. But how do you know—"

"He made the most fascinating fishing pole," she said. "Perhaps your friend would be interested in that as well."

"I've seen the pole." Chase eyed her pretty face. He'd never met a woman who recognized the potential of an invention like this before.

She stepped away from him. "Thank you for letting me look through

your telescope, Mr.—"

"My friends call me Chase."

She watched him as she backed toward the stairs. "Then it was nice to meet you, Chase."

He didn't want her to go. "You can't leave, not until I know your name."

"My name?" She asked as if no one had ever asked her the question before.

"Most people get one when they're born."

She hesitated again. "I happen to like the name Andromeda."

"Andromeda?" He grinned. "That's much too hard to say."

"Plenty of names are difficult to say."

"Hmm…I think I shall call you *Andy*." He watched her face, not wanting her to leave. "I hope to see you again—Andy."

She gave him a smile, tentative at best, before she rushed down the stairs.

Chapter Fourteen

Elena pedaled her bicycle slowly through the trees, smiling in spite of herself. Who was this man who owned such a powerful telescope? A man who marveled at the stars alongside her?

Her mother would think it scandalous, her meeting a stranger—a soldier—at the lighthouse, even in the middle of the day. But it was the middle of the night, and she had enjoyed every moment of talking with him about God's creation.

None of the society men she met ever once talked to her about such things. They seemed to view the stars as a way to romance the women they were with, using creation instead of appreciating it.

But Chase hadn't been trying to romance her—or at least, he didn't seem to be. She didn't feel a bit of remorse about tonight. Even if Chase wasn't part of the circles her mother deemed proper, he had somehow learned how to be a gentleman, more so than some of the men she'd met recently. Perhaps he had a good mother.

She should have been afraid of Chase, but she wasn't. At first, she was furious at him for stealing her sketches and invading her space. But he was just as surprised tonight to see her as she was to see him, and perhaps just as annoyed.

She hadn't wanted to be intrigued by him in the least, only in his telescope. But the more he spoke, the more he interested her as well. He was a handsome man, to be sure, and maybe a little too charming. The girls in the village must swoon every time he came to town.

She wished she could have been honest with him, even if she only shared her first name, but she couldn't possibly tell him who she was. If her fall on the pier had crippled her reputation, meeting a soldier at the lighthouse—at night—would ruin it. Even if nothing inappropriate happened between them, her mother's friends would assume that she was just like Hilga, and her indiscretion could cost her and her family dearly.

No one could know about tonight, not even Jillian. She trusted Jillian completely, but sometimes it seemed like the walls in her house had ears. She wouldn't do anything, intentionally at least, to harm her family's reputation.

She might never see Chase again, but she would never forget this night. Nor would she forget him. The man liked the stars, and he had even liked her sketches. When she left tonight, she'd hidden her sketchbook in a different place, but the next time he came, if he looked hard enough, he could find it.

If he ever came back—

She shook her head. She didn't want Chase to come back to her lighthouse…or, at least, she shouldn't want him to return.

For six summers now, it had been her private escape to meet with God and enjoy His creation even as she created with Him. This man had done nothing to harm her, but she should still feel violated. Or angry at him, at the very least, for invading her privacy.

Yet she couldn't seem to help herself. She liked the thought of him returning to the lighthouse, of seeing him again.

She groaned as she pedaled down the lane to her home.

She couldn't possibly think anything more of Chase than a friendly acquaintance during a chance meeting. She was destined to marry someone of connection and wealth for her family's sake, and she wouldn't forsake her role in helping her family.

Even so, she'd enjoyed the moments of his company the way she hadn't with any other man. He teased her as Parker did, and yet he appreciated her sketches. Art, he'd called them.

She'd never thought of herself as an artist before.

As she drew close to her back gate, she extinguished her lantern and hid her bicycle behind the hydrangea bush. She tiptoed down the stone steps and heard the dog barking again from their neighbor's house. The exhaustion after the masquerade party, the irritation at Mr. Darrington's words, had disappeared. Her heart felt as if it were soaring like an osprey above the water.

She hurried as quietly as possible down the pathway to the back porch.

Stepping onto the porch, she heard a low rumble behind her. Her heart stopped for a moment, and she turned slowly.

It sounded as if her neighbor's dog was growling at her.

She scanned the moonlit yard, but nothing moved. The groaning sound grew louder.

She listened closely in the shadows, but the noise no longer sounded like a growl. It sounded more like a…snore.

Was someone sleeping in their backyard?

She tiptoed across the patio and grass. The sound seemed to be coming from one of their lawn chairs. Often she'd seen people sleeping on the streets of Chicago or in a park, but she'd never known of anyone spending the night in their yard, either here or at home.

She moved around the chair quietly, not wanting to wake the sleeper. If he were a stranger, she'd get Claude or someone else to help.

But he wasn't a stranger at all. Instead, her father sat partially upright on the chair, sound asleep.

What was he doing outside?

She nudged his shoulder, whispering to him. "Papa?"

Startled, he leaped to his feet, staring at her for an instant before seeming to realize where he was. He sighed as he sat down again. "When did you get home?"

She blinked and then watched him for a moment. "How did you know I was gone?"

He chuckled softly, running his fingers over hair that had begun to turn silver in the past months. "I always know when you go to the lighthouse."

"Lighthouse?" The question sprayed from her lips. She'd thought Claude, Jillian, and Parker were the only ones who knew her secret.

"Do you really think Claude would let you go out at night without telling me?"

She clutched her hands together, the question ringing in her mind. After Claude had told her about the lighthouse, she'd sworn him to secrecy along with the others, but she should have known he wouldn't keep the secret from her father—Claude was much too loyal to him and much too protective of her.

Part of her wanted to be irritated at him for sharing her secret, but she couldn't muster any anger—not at Claude for sharing her secret or at Chase for stealing it.

"At first, I followed you every night you went. Every night I thought it would be your last time, thinking you would get bored with the place."

She shook her head. "I could never be bored with it."

"I figured that out after the second or third year." He sighed. "I followed you for three years, but then my knee started to go bad on me. The year after you turned sixteen, I finally determined that you were old enough to go on your own."

She leaned back against a tree. "So you wait out here for me?"

He nodded. "Every time."

All those nights she had returned from her bike ride, at two or three or sometimes even four in the morning, tiptoeing back to the house so she wouldn't waken anyone...all those nights she'd been so careful to sneak out of the house so no one would hear, thinking she was alone, when all along her father was following her.

"But you were sleeping, Papa. How would you know when I return?"

"I don't always fall asleep," he said. "But if I do, I just go look for your bicycle when I wake up."

Her heart softened. She was glad he still worried about her. "You don't have to keep waiting up for me."

"Maybe so, but it makes me feel better to know when you're home."

She stepped forward and sat in the chair next to him. The breeze fluttered across her skirt and ruffled her hair, but she didn't care the least what it did tonight.

"Does Mama know?" she asked.

He leaned back in the chair, looking up at the sky with her. "What do you think?"

"She'd never let me go if she knew."

"Your mother—she loves you very much."

Elena edged her knees up to her chest, putting her arms around her legs like she had when she was a girl. "I know."

"She wants what is best for you, Elena—your safety and your health and a husband who can take much better care of you than I can."

She reached over and squeezed his hand. "You've always taken good care of me, Papa."

"But not good enough, at least not lately."

She pulled her legs even closer to her. "It doesn't matter to me if we lose our house or our money. As long as our family is together."

He took a long breath. "You may think that now, Elena, but you don't know what it is like to be poor. You know how your mama grew up—she doesn't want the same thing for you."

Elena put her chin on her knees. Mama rarely talked about her childhood, but the bits she did talk about, like the piecework Elena's grandmother took into her home to supply their family with basic food and shelter, made Elena sad.

Mama had slaved endlessly alongside her mother to make pretty clothing, and as she sewed, she was very deliberate in pleasing the right women, those who could help her escape the chains that kept her bound to the working class. She studied these society ladies as a young woman, mimicking their style and manners. One of them invited her to her home for a special fitting, and during tea, she met a young businessman named Arthur Bissette—a man following his father's legacy as a successful factory owner and real-estate mogul.

Arthur was looking for a wife who could help him manage his household. An elegant woman who could also attend society functions with him and put their guests at ease. When Arthur proposed the idea of marriage, she never seemed to look back. They married, and the role of socialite fitted her like the perfect glove. Thirty years later, she remained stalwart in this role.

"Did you love Mama when you married?"

He hesitated before he answered. "I don't regret marrying her."

"But did you love her?"

"We grew to appreciate each other over the years."

She blinked. "I'm sorry, Papa."

"There's no reason to feel sorry for me," he said. "Your mother has been an excellent mother to you and a good wife to me. She's worked tirelessly to help our family's business and reputation."

"But she's practically killed herself while doing it."

"She only wants what is best for you, Elena."

She wanted to tell her father about the soldier she'd met tonight, of the pattering in her heart, but no matter what she said, she wouldn't be able to convince him that Chase was a good man. That someone like Chase might be best for her.

"I know that." She wiggled in her seat. She should be exhausted, but the night had exhilarated her. "But she wants me to marry a man I've never met before."

"She wants you to marry someone who will provide well for you."

"Is that what you want, Papa?"

"I want—" He paused. "I want you to marry someone you love."

She turned toward him quickly. "Are you certain?"

He nodded. "Someone you love and someone who loves you."

She mulled over this information. Neither of her parents had ever talked about marrying for love.

"But what if he isn't wealthy?"

"It will be hard, Elena. You'll have little time for leisure, but I know you can learn how to care well for a home."

She glanced back at the dark cottage behind them, towering among the trees. Could she take care of a house by herself? She'd been groomed her entire life to manage a household, but she'd never learned how to cook or launder clothes or even clean. If she married someone with a lower income, someone with the military even, could she do the household tasks without much—or any—help?

If she married a soldier like Chase, her home wouldn't be nearly as large as this cottage, but no matter where she went, Jillian would surely go with her. Jillian could teach her what she needed to know, even as they worked alongside each other.

Oh, it would be worth the work to marry a man who loved her. To marry a man she wanted to welcome home every night instead of feeling like wanting to run away from their home. Or perhaps they could even run away together and look at the night sky, like she and Chase had done tonight.

Her mind wandered back to the hour or so at the lighthouse, marveling at the skies with Chase. Instead of critiquing her or coddling her, he had treated her like an equal, and not once did she dream of being someplace else. If someone like Chase loved her, if she loved him, then it would be a privilege to care for him and their small home.

Papa leaned forward. "Are you asleep?"

She shook her head. "If God gives me a husband who wants to marry me for love instead of position, I think I could learn to care for our home on my own."

He studied her face for a moment in the dim light before he spoke again. "I'm proud of you, Elena."

"Thank you, Papa."

"I will pray with you that God will bless you with a man who loves you…*and* a man who can provide well for you."

"Mama thinks Mr. Darrington is the best man for me."

"Perhaps your mother is right."

She shuddered. "I can't marry a man I don't know."

"Would you like me to invite Chester Darrington over for dinner?"

She wiggled her toes in her boots. Did she really want to meet this Chester Darrington, after what he'd said about her?

It was inevitable, she supposed, that they would have to meet, but when it happened, she hoped it would be at one of the balls or another public setting. A place she could easily flee.

"I don't know," she replied honestly.

Papa scratched his chin. "I think I'll wait before I invite him to our home, then. Whenever you are ready."

Relief flooded through her as she thanked him again.

He stood up and brushed off his pant legs as faint rays of sunlight stole over the top of their house. Then he reached for his cane, pointing it toward the house. "I suppose we should try to sleep a few hours before breakfast."

She agreed even though she didn't know if she could sleep with all the thoughts racing through her mind.

They crept up the back staircase silently in the darkness, not wanting to wake Mama—but when Elena reached for her doorknob, her mother's door opened. Her hair was hidden under her nightcap, and a candle made her emerald wrapper and face glow.

She looked back and forth between them. "What are you two doing?"

Papa cleared his throat. "We were both awake, so we decided to get some fresh air."

Mama looked back into her room, at the clock on the mantel. "It's barely five o'clock."

He yawned. "We couldn't sleep."

Her eyes traveled down Elena's old dress. "What are you wearing?"

Before she answered, Papa spoke. "I think Elena and I both need a bit more rest before we start our day."

"But—"

He leaned in and kissed her cheek. "We're sorry for waking you."

Mama didn't move. "I'm afraid we've ruined our chances to meet Mr. Darrington."

He leaned back against the doorpost, looking down at Elena. "I believe Mr. Darrington might have ruined his chances to meet Elena."

She smiled.

He nudged Mama toward her room. "You need to get some more sleep, Deborah."

Before Mama said anything else, Elena slipped inside her bedroom.

After she changed into her nightgown and climbed under her covers, Chase's handsome eyes danced in her mind.

She didn't know when she would see him again, but she knew that she must.

She turned over, trying to rest, yet the thought of this man robbed her sleep. Her mother would tell her not to be too anxious to see him again. If she encouraged him too much, he might run.

As she closed her eyes, sunlight streamed softly through the window, warming her face.

Neither of her parents could know about him, at least not right now, but if her father was telling her the truth, if he really did want her to marry for love, perhaps there was hope for her and a man like Chase.

Chapter Fifteen

Dozens of people stood on Mackinac's pier, waiting to board the *Manitou* before it embarked for Chicago. Chase scanned their heads just as he'd found himself searching faces on his carriage ride to town, looking for her.

He'd stayed for another fifteen minutes at the lighthouse last night, not wanting to frighten Andy by following her. Even though he'd promised her he was a gentleman, he was keenly aware that not all men kept their promises.

Andy's presence lingered in the lighthouse after she was gone, and then she'd stolen into his dreams during his few hours of sleep. He'd awakened late this morning with his heart pounding in fear, afraid he would never see her again.

One of the women on the pier wore light brown ringlets that cascaded down her shoulders, and Chase elbowed his way through the crowd, his eyes on the woman's hair as he tried to reach her.

He had lifted his hand to tap the woman's shoulder when someone clutched his arm. Chase was tall compared to most men, but when he turned, the man who squeezed his arm was at least an inch taller. And his face was beet red.

The man's nostrils flared. "What do you want?"

"I—"

"Leave my wife alone."

His chest burned for a moment until the woman turned, her blue eyes narrowed at him. She wasn't nearly as beautiful as Andy, nor was she smiling as Andy had done last night.

"I'm sorry." Chase backed away. "I thought you— I thought she was someone else."

The man released his grip and turned to quiz his wife. Chase sighed as he walked to the other side of the pier. He hadn't meant to scare the woman or worry her husband. He only wanted to find Andy.

Why hadn't he persisted like his mother would have done and discovered Andy's real name?

Mackinac wasn't that big of an island. Surely if he asked enough people, someone could tell him where to find her. But then again, what was he supposed to say? If he told people about a beautiful girl spending her night hours drawing at the lighthouse, he might embarrass her like he had the woman across the pier—or even destroy her reputation.

He would have to harbor her secret, just as she'd promised to harbor his. They would have to trust one another...until they met again.

The steamer to his left pushed away from its berth as another ship waited behind it with new tourists to explore the island. His parents' yacht should arrive in the next hour.

He sat down on a bench, watching the steamer cruise across the strait.

What if Andy left Mackinac before he was able to find her?

He couldn't allow himself to think about her leaving, not without seeing her again.

* * * * *

Elena hummed over her family's late breakfast. The warm biscuits and fresh strawberry jam and poached eggs tasted so extraordinary that she asked Claude to give Nell her compliments.

Her mother eyed her warily. None of them ever complimented their cook at breakfast. "Are you feeling ill again?"

"I haven't been ill, Mama. In fact, I feel fantastic."

Her mother nodded at Papa's empty chair. "I thought you would stay in bed a couple of hours longer as well."

"I wasn't tired."

She'd tried to rest during the hours before breakfast, but even though she'd been up all night, she hadn't been able to sleep. Whenever she closed her eyes, Chase appeared in her mind, and the sight of him made her smile. It was childish, she knew, but she couldn't seem to help herself.

She had to stop being so ridiculous. She knew nothing about the man…or very little, at least. For all she knew, he could be in trouble with the law or running away from an angry boss. Or hiding from his wife.

She spread a thick layer of jam over a second biscuit as her thoughts collided in her head. Edward Powell had misled her at the dance, and she didn't need that kind of trouble haunting her. Chase had been nothing like Edward, though—or any of the other men she met at society events. Chase seemed like a man who cherished freedom as much as she did, and he had some knowledge of art—or at least of flattery. But she was more struck by his fascination with the masterpiece that God had created than by his kind words about her sketches. She didn't know of any man other than perhaps her father who enjoyed the intricate beauty in the stars.

Her father walked into the room, and as he pulled back his chair, he winked at Elena. "I enjoyed our early morning chat."

"Me too, Papa."

"Did you get any extra sleep?"

"I tried, but I couldn't seem to rest."

"Then you shall need a nap this afternoon."

"I don't know—" Mama said.

"Ah, Deborah, let the poor girl have a bit of vacation." He reached for his juice glass and drained it. "If she wants to get up early and sleep in the afternoon, she should do it. For that matter, she should stay up all night and enjoy her freedom before she settles into marriage."

Elena washed down her smile with her milk. Papa knew good and well that she'd been up all night enjoying her freedom at the lighthouse. What he didn't know was that her stomach was still in knots because of the man she'd met there.

She picked up her biscuit and then put it down. Chase said he'd hoped to see her again, but what if she went back and he'd already left the island with a company of soldiers?

As her parents watched her, she lifted her biscuit again and bit into the clumps of fruit spread over the biscuit. She couldn't entertain the thought that last night was the first and only time she would see this man.

She began to hum, and her mother cleared her throat. "Mr. and Mrs. Darrington are supposed to arrive today on their family's yacht."

Elena stopped humming. The arrival of the senior Darringtons no longer concerned her. Since their son was avoiding her, she decided that she would avoid him too.

"Arthur—" Mama began. "When are you going to invite Mr. Darrington over for supper?"

Papa stole a glance at Elena before he looked back at her mother. "Now, Deborah, I don't see any reason to rush this—"

"No one can accuse us of rushing," she insisted. "We've been here for almost a week now, and neither Elena nor I have met him."

"Perhaps you should invite his mother over first," he said. "If you two ladies make a good acquaintance, then surely she will want to introduce you to her son."

Elena didn't want to meet the man's mother, but her own mother seemed to be considering his words. "Perhaps I shall."

Elena picked up her knife and swirled the jam around on the remaining surface of her biscuit. She didn't want to think another moment about this Mr. Darrington or his mother, even if Mrs. Darrington was the nicest of women. She wanted to think about a man like Chase—someone who was considerate and strong, interesting without being cocky or absurd.

"Why aren't you eating?" her mother asked.

She looked up quickly, her mother's words interrupting her musings. "I'm getting full."

"But you just said you liked the jam."

"I do like it."

Her mother set down her knife. "The flu might be going around the island again, like it did in '88."

Elena glanced at her father, and he looked worried. She forced herself to take another bite of the biscuit even though she was no longer hungry. He wouldn't let her leave the house if he thought she was sick.

All she could think about was going back to the lighthouse, tonight if possible. She would make herself rest this afternoon. No matter how alive she felt in this moment, she would be exhausted by the evening, and she didn't want to feel the least bit tired tonight.

Mama straightened her silverware on her plate and then picked up her spoon. "I suppose I should wait a day or two before I send Mrs. Darrington an invitation, so she can settle into the hotel."

Papa nodded his head. "I suppose so."

"But if I wait too long, Elizabeth Frederick might invite her to their house first."

"Perhaps you can send her the invitation in the morning."

She nodded. "An excellent idea. In the meantime, I need to go down to the market and order supplies."

"Excuse me, sir." Claude interrupted them. He held out an envelope. "A telegram just arrived for you."

Papa thanked Claude as he took the telegram, placing it beside his plate. Then he nodded toward Elena. "What would you like to do today, Elena?"

"I think I should sleep."

"You should come with me," Mama proposed. "The fresh air will do you some good."

Elena studied the remains of her poached egg, trying to think clearly. "Maybe you and I should go visit the fort."

Mama lowered her spoon. "The fort?"

"I heard that some of the women take baked goods up to the soldiers."

Mama shook her head. "Only women looking for a husband."

"Then I suppose I qualify."

"You are in no way looking for a husband," Mama huffed. "Your father and I are selecting a good man for you."

Elena put down the biscuit. "Maybe my future husband lives up at the fort?"

Mama's spoon clattered on her dish. "For heaven's sake, Elena. Go back to bed."

Chapter Sixteen

Chase waved to his mother from the pier. She was standing on the bow of their yacht, waving wildly to him as they approached Mackinac.

His parents had left for Europe almost four months ago, traveling across the continent for business, but he was certain that his mother had convinced his father to play as well. Lydia Darrington—"the lovely Lydia," as the papers liked to call her—made sure the Darrington family stopped on occasion to enjoy some of the many blessings God had given them.

"Chase!" she called, her wave widening in case he didn't see her. He lifted his hand again and tried to hide his grin as he waved back.

Sarah would be mortified at her display, but neither of their parents concerned themselves with society's norms. He'd never heard anyone comment about his mother's actions. Most people, he assumed, were too discreet to chastise the Darrington family in public, but they probably whispered behind closed doors about his mother's lack of societal inhibitions. He was also sure that his mother didn't care what they thought.

After the boat docked, Chase helped his mother onto the pier and then lifted her from the ground in a big hug. "Welcome home, Mother."

She kissed his cheek, and then his father—Samson Darrington—climbed off the boat and clapped Chase's back in greeting. "It's good to see you, son."

Lydia glanced over his shoulder. "Where's your sister?"

"Sarah and Edward are waiting for you at the hotel."

"Ahh, well—" Her smile slipped, and he hated hearing the disappointment in her voice.

"Sarah wanted to make sure you had a proper welcome when you arrived at the Grand."

Her warm smile returned again. "That was kind of her."

"You deserve the royalest of welcomes, Mother. Four months is a long time."

"Too long," she concurred.

Chase turned to his father. "Was it a productive trip?"

"Very," his father said as they walked down the pier. "We have a lot to talk about."

Chase loved it when his father came back from these trips. He was always brimming with new ideas to replicate in the States.

"We were in Italy for three weeks." He lowered his voice. "I met a man named Guglielmo Marconi. He's working on transmitting electrical signals without wire."

"Without wires?" Chase glanced around him, hoping no one had heard intensity in his voice. Many people had talked about the possibility of wireless communication over the past decade, but he'd never met anyone who thought it really possible. The latest inventions for communication—the telephone and the telegraph—required wires to transmit information.

"I'd like us to consider investing in his work," his father said as they walked up the pier, toward the bustle of the village.

"Do you think it's possible to do this?"

"I'm not certain, but Mr. Marconi is convinced that he can do it. And he's working harder than anyone I've met to transmit these signals."

"Is he in his right mind?"

His father laughed. "He seemed to be."

Few people had a keener sense for innovation and business than Chase's father, though he usually invested in people, not products. If he believed in an inventor—even more than the actual invention—he would put his money into it. Rarely did he invest in someone who didn't eventually turn a profit for them.

"Did this Mr. Marconi make a drawing of what he wants to do?"

His father patted his briefcase. "I've got it right here."

"I will review it with you."

As the three of them stepped off the pier and onto the sidewalk, a woman bumped into Chase's shoulder. "Oh, I beg your pardon," she said.

The woman was a few years past middle age and a few pounds overweight as well. A basket hung over the sleeve of her walking dress, swinging like a pendulum. She studied Chase for a moment and then looked back at his mother. "I don't believe we've been introduced."

His mother put out her gloved hand. "My name is Lydia Darrington, and this is my son, Chester, and my husband, Samson Darrington."

"Oh," the woman stuttered. She quickly regained her composure, shaking his mother's hand with enthusiasm. "It is an honor to meet all of you. My name is Bissette. Mrs. Arthur Bissette."

Bissette? Chase suppressed his groan. This was the mother of the woman who Mrs. Frederick claimed was trying to marry him. The same woman who had been flirting with Edward.

Mr. Bissette had seemed perfectly normal when they met at the Grand—a pleasant fellow, even—and he'd never once even hinted that Chase might want to meet his daughter. His wife, however, studied him like he was the fox being released for a good chase. Like any hunted animal, he wanted to run.

He stole a glance toward his mother, and in the flash of her green eyes, he could see a mixture of admiration and amusement at the woman's boldness. The lovely Lydia never thought herself any higher than another person. Instead it seemed to entertain her when others coddled and esteemed her as an influential society woman.

"It's a pleasure to make your acquaintance," his mother said as she released the woman's hand. "Your name sounds familiar to me."

Mrs. Bissette nodded. "My family spends every summer on this island."

"This is our first summer here." His mother gazed at the village and then looked up at the hills. "But it seems like such a lovely place."

"We winter in Chicago."

"How lovely. My sister lives in Chicago."

Mrs. Bissette shifted her basket onto her other arm. "What is her name?"

"Lottie Ingram."

"Oh, I know your sister," Mrs. Bissette said with a light clap. "She and I are on the mayor's gardening committee together."

Chase opened the door on the waiting carriage, and his father climbed inside. He wished he were as courteous as his mother at times, but his graciousness ceased at the mention of gardening committees.

He nudged his mother ahead. "It's a pleasure meeting you, Mrs. Bissette, but my parents have had a long journey. I must get them to the hotel."

"Certainly." Mrs. Bissette stepped alongside his mother as she moved toward the carriage. "It would be my pleasure to have you lunch at our cottage while you're on the island."

"I would love to come and visit, but at the moment, I'm not sure about my availability."

Chase took his mother's hand and helped her into the enclosed carriage.

"Perhaps tea would be better?" Mrs. Bissette asked.

His mother straightened her skirts, still smiling at the woman on the sidewalk. "I would love to stop by for tea."

Mrs. Bissette smiled at him now. "Perhaps you could join us as well, Mr. Darrington."

"I'm certain that it would be an entertaining experience, but I am preparing to leave for Chicago soon."

Her eyebrows rose in worry. "Will you be returning?"

"I haven't decided yet."

His mother took his arm as he climbed in beside her. "We certainly hope so."

Mrs. Bissette eyed him and then looked at Chase's mother. "I will send an invitation to the Grand this afternoon."

The carriage moved forward. "I'll look forward to receiving it."

Mrs. Bissette waved her hand as the carriage rode away.

Chase put his hat on his lap. "You don't have to go to tea, Mother."

"Of course I don't have to, but why wouldn't I? She seems perfectly delightful, and I want to hear about Lottie."

He turned his hat. "I believe she already knew that Aunt Lottie is your sister."

"Perhaps," his mother said as she arranged her ruffled skirt again. "But she might have been embarrassed to tell me."

Chase thought for a moment about telling her that the woman and her daughter were conniving to become part of the Darrington family, but his mother would reprimand him for listening to gossip. He wasn't one who usually concerned himself with gossip either, but judging by the actions of the mother, he wondered if the Fredericks were right.

He opted for a more general approach.

"I'm told the Bissette family has a daughter they are looking to marry off."

His mother reached for his hand. "Perhaps you should join us for tea, then."

He laughed. "No, thank you."

His mother sighed as she released his hand. She no longer haggled him about marriage, but he knew she was as anxious to have him married as Sarah was. She never suggested specific women for him to marry like Sarah did, but she often implied that she wanted to be a grandmother.

"When do the festivities begin for Independence Day?"

"On Wednesday."

His mother clapped. "It will be spectacular, I'm sure."

He smiled. His mother was really a girl in a woman's body. She loved dancing and playing games and listening to music for hours.

"They have a new sport at the hotel you might like," he said. "Something called lawn tennis."

She clapped her hands again. "I shall have to try it."

Across from them, his father opened his briefcase and riffled through the stack of paperwork.

While he appreciated his mother's zest for life, Chase admired his father for his good business sense. Like his father, he wanted to be married to a woman he could trust, a woman who delighted in life alongside him. When he married, he wanted to be more deliberate about breaking from his work to share the frivolities of life with his wife.

Of course, he was terrible at taking these breaks now. He'd been practically forced to go to the beach with Sarah and her friends, and the dog race wasn't a bit of fun until the dogs went berserk. Then he was amused.

The most enjoyment he'd had on the island wasn't advertised on the hotel billboard. It was the pleasure of Andy's company last night, of being able to enjoy the sky and the woman at his side.

Some men were frightened by a beautiful woman, but beauty didn't scare him. It was the confidence in a woman that intimidated—and intrigued—him. Not confidence in pursuing him—plenty of women did that—but confidence in her own opinions and in being honest with him.

So few of the women he knew could actually communicate what they thought or even felt. Instead, it seemed to him they were constantly looking for approval from their parents or husband or circle of friends. As long as their words met with approval, they would speak.

Andy, however, didn't need him or anyone else to approve her words last night.

Of course, she didn't know who he was, but even if she did, he felt she would still speak her mind. It was refreshing to hear a woman speak what she thought, and it was refreshing not to have a woman pretending to be someone she was not in order to catch him.

"I found it," his father said as he handed over the paperwork from Mr. Marconi.

Chase took the papers, and they began to review them together.

Even as they worked, he couldn't help but wonder—what would Andy think?

*****

Elena watched Parker from the upper window as he tucked an envelope under the cushion on a veranda chair. How long had he been sending letters to Jillian? She smiled and rushed down the stairs to open the door before he knocked.

He leaned back against the door frame. "How are you, Lanie?"

"Splendid. And you?"

He shuffled his feet awkwardly for a moment, and she directed him into the drawing room.

"Would you like some tea?"

"I suppose."

She rang a bell, and Claude hurried into the room.

"Mr. Randolph would like some tea." Elena paused. "Could you find Jillian and send her in, as well?"

"Certainly," Claude said.

"What brings you to Castle Pines today?" she asked.

"I wanted to visit you."

"But we just visited last night."

"I suppose we did." He picked at his trousers.

"You need an occupation, Parker."

He looked up at her. "The only occupation I'm good at is entertaining people."

She didn't smile. Parker was supposed to be learning his father's business, but Mr. Randolph seemed just as reluctant to give Parker work as Parker was to take it.

"You are good at plenty of things," she insisted.

Before he probed further, Jillian walked into the room, glancing uncomfortably at Elena and Parker.

Elena stood up. "Would you be so kind as to keep Mr. Randolph company for a few moments while I—while I fetch something to eat with our tea?"

"I don't think—" Jillian began.

Elena leaned toward Jillian, her voice a mock whisper so Parker could hear. "That way you can return his letter in person."

Both Parker's and Jillian's faces colored red.

Elena lingered for a moment at the archway, watching her two friends. Jillian sat down across from Parker, fidgeting with her hands.

"How are you today, Mr. Randolph?"

"Fine. And you?"

They both reached for the teapot at the same time, their hands colliding, and Jillian pulled away.

"Let me get it," she heard Parker say.

Elena slipped into the kitchen, opening cabinet after cabinet until she found a box of almond biscotti. With great precision, she arranged them on a plate. She was in no hurry to return to the drawing room.

About twenty minutes later, Mama stopped her in the hallway with a basket full from the village. Mama eyed the dish of biscotti in Elena's hands. "Why exactly is Parker Randolph sipping tea with Jillian in the parlor?"

Elena glanced toward the parlor door and then looked back at her mother. "I asked her to wait with him while I retrieved the biscotti."

"Retrieved the biscotti?" Mama's voice began to climb. "That's Jillian's job. You are supposed to entertain our guests."

"Yes," Elena whispered, "but I was tired of talking with him. You know how Parker can be, always making a joke out of everything."

"So you decided to get Jillian?"

"Only for a few minutes—" She scooted around her mother, moving toward the drawing room. "I think they've been in there long enough, don't you?"

"Elena," her mother called, stopping her. She was smiling now. "Guess who I just met in the village?"

January 2, 1813

Nickolas Westmount visited us late last night, dressed in his black cloak and carrying a basket with a half loaf of bread, a block of cheese, and smoked pork.

I don't know what he expected to find, but he seemed surprised that the children and I were still at the lighthouse. Or maybe he was just surprised we were alive. He offered Thomas what was left of his meal, and my son devoured the food while Nickolas hovered by the door.

"Magdelaine." He said my name twice, as if he were checking to see if I was an apparition. "What are you doing here alone?"

When I told him that Jonah was gone, that he'd disappeared three months ago and never returned, he didn't display one bit of surprise.

I asked Nickolas if he knew where Jonah was. I asked him if he'd seen Jonah, if he knew whether Jonah was still alive.

Nickolas shook his head, evading every one of my questions.

Some people are scared of me because of the Indian blood in my veins, but neither Nickolas nor his wife ever seemed frightened of me. Perhaps he is worried now about what will happen if I find out the truth.

Perhaps he is right to be worried.

Nickolas said he would be back again soon with more bread and some jam. I thanked him for it.

Chapter Seventeen

When Elena stepped into the dark hallway that night, as quietly as she could, her father opened his door. He held a candle in one hand and his cane in the other, but instead of his nightclothes, he was dressed in his waistcoat, shirt, and trousers. Perhaps he was relieved that she was finally aware of his secret. Their secret. He no longer had to sneak around or hide from her.

Her father yawned as he eyed her worn riding dress. "Are you going out again?"

"I am."

"But you just went last night…and the sky isn't clear this evening."

"The rain has stopped, Papa." She didn't want to sound desperate, but anxiety laced her voice. "I want to get away from the house."

"But you've barely slept today."

She leaned back against the paneled wall. "It was a rather difficult day to sleep."

"Ahh—all the noise."

She nodded. Mama talked for an hour after she returned from her shopping trip into town. Not only had Mama finally been introduced to Chester Darrington—by far the most handsome man on the island and probably in all of Detroit—but Mrs. Darrington had agreed to visit their house for tea. In anticipation of the visit, Mama had sent the household staff into a frenzy of dusting, washing, and scrubbing of both walls and floors.

Mr. Darrington wasn't only handsome, he was refined and took good care of his mother. Any man who cared for his mother, Mama had informed Elena, would care well for his wife.

But they must hurry, Mama said, for Mr. Darrington was preparing to leave the island on business. They would have Mrs. Darrington here for tea and then find a way for Elena to meet her son before he left. If Mrs. Darrington liked Elena—and according to Mama, how could she not?—she would secure an invitation for her to meet her son.

Elena was sent off to rest before lunch, but no one bothered to curb the amount of noise in their house. Doors banged below her, and furniture was scraped across the floor. Servants were talking loudly, and her mother's voice trumped them all. Even as she tried to sleep, the smell of lemon polish drifted into Elena's room along with the noise. One would have thought President Cleveland and his young wife were coming to visit them for the week.

She'd leaned back against her pillows and tried to read, but her mind kept traveling back to her refuge and the stranger who had wandered into her space. It almost felt like she'd dreamed of him last night, but it hadn't been a dream. She remembered well the brief touch of his hand when she had leaned down to look through his magnificent telescope.

In the midst of her unsuccessful attempts to rest, the doorbell rang below her. Her mother had rushed up the steps and burst into her room, Mrs. Darrington's reply flitting about in her hands. Mrs. Darrington would join them for tea on Tuesday. Only three days from now.

It would be a long three days.

"If the rain has stopped—" her father hesitated, blinking in the candlelight. "Why don't we go for a walk instead?"

She studied her father for a moment. It had never occurred to her that perhaps her father enjoyed escaping from their house as much as she did. He might have allowed her to sneak away to the lighthouse in secret because it gave him a good reason to leave too.

"We could walk down to the lake," he offered.

As much as she wanted to see Chase, Papa would be hurt if she refused to go with him, especially since he didn't know she was planning to meet someone at the lighthouse. She would never willingly wound him.

She looped her hand through his arm. "I would love to walk down to the lake with you."

Papa moved slowly, relying on his cane as he limped beside her, and the two of them walked away from the city lights, along the coastline that alternated between rocks, pebbles, and sand.

A boat was anchored between their island and Bois Blanc, and she watched it for a moment. What would it be like to climb aboard one of those and sail away? And what would it be like to steal away with a man like Chase?

Her cheeks grew warm in the darkness, and she was glad that her father seemed to be lost in his own thoughts. He didn't know what she was thinking, nor would he ever. She could never leave her family like that, but still she wondered.

They walked closer to the shoreline and she let go of his arm, dipping her hand into the coolness of the lake. The water trickled off her fingers, and it seemed to awaken her heart to the realness of God's creation, the substance of it. It was so different than the falsities that threaded through her life.

She wanted to jump into the water and splash it with her feet. She wanted to twirl around like a girl and feel the wind in her hair. She wanted to draw.

And not just any picture. Her fingers suddenly itched for her pencils, her paper. She wanted to draw Chase while she remembered what he looked like. She didn't want to forget a single detail of his face or the warmth in his eyes.

"I have some bad news," Papa said.

Her hands trembled, and she clasped her hands behind her back. "What is it?"

"Your mother—she doesn't know yet."

When he paused, she prompted him to continue. "You got a telegram today."

He looked out at the dark waters again. "Last fall, when my partnership with Oliver Randolph crumbled, I had to take out a loan from the bank."

She nodded. A lot of people had to secure loans after the panic last year.

"I thought the business would recover quickly, but we're not even close to recovering. If I don't pay the loan back by August—" He paused. "The bank will be taking the factory first and then our home."

For a moment, Elena felt as if her legs might fail. She'd known they might lose their cottage on Mackinac, but she never thought they would lose their home in Chicago. She didn't dare ask where they would live, for fear of what the answer would be.

"But you have other bonds and stocks," she persisted.

"Most of them are almost worthless, and the ones that are still good—it isn't enough to cover the loan."

She sighed. With their family finances in such a dreadful state, the pressure to marry someone like Mr. Darrington would only increase now. It wouldn't matter if she wanted to marry another man for love.

"I need to tell your mother soon."

She nodded.

"I will do everything I can to save our home," he assured her.

She didn't tell him, but she would do everything she could to help save it as well.

The rain started to fall again, splashing on her nose and soaking her dress.

Papa opened their umbrella. "We'd better hurry home."

She held the umbrella for them in one hand and lifted her skirts with the other as they hurried as quickly as they could back up the bluff. As soon as they stepped under the roof of the patio, her father took the umbrella from her, shook it off, and left it by the door. She collapsed onto one of the patio chairs.

Papa opened the door into their house and then tapped on the floor with his cane. "It's time for bed, Elena."

The rain pattered on the rooftop as the fresh air drifted through the open windows. She didn't want to move. "I think I'm going to sit here for just a few minutes longer."

"You need to get some sleep before church."

"Just a few minutes, Papa."

Her father kissed her wet hair and then stepped back, looking at her. "Promise me you won't sneak away tonight."

She thought for a long moment and then kissed his cheek. "I promise, Papa."

* * * * *

Andy wasn't at the lighthouse. Chase called her name several times when he stepped into the parlor, not wanting to frighten her, and then he jogged up the circular steps to see if she was waiting upstairs.

The clouds hid the stars tonight, but he'd still hoped she might want to see him again, as much as he'd wanted to see her.

There might have been a reason for her to be detained. Or perhaps she never intended to come back. She might have run away quickly from the lighthouse last night, away from him.

He leaned back against a post and clutched his hat in his hands. He wasn't used to women running away.

His parents had gone to bed early after their long journey, and Sarah and Edward were out dining at the home of another potential buyer for Edward's newly acquired land. They hadn't bothered to invite Chase this time. He would wait for a bit tonight, just in case Andy came later. He'd hoped she had enjoyed his company enough to return—or, at the very least, enjoyed his telescope.

He twisted his hat in his hands. As the minutes passed, he grew more anxious. He couldn't bear sitting here alone another moment, waiting for her.

Standing, he moved downstairs into the lighthouse keeper's old residence and opened the desktop to look at Andy's artwork, but her drawings weren't there. He smiled to himself. Andy might pretend to be strong, but she was still a little scared—not of him taking her work as much as of him exploring the emotion in them. Which was exactly what he intended to do.

He stepped back from the desk and looked under the braided rug and the davenport, but her book wasn't in either of those places, so he pulled out the drawers on the sideboard and then got on his knees to look underneath it, as well.

Perhaps Andy had taken her sketches with her if she'd come back earlier tonight, but if she hadn't...

Surveying the room, he tried to determine where else she could have hidden the sketchbook, but the options were few in the parlor. He moved on to the bedroom, looking under the bed and then opening the dresser drawers. There were clothes inside the dresser—women's things—and he felt strange rummaging through the clothing of a woman who'd probably died long ago.

When he stepped back, he looked around the room again. Besides the double bed in the room, there was a crib and a trundle. He'd imagined a lightkeeper would live in solitude, but this man must have had a family with him. What kind of family lived out here, on the edge of the island? And how had Andy discovered their home?

He hung his lantern in the middle of the room and sat down on the side of what was probably once a straw mattress. There was no straw or any stuffing left over the bands. He hadn't planned on coming back to the lighthouse after tonight, but now he couldn't imagine not returning.

It seemed crazy, but he wanted to learn more about Andy. Not just her real name or who she worked for on the island, but why she drew herself on the beach, looking out at the lake—like she wanted to be set free.

Walking to the corner, he opened a trunk. Inside was a quilt, and he riffled through the clothing under it to look for her drawings. There was some sort of book at the bottom, though it felt much too small to be Andy's book. He pulled it up, and in his hands was a brown booklet not much wider than an envelope, with leather cracked along the edges.

Chase held it up to the light and flipped through the handwriting on its pages. It looked like some sort of journal.

He read the first line.

Where are you, Jonah?

Chase lowered the book to his side and sat down on the bed frame, brushing his hands over the cover. Someone had written this plea more than eighty years ago, but even so, he felt strange reading it, like he was invading someone else's story.

But someone had left the journal here. Perhaps whoever wrote their story wanted it to be read.

He moved to the parlor with his lantern and opened the book again. The pages were filled with writing, but some of the words were smeared, as if tears had mixed with the ink.

He read the first entry. And then the second and third.

The lighthouse keeper's wife was the writer, he assumed, and she was searching for her husband.

When Chase looked around the parlor again, he could almost imagine this Jonah and his family in the evening hours, singing or reading together around the fireplace before he disappeared. Eighty years ago Jonah's wife had still been here, worrying and wondering what happened to her husband. Had her children been playing while she wrote this journal? Or were they sleeping in their beds? The lighthouse was now a beautiful refuge, but it must have felt like a prison to her at the time. Or maybe more like a fortress, protecting her from whatever had happened to her husband.

He slowly closed the dairy. He didn't want to read anymore without—

The very thought startled him. He didn't want to read anymore without Andy.

She might have already read the diary, but if she hadn't, he wanted to share it with her, like he had shared the telescope and the wonders in the sky.

He started to tuck the journal into his satchel but took it back out. If the writer of the diary had left her story behind, it needed to stay in this place. He would leave it here, and perhaps if Andy decided to return, they could read the story together.

He took his watch out of his pocket and checked the time. It was almost two. He sighed. Andy wasn't coming tonight, and he was supposed to meet his family for breakfast before church in the morning.

He put the diary back in the trunk and covered it with the clothes and the quilt.

When he stood up, he heard something brush against the door. He turned his head sharply toward the parlor. Perhaps Andy had come to see him—or at least to visit the lighthouse. He didn't want to startle her, but surely she'd seen his light through the window.

Something moved against the door again, but no one opened it.

Why wasn't she coming into the house?

Perhaps someone else was coming to visit the lighthouse, or maybe Andy was debating whether she should come inside.

He moved quickly to the door, afraid she would leave, and threw it open. His gaze dropped quickly to the animal on the forest floor. The dog who'd befriended him in town.

The dog looked up at him, his tongue hanging out.

Chase may have been surprised, but this animal wasn't the least bit surprised.

"You're following me, aren't you?" Chase asked.

The dog replied with a short bark.

Chase stepped outside and pulled the door shut. "Well, you might as well follow me home."

He picked up his lantern and slipped back into the darkness with the dog at his side. And the mysteries of two women on his mind.

Chapter Eighteen

"There he is," Mama said, nodding ever so slightly toward the front of the sanctuary.

Elena stretched her neck, looking over the rows of people streaming into the pews. She didn't know which man her mother was referring to, but she didn't dare tell her this for fear that she would point to him. Most of the attendees were facing the front of the sanctuary, but someone would certainly see her mother pointing and wonder.

The Bissette family had arrived early at church this morning, securing a seat on one of the back pews so they would have a view of most of the sanctuary—and the Darrington family—but Elena no longer wanted to meet this man, not even out of curiosity.

Had Chase gone to the lighthouse last night?

She'd awakened on the patio this morning, regretting her promise to her father about not going to the lighthouse. Now she hoped—prayed—that if Chase went last night, he wouldn't give up. She wanted him to come again.

Fourteen men and women made up the choir, and as they moved onto the platform, the church quieted. Elena scanned the twenty or so rows in front of where she sat, searching for Sarah Powell's auburn hair to see if her brother was nearby. But she couldn't find Mrs. Powell in the crowded rows. Perhaps the woman was sitting behind her.

If only one were allowed to turn around in church.

As the organ began playing "A Mighty Fortress Is Our God" and the choir sang, the floor trembled under her feet. It was still raining when they left the house this morning, a light rain that would refresh the island roads and awaken the gardens. As her lips joined the others in their singing, her gaze wandered to the stained-glass window beside her. The image of a sheep with a lion was dimmed by the gray sky. After the rain finished, perhaps the skies would clear again.

The choir began a slow hymn, worshipping God in their own way. Her eyelids grew heavy from the music. Some people found God in church, but she didn't feel Him here, not like she did when she was at the lighthouse. It was as if His Spirit breathed in and out of nature, like He spoke directly through His creation to her.

She scooted up in her seat, tapping her shoes together to keep herself from drifting to sleep.

The minister read from his notes, his voice as soothing as the water lapping against Mackinac's shores. The man next to her yawned. She wanted to stand up and yell. Instead of being crowded into this warm building, listening to someone drone on and on about religious matters, they should be outside, arm in arm, shouting His praises together.

God was wild beyond their imaginations, able to breathe out wind and storms and fire, able to mold planets and carve valleys. She couldn't imagine God in the box of a church building, not when He was so big. How could one confine the mighty Creator?

In this building, men talked about God and sang about Him, but she didn't feel the marvel in it, the awe. Not like when she gazed up at the stars and saw God's wondrous handiwork in them, as if He took much pleasure in His design.

Her eyes closed again, the battle to fight it an impossible one.

Why did their church inspire sleep instead of celebration?

Her mother elbowed her, and her eyes flashed open. She sat a little straighter, trying to listen out of respect as the minister spoke about seeking God. *She* knew where to find Him. He was all around them. Didn't the minister know He was so much bigger than this?

She continued watching the rain through the window, trying to stay awake, and then her eyes roamed the backs of the men in front of her. Which one of these men was the great Mr. Darrington? Did he understand the power and beauty of God, or was religion a once-a-week obligation to him?

His hurtful rejection at the masquerade party replayed in her mind. Had Mr. Darrington's sister told him that Elena had been flirting with her husband? If not, Elena didn't know what she could have done to make him disregard her so. Perhaps it was better that she didn't know. No society man could ever contain her anyway, just like none of them could contain her Maker. There was too much to do and see outside the boxes her society liked to create to keep their life orderly and controlled.

Was Chase worshipping God this morning? Surely the soldiers had some sort of church service at the fort. Perhaps it was outdoors, overlooking the water. Even in the rain, she wished she could worship with them.

The service ended with a long prayer, and Elena began to doze off again.

"Stand up now," her mother coaxed when the prayer finished. "I'm going to introduce you to the Darringtons."

Elena glanced at the cluster of people crowded into the aisle, most of them standing and talking instead of streaming out for Sunday dinner.

Parker Randolph slid into the row behind her. "Remember when we used to go puddle-jumping on days like this?"

She smiled. Those wonderful days of playing with Parker were long before they had chaperones and social calendars. Until they were ten or so, they were allowed to be children, playing in the backyard while their mothers visited.

"I remember getting into trouble for puddle-jumping with you," she said.

He cocked his head. "But it was worth it, wasn't it?"

"Absolutely," she whispered. Even with her muddied skirts and her mother's reprimands, those days had been some of the most fun of her life.

Parker eyed the growing cluster in front of them. "Apparently, no one wants to leave church this morning."

"Perhaps because of the rain."

"Most likely the clamor over the arrival of you-know-who."

She watched the younger women and their parents huddled together around the Darrington family like hens in a roost.

She sighed. "I wonder if you-know-who might enjoy jumping in puddles too."

Parker laughed. "I doubt it. The man is nice enough, but he seems more reserved than a member of the clergy."

She groaned inwardly. She didn't want to marry a man who knew how to talk about God but didn't know how to enjoy all He'd created.

"Did you and Jillian have a pleasant talk yesterday?" she whispered.

His laugh faded away. "We have to be careful. If my parents found out—"

"They won't hear it from me." Her hand slipped into her pocket, and she drew out an envelope folded into thirds. "Jillian asked me to give you this."

He hesitated, glancing around them before he took it and stuffed it inside his waistcoat.

Her mother nodded at Parker and then nudged Elena toward the aisle. Two rather large ladies blocked them from moving toward the front of the church, and her mother tried to force Elena between them. The ladies didn't move.

"Pardon me," her mother said. "We're trying to say hello to the Darringtons."

The women looked at her as if she'd lost her mind. "We're all waiting to speak with them," one of the ladies said.

Mama tried to press Elena forward again until Papa joined their side. "You're making a fool out of yourself, Deborah," he whispered.

"But Elena needs to meet him."

"In the proper place and time, my dear."

"He is leaving soon," Mama insisted, her voice panicked.

"But he won't remember meeting her here, not with this crowd of people."

This time her mother didn't listen to reason. She took Elena's wrist and continued to move forward until there was a barrier of shoulders and arms that she couldn't pass, not without, as her father put it so bluntly, making a fool out of herself.

Elena turned to appeal to her father, but she only saw his back as he went toward the door. For a moment, she felt abandoned by the one man who was supposed to take care of her, the man who had told her that he wanted her to marry for love. But then she realized he had already tried to stop his wife from her foolishness. It was time for Elena to stop her now.

"Papa's right," she whispered. "He'll never remember meeting me, with this crowd."

Her mother was trying to edge around another woman, but there was no room for her to pass. "He most certainly will."

"We'll seem desperate, Mama."

Even if her mother was desperate, she knew quite well that they could never let Mr. Darrington know this. Her mother didn't seem so concerned at the moment about their appearance, perhaps because Mr. Darrington was preparing to leave the island. If she didn't introduce Elena soon, she might not have an opportunity to do it.

But that didn't mean Elena must show her desperation as well.

Elena took a step back, away from the crowd. Mama tried to nudge her forward again, but she shook her head. They would have to meet Mr. Darrington another time.

Elena shook the minister's hand at the doorway, and her mother moved slower than normal toward their waiting carriage, lingering first by the doorway and then by the side of the building before she reluctantly got into the carriage with her family.

February 13, 1813

Winter lingers on, but I have begun singing again. The music sustains me in the darkness.

Thomas and Molly sing with me about God's goodness even when we don't feel it, about His joy even when we are sad, about His peace even when we worry so.

Nickolas Westmount came again last week, carrying bread and jam for the children. This time I was ready with my questions. At first he avoided answering, as he had the time before, but when I persisted, he finally told me some of what he knew.

The British, he said, might have taken my Jonah to the fort. They've demanded every islander renounce their citizenship with the United States and take an oath of allegiance to their king.

Jonah Seymour would never renounce his allegiance to our country. His father died fighting for this country during the first war with the British. If he'd been old enough, Jonah would have fought too. What would the redcoats do if he wouldn't swear his allegiance to the motherland? Nickolas couldn't answer that question.

If Jonah is at the fort, perhaps the British will return him soon. Once the weather turns warm again, won't they need him to care for the light?

Nickolas couldn't answer those questions either, but this time his visit filled me with hope. Perhaps Jonah hadn't been killed or wounded or trapped in a cavern. Perhaps he was safe at the fort, biding his time.

As Nickolas hurried away from the house, I realized there was one more question I hadn't asked. And he never volunteered the answer.

If they were imprisoning those who wouldn't swear allegiance to the crown, why had the British allowed Nickolas Westmount to remain free?

Chapter Nineteen

Elena stepped through the doorway of the lighthouse and waited as the mice scurried away. Her heart pounded as she walked toward the spiral steps.

"Chase?" she quietly called up to the tower.

Silence was her only answer.

She shouldn't want him to be here, not as much as she did. Nothing could happen between them except friendship. Yet what was so wrong with their being friends?

It had been three nights now since she'd met Chase. Three nights since she'd been able to escape the house on her own. Last night it had been raining too hard for her to leave their house—her father would have guessed something was amiss if she'd tried to go in that weather. Clouds had lodged themselves over Mackinac tonight, swallowing even the smallest star, but the rain was gone.

Tonight she would wait. And she would draw. She hadn't seen her father in the hallway tonight, but she suspected that he knew she'd left.

Had Chase been back here since their first meeting? On her entire bike ride over, she prayed that he hadn't given up on her, that he would come again. They'd never made any promise to continue to see each other, but he'd said he wanted to see her. She hoped it was true.

Her lantern lit the walls of the kitchen, and she climbed on a chair to the top shelf above the table to retrieve her sketchbook and pencil box. If Chase had found it, at least he had returned it to her new hiding place.

Instead of going up the steps to the tower, she moved back into the parlor and sat down at the desk. Picking up one of her charcoal pencils, she began to draw. She drew a man on a dark horse riding along the shore, his strong profile facing the lake. Lightning flashed behind him, and she felt its power as she drew it, just like the power of the man.

Lost in her world, she didn't hear the door open. When she looked up, Chase was studying her with his easy smile.

She caught her breath, words escaping her.

He flung his hat on the post. "Hello, Andy."

Trailing behind him was a white dog spotted with black. The dog scooted up beside her and she set her pencil down, petting his damp fur before she looked back up at Chase. "I didn't think you would come."

He leaned back against the doorpost. "It seems to me that you're the one who didn't come on Saturday night."

"You were here?"

"I was, and I have to admit, I was a bit lonely."

"I was with my—" She hesitated. She wanted to see this man, but she wasn't ready to tell him about her parents.

He studied her for a moment. "I missed you."

The dog nudged her hand, prompting her to keep petting. She laughed as she brushed her hand over his back again. "Who is this?"

"My new companion," Chase said simply. "I tried to take him back to where I thought he lived, but the people at the house said it looked to them like he'd found a new owner."

"He's a smart dog, then." She leaned back in her chair. "What did you name him?"

"I was going to call him Andy, but the name was already taken." He shrugged. "Now I can't decide what to call him."

The dog licked her cheek, and she laughed. "He's friendly."

"What should we name him?"

Her heart leaped at the word "we," and then she felt silly. Chase was only asking for her help.

"Something practical, perhaps, like Spot or Moses."

"I can hardly believe the word 'practical' just came from your lips."

She laughed again. "Or something more exotic…like Akiko."

"Sit, Akiko," he tried to say, but he butchered the name. "I can't say that."

"If he were my dog—" When she hesitated, he stepped closer, watching her.

"What would you name him if he were your dog?"

She looked toward the window. "Something that reminded me of the stars, of the people who love watching them as I do."

He turned a wooden chair around and sat in it. "How about Galileo?"

She smiled. "That's the perfect name."

Chase leaned over to pet him. "How do you like that name? Galileo."

The dog barked once, as if he agreed.

Chase moved his chair toward her, looking down at the desk. "What are you drawing?"

Her eyes traveled down the pad and she slammed her book closed. But it was too late, and she knew it. He'd seen what was on her paper.

The grin edged further across his handsome face.

"It's a picture of a friend," she tried to explain.

"A good friend?"

She felt the heat climbing her cheeks and hoped he wouldn't see the pink tint of her skin in the shadows.

"I didn't expect you to return so soon," she stammered. "It's been too cloudy to see the stars."

"The stars weren't the only reason I wanted to return."

"I—" Surely he could see her red face now, even in the dim light.

He crossed the room, waving her to join him. "Let me show you something."

She followed him to the other room. The bedroom. Even though there was no mattress left on the bed, she felt strange, being here with him. What had she been thinking, hoping to meet this stranger here? She'd been so silly, wanting and wishing to see him again.

He opened the trunk and pulled out the book. "I wanted you to see this."

She stared at the cracked cover and her heart sank. She had thought he had meant her, that he had returned tonight to see her, but he had come back for Magdelaine's diary.

She was being so foolish, hopelessly opening her heart to a stranger who wanted to be her friend. Just a friend.

Rain began to patter against the windows, and lightning flashed through the room. If the storm continued, they might be stranded here for hours.

He motioned for her to sit on a rickety-looking chair beside the bed. She tested the chair, and it seemed sturdy enough. As she sat, she avoided his gaze so he couldn't read all that was in her eyes, in her heart. For if he looked too closely, she would be exposed—all her hopes, relief, even desire was there, as transparent as the air they breathed.

It wasn't for him to see.

"You found Magdelaine's journal."

He nodded.

"How did you find it?"

He shifted on the bed frame like a schoolboy caught telling a fib. "I was looking for your drawings."

"Ahh—" She should at least pretend to be angry, but his compliment made her smile instead. Even if she wanted to keep her work hidden, he'd wanted to see it.

"I read a few pages, and then I stopped."

"Why didn't you read it all?"

His smile faded as his eyes grew serious. "I wanted to share her story with you."

It felt so warm in the room, as if the ghost of the lightkeeper had returned to light the stove. Heat flickered on Elena's cheeks, but she didn't dare break from his gaze. He would think she was scared, and she wasn't scared…at least not of him harming her.

The only thing she feared tonight was that he might hurt her heart.

As thunder cracked in the distance, she reached out and brushed her hands over the cover, honored by his gift.

"I wanted to share it with you," he said, "but it seems you've already read her story."

She sighed. "It's a story without an ending."

He put the journal on the bed by his side. "Do you think this Magdelaine would mind if I took her story home to read?"

"I don't believe she would mind at all."

He looked around the dusty room, seeming to take in the sights of the bare furniture and the curtains that had been chewed by mice. "I like being here with you."

She caught her breath. "I like it too."

"But I'd still like to know your real name."

Panic wrapped itself around her heart like a noose. The truth would change everything. "I can't tell you."

He leaned forward. "We could spend time away from the lighthouse as well as here."

"I'm a much different person away from the lighthouse."

He stretched out his legs and then scratched Galileo's neck. "But why must you be so different when you're away?"

"It's what is expected of me."

"You don't seem to be the kind of woman who worries about what is expected of her."

She shook her head. "You don't know me very well."

"Something I'm trying very hard to change."

She nodded at the book beside him. "It's not like you've been an open book to me."

"What would you like to know, Miss Andy?" He hesitated. "It is *Miss*, isn't it?"

A smile flickered on her lips. "It is."

"I hoped as much." His eyes softened again. "Now, what would you like to know?"

Part of her wanted to probe him for specifics, but part of her was terrified to ask even the simplest of questions, in case he expected her to reciprocate.

"Where are you from?" she finally asked.

"You probably never heard of it." He cleared his throat. "It's a small town called Brush Park."

"Brush Park?" She thought for a moment but didn't remember ever hearing the name before. "Is it in Illinois?"

"No, I'm from Michigan." He rubbed the dog behind his ears. "Where are you from, Andy?"

"It depends on the season," she said. "But this lighthouse is my favorite place in the whole world."

"It's becoming my favorite place too—if you're willing to share."

"I'm willing to share." She paused. "With Galileo."

Chase laughed. "Then I'm a bit jealous of this dog."

"Where is your family?" she dared to ask.

"I only have one sister, and she is like you and me, a bit of a runner."

"I don't run."

He cocked his head.

"Well, I don't run very far."

"Your feet may not run far." He touched his chest. "But I think your heart does."

He was right. Her heart often ran far from where it was supposed to be, and it wouldn't get any better, not if she married the society man her mother had chosen for her. Her life would be full of parties and meaningless, endless chatter with the daughters of her mother's friends.

Perhaps she would steal away on one of the steamers heading north.

"When did you arrive at the fort?"

He tilted his head again. "The fort?"

"Fort Mackinac," she clarified and then felt silly. There was only one working fort on the island.

His eyebrows arched. "You think I live at the fort?"

She shrugged, not wanting to insult him. "I've heard that some of the officers live outside."

His laughter erupted so suddenly that even Galileo looked concerned.

"What's so funny?" she asked.

"You think I'm in the army." It wasn't a question, just a statement that he seemed to find terribly humorous.

She wrapped her arms over her chest. "I don't see what you find so amusing."

He wiped his eyes with the back of his hand. "I have all the respect in the world for our military."

She sat up a little taller. "As do I."

He looked down at his gray trousers and stained shirt. "I'm not wearing any military attire."

"The soldiers don't *always* wear their uniforms. Not when they're playing on the island."

"And you have experience with this?"

"I've seen a few of your men out during the day, yes, but I have no firsthand experience, if that's what you're implying."

"They're not 'my men,' Andy."

Now she was confused. "What do you mean?"

"I'm not in the army."

"Then what are you doing on the island?"

He thought for a moment. "I work at the Grand Hotel."

Her heart sank. A military officer didn't make much money but the position was respectable, even in her parents' eyes. If she married an officer, she would be able to afford at least one servant.

But a laborer at the Grand? It didn't matter what his position. Neither of her parents would think of letting her marry a man who served at a hotel, no matter how much she loved him.

Not that Chase had proposed marriage to her or even hinted at it. She groaned inwardly. Her heart was becoming entangled with a man she didn't know.

Chase was studying her again, watching for her reaction. She wanted to cry but refused to insult him with her tears. She swallowed hard. "I'm sure it is interesting work."

"Most interesting," he replied.

"And respectable."

"I suppose." He brushed his hands over his trousers. "If you could do anything you wanted in this life, what would you do?"

She didn't hesitate this time. "I would fly."

He laughed again, but this time it didn't feel like he was insulting her. It sounded like he was delighted with her words. "Perhaps one day you will fly, Andy."

She smiled at him. They were both crazy.

He eyed her again in that way that made her heart leap. "Do you think you will marry one day?"

Her smile vanished, and she looked down at her hands in her lap. "I know I will."

The joviality in his voice washed away. "Are you promised to someone?"

"Not promised as much as prepared."

"Do you want to marry this man?"

She shook her head. "Nor does he want to marry me."

"So you're planning to marry a man you don't love?"

Her father's words came back to her. Her father thought she should marry for love, but if she loved someone like Chase...he would never agree.

"Sometimes life doesn't happen the way we want it to, Chase."

He watched her closely. "Are we still talking about marriage?"

She shrugged.

"Because if we are, you should never marry a man who doesn't want to spend every moment possible with you. His heart should ache when he's not with you. And your heart should ache too."

She stood up. The thunder had quieted, the rain no longer pattering the roof. "I must be getting home."

"I hope you marry for love, Andy."

"I—I do too, Chase, but it's not my choice."

He stood up beside her. "Will you come back tomorrow night?"

The dance of the season—the Independence Day ball—was Wednesday night. Tomorrow she should be preparing for their tea with Mrs. Darrington and then resting well for the ball.

He studied her face for a moment. "I must leave the island on Thursday."

Her heart seemed to stop. "Where are you going?"

"Not far," he said. "But I may be gone for a few days."

"So you'll be coming back?"

He leaned toward her, and for a moment she thought he might kiss her. Instead, he breathed into her ear. "Do you want me to return?"

She thought for a moment, not wanting to encourage what could never be. Yet she wanted to be honest with him. They could be friends for the remaining weeks of the summer, couldn't they? They could look at the stars and read Magdelaine's diary and rejoice in God's creation together.

"I believe I do," she whispered.

He held out his hand to help her stand, and she took it. His touch made her tremble.

"I'm glad you came tonight," he said.

"Me too."

"Will you come back tomorrow night?" he asked again.

"I will," she whispered before she scrambled out the door.

Her father would probably be waiting out back for her, on the porch, and she hoped he was asleep again. She didn't think she could constrain the smile on her face.

Chapter Twenty

Elena waited by the window in her nightgown. She couldn't see the stars with the lights nearby, but it was a clear night. As soon as her mother was asleep, she would leave, and perhaps she could even sneak out before her father stopped her. If he asked why she was going out again, she would tell him the truth—that she wanted to watch the stars.

Someone knocked on the door, and she turned to see Jillian peeking into the room.

"Do you need anything else this evening?" she asked.

Elena pointed to the lounge chair beside her. "I'd love to talk with you."

Jillian closed the door and sat down.

"How are you doing?" Elena asked.

"I'm well."

"Parker—he's quite enthralled with you."

"He shouldn't be," Jillian said with a shake of her head. "Are you going out tonight?"

"As soon as I can," she whispered.

"You have to be careful at night, out all by yourself."

Elena eyed the closed door, and for a moment, she wanted to confide in Jillian about Chase. But if someone heard her talking about him, she would never be allowed to see him again.

"I'm very careful." She leaned forward. "One day, perhaps, you will be Mrs. Parker Randolph."

Jillian giggled. "And you will be Mrs. Chester Darrington."

Elena groaned. "If I have to marry that man, you're not allowed to marry Parker. I'll need your company every day."

"I'll come visit every day...for tea."

They laughed again.

The doorbell chimed below them, and Elena jumped. She glanced at the clock and saw that it was after eleven.

"Maybe it's a telegram," Jillian said.

No visitor—or telegram—coming so late at night could bring good news.

Seconds later, Elena heard a voice below them, a woman's voice. She sounded angry.

"Wait here," she told Jillian as she tugged her wrapper with its puffy sleeves and ribbons over her nightgown. Then she opened her door, preparing to go downstairs.

Claude was across from her, knocking on her mother's door. When Mama opened it, her nightcap rested just below her eyebrows and she clung to the edges of her wrapper. Claude cleared his throat. "Mrs. Randolph is here to see you."

Mama hugged the wrapper closer to her chest. "It's almost midnight."

"She says it's urgent."

Mrs. Randolph was in the entryway below, gripping a half dozen or so envelopes in her hands. Dread filled Elena as she followed her mother down the steps. She knew exactly who the letters were from. She'd delivered one herself that very morning.

Mama squinted her eyes like she didn't recognize the woman. "Francis?"

Mrs. Randolph stepped forward, her gaze shifting between Elena and her mother. "I want to see your maid."

"Whatever for?" Mama asked, her voice strained but polite.

"It's a personal matter."

"Our entire household is asleep," Mama said with a shake of her head. "Surely this can wait until morning."

"It most certainly cannot."

"Jillian is my maid, Francis. I will not wake her without knowing the reason for this disruption."

Mrs. Randolph waved the envelopes in front of her, and Elena's fear turned into fury. How could she be so appalled at her son caring for a woman considered beneath him by the world's standards but every bit his equal in the sight of God?

Mrs. Randolph took another step toward Mama, her nostrils flaring. "I want to know why your maid is writing such atrocious things to my son."

"Writing—" Mama stopped for a moment, seeming to organize her thoughts. "She's writing letters to Parker?"

"Almost every day, ever since we've been on this island, at least."

"Surely this is a mistake."

Elena turned toward her mother. "It's no mistake, Mama. She cares for Parker."

Mrs. Randolph glared at her. "This is none of your business."

"I delivered one of her letters."

Mama stared at Elena like she didn't recognize her. "Why would you do that?"

"Because Parker cares for her too."

"He does no such thing," the woman insisted.

Elena's voice quieted. "Did you ask him?"

Mrs. Randolph cleared her throat. "Parker may think he fancies her for the moment, but it's nothing more than a fascination. He doesn't know what or who he needs."

"But what if Jillian is who he needs?"

Elena's mother stepped up the staircase, calling up to the next level. "Jillian?"

Jillian stepped into the hallway. The electric light made the blotches on her pale face glow. It would have been impossible for her not to hear Mrs. Randolph's harsh words. The whole house had probably heard them.

"Yes, ma'am." Her voice cracked on the last word.

Mrs. Randolph clutched the banister. "I want you to leave my son alone."

"But—"

"I don't care what he's said." She waved the envelopes again.

"He doesn't love you—only the idea of you."

Jillian's voice strengthened. "The idea of me?"

"Plenty of men pleasure in the conquest of consorting with ladies' maids and such, but I won't stand for it in my family."

Other men might enjoy the pleasure of the conquest, but not Parker. Elena knew he was a genuine soul.

Elena stepped forward, ready to defend her friend. "Parker isn't like other men, Mrs. Randolph. He cares about Jillian."

Mrs. Randolph's eyes remained on Jillian. "Has he proposed marriage to you?"

"No." Her voice was still strong.

"Has he made any promises?"

"No." This time her voice was weaker, and Elena wanted to tell her to fight.

"Nor will he propose, my dear, because he's already been promised to Miss Grunier."

Elena gasped. "Trudy?"

Mrs. Randolph glanced at her. "Of course, Trudy."

"Does Parker know this?"

Mrs. Randolph ignored Elena's question. How was it that, often in her circle, the last people to find out they were marrying were the bride and groom?

Mrs. Randolph took another step up the staircase. "You will stay away from him."

Jillian stood a little taller. "Only if he asks me to."

"Oh, he will," Mrs. Randolph assured her before she turned. She faced Elena's mother again. "You know she has to leave."

Elena felt as though the floor were about to crack under her feet. Her mother couldn't let Jillian go.

She saw the look of regret in Mama's when she looked at Jillian. The resignation. Perhaps her mother felt a little sorry for her too. It wasn't so many years ago that her mother had left her position to marry a wealthy man.

"I have to let her go," she said to Elena.

"No, you don't, Mama."

Mrs. Randolph looked up the steps. "She needs to go tonight."

Her mother shook her head. "Morning will be soon enough, Francis. Enough damage has been done already."

No matter what Elena said to try to convince her friend, Jillian refused to stay the night. Tears flowed down Elena's cheeks as she helped Jillian pack. She wanted to be angry at her mother for forcing Jillian to leave, but she was more angry at the society in which they lived. What was so wrong with Jillian caring for someone above her in status but quite compatible with her in personality and spirit?

Elena's mother hadn't been wealthy when she married, and her parents' marriage had worked. Sort of.

Perhaps it was better for Jillian to leave before both their hearts were broken.

Mama wasn't around when Elena changed into her old dress, nor did she appear when she and Jillian crept off the back porch like outlaws. Elena didn't take the bicycle with her this time. In one hand was a lantern, and over her back was strung a makeshift knapsack filled with most of Jillian's belongings. Her friend carried the rest in a blanket.

Part of her wanted to go straight to the Randolphs' house and knock on Parker's door, but what would he do? Give them money, perhaps, so Jillian could stay in a hotel until she returned to Chicago? She suspected that Jillian wouldn't take his money. And even if Parker did pay for it, all the hotels would be booked for the Independence Day celebrations.

"Where should we go?" Jillian whispered.

"Don't worry," Elena told her even though she herself felt terrified.

If Chase wasn't at the lighthouse, she didn't know what she would do. She certainly wasn't going to let Jillian stay out on the island by herself, even at the lighthouse, no matter how safe she knew it to be.

"I have a little money saved," Jillian said. "Enough to get me back to Chicago."

"In the morning, my mother will rethink everything. Perhaps she will even ask you to return."

"It doesn't matter what she wants. She can't take me back."

Elena's stomach rolled. She understood her mother's need to protect their family's reputation, but Jillian hadn't done anything wrong. If only her mother would take a stand and tell the other ladies that as well. It was exhausting to be driven by what others thought of you.

"Parker's mother...," Jillian said. "She was never supposed to find those letters."

"I know."

"Parker said we should burn them."

"But you didn't."

Jillian shook her head.

"Apparently he couldn't burn your letters either."

They stopped along the road, and Jillian eyed the narrow trail ahead of them. "Where are you taking me?"

"There is a man I met at the lighthouse, a nice man named Chase. He works as a laborer at the Grand Hotel, and he doesn't know—" She took a deep breath. "He calls me Andy."

Jillian reached out and stopped her. "I understand."

Elena sighed. "I suppose we've both given our hearts to someone we should not."

The women hiked through the woods until they came to the lighthouse. A light burned in the window, and Elena's heart leaped at the sight of it. They found Chase inside the parlor, holding the diary in his hands.

He stood up quickly, smiling when he saw Elena. But his smile quickly faded to worry when he saw Jillian.

"Did something happen?"

"My friend," Elena began. "She lost her position and needs some place to sleep for the night."

Chase opened his mouth to speak, but Elena didn't let him. She was afraid he was going to refuse her. "I was hoping that perhaps she could stay with one of the women you work with at the Grand."

Chase blinked. "I don't know...."

"Just for the night," she insisted. "Tomorrow we can find her a new position, perhaps even at the hotel."

Jillian shook her head. "I don't want to be an inconvenience."

Chase looked at her. "You're not an inconvenience."

His words were spoken with such sincerity that Elena wondered if he was flirting with Jillian. The very thought dismayed her. She'd created her own world in her mind, and in this world, Chase was devoted to her. Perhaps he was just as friendly to all women as he had been to her, or he could even be married like Edward, who roamed in spite of his marital vows.

But as Chase turned back to Elena, she realized he was serious. He saw worth in Jillian just as she did.

He tucked the diary into his satchel. "I believe I can find a place for her to stay tonight."

Elena clasped her hands together. "Thank you."

"Are you certain, Mr.—" Jillian asked.

He nodded. "Quite."

Galileo escorted them the mile to the Grand Hotel. As they walked, Chase stole a glance at Elena, and she warmed at his gentle smile.

"Thank you," she mouthed.

He acknowledged her words with a slight bow of his head. The perfect gentleman.

She looked at the path ahead of them, washed yellow in lantern light. Her mother might have plans for her to marry someone in their society, but there had to be another way to provide for her family. Perhaps her father would find a way to improve their family's financial situation that didn't involve her marrying a man she didn't love. She didn't know how she could marry another, not when her heart belonged to this man.

As they drew closer to the hotel, Elena stopped, remembering how she was dressed. She looked up at the imposing structure with new eyes.

"I can't go in there," she whispered.

Chase reached for her arm, and his touch enflamed her. Part of her wanted to run into his arms, and the other part screamed at her to run away.

Jillian cleared her throat. "I'll wait over there." She pointed toward a lamp standing along the wide drive leading to the porch.

Chase leaned toward Elena, his cheek touching her hair. "Why can't you go into the Grand?"

"I can't explain it."

"The people who stay here—they are just like you and me."

If he only knew how much they were like her...

"I'm not afraid of them. I'm afraid of..." Her voice trailed off. How could she tell him that she was more afraid of him than the people in the hotel, or at least of losing him when her mother found out? Mama wouldn't make her leave the house as she had Jillian, but the next morning they would be on a boat back to Chicago.

He lifted his finger, and she trembled when he trailed it over her lips. "You don't have to tell me, Andy."

"I wish I could."

"I will take Jillian to a safe place, and then I will walk you home." He looked down at Galileo. "You keep her safe for me while I'm gone."

Elena hugged Jillian and watched Chase escort her up the steps, into the beautiful hotel. Elena had visited countless times, but it occurred to her that Jillian had never been inside.

When they disappeared through the doors, Elena bent down to Galileo and scratched behind his ears. "I know what Chase told you, but I can't possibly allow him to walk me home, and I can't let you follow me either."

She stood back up. "Tell that master of yours that I've never met a gentleman quite as fine as him."

"Good night, Chase," she whispered as she hurried through the back streets and up the eastern bluff to her house. It wasn't until she got home that she realized she couldn't help Jillian find a new position without returning to visit Chase at the Grand.

Chapter Twenty-One

Chase's gaze kept slipping from the stack of papers on his desk to the lake view outside his window. The visit to Mackinac began out of obligation for him and then became quite practical to test Nelson's telescope. He thought he'd be counting the days until he could leave for Chicago, to be back in the business world, but now he didn't want to leave.

He'd peppered Jillian with questions about her friend, but Jillian refused to share Andy's secrets, and he admired her for it. Most women knew who he was, even if they pretended they did not. They would subtly follow him around a dinner party or a ballroom, but he knew exactly what they were doing.

Andy didn't follow him around. Last night, she'd even left him at the hotel without a good-bye. He'd met hundreds of debutantes over the years, at dances and dinners and parties, but there had never been a woman like this, a woman who wasn't feigning to be something she was not or expecting him to propose marriage after their introduction. They could simply enjoy each other's company.

The women he met at the balls and banquets cared very much about the legacy of S. P. Darrington & Company and the inheritance that would one day be his. Even if they pretended to be enthralled by his every word, they didn't care one iota about his thoughts or dreams or the secrets he held in his heart. He could say he wanted to live among the headhunters in New Guinea one day, and they would nod their pretty heads and smile and tell him that their dream was to live among the headhunters as well.

He could say he'd hung the moon in the sky, and they would probably congratulate him on his success.

It was disturbing, really.

Was Andy the only woman in the world, besides his sister, who dared to disagree with him? Who was confident enough to walk away?

He tapped his palm on the papers and smiled.

Sarah wouldn't believe him if he told her he wanted to stay longer on Mackinac. She would be pleased at first, until he told her the reason. But if his mother knew there was a young woman who intrigued him, a woman who loved God, she would be happy. She would love Andy's spirit.

He hadn't made any promises to Andy, but there was nothing wrong with seeing her again, was there? His only fear was what would happen when she found out he was a Darrington. Hopefully she had never even heard of his family.

There was a knock on his door, and Galileo barked.

When he opened the door, his mother soared into the room, and then she stopped and stared at him. "Why are you smiling?"

He shrugged. "I'm happy."

She watched him for another moment. "Did something happen?"

He petted Galileo. "Why can't I just smile?"

"Hmm." She strolled to the window, looking outside before she turned. "I wish you would attend this tea with me today."

"I actually have a good excuse not to attend."

His mother laughed. "You must have put a lot of effort into finding an excuse."

"I'm meeting with a local man about a fishing pole he's made."

"A fishing pole?"

He put on his coat. "A lot of people fish, Mother."

"You are just like your father."

"Is he going to this tea?"

She reached out and fixed his collar. "Of course not. He's working, just like you."

"Then surely Sarah can accompany you."

But even as he said it, he realized Sarah wouldn't be there. First of all, because she disliked Miss Bissette and her family. Secondly, because she'd been doting on Jillian all morning like the poor girl was her new pet.

"I wish you weren't going to Chicago on Thursday." His mother sighed. "We've only begun to see you."

"I think—I might return after my trip."

She studied him again, as if she were trying to determine whether he was teasing. "Why would you return?"

He shrugged. "You've been gone for four months, and I would like to see you a little more as well."

"But we will see you in Detroit in August."

He crossed his arms, leaning back against the davenport. "Are you trying to talk me out of returning?"

"I'm not, it's just—" She paused. "You're not coming back for a fishing pole, are you?"

"Of course not." He stood up. "Perhaps I want to spend more time on the island."

"Sarah said the women on the island have become quite enamored with you."

He glanced out at the lake before looking at his mother again. "I've met a few of them."

She hesitated again. He knew she didn't want to press him. "And have any of these young ladies caught your attention?"

He smiled. "Perhaps."

She clasped her hands together but did an admirable job of containing her excitement otherwise. "Are you planning to tell me which one?"

He leaned down and pecked her cheek. "Not yet."

"Perhaps I shall meet her tomorrow night."

"I don't believe she'll be attending the ball."

Disappointment flashed across her face.

"But when you do meet her…I promise you that you will like her as much as I do."

"I'm sure she's splendid, Chase."

"She is."

"Then one day I'll look forward to making her acquaintance."

His mother stepped toward the door, and he stopped her. "If Mrs. Bissette or her daughter inquires about my status, please tell her I'm otherwise engaged."

"Engaged?" his mother asked, a mixture of horrified and pleased.

He sighed, wishing that every young woman on the island thought he was engaged to be married. "Not engaged to be married, Mother. You can tell her, though, that my interests lie elsewhere."

"Are you certain?"

"Absolutely."

As his mother waved good-bye, he looked back out at the lake.

Galileo slipped up beside him, and he rested his hand on the dog's head. "She'll like Andy, won't she?"

His mother wouldn't care if Andy didn't have connections as long as she made him happy.

If only he knew where Andy came from and where she was going.

If only he could go with her.

* * * * *

Elena turned back the edge of the curtain and watched Mrs. Darrington step down from the Grand Hotel's carriage. She was a beautiful woman, looking very much like her daughter with her slender frame and neatly pinned auburn hair. She hoped Sarah hadn't told her mother that Elena had acted improperly toward Edward. She'd be mortified if this woman thought she had been flirting with her son-in-law.

Mama spent the first hour of their visit telling pleasant stories about the gardens she and Mrs. Ingram had overseen, and Mrs. Darrington seemed to relish the connection with her sister. As the women talked and sipped tea, Elena thought about Jillian at the Grand. She wished she could walk into the hotel and ask for Chase, but that would ruin everything. As much as she wanted to see him, she would have to avoid him today and at the ball tomorrow night.

But how was she supposed to help Jillian if she couldn't go to him?

She should have thought this through more before she took Jillian to him.

When there was a lull in conversation, Mrs. Darrington turned to her. "Do you draw, Elena?"

Elena blinked. "Why do you ask?"

"You have that look in your eye of a woman who likes to dream."

Elena didn't look at her mother. "I suppose I do enjoy drawing a bit."

Mrs. Darrington's green eyes sparkled with her smile. "Indeed."

Mama refilled Mrs. Darrington's cup. "She hasn't had time to draw in a long while."

"Oh, that's unfortunate," Mrs. Darrington said. "Every artist should make time to create."

Elena turned the teacup in her hands. "I suppose."

"What is it that you used to draw?"

"I—"

"Landscapes," her mother replied.

Elena didn't bother to dispute her mother's words. Mama thought it was improper for a lady to draw portraits of people, as if it were the height of impropriety to notice the beauty and flaws of another.

"Well, God certainly created some beautiful landscapes for us to draw." Mrs. Darrington was watching her instead of Mama. "And He created beautiful people as well."

"Speaking of beautiful people," her mother asked, "have you met Gracie Frederick?"

"I don't believe I have had the pleasure of making her acquaintance."

Elena didn't have to look at her mother to know that there was a smile on her face.

"Miss Frederick is quite beautiful, and bright as well."

Elena lifted her head. What was her mother doing?

Mama sipped her tea. "Of course she's also known for making and breaking her promises. She—"

"Oh, I don't believe I need to know that." Mrs. Darrington replied with such grace and strength that Elena watched her in a bit of awe. "The Good Book, as I'm sure you know, instructs us not to say spiteful things about one another."

"Of course not." Mama stumbled on her words. "I mean—of course."

"And it says we reap what we sow. I'd rather not reap having people talk about me or my family, so I try to avoid gossip all together."

Elena nibbled her biscotti. She'd never heard anyone refuse to bite on the enticement of good gossip before. And this woman had done it with such resolve and dignity. Elena hadn't realized it was possible to repudiate gossip in polite society.

Mama didn't seem to know what to say next, so Elena leaned forward. "I heard that you just returned from Europe."

"I did." The smile returned to Mrs. Darrington's face. "We were there four months."

"What was your favorite place?"

"The museums in Florence."

Elena's heart sped up. "That was mine as well."

"You've been to Florence?"

She nodded. "My parents took me there when I turned sixteen."

"Did you go to Venice?"

Elena nodded again. "I loved riding on the canals."

Mrs. Darrington placed her teacup on the saucer. "It's wonderful, isn't it?"

"Magical."

Mama finished her second cup of tea and refilled their cups. "Will you be attending the ball tomorrow night?"

Mrs. Darrington nodded, adding a sugar cube to her tea. "I love nothing more than dancing."

"And will your family be there?" Mama asked.

"Absolutely."

"Elena has met your daughter."

She turned toward Elena. "I didn't realize that."

Perhaps Sarah had honored her mother's desire to avoid gossip.

Mama shifted in her seat, taking another slow sip of tea. "She's met your daughter, but Elena has yet to meet your son."

"I shall have to introduce you to him."

Her mother took another sip of tea. "Is he courting anyone?"

Mrs. Darrington nodded. "He tells me he is quite enamored right now with a certain young lady."

"Enamored." Her mother's teacup clanked against the saucer as she repeated the word. "Has he proposed marriage?"

"Oh, no," Mrs. Darrington replied with a wave, but Mama looked crestfallen.

Elena felt nothing but relief. If another woman occupied Mr. Darrington's mind, then perhaps it was okay if another man occupied hers.

"To Gracie Frederick?"

Mrs. Darrington ignored the question. "When did you meet Sarah?"

"At the dance last week," Elena said.

"Did you meet her husband as well?"

Elena pulled her hand close to her side. She could still feel Edward's fingers on her, and it made her shudder. "I made his acquaintance."

"I hope he was—pleasant to you."

"Pleasant enough."

When Mrs. Darrington left, her mother fled upstairs to her room, pleading a headache. The news about Chester Darrington's affections might keep her mother in her room until the ball tomorrow night.

Chapter Twenty-Two

Chase met Silas Hull in the lobby, and a few heads turned at the unusual sight of a soldier carrying a fishing pole into the Grand Hotel. Chase led the lieutenant to a quiet corner with two chairs and a couch. It wouldn't pay for any of the other men in the room to discover the novelty of Silas's invention.

Silas put the three sections of his bamboo pole on the couch. "I have to be back on duty in an hour."

"I won't keep you long," Chase said, before nodding at the rod. "But I wanted to know, why did you make that?"

Silas shrugged. "The sections make it easier to carry."

"I'm sure others would agree with you." Chase tapped his hand on the table next to him. "Sometimes the simplest things sell the best."

"Sell?"

"I invest in new inventions," Chase said, leaning forward. "And I think I could sell thousands of your fishing poles."

Silas slowly registered his words. "Are you serious?"

Chase leaned back. "We'd have a lot of details to iron out, of course. You'll have to get a patent right away so no one can take your idea, and then we'll have to figure out a way to produce them."

Silas picked up the sections and looked at them. "You really think people would buy this?"

"There's never any guarantee, but I believe they would." Chase took a deep breath. "But until you get the patent, you can't go fishing with this pole."

Silas's face fell. "Why not?"

"Someone might steal your design."

Silas seemed to contemplate the choice—either fish with his pole for the remainder of the summer or put it aside to make income for his future.

"It would just be for this season," Chase said. "You can fish with another pole."

"I suppose I could."

Chase patted the couch. "And next year, you can fish with this one again."

He began to discuss the next steps of how he and Silas could partner together. As he talked, Silas's gaze wandered over Chase's shoulder, and his eyes grew wide.

Chase turned and saw Sarah walking toward them with Jillian. The girl looked like a completely different woman than the one he'd snuck into the hotel last night. Her blond hair was perfectly curled, and she wore one of Sarah's day gowns, a mixture of light blue silk and lace. As pretty as Jillian was, he was surprised that Sarah didn't seem to see her as competition. Maybe his sister had finally found a friend.

Sarah put her hand on his chair. "I've been looking all over for you."

"Hello, Jillian." Chase nodded at her. "You look lovely."

Sarah reached out and took the younger woman's hand. "We've been playing."

Chase nodded at Silas. "This is my friend, Lieutenant Silas Hull."

"I've seen you before," Silas said. "At Arch Rock."

Jillian blushed. "I remember."

Sarah tugged on Jillian's arm. "Now that we've taken care of that business, Jillian and I are off to lunch."

"It was nice to see you again," Silas said.

Chase leaned forward, talking to Silas. "Jillian is looking for a position as a nursemaid. You wouldn't know if there is a position available up at the fort, would you? Just until the fort closes."

"I can inquire about it."

"She is in no rush to get a position here," Sarah said, patting the younger woman's arm. "When she gets to Detroit, perhaps she can find work as a governess."

Chase wondered what Jillian wanted but thought better of asking right then.

Jillian nodded toward the men, but before she turned, Edward walked into their circle. Chase braced himself, not knowing whether the man had been drinking again.

Edward looked between the two men. "What am I interrupting?"

"We were finished," Chase said, relieved that he appeared to be sober.

Edward turned his head, and Chase watched the slightest of smiles creep up his lips the moment he saw Jillian. Edward's gaze traveled down and then back up Jillian's gown.

He almost wished the man were drunk.

"Your gifts astound me, Sarah." Edward might have been talking to his wife, but his eyes were still focused on Jillian. Jillian's face turned red at his open admiration. "I believe you've made her into a lady."

Sarah's voice hardened. "It is your appreciation of my gifts that astounds me."

Edward offered Jillian his arm. "May I join you both for lunch?'

Sarah shook her head, releasing her hold on Jillian. She scanned over Chase, and her eyes locked on Silas. She nudged Jillian forward. "Jillian was preparing to accompany the lieutenant here to see about a position."

"Surely that can wait," Edward replied. He dropped his arm back to his side when Jillian didn't take it.

Silas stood up. "No, I don't believe it can."

Jillian didn't look back at either Sarah or Edward. "I am ready to see about the position."

Chase stood beside Silas and clapped him on the back. "Lieutenant Hull will take good care of you."

She nodded.

He leaned down, whispering to Jillian, "Andy—she doesn't know my last name."

"You must tell her."

"I will," he said. "Soon."

He stood tall again. "If there isn't a position available at the fort"—he stole a glance back at Edward and then looked at Silas—"come and talk to me."

*****

After Mrs. Darrington left, Elena picked up the tea set and carried it into the kitchen.

It seemed as if Mr. Darrington had chosen someone to be his wife, and she was happy for him as well as his family. And she was quite pleased to be released from the idea of marrying him.

But what was she supposed to do for her family now? Her father was about to lose the factory, and they were on the verge of losing both their homes. If she didn't marry someone who could help them, where would they live? If she married a man like Chase, he might be able to care for her but not for her parents as well.

She didn't have to marry for love to live in poverty. She was already destined to be there.

Filling the sink with water, she began washing the cups. The birds outside the window flitted from one tree to the next, oblivious to the concerns of the world. She envied their freedom to go wherever they wanted as they sang such beautiful songs. It was too early for her to go to the lighthouse and too late to walk down to the town.

Her father had told her to marry for love, but she had no choice. She had to marry to help their family—but whom would she marry? Certainly not Parker. And none of the other young men on the island interested her.

It didn't matter, she supposed. She couldn't be too selective.

Someone stepped into the kitchen, and she turned to see Claude.

"What are you doing, Miss Elena?"

She looked down at the soapy water in the sink. "Dishes."

"Your mama would have my head if she saw you doing that."

"I—I needed to do something."

He reached for the cloth in her hands and then held out an envelope. "You got a letter."

She dried her hands and took it from him. Ripping it open, she began to read Jillian's words. Lieutenant Hull had found her a position as a nursemaid for an officer who had seven children. She thanked both Elena and Chase for helping her.

She looked back up at Claude. "Jillian found work at Fort Mackinac."

Relief washed over his face as well. "It should be a good position until the fort closes."

After the fort closed, she would help Jillian get a position back in Chicago, at least until Elena married. Then Jillian could come live with her.

Claude washed a cup. "Why don't you go rest?"

She shook her head. "I'm not tired."

He turned a kitchen chair around and motioned for her to sit on it. Then he sat on a second one. "Are you still angry with me?"

"I was never angry with you."

He didn't seem to hear her. "I had to tell your papa about the lighthouse."

"I know."

"If anything happened to you—"

She stopped him. "You did the right thing."

Her gaze drifted back toward the window before he spoke again. "You look like you're carrying the weight of the whole world on your shoulders."

She sighed. "I believe I am."

He leaned back in the chair. His eyes wandered to the window and then he looked back at her. "I bet that's a pretty heavy load."

She nodded slowly.

"You know as well as I do, Miss Elena, that there's only one way to get rid of that burden."

She glanced at him. "It doesn't feel like there's even one way right now."

Claude pointed toward the windows. "Jesus says He doesn't want us to worry. He wants us to be like those birds in the air or the flowers in your mama's garden, living in the moment of beauty and trusting in Him."

"I can't stop worrying."

He leaned toward her. "You have to give that burden to Him."

"He wouldn't want it."

Claude lowered his voice. "Why do you go to the lighthouse?"

"To escape to a quiet place by myself to look at the stars," she said. "And to draw."

"And why else?"

She didn't like to talk about this, not with anyone, but Claude had been like an uncle to her for more than a decade now. "To spend time with God."

A bird landed on the limb outside the window, chirping at them. "You don't have to go away to spend time with God."

"But I don't feel Him anywhere else, not like I do at the lighthouse."

"You think God is out there in the universe, Miss Elena, but His creation is all around you. And He's right here with you too."

She blinked. "But I don't feel Him here like I do at the lighthouse."

"The Bible says He'll never leave us nor forsake us. He's at the lighthouse and in this cottage and even at your home in Chicago.

"It also says to pray on all occasions, with all kinds of requests." He stood up and began to dry the cups. "Why don't you talk to God right now and ask Him to take away that burden of yours?"

She walked out of the kitchen to the back porch and leaned against a post.

She always went to the lighthouse to seek God, but perhaps Claude was right—perhaps she didn't have to go anywhere else to find Him. Perhaps she could talk to Him right here.

Did He care enough to take away the burden of her worries? Or perhaps He would help her carry it?

Quietly she clasped her hands together and began to pray that God would help her know what to do. That if He wanted her to marry, He would give her a husband like Chase, who cared for her. And a man who could also help support her family.

She was desperate—desperate to talk to Him, desperate for answers, desperate to know what she should do. So she began talking, pouring out her heart in whispers about whom she was supposed to marry, about Chase. Even though her father had told her to marry for love, she guessed he was secretly harboring the hope that she would marry someone who could provide well for her.

But what did God want of her?

Minutes passed as she talked to God on her back porch, and she knew Claude was right. The God who created the majestic heavens was here as well. She could feel Him in the wind and hear Him in the calls of the birds. She loved her lighthouse, and she loved seeing the beauty He created above it, but perhaps she didn't have to go there any longer to talk to Him. She could talk to Him here and trust that He was listening to her and would guide her when she didn't know where to go.

The door opened with a *bang*, and she jumped. Her mother stepped outside, her hair askew. She collapsed onto a wooden chair beside the door.

"Did you get some rest?" Elena asked.

Mama shook her head. "I couldn't sleep."

"I'm sorry about Chester Darrington."

"All is not lost," she said. "Mr. Darrington hasn't met you yet."

"It sounds like he's already decided to marry another."

"He will change his mind," Mama said as she scanned the backyard, as if she had just realized where she was. "What are you doing out here, Elena?"

"Praying."

"That's good, I suppose." Mama shifted in her chair. "Right now we need a miracle."

Chapter Twenty-Three

Music flooded through the walls of Chase's room and shook the floor. The ball had begun below, but he was in no hurry to make his appearance. He reluctantly packed the last of his clothes into his trunk and stepped toward the mirror, straightening the satin knot of his cravat.

He stared for a moment into the glass. The past week, he'd changed from a man anxious to rush on to the next business proposition to a man who wanted to linger a bit longer and savor the moments with a woman who had captured his heart. Instead of fleeing the island, now he didn't want to leave, not without Andy.

If only Andy could come to Chicago with him.

He shook his head. The thought was an impossible one, currently, at least, but she'd said she was a wanderer. Perhaps she would enjoy traveling with him one day.

Galileo put his head on the dresser. While Chase was in Chicago, the dog would be staying at the hotel with his sister and parents and spending his evenings in the hotel kennel. Chase sat on the floor, leaning back against a chair as he rubbed Galileo's ears.

"Do you think she would like Chicago?" Then he laughed at himself, for talking to his dog.

Andy liked the fresh air, watching the skies—but she also liked art. If she went with him, he could take her on a tour of private art collections and watch her marvel at the artwork. They could visit a dressmaker to make a new gown for her…or gowns. Had she ever had a new dress? As much as she enjoyed beauty, she would surely enjoy selecting the fabrics and ribbons.

He could almost see the sparkle in her eyes from being able to choose—and then wear—such an elegant costume. He could take her to the gardens in her new gown...and one of the finest restaurants and the theater.

The more he mulled over the thought of indulging Andy for a few days—a week, even—and introducing her to the beauty in the city, the more he liked the idea. He could talk to her employer—or her parents—and ask for permission to escort her, along with a chaperone, to Chicago. Once they knew who he was...hopefully they would agree.

Richard would think he was crazy, of course, bringing a woman and perhaps a dog to Chicago, but other people were allowed to lose their minds for a bit. Why couldn't he lose his as well?

He donned the black evening jacket and cummerbund that Sarah had selected for him. Tonight he would dress up for his family's sake and spend a few hours hobnobbing before he went to the lighthouse. Or perhaps he would just stay an hour.

"Don't cause any trouble," he told Galileo as he walked to the door. He'd meet whoever it was that his parents wanted him to meet downstairs, dance a time or two, and then bow out with the excuse that he needed to check on his dog. Then he and Galileo would escape to the lighthouse.

He brushed his hand over his jacket, making sure every button was secure before he stepped out into the hallway.

No, he wouldn't stay long at the ball. He had to see Andy one last time before he left Mackinac.

* * * * *

Red and blue balloons arched across the ballroom entrance for the Independence Day ball. Light shimmered over the ribbons and bows that climbed the railings and posts around the room. Jewels and beads sparkled as the elegantly clothed men and women danced under the chandeliers. A swan made of carved ice was the centerpiece of a table towering with fruits, chocolates, and sliced meats.

As Elena stepped into the room with her parents, she stopped and admired the splendor of it all. It didn't compare to God's splendor above them, but it was still breathtaking.

Hundreds upon hundreds of people crowded into the room, the waiters blending in with the guests. She sighed with a bit of relief. There were so many people that Chase might not see her. Even then, he probably wouldn't recognize her in her evening attire, with her hair up.

She looked down at her gown, designed at the prestigious House of Worth in Paris. It was made of a pale blue taffeta to match her eyes and accented with ivory lace. On her neck was a strand of pearls—Mama insisted that she wear it instead of the locket for this one night. The gown was beautifully stitched, but she didn't feel comfortable in either the dress or the expensive jewelry.

Chase had tapped into her heart and mind, and she didn't want to muddy their friendship by letting him see her in society dress. She would feel ridiculous, meeting him at a ball like this, and he would surely feel uncomfortable as well, serving guests while she danced.

And if her parents found out about him—

She couldn't let him see her.

Someone called her name, and she turned to see Mrs. Darrington motioning them toward her. She took a deep breath and donned the perfect smile. Her son might not want to meet her, but she would be courteous, for the sake of his mother and hers.

"He won't be able to take his eyes off you," Mama whispered.

Elena walked slowly between her parents and as gracefully as possible toward Mrs. Darrington and the small crowd gathered around her. Mrs. Darrington shook her gloved hand and then kissed her lightly on the cheek. "I want you to meet my family."

Sarah's friendly gaze turned to ice as Mrs. Darrington introduced them. Edward's lips turned up under his mustache into something like a smirk.

Elena gave a slight curtsy. "It's nice to see you again, Mr. and Mrs. Powell."

Sarah's eyes found Elena's face. "Have you recovered from your terrible fall?"

She could feel heat climbing to her cheeks. "It wasn't so terrible."

"I heard that you—"

"Now, Sarah," Mrs. Darrington stopped her, "we can all rejoice that Miss Bissette is fine."

Sarah tugged on Edward's arm. "Let's go dance."

Edward was still watching her with that terrible smile. "I don't want to dance."

"Right now, Edward."

When they left, Mrs. Darrington turned to the man next to her. "Let me introduce you to my husband, Samson."

The senior Mr. Darrington shook Elena's hand, his smile friendly and somewhat familiar to her. Perhaps she had seen him at one of the parties in Chicago. "My wife has told me about you," he said. "She said you love to draw."

"It's true."

"She used to draw as well, but she rarely does anymore."

Mrs. Darrington patted Elena's arm. "Perhaps we shall do it together one day."

"I would enjoy that."

"What is your business?" Mr. Darrington asked her father.

"I have a factory in Chicago," he replied. Elena was glad to hear him say "have" and not "had."

The two men stepped aside to talk.

"If I can find him—" Mrs. Darrington scanned the crowd behind them. "I wanted you to meet my son."

Someone touched Elena's arm and she turned to see Parker, but there was no smile on his face. "Would you like to dance?"

"Yes," she said as she started to step away from the circle, grateful for the excuse not to have to meet Chester Darrington.

Mama stopped them. "Elena has to stay with us for the moment."

"Perhaps I can have the next dance."

Mama gave him a tentative nod and then resumed her conversation with Mrs. Darrington.

Elena turned and whispered to Parker. "How are you?"

"*Rotten* is the first word that comes to my mind."

"I'm sorry, Parker."

"Mother said she left your house."

"She didn't want to leave."

He glanced quickly on both sides of him. "Do you know where she is?"

"Yes, she's—"

Elena's gaze wandered over Parker's shoulder, and her heart flipped at the sight of Chase across the room. She hadn't wanted to see him, but now...now she couldn't seem to look away. Instead of wearing his work clothes, Chase was dressed in a black evening suit, his hair combed neatly behind his ears. He didn't look like a regular hotel employee. Perhaps he was the maître d'hôtel.

"Where is she?" Parker repeated.

She took a deep breath, trying to concentrate.

Parker turned to see who she was looking at. "I've lost your attention, haven't I?"

"No, I—" She tried to focus on Parker, even as her whole body trembled. Her heart warred with itself, wanting to see Chase tonight and yet wanting to run. "Jillian's up at the fort."

"Thank you," Parker said. "Apparently I'll be asking someone else for the next dance."

She gave a slight nod, her gaze stolen by the man across the room. As Chase strolled toward her, she blinked in disbelief. This was the same man she'd met at the lighthouse, and yet he seemed to be only a shell, a ghost of the man she knew. There was no easy smile on his lips nor the light in his eyes that had become so familiar, so comfortable to her.

In that moment she realized—Chase wasn't looking at her.

"Oh, finally." Mrs. Darrington waved her hand, motioning Chase toward them.

Chase kissed her cheek. "Hello, Mother."

Elena stared in horror at Chase…and his mother.

It wasn't possible.

She grasped for Mama's arm, her legs teetering under her gown. If she weren't wearing this blasted corset, she would run—out of the hotel, back to their cottage, all the way home to Chicago.

"I want to introduce you to my new friends," Mrs. Darrington said.

Elena dropped her gaze to the marble floor.

How could he—how dare he lie to her? He had said his name was Chase, that he worked at the hotel. He liked stars and art and talking about things that mattered.

She was going to faint, right here in the ballroom, in front of every society member who was important to her mother. And the man who was most important to her.

"This is Mrs. Bissette," Mrs. Darrington said.

"It's nice to see you again," she heard Chase say.

Elena didn't dare look at him. What would he say when he saw her? Would he pretend he didn't know her?

Oh, how could they pretend?

"And this is her daughter, Miss Elena Bissette."

"It's a pleasure to meet you." The way he said it sounded so smooth, so like the society men who frequented her circle. She'd thought he was different, but this man…he was just like the others.

The music played behind them and people were dancing and drinking, but she couldn't move. She stood as frozen as the swan on the dining table, and she didn't want to thaw until she could fly away.

"Elena," her mother prompted, nudging her elbow.

Elena tugged on the fingers of her glove.

"Elena!" This time it was a command.

She took a deep breath and willed herself to lift her hand to shake his. And then she slowly lifted her head.

His gaze collided with hers like an asteroid hitting earth. Admiration flickered in them for an instant, and then came the shock.

"I—" His voice was so low she barely heard him. "Andy?"

"My name is Elena."

The transformation in his eyes frightened her. The hardness of his voice matched the realization on his face. "You don't look a bit like a governess."

"I'm sorry," Elena said, standing a bit taller. "You must have mistaken me for someone else."

"Your name is—Elena," he repeated. "Elena Bissette from Chicago."

"And you are Chester Darrington from Detroit."

"Brush Park," he muttered. "It's outside of Detroit."

"Chester Darrington from Brush Park," she stated, like she was a judge reading a guilty verdict.

"My friends call me Chase."

Mama broke the awkward pause that followed with a nervous laugh. "Does that mean we're all friends now?"

Elena didn't return the laugh. "Why do they call you Chase?"

When he didn't answer, his mother spoke. "When he was young, he was always running after something. Instead of calling him Chester, Samson began to call him Chase."

Even as she spoke to Mrs. Darrington, Elena's eyes remained on the man in front of her. "Did he ever catch what he was chasing?"

Mrs. Darrington hesitated. "I don't suppose I know."

Elena could feel the tears coming, disappointment and frustration and hurt at how this man had tricked her, but she had to be strong for just a little longer. "What is it that you do, Mr. Darrington?"

"My name is Chase."

"He's a financier," Mrs. Darrington began to explain.

Chase interrupted her. "I do my work at the hotel."

Mrs. Darrington was not to be deterred from bragging about her son. "He invests in all sorts of wonderful ideas and inventions for the future, just like his father."

"I've heard you are a fine artist, Miss Bissette," Chase said, searching her face.

Tears brimmed in her eyes, her gaze dropping back to the floor. "I'm not quite sure what you mean."

"Or was it actress?"

If she dared to look back up, dared to look at him, there would be a flood. Her mother would be horrified at her tears, and Chase—she didn't know if he would gloat or feel sorry for her. She thought she knew this man, but she didn't know him at all.

She stepped back. "I must go."

Mama stopped her. "I'm sure Mr. Darrington would like to dance with you."

He shook his head. "I don't want to dance."

"Chase!" Mrs. Darrington exclaimed.

Mortified, Elena spun around. Gathering up her gown, she rushed across the room.

"Elena," her mother called—but she didn't stop.

She didn't care what her mother said. She never wanted to see Chase—Chester Darrington—or any of his family again.

March 22, 1813

The snow has protected our home from friends and foe alike this winter. Nickolas stopped coming weeks ago, after I insisted he give me an answer about his allegiance to the British. He never answered my question, nor did he return. In reflection, I almost wonder if someone else sent him to visit us, to see if we were all right.

The lake remains frozen, and the deer cross over from the mainland. I killed a doe last night with Jonah's bow and arrow, and the children and I feasted on her. Even though my stomach was full, my heart ached. Jonah was with us the last time we ate venison.

I should assume my husband is dead now, but I cannot do so, not until I know what happened. Someone must be able to tell me the truth.

I spend my days making clothes, playing with the children, and reading the Bible from Jonah's family. We sing, and we pray for Jonah.

Would the British kill him for refusing his allegiance?

If only they would send someone from the fort to tell me. If I don't have an answer by spring, I will go and demand it.

Chapter Twenty-Four

Voices chattered in the ballroom behind Chase, the orchestra's music blaring, but Elena's exit silenced everyone around him. Or maybe it was his refusal to dance with her.

He didn't call out to her, nor did he run after her. How was he supposed to talk or dance with the woman who'd tried to seduce Sarah's husband—the woman who'd determined to become his wife?

The woman who had stolen his heart?

When he met his mother's eyes, she looked at him as if he'd gone mad.

The Andy he knew was a young woman who smiled at the stars and spoke in awe about God and His creation. Andy was different than the other women he'd known, caring for *him* instead of his money or position or status in society.

But the Andy he'd loved was only a mirage. The woman who'd raced from the room was really Elena Bissette, a woman scheming to marry him.

He'd trusted her with his secrets, but she'd deceived him. All along she knew exactly who he was.

His stomach rolled, and he thought he might be sick.

Forget taking Andy to Chicago with him one day. Forget meeting with her at the lighthouse one last time. She had tried to trap him, but he refused to be caught.

Mrs. Bissette stepped forward. "You—you just insulted my daughter."

He dug his hands into the pockets of his jacket. "I suppose I did."

"How dare you—" She lifted her hand, and for a moment he thought she might slap him. He welcomed the pain. But instead of hitting him, she waved for her husband to join them.

Chase moved past his mother. "I've got to get some air."

His mother shoved him forward. "Quickly."

The air was muggy tonight on the long porch. Most of the people were inside dancing, and Chase was glad of it. He needed to think.

Ever since he'd been of marrying age, young women had pursued him. The mothers of these debutantes hinted, manipulated, and even stalked him. If he thought for a moment that their intentions were pure, he might be complimented at their persistence, but he knew they wanted to marry him for his family's money, as Edward had done with his sister.

Never before had a woman so completely and utterly deceived him. He'd trusted Andy, even thought she might care for him as he did for her, but it was all a ruse, a sleight of hand by a ruthless actress.

He walked the length of the porch, his emotions churning like the lake water after a storm. He'd prided himself on being nice but yet aloof with most women, offering no expectations for the future. He hadn't promised Andy anything for the future either, but in his heart, he'd hoped that she might become his wife.

She'd fooled him like no other. Even tonight, even when he'd called her bluff, she'd still tried to pretend that she didn't know who he was.

What an idiot he'd been.

He wouldn't be manipulated into marrying, not by his sister or Elena or Elena's mother.

He blinked, and ahead of him he saw Elena, the blue of her gown shimmering in the glow of the electric lights. When she turned, he saw tears streaming down her face—disappointment, he assumed, at having her plans dashed.

What had she thought would happen when he found out the truth? She couldn't hide forever behind the anonymity of *Andy*.

Perhaps she thought his heart would be so entangled with hers that he wouldn't care about the deceit. Perhaps she thought he would still marry her.

She started to walk away, but he moved quickly toward her. With the absence of an audience, there were some questions he wanted her to answer.

* * * * *

Elena stopped, her back to Chase. She didn't want to face him, couldn't face him, but she couldn't walk another step, either. Her chest burned as she tried to stop her tears and breathe stunted breaths inside her corset.

She could see his shadow on the rail in front of her, but she didn't turn around.

"You tricked me."

She shook her head. "I never tried to trick you."

The music from the orchestra spilled onto the porch, but she and Chase were alone out here, like they'd been at the lighthouse. Except that everything had changed.

His voice was barely a whisper. "You can stop the pretending."

"No, I can't, Chase—Mr. Darrington." She spun on the heels of her slippers, the hem of her gown floating with her. "Don't you know we're on stage, performing for an audience that's always watching, always criticizing? The lighthouse is the only place I can stop pretending."

He slapped his hand on the railing. "You're no different—no different from the rest of the women."

"I'm very different."

"You were trying to marry me—"

She shook her head. "I wasn't."

"Marry me for my money."

She swallowed hard, the reality of his words crashing down on her. It was true. She had been trying to marry him for his money. Marry Chester Darrington, at least, the man her mother wanted her to marry. But that's not why she had fallen for Chase—and she had fallen hard—for a man she thought she knew.

She stepped away from the railing. "I don't know what game you're trying to play, Mr. Darrington, but I'm not playing along."

"Game?" he choked. "I'm not the one playing."

"Did you follow me to the lighthouse?"

His voice grew stronger. "Most certainly not."

"Did my mother convince you to marry me?"

"I've barely spoken three sentences to your mother," he huffed.

"Because I can assure you, marrying you is the last thing I want to do."

"You said you were going to marry a man you didn't love."

She crossed her arms over her chest. "I'm certainly not going to marry the man I do love."

He stepped closer. "Did your father send you to the lighthouse?"

Her heart beat harder. "What?"

"Back at the dance last week," he pressed, "your father asked me what I was working on."

"He always asks people what they're working on."

"Did he send you to check on me...or did your mother send you to lure me into marriage?"

She felt like a child, defending herself when she'd done nothing wrong. "No one sent me."

"How did you know where to find me?"

Fury bubbled within her, and she felt like she was about to explode. "You found *me*, Chase. That lighthouse has been my refuge for six years."

He didn't stop. "Do you know Henry?"

She glanced around her, wondering if anyone was listening to their conversation, but no one seemed to notice. "I know plenty of men named Henry."

"He's a carriage driver at the Grand."

"What does this have to do with—"

"Maybe you or someone in your family paid him to take me to the lighthouse."

She put one hand on her hip, leaning toward him. "You are so full of your own importance, Mr. Darrington, that you can't fathom that someone might actually love you for who you are instead of for your money."

Even as the words escaped her mouth, she wished she could swallow them. She didn't want to talk about love, not with him.

A firework went off in the air, showering the night sky with blue and yellow. Elena's heart leaped with the explosion.

People flooded out of the hotel to watch the display and crowded around her and Chase, pressing them together.

He whispered in her ear, "Do you love me, Elena?"

Another firework colored the sky green and yellow. People clapped around them.

She pushed away from him. "I don't know who you are."

* * * * *

He didn't believe Elena, couldn't believe her. He knew that she had set her sights on marrying him. He knew that Mr. Bissette was interested in investing. He just didn't know how exactly they'd accomplished the feat of trapping him.

How did they know he would be intrigued by her artwork? How did they even know he might go to the lighthouse?

Perhaps Parker Randolph had set him up, when he pointed out the lighthouse on the bluff.

He left Elena standing on the porch with her mother beside her. This time Mrs. Bissette told him to leave.

At least she wouldn't be pushing him to marry her daughter anymore.

He rushed through the lobby and up the steps. His room was three doors down the hallway.

"Chester, wait!"

He turned to see Gracie Frederick holding up the folds of her yellow gown as she rushed after him. The last thing he wanted to do was talk to her—the woman who'd told him about Elena's intentions.

He pointed toward the tall windows. "You're missing the festivities, Miss Frederick."

"I don't care one bit about fireworks."

Galileo barked from his room.

"You'll have to excuse me." He stepped toward the door. "I'm going to retire for the night."

She eyed the door slyly. "Do you want company?"

He cringed at the blatancy of her offer. "I'd rather be alone."

"I saw you with Elena Bissette." She drew closer to him, a mischievous smile playing on her lips. "She's no good for you."

He shook his head. "Please don't presume to know what is good for me."

Her smile grew bigger. "Oh, but I do know."

"I'm going to take my leave—" He put his key into the door.

She stepped closer. "Elena is a master at manipulating people, just like her mother."

"And I am a master at sorting out the truth."

She leaned against his door, and it was clear in her eyes, in the tilt of her hips, that she desired more than conversation on the other side. He pushed open the door over her shoulder and scooted around her without a word.

"Chester," she started, stepping into his room. Galileo growled at her, and she eyed the dog as if she were trying to determine whether he would bite her. Apparently she thought Galileo was serious in his intent, because she slowly backed out into the hall.

Chase locked the door without another word to her. Then he sank into a chair.

What was it with the society women on this island? When they vacated the city for the summer, they seemed to lose all sense of protocol and propriety. Not that he approved of all the intricacies of society's rules, but downstairs was one woman sneaking to a lighthouse in the middle of the night without a chaperone, and in the hallway was another woman,

proposing to escort him into the privacy of his bedchamber.

Not that Elena had proposed anything of the sort.

Galileo nosed his hand, and he petted him. His dog was usually an excellent judge of character. Why did he have to like Andy so much?

He leaned his head back against the chair, muttering to himself. "We both judged her wrongly."

He didn't want to stay in his room for the night, alone with his thoughts about Elena, but he waited for a good ten minutes before he cracked the door to make sure that Gracie Frederick was gone. The hallway was empty, so he and Galileo raced out the back door of the hotel and hiked quickly through the woods, away from Gracie and Elena and the others.

How did Elena know how much he liked the stars or even about Silas Hull's fishing pole?

He had trusted Andy with his secrets. Not just with the telescope—he'd shared his heart with her too. If he lost the bid for the telescope, he would recover, but if he lost Andy—

He stopped and leaned against a tree. His heart fell.

There was no Andy.

Galileo barked, and he turned and trudged up the narrow trail until he was staring at the stones of the lighthouse.

He hadn't been able to keep himself from dreaming about her, from dreaming about what life would be like with Andy at his side, but the facade was over. Elena had done what she'd intended. She'd hooked him and tried to reel him in, but he wasn't a fish to be caught and filleted. He'd gotten away and would keep on swimming, upstream if necessary.

He opened the door and retrieved Elena's drawings from where she'd hidden them.

How had she known these pictures would speak to him? That the picture of her on the beach would draw him to her like a moth to light?

He tossed the book onto the desk.

Either she was a master manipulator...or she was caught up in this web as well.

Maybe Aunt Lottie or even Sarah had told the Bissettes he liked art. He wouldn't put it past his sister to pretend to dislike Elena, thinking it might make him like her even more.

Perhaps he would never be ready for marriage. If this was what love felt like, this miserable wrenching in his gut, then he didn't want it at all.

He wanted to be left alone.

But he wasn't alone. The memory of Elena lingered in the parlor and on every step that led to the top of the lighthouse. He could see Elena sitting at the desk, working on her sketches. If he dared to go up their stairs, he would see her in the broken glass panes above.

He slapped his fist on the desk, and Galileo yelped.

God help him, he had to get out of here.

Turning, he took a step toward the door but stopped. Picking up the sketchbook, he flipped through the pages until he found the picture of her walking on the beach with her hair blowing in the wind...and he tore it out.

He was a fool, that was for certain, but he couldn't seem to help himself.

* * * * *

Long after the orchestra stopped playing and the dancers stopped gliding across the floor, Mama sat down on the side of Elena's bed, resting her hand on the mound of pillows around Elena.

"What happened?" she asked softly.

Elena bundled a pillow close to her chest. "Nothing."

"Something must have happened between the two of you. I didn't think you had met before."

"I didn't know it was him before.... We were confused."

"You ran away, Elena. And then he chased you out the door. This is more than confused."

"He was extremely rude."

"Indeed."

Elena buried her head in the pillow for a moment and then looked up again. "I didn't know what to say."

Chase had made himself perfectly clear. He thought she had tried to snag him like the other young women on the island, and the irony was that she had tried to catch him—just not in the way he thought. She hadn't orchestrated their meeting at the lighthouse, but she would never be able to convince him of that. He'd already made up his mind.

She hadn't orchestrated it, but there was that slimmest of possibilities—

She knew her father had nothing to do with their meeting, but if Chase was right, if her mother had somehow arranged all of this, Elena would find Jillian and sail far away from this island and its craziness.

She sat up and met her mother's eyes. "Did you know?"

"Know what?"

"That Mr. Darrington and I had met before."

"Of course not, though the Lord knows and so do you that I tried my hardest to get the two of you together. You both kept disrupting my plans."

It seemed the Lord had had another plan for them to meet, outside her mother's control, but if that was so, why did it have to end like this? She'd seen the anger in Chase's eyes...the disappointment. No matter what her mother said or did, Elena would do nothing to pursue him again, and she was certain he wouldn't try to pursue her.

There were plenty of other wealthy bachelors in Chicago and Detroit. If her parents couldn't find a man in either of those cities who was interested in marrying her, they could try Cleveland or Philadelphia or New York City. Her mother could pick a decent man from the flock and she'd marry him. She could never care for another man, not like she had Chase, but perhaps marriage would help to mend her heart.

"I thought—I didn't know he was Mr. Darrington."

"Who?"

"The man I met—"

Her mother hushed her. "You can't marry a man who tried to

deceive you."

Her mind spun. Had he tried to deceive her? She wasn't sure. He had told her his name, or his nickname, at least, even if he hadn't said his last name. She was the one who had hidden her name.

"I don't know if he meant to deceive me."

"Well, he was certainly unkind to you."

"But you want me to marry him, Mama."

She shook her head. "There are other eligible men."

Papa must not have told Mama yet that they were on the verge of losing their home in Chicago.

Her father walked into the room and leaned against one of the bed-posts, compassion heavy in his voice. "How's my little girl doing?"

"Not well."

He sighed. "And Chase seemed to be such a nice chap."

"He was a bit too dapper for me," Mama replied. "There are other bachelors on the island, much nicer ones. The man she marries doesn't have to be as rich as the Darringtons."

"Deborah." Papa turned to face her. "There will be no more talk about marrying in this house."

"But—"

He shook his head. "Elena will let us know when she's ready to marry."

Elena wanted to applaud her father's mandate, but she felt sick instead. How was she supposed to know when she was ready to marry another man? She didn't want to marry anyone except Chase.

She fell back against the cushions. If only she could escape tonight... But there was no place left for her to escape to.

Chapter Twenty-Five

The wind ruffled Elena's walking gown as she gazed at the colorful window display of confectionaries at Murdick's. Buckets of saltwater taffy, trays of hand-dipped chocolates, and mounds of fudge were displayed behind the glass.

After the week of parties, concerts, and a grand rowing regatta, the quietness on Main Street was almost eerie. Hooves of a horse clip-clopped behind her, pulling a wagon that coated the dusty streets with its barrel of water. The wind blew the water across the sidewalk, spraying the hem of her walking gown.

Days ago, the fort's remaining soldiers paraded down this street while tourists and food vendors crowded the sidewalks. Hundreds of balloons were released into the sky, and the aroma of candied apples and caramel corn sweetened the air. But there was also a sense of sadness among the society mothers and their unmarried daughters during the week. Chase sailed away the morning after the ball, without a promise to call on any of the debutantes in the future or even to return to the island.

Now that Chase was gone, her mother stopped insisting that Elena stay caged at home all day. There were still the afternoon teas and social calls, but when Elena wasn't visiting a neighbor, she was free to roam the village like she'd done when she was younger. Her mother seemed to have given up any hope that Elena would secure a husband over the summer.

No one except her parents and perhaps Mrs. Darrington had any notion that she and Chase had known each other outside society events. When she and Mama went calling, Elena had to endure endless discussion about whether or not Mr. Darrington would return, but her mother kept her promise and hadn't mentioned again the possibility of her marrying Mr. Darrington or anyone else. For that, she was grateful.

She'd visited Jillian several times at the fort, but even when Elena tried to help, the general's wife thought her visits distracted Jillian from the children. Elena understood, but she missed her friend.

A bell chimed when Elena opened the door to the candy shop, and it chimed again when she walked back outside with a half pound of chocolate fudge in a paper box. Opening the lid, she broke off a piece, and the buttery chocolate mixed with sugar and walnuts tasted heavenly. She eyed a bench to sit down and enjoy her treat, but she decided to walk instead, away from the village.

She missed her nighttime escapes to the lighthouse, but she didn't want to return, knowing Chase would never come again. One time she'd started to go but turned around when she reached the trail. It didn't feel right, enjoying God's creation without Chase at her side.

She took another bite of fudge.

Instead of walking toward the East Bluff, she turned up the street by Fort Mackinac and began to climb the hill toward the white walls that protected the fort. At one time she had thought Chase an officer, until he had laughed at her. Now she could understand his laughter. He was Chester Darrington of S. P. Darrington & Company, quite above military service. How could she have missed the pride in his heart and words?

She should have run away the first time she saw Chase in the tower. If only he had told her that he was Chester Darrington, she would have stepped right back on the stage. She never should have allowed him to have a glimpse of all that was in her heart and then crush it. The pain was as real as any she'd ever felt before, except that no one could see the bruises.

Near the top of the hill Elena turned away from the fort, wandering left into the trees. She'd allowed Chase to become part of her refuge, part of her communion with God. But Claude had been right; she didn't need to go to the lighthouse to talk to God. She'd done so every night during the past week on the back patio. He was there...and He was here right now, in the shadows of the sugar maple and wild cherry trees, in the knocking of the woodpeckers that echoed through the leaves. She could feel His peace filling her, and she was grateful for it.

Ahead of her she saw tombstones tucked into the forest. She stopped, reading the epitaphs of the old stones until she came upon one with an angel carved into it.

MAGDELAINE SEYMOUR
MARCH 8, 1783—JULY 6, 1813
SINGING WITH THE ANGELS

Elena rubbed her fingers over the lovely words and imagined Magdelaine singing at that moment. She'd only been thirty years old when she died, and Elena couldn't help but wonder if she'd found Jonah before she left the earth.

There was no stone for Jonah or their children.

Were her children still alive? Had they ever come to honor her grave? She and Chase were supposed to share the woman's story together, but it was too late for that now.

When Elena looked up from the grave, something moved near the trees. At first she thought it was an animal, and then she realized that the movement was from a lone man, stumbling toward her and swinging a brown bottle in his hand. She stood to greet him, but when she saw his face, her smile faded.

Edward's gaze didn't quite make it up to her face. "Don't ya look pretty today, Miss Elena?"

She stepped away from Magdelaine's grave and stood as tall as she could so he wouldn't think she was afraid. "It's time for me to go home."

"What's the—what's the hurry?" His words slurred together.

She eyed the brown bottle. "You've been drinking, Mr. Powell."

"That I have." He laughed, but there was no joviality in the laughter. "You're a very perspective woman."

"Perceptive," she muttered.

"And you've become quite enamored with my brother-in-law."

"I am no such thing—"

"Sarah thinks Chase hung the stupid moon." He threw the bottle against Magdelaine's tombstone and the glass shattered. Then he sneered. "You love him, you know. Everyone who saw you run out of the ball... everyone knows."

"I don't," she whispered.

"He might care for you now, but not for long. He runs faster than any scared animal when a lady shows a little interest in him."

She wanted to say something, to protest his lunacy, but her words were trapped in her throat.

Edward stepped closer to her, his gaze fixed on her like she was one of the chocolates on display in the candy shop. "Chase is foolish that way."

Her skin crawled. She'd never been afraid on the island before, even roaming at night, but the woods were so quiet here. And isolated. If she screamed now, no one would hear.

Even though Edward was drunk, she couldn't run fast enough, not with her heavy skirt and corset. If only she were wearing Jillian's old dress, she might be able to outrun him.

She stepped to the side. "It was a pleasure to see you, Mr. Powell, but I must go home."

"A pleasure." He laughed at the word and then reached out, touching one of the curls that dangled over her shoulder. "You don't need to go home."

"My parents—they will be waiting for me."

"Don't lie to me." His face was too close to her, his smile smug. She felt sick. "I don't li–like it when people lie."

She locked onto his eyes and saw the threat in them.

"There's no reason to be afraid."

"I'm not afraid." She held her shoulders a bit higher, trying to hide her fear. "Where is your wife, Mr. Powell?"

"Having lunch with Gracie Frederick—Gracie's going to marry Chester."

"It seems like every woman on the island is planning to marry your brother-in-law."

"You jealous?"

"Not particularly," she said, even as her heart ached at the thought of Chase marrying Gracie or any other woman. But she wouldn't confide in Edward Powell, even if he were sober.

He glowered at her. "You can hurt him back, you know. Even more than he is hurting you."

Her shoulders crumbled. "I don't want to hurt him."

At her words, hatred flashed in Edward's eyes. "You and I—we could destroy him."

She was angry at Chase, at the wounds inflicted by his doubt and maybe pride, but she would never want to destroy him. Even if she gave in to Edward, it wouldn't destroy him. Chase might have cared for the girl at the lighthouse, but he didn't love Elena Bissette.

She turned to walk away. "I don't want anything to do with you or your plans."

Edward reached for her arm, squeezing it in his grasp. "I don't care one bit about what you want."

Elena balled up her fists, praying that Claude was right, that God didn't just dwell in the skies or the walls of a church, that He dwelt with her in the forest.

And she begged Him to protect her.

Edward shoved her shoulders against a tree. She couldn't run, but she would fight him with everything she had, for her…and for Chase.

She kicked Edward's shin, and then she pummeled him with her fists. He yelled at her to stop, but he didn't let her go. Her mind screamed as she struggled against him, telling her to run. If only she could break free—

The breeze called out her name, so softly at first that she almost wondered if God Himself was speaking to her and answering her cries. But then over Edward's shoulder, she saw a familiar face sprinting toward her—the same face that had rescued her from her fall on the pier—and there were two soldiers running behind Lieutenant Hull.

God had sent guardian angels.

Silas grabbed Edward's shoulders and pulled him away from her, throwing him toward his companions.

"Take him to the fort," he commanded the other men.

Edward resisted the soldiers, but they overpowered him and, minutes later, led him away.

Elena slumped down the tree and Silas turned back to her, sitting quietly on the ground beside her.

"Thank you," she whispered.

His voice was gentle. "Did he—did he hurt you?"

"No." She paused. "But only because of you."

Silas stood, offering her his hand. "Let me take you home."

"It's not necessary—"

"I believe it is."

Her legs wobbled as he helped her to her feet, and she wiped her hands over her hair, brushing the leaves from it. Thank God for Silas and his men.

Claude answered Silas's knock, and his eyes widened when he saw Elena's tangled hair and muddied dress. He looked back and forth between Elena and Silas, as if he were afraid to ask what happened.

Elena's lips trembled as she spoke. "Silas rescued me."

Claude helped her to a chair in the drawing room. "I'm going to get your mama."

If only Jillian were here to help care for her. She would know what to do.

Silas stood in the door frame of the drawing room as Elena curled up on the chair, her tears erupting like a fountain from a well deep within her...tears of fear and gratefulness, of love and loss. She cried in her hands for what Edward had almost done, for Chase leaving, for disappointing her parents, for disappointing God. All her emotions, the ones she usually poured out on paper in the privacy of the lighthouse, poured down her cheeks.

She heard a door slam in another room before her mother rushed into the drawing room.

"What did you do?" she yelled.

Elena looked up, thinking at first that her mother was angry with her. Then she saw Silas backing toward the hall.

"Don't, Mama," she said. "Lieutenant Hull—he saved me."

Mama stopped, looking at Silas speculatively. "Saved you from what?"

"Is Mr. Bissette home?" Silas asked.

"I'll get him," Claude said.

Mama helped Elena stand, and Elena leaned against her as they went up the stairs to her bedroom. As her mother loosened the bands of her corset, Elena heaved in deep breaths that helped to clear her mind and strengthen her body. Mama drew a bath and sprinkled drops of jasmine and lavender oil into it before she helped Elena into the warm tub.

"What can I do?" Mama asked, her voice cracking.

Elena wasn't sure how to respond. Mama always knew what to do. "I want to rest."

"I never should have let Jillian leave." Mama screwed the lid back onto the lavender oil and placed it on the pedestal sink. "Perhaps she would return."

Elena shook her head. "She's working up at the fort."

"I'll talk to the lieutenant."

Elena slipped farther down into the soothing folds of the water. "You should apologize to him first."

Mama nodded before she shut the door behind her.

Silas would make it clear that Elena hadn't done anything wrong, but her innocence wouldn't keep the circuit of society ladies from talking. If her fall had been discussed and elaborated on in detail, she couldn't imagine how quickly this encounter with Edward would spread.

She cringed at the thought of Chase hearing the story through the gossip of society women.

She sank deep into the water, submerging her face, as her hair floated around her.

She never should have encouraged Edward on their first meeting at the Grand. Nor should she have gone walking alone in the woods.

She'd tried to stop Edward from forcing himself on her, and yet Edward's actions would still wound Chase. He would be devastated at what Edward had attempted to do, for his sister's sake.

If only she could stop the story from reaching him in Chicago. Or at the very least, she wished she could shield him from the blow.

May 1, 1813

Flowers have replaced the snow, and I have been busy sewing new clothing for Molly and Thomas. When I am finished, I shall take them to the British fort to see if the soldiers can tell me what happened to the children's father. My husband.

My greatest fear is that they will demand my allegiance as well and take the children from me.

Nickolas knows what happened to Jonah. I saw it in his eyes, and yet he refused to tell me. How can a man live with himself after betraying his loyalty to his country—and hiding what happened to an innocent man?

My hands hurt as I write this, from sewing and cooking and making repairs in the house. There is no longer any fuel for the lamp.

I can't stop working, for the sake of my children and for Jonah when he returns.

Even if I had a way to leave Mackinac, I wouldn't. Not until I find out if Jonah is still alive.

Chapter Twenty-Six

"You have another telegram, sir."

Chase looked up from his rented desk on the fourteenth floor in the Owings Building. The boy seemed to space out his deliveries, one every hour or so, instead of bringing the telegrams all at once. Chase certainly encouraged a budding entrepreneur, though he wasn't sure he should encourage such misuse of the boy's time.

The messenger held out the envelope, and Chase tapped on the stack of unopened messages piling up since early this morning. "You can put it here."

Chase dug into his pocket and pulled out a dime. The boy took it and scurried off for his next delivery. Chase glanced out the window, where the lake and sky blended together in the distance. Whaleback steamers dotted the horizon, hauling coal, lumber, and grain to and from the city. As one industry faded away, others were budding to take its place. The world was changing so quickly, it felt almost impossible at times to keep up with progress.

But it was his job to stay one step ahead, so he picked up his pen once more to finish his letter to Guglielmo Marconi inquiring about his proposed wireless signals. He'd barely completed two sentences before Richard cleared his throat from the door.

"Nelson Reese is here to see you."

Chase waved his pen. "Send him in."

He completed one more sentence and then looked up. Nelson was a lanky man with thick spectacles on his long nose. His gaze darted from the window to Chase and then to the floor. Most of the inventors Chase met didn't know the first thing about business or business meetings, but he didn't mind educating them. He didn't know the first thing about inventing.

Chase pointed toward a chair on the other side of his desk. "Have a seat."

Last night, out on Lake Michigan, he'd seen ridges on the moon and dark spots that astronomers believed to be bodies of water. Brilliant white spots dotted the moon's surface, as well, and what appeared to be rocks… or perhaps they were mountains.

Only a handful of astronomers had seen such a close view of the moon before, and now he joined them. If he and Richard could work with Nelson to produce more of these telescopes, thousands of others could see the majesty of the skies.

If men like the ones before him persisted, they might find out in his lifetime what was on the moon.

"I've been testing your telescope," he explained. "On Mackinac Island and then last night on Lake Michigan. I wanted to be sure, you see."

Nelson fidgeted in the chair. "Sure of what?"

He nodded toward Richard, standing beside Nelson. "Richard and I want to partner with you, to make and distribute your telescope."

Nelson crossed his arms, his eyes shifting between the men. "I was looking for an investor, not a partner."

"I understand, Mr. Reese." He crossed his legs. It wouldn't pay to let this man think he was nervous, but the reality was that he really wanted to be part of making this telescope even if it didn't generate a profit. "Some companies do just invest, but my father and I—we like to have an active part in making sure our investments are successful."

"How does that work?" Nelson scooted the chair closer to the desk, and Richard sat in a chair beside him.

His assistant was even more anxious for the company to invest in this telescope, but Chase wished he would stop tapping his foot on the carpet. It wouldn't pay for any of them to be nervous.

Chase shuffled through another stack of papers on his desk and pulled out a contract that he and Richard had written with their attorney. Nelson took it from him.

"You patent this telescope and we will find a manufacturer to make it," Chase explained. "Then we sell them to department stores and put advertisements in the major newspapers across the country so people can see the wonders of the heavens for themselves."

Richard cleared his throat. "The wonders of the heavens?"

Andy would have said something much more eloquent than that, but it was the best he could do. "What's wrong with wonders?"

"Nothing, I suppose." Richard glanced at Nelson and then looked back at Chase. "It just doesn't sound a bit like you."

Chase nodded at the papers. "Can we focus on the business at hand?"

Richard scooted to the edge of his chair, looking over Nelson's shoulder at the contract. "After the cost of making and distributing the telescopes, this says that you and S. P. Darrington & Company will split the profits in half."

Nelson pushed the spectacles up his nose. "Half the profits?"

Chase shifted on his chair. He'd been through this conversation many times with inventors. They often wanted more than half of the profits, but they didn't take into account the risk S. P. Darrington & Company was taking. Chase wanted to invest in the telescope, but his father would never allow them less than a 50 percent partnership.

He reached for the contract. "I'm sorry it's not satisfactory."

"Oh, no." Nelson tugged the papers closer to him. "So if you sold, say, a thousand of these, what would our profits be?"

Richard reached across the desk for another paper outlining the potential profit margin. He slid the paper toward Nelson.

"Here's what you would make if we sell a thousand." Richard pointed down the column. "And here is the amount if we sell ten thousand."

Nelson gasped. "Do you think we can sell ten thousand?"

Chase nodded. "If we do our job right by pricing and advertising it well.

And then we hope people start telling their friends how amazing your telescope is."

Nelson held out his hand. "I'd like to sign."

Chase handed him the pen. "Do you have a plan on how you would use this money?"

Nelson studied him for a moment, as if Chase should know the answer. "I'll build a stronger telescope."

Chase leaned back, pleased with his words. "Of course."

He and Richard shook Nelson's hand, exchanging the satchel with the telescope for a signed contract to make many more. After he left, Chase swiveled in his chair and watched the man and his worn bag climb onto a streetcar along Dearborn Street. He was almost sad to say good-bye to it.

"Andy would be pleased," he said, so quietly he didn't think anyone heard him.

"Who's Andy?" Richard asked.

He glanced back at his assistant in surprise. He'd promised himself he wouldn't talk about Andy or Elena, not with Richard or anyone else, yet her name flowed naturally from his lips...even as she haunted his thoughts.

He picked up the stack of messages on his desk and began thumbing through them. "Don't you have something to do?"

Richard watched him for another moment. "Nothing pressing."

"Surely you can find something of moderate importance to occupy your time."

Before Richard could respond, someone knocked on the door. Chase expected the messenger boy again, but instead the doorman stood in front of him, a panicked look on his face.

"Your father is on the telephone, Mr. Darrington. He said it's an urgent matter."

Chase dropped the stack of messages. His father never used the telephone.

The doorman led him quickly to the booth in the lobby.

*****

The afternoon sun warmed the bedroom, but even with the sunshine Elena shivered under her covers. No matter how many wool blankets her mother piled on top of her, the coldness still clung to her skin. She closed her eyes in the light, the rays warming her face.

God had been there in the woods. She felt Him just as strongly as she'd felt His presence in the lighthouse. He had protected her from the hands of a man who wanted to hurt her.

God had been there, and He'd listened to her. Now she prayed a new prayer. She prayed that God would protect Chase, as He had protected her, from the man who wanted to ruin him. According to the Scriptures, the enemy meant to steal, kill, and destroy, but if they followed God's voice, He could use this situation for good. If only Chase would let Him.

She rolled away from the sunlight, Edward's words playing over and over again in her mind. Did Chase always run when a woman began to love him? Perhaps his leaving her had nothing to do with either her father or her mother. Perhaps he'd been planning to run even before they saw each other at the Grand.

She could pray for Chase, but she never should have allowed her heart to get entangled with a man she didn't know.

Mama walked quietly into her room and sat down on the bed, holding out a cup of tea to her. Elena could smell the gentle aroma of chamomile. "Nell made it for you."

Elena took a long sip. Perhaps it would ward off this chill that plagued her.

Her mother took the cup from her and cradled it in her hands. "Are you all right?"

Elena leaned back against the pillows as the tea began to warm her from the inside. She didn't quite know how she was, nor could she find the words to express it. "I'll recover."

"Of course you will." Mama placed the cup on the nightstand

and then tucked the blankets around Elena, like she had when Elena was a child.

Elena's smile flickered, and then she swallowed hard. "The women will talk, won't they?"

"Probably."

Her stomach plummeted again. "I'm so sorry."

She heard footsteps and turned her head as her father slipped into the room.

Mama patted her hand. "There is absolutely nothing for you to be sorry about, Elena. It wasn't your fault."

She shook her head. "If I hadn't been there alone..."

Papa sat down on the other side of the bed. "You should be able to go anywhere on this island you like, Elena, without worrying."

She swallowed, wishing she could believe his words. "What are the soldiers going to do with Mr. Powell?"

Papa glanced down at his folded hands before he looked back at her. "They'll have to let him go tonight."

"Let him go!" Mama exclaimed. "But the lieutenant—he saw what the man did."

"What he tried to do," he corrected her. "Thank God he didn't hurt her."

Mama glanced at Elena. "He hurt her plenty."

The room felt as though it were swimming around her, the walls closing in tight. It was true; he hadn't committed a crime—but he'd intended to hurt her.

She wiggled herself up on her elbows. "I want to go to my lighthouse."

"Your what?" Mama exclaimed.

"My lighthouse, over on the eastern bluff."

"Lightho—" Mama stammered. "You'll do no such thing."

Papa stood up. "Claude can go with you."

She took a deep breath. "Thank you."

Mama trailed him out the door. "What lighthouse?" she asked him again before she shut the door.

After the fort's cannon saluted the sunset and the world melded into black, Elena and Claude walked together out the back door. No one would see her in the darkness, and with Claude at her side, she wasn't afraid of Edward or any other man. She didn't comment about the pistol Claude carried on his waist. At one time she might have been afraid of the gun, but tonight she was glad of it.

There was no reason for her and Claude to hurry as they walked down the alley or the wider lane that led to the trail. Both her parents knew where she was going tonight.

Years ago Claude had told her about the lighthouse he'd found when he was a boy, but he'd never told her how he'd come to find it. After that day he'd led her to it, she'd rarely spoken of it to him, afraid someone else might hear.

As she stepped onto the trail a few steps behind Claude, she spoke. "When you were a boy...how did you find the lighthouse?"

"My granddaddy told me all about it."

She took a deep breath. "Was Jonah Seymour your grandfather?"

He lifted a branch along their path, and she ducked under it. "Mr. Seymour wasn't my granddaddy."

"What were the names of your grandfathers?"

"Nickolas Westmount and—"

She interrupted him. "We—I found a journal written by Magdelaine Seymour. It talked about Nickolas."

He stopped walking. "What did it say?"

On the bluff in front of them was the lighthouse. She nodded toward it. "If it's still here, I can show it to you."

As they stepped into the lightkeeper's home, a scurry of mice feet rushed into the shadows. Claude hung the lantern on a hook and surveyed the room.

"How long has it been since you were here?" she asked.

"Since I showed it to you in '87."

"But how long before then?"

He paused. "A good thirty years."

She sat down at the chair beside the desk. "Why haven't you come back?"

"This place brings joy to you, Miss Elena, but it brings nothing but sorrow to me. My granddaddy died in 1818 a broken man."

She hesitated by the dresser. This beautiful tower had been a place of sadness for Magdelaine as well. Perhaps reading the journal would also bring Claude nothing but sorrow.

She opened the trunk and searched through the clothes, but the journal wasn't there.

"He didn't bring it back," she muttered.

He watched the trunk like it might share its secrets with him. "What did Magdelaine say?"

"She talked about missing her husband," Elena said. "And how your granddaddy brought her and her children food."

Claude leaned against the stone wall. "He wanted to help them, and I suppose he did at first. But then he did something terrible."

A shiver chilled her. "What did he do?"

Claude heaved deeply, in and out. "He reported to the British that Mrs. Seymour was living at the lighthouse."

"How could—why would he do that?" Especially to someone like Magdelaine Seymour, who needed him.

Claude took his watch out of his pocket and twisted the timepiece in his hands. "He got scared, I think, about what would happen to his family if they found out he was keeping this secret. And the British offered rewards to those who turned in people who hadn't pledged their allegiance to the king."

"So he took their money—"

"I'm not proud of it, Miss Elena."

She tried to smile, to reassure him. What a terrible thing it must be, to carry the weight of what an ancestor had done.

"What happened to Jonah?" she asked.

"I'm not certain," he said with a shake of his head. "I was told Magdelaine went to the fort to search for Jonah. The fort was struck by lightning and there was a fire. Magdelaine was killed."

Her voice caught. "And her children?"

"Legend has it that they disappeared, killed in the fire maybe, but I sure wish I knew what happened to them."

Tears stung Elena's eyes. She was silent for a moment, her heart grieving for Thomas and Molly. "We're both carrying a heavy burden for bad choices that others made."

He smiled at her. "I guess I need to listen to my own advice and ask Him for freedom."

Freedom.

Elena raced across the room, to the desk in the parlor, and rolled back the top. She sighed with relief when she saw her sketchbook. Not that she thought Chase would take it too...

She opened to the last page in the book, her drawing of him with the horse. She should rip it out, throw it away, but she couldn't bring herself to do it. Thumbing through the rest of the sketches, she stopped. Someone—Chase—had torn out the picture she'd drawn of the woman standing barefoot on the beach. The picture of her.

She wanted to be angry with him for stealing her picture, but she was just confused. Did he want to keep her picture, or did he want to burn it?

She pushed the sketches away and closed the roll top. If only they had met a different way, even at one of the parties or balls, perhaps it would be different now.

Claude stepped up behind her and put his hand on her shoulder. "Miss Elena?" he said softly. "Who else has been up here with you?"

She sighed. "Chase—Chester Darrington."

Claude sat down on the chair. "Do your parents know?"

She shook her head. "I didn't know it was Mr. Darrington, but he—he was nothing but honorable to me."

"You must tell your father."

"One day."

"Though you might not want to tell your mother."

A smile edged up her lips. "Mama would hunt him down."

"It sure is good to see you smile again."

"I'm sorry about the journal, Claude."

He checked the timepiece and then slid it back into his pocket. "I'm sure it will turn up."

She wasn't so certain.

Chapter Twenty-Seven

Chase elbowed his way through the crowd of people until he saw his father on the pier.

"Where's Edward?" he demanded.

There were people all around him—vacationers, residents, and soldiers alike—but he didn't care if they heard. He wanted to find his brother-in-law—and pummel him.

His father shook his head. "Edward's gone."

Chase pressed his fingers against his temple. The trip had taken the longest two days of his life. With every mile the steamer traveled, the pain in his head grew more persistent, until his entire body felt like it might explode. "Where did he go?"

"Let's get away from the crowd." His father directed him off the pier and toward the waiting carriage. He still couldn't believe the little his father had told him on the telephone, that Edward had tried to—

His stomach rolled.

Even if Sarah pretended all was well, he'd guess Edward had had a number of trysts during their marriage. But had he ever tried to force himself on another woman?

At the lighthouse, Elena had used every wile possible to try to win Chase. After he left, was it possible that she'd tried to urge Edward away from his wife? She might have hinted at her interest, led Edward to believe…

He shook his head. It was all wrong. Elena hadn't used her body to seduce Chase. It had been so much deeper than that, a meeting of their minds and hearts. Her deception—it was nothing like Gracie Frederick's trying to capture him. Elena's deception wounded his core.

But still, even though he knew so little of the real woman, he couldn't reconcile the unassuming Andy in the lighthouse and the scheming Elena seducing Edward away from his wife.

Edward, on the other hand—

He pressed his fingers against his temple again. He couldn't allow himself to think of what Edward could have done to Elena.

The driver clicked his tongue and the horses moved forward.

Chase lowered his voice. "Tell me, please. What happened?"

"Edward and the Frederick girl..." His father cleared his throat. "They ran away."

"Ran away—" He stopped. "He should be in jail."

"They locked him up for a few hours, but they couldn't keep him there."

"He tried to...he tried to hurt Ele—Miss Bissette."

"Well, he won't do it again. I'm told he and Gracie took the last boat out last night, on their way to Canada."

Chase never thought he would feel sorry for Gracie Frederick, but he did. Sorry for her and her parents. The Fredericks would hear from Edward again, he was certain of that. Probably with an offer to buy his property in Ohio and, with the sale, marry their daughter. After he secured a bill of divorce from Sarah, Chase hoped.

Chase took off his gloves and placed them beside him then leaned his head back against the seat. "How is Sarah?"

"Better than we expected."

"And Miss Bissette?" he ventured as the carriage climbed the long drive toward the hotel. Just a little over a week ago, he'd left here angry at Elena for deceiving him and angry at himself for letting her steal his heart.

His father shook his head. "I don't know."

He didn't ask about his mother. He knew she couldn't be doing well, or she would have been at the pier to greet him.

When he walked into his parents' suite at the hotel, Galileo greeted him with a lick and jumped onto his trousers. He petted his dog and then hurried into the next room to find his mother. She was propped up on the davenport, sipping a cup of tea.

She nodded at Galileo. "I've grown quite fond of that dog."

Galileo lay down on the floor beside her.

"It appears that he is quite fond of you as well." Chase kissed her cheek. "It's been a trying week for you."

She moved her legs off the davenport and patted the seat beside her. "For all of us, but for Sarah most of all."

He sat. "Where is she?"

She nodded at the doorway to the adjoining room. "Sleeping for a moment."

"Is she angry?"

"I believe she is humiliated more than anything."

"Humiliated?" Sarah asked from the open doorway. "You think I'm humiliated?"

Mother sighed. "I don't know what you are."

Sarah's face was splotched with red, her long hair tangled around her shoulders. "Please don't talk about me, at least not when I'm not here. You can say anything you want while I'm in the room."

Chase stood and stepped forward, wanting to hug her but not sure of what he should do. "I want to shoot him."

"It would only make things worse." She swirled the drink in her glass. "He wants nothing more than to hurt you. If you were sent to prison, he'd get exactly what he wanted."

"What did I do to make him so angry?"

Her laugh was bitter. "You made something of yourself, that's what. You're determined and hardworking and honest. Everything my—everything Edward is not."

After years of listening to his sister justify Edward's sins, he was shocked to hear honesty flow from her mouth. For so long, Sarah had supported her husband in spite of his many flaws. As far as Chase knew, she'd never betrayed Edward's confidence, nor had she spoken an ill word about him.

She sat on a chair, and Chase returned to his seat on the couch. "You didn't have to come," she said.

"Yes, I did."

She sipped her drink slowly and then spoke, her voice like a child's. "Thank you."

"What can I do to help you?" he asked.

She paused for a moment, staring at her glass. "Our—my finances are a mess."

"I can help you get your affairs in order." He glanced at his father, who was working at the corner desk. "What else can I do?"

"Go see Miss Bissette," his mother said. "On behalf of our family."

"I—I can't do that."

"For heaven's sake, why not, Chase? You were perfectly rude to her at the ball. This will give *you* an opportunity to make amends as well."

He hated the thought of what Edward had tried to do to Elena, but she was not the woman he thought he knew. How was he supposed to make amends with someone who'd lied to him? And after what he'd said to her, for that matter?

"Perhaps I shall go with you," his mother offered.

"I don't know—"

"We'll go first thing in the morning—and I can make sure you apologize."

Sarah retreated to her room as Mother leaned over, whispering to him, "What happened to that woman you told me about, the one who captured your attention?"

He shook his head. "She wasn't who I thought she was."

"Hmm. That's too bad."

"Yes, it is." He paused. "She was a beautiful artist. I think you would have liked her."

His father looked up from the desk. "Did you finalize the contract in Chicago?"

Chase nodded. "I did."

"We have a few matters to discuss, then."

Chase moved to a chair closer to his father as his mother followed Sarah into her room.

"Nelson can help Richard oversee the production of the telescopes," he said, "but we haven't yet been able to find a factory to produce them."

His father blinked. "A factory?"

Chase nodded. "Someplace reliable."

His father tapped his pen on the desk, thinking for a moment, before he spoke again. "I have an idea."

* * * * *

From the upstairs window, Elena watched a yacht glide across the lake. More than two days had passed since Edward had assaulted her, but she still didn't want to go outside, afraid that people would be watching her and wondering. However, she couldn't stand to be inside, either. At least she could sit here and pretend that she was free to go where she wanted.

Papa was in his patio chair in the backyard, Mama resting in her bedroom. Papa didn't seem to know how they would recover all they had lost and were continuing to lose. She wished there was something she could do to help him save his factory, save their home, but now there wasn't even anyone for her to marry.

A carriage pulled up in front of their house, and she watched Parker emerge from the door. He sauntered up the walk, to the door below her, but this time he didn't hold an envelope to tuck under the patio chair.

There were few people she wanted to see, but now with Jillian gone, it was good to see a friend. She stepped down the stairs slowly after he rang the bell, meeting him in the drawing room.

He stood up when she walked into the room, his eyes full of pity. "How are you, Lanie?"

She didn't want his pity. She wanted Parker to make her laugh like he always did.

She smoothed her fingers over her skirt. "Is everyone talking?"

"About what?"

She smiled. "That's what I love about you, Parker."

He smiled back at her, but she saw the misery in his eyes.

"Everyone is talking," he said, "but not about you."

She watched him closely as she sat on the floral davenport. He tossed his hat onto the sideboard and sat in the upholstered chair across from her, his fists curled up under his smooth chin.

She couldn't imagine what could possibly be more tantalizing gossip than the disgrace of Deborah Bissette's daughter. "What happened?"

"Edward left the island...with Gracie Frederick."

"Gracie?" she gasped. "But—how could they—? How could he? He's already married."

Parker shrugged. "It doesn't seem to matter much to him."

"I thought Gracie wanted to marry Chester Darrington."

"Apparently she changed her mind."

Elena shifted in her seat. There was no relief in the fact that the ladies were talking about Gracie and Edward instead of her and Edward. Poor Sarah Powell...and the Frederick family.

He leaned toward her, whispering, "Our mothers are talking, plotting for our future."

She sighed. "I guess I should be glad they're friends again."

"I don't know about friends. More like conspirators."

Nell placed the tea set and a plate of homemade oatmeal cookies on the table between them. As Parker thanked her, Elena studied his face with its laugh lines that were so free to spread joy, eyes that were honest and real. He would be truthful with her for the rest of their lives, she was certain, and he would make her laugh. Her family would have a pleasant future again, and probably a profitable one.

Parker would imagine himself to be all she needed. He wouldn't understand why she needed more. He wouldn't understand that longing inside her to escape to a place where she could draw and commune with her thoughts... and most of all, with God. Parker was a good companion to her. A brother. But she couldn't marry him.

Even if Chase would have her—which he had made quite clear that he would not—she couldn't marry him either. Not only had Mama evolved into a stalwart opponent of this marriage, but Sarah Powell would despise her, as would the rest of the Darrington family. She couldn't blame them. In their minds, they would always wonder if she had done something to provoke Edward.

She leaned forward. "Do you want to marry me, Parker?"

His gaze fell to his hands clasped in his lap. "It's not that I don't love you—"

"But you love me like a sister."

A light sparked in his eyes. "Exactly."

"And you love Jillian like a wife."

"It doesn't matter what I feel about Jillian." He shook his head. "It would never have worked out—you know that."

"But why wouldn't it have worked out?"

"She is—" He paused. "My parents said they would disinherit me if I married her."

"So you make your own money, Parker."

He shook his head. "I'd be no good as a working man."

"For Jillian's sake—"

"I would if I could do it, but I can't. This isn't like you and Chase."

She leaned back. "There is no me and Chase."

"You don't have to pretend with me." He crossed his arms. "You are the consummate socialite, Lanie, and I've never seen anyone else break that facade, not like Chase did at the ball."

"You think I should marry him because I'm angry with him?"

"I think you should marry him so you can stop hiding. It's not too late for you and Chase."

She shook her head. "You're crazy."

"And you're clearly denying the truth."

He leaned forward and poured himself a cup of tea. "Chase asked me about your lighthouse."

Her mouth dropped. "You told him about the lighthouse?"

"My guess is that he found it."

"You promised, Parker, never to tell anyone about it."

He took a sip of his tea. "But he asked me what was on the bluff. I couldn't lie to him."

"You could conceal the truth."

"Nah," he said with a little wave. "He needed to find it."

His words registered slowly. "You set us up!"

Parker didn't seem to hear her. "I told him about the ghosts."

"There aren't any ghosts there."

"I warned him they might not be friendly."

Since Chase left for Chicago, she'd refused to linger over the memories, the hours they'd spent together. Now they came rushing back. The first time she'd seen Chase at the lighthouse, she'd been so frustrated at him for taking her sketches and encroaching on her sanctuary, and yet he had returned to the lighthouse and wanted to see her again...until he found out who she was.

"I'm betting that the only thing obstructing you and Chase is pride."

She shook her head. "I'm quite sure he hates me."

"Hate is often a mask for something else."

"Like ignorance."

"Nope." The familiar grin returned to his face. "Like love."

She and Chase—they were too far gone to even think of love. What they had, whatever it was, had been splintered into pieces. They could never put it back together.

The doorbell chimed, but she didn't move. If it was a messenger—

or a caller—Claude would send him away. He knew she didn't want to see anyone except Parker or Jillian.

"You and Jillian loved each other," she said.

He fiddled with the teacup. "I was smitten, that's for sure, but—I can't love her enough to give up everything, nor can I ask her to join me in a floundering attempt to make it in the industrial world."

"Parker—"

He pushed the teacup away. "Trudy Grunier isn't too bad, is she?"

How could she argue with him? He was as trapped as she was, in this crazy world where life was planned for them no matter how much their hearts protested.

She couldn't blame Parker, but she did feel sorry for him. Marriage—it was a sacrifice for all of them. Only a few people in this world actually got to marry the man or woman they loved.

He looked back up at her. "However, you and Chase—"

Claude opened one of the pocket doors and cleared his throat. "You have callers, Miss Elena."

She turned, her eyes flickering with questions. She'd told him very clearly that she didn't want to see anyone today except Parker or Jillian.

Claude looked over her head, at the piano behind her, as if he didn't want to meet her gaze. "Mrs. Darrington and her son, Chester Darrington, are here to visit you."

The protest reared up in her throat, but before she could speak, Claude opened the other door and motioned Chase and his mother forward. The room seemed to tilt under her feet. Chase wasn't supposed to be here. He was supposed to be far away. In Chicago.

He looked so handsome in his brown pinstriped coat and trousers, his tweed vest and satin tie, and the felt derby in his hands. Like a gentleman.

Instead of rising, she sat frozen in her chair.

Parker leaped from his seat, extending his hand. "It's nice to see you again, Chase."

"And you as well."

At the sound of his voice, her heart seemed to collapse inside her. She looked away from him, at the window behind Parker. If she had to speak with him—she would collapse as well, in front of all of them.

"Are you here to visit Miss Bissette?" Parker asked.

"I—" Chase's voice faltered, and she wanted to take his hand and tell him that everything was all right. "I'm here to visit with her father."

Mrs. Darrington hurried forward toward the davenport, reaching down to take Elena's hands. "I'm here to see Miss Bissette."

Elena had thought the woman would be angry at her, but she kissed her cheeks instead.

"Mr. Bissette is out back," Claude announced.

Elena didn't dare turn her head, not even to watch Chase leave. *Is this what love feels like,* she wondered, *this tilting, whirling, out-of-control feeling that puts one off-balance?*

What must he think of her, first pursuing him for marriage and then all that happened with Edward? Did he think she'd tried to seduce his brother-in-law?

Mrs. Darrington released Elena's hands and sat on the chair next to where Parker had been sitting.

Parker picked up his hat. "I believe it's time for me to say my good-byes."

When Elena looked up at him, the room seemed to right itself again.

"Remember what I said, Lanie."

But Parker was wrong. It was too late for her and Chase.

*****

Chase found Arthur Bissette in a lawn chair, sipping iced lemonade and watching a purple finch flit from one branch to the next. Chase wondered if the man was going to ignore him like his daughter had, but Arthur offered Chase his hand, and then he offered him a chair.

Arthur leaned back in his chair. "My wife thinks you might be the devil himself."

Chase didn't dare agree or disagree. He didn't want to speak ill of the man's wife or daughter or how they'd conspired against him.

"I never wanted to upset your family."

"I know you didn't, son."

"I just— I was misinformed."

"Are you certain?" Arthur handed him a cigar.

He took it. "I'm certain of very little right now."

Digging into his pocket, Arthur removed a book of matches and held it up. "My wife thinks you invented these."

Chase laughed as the man lit his cigar. "I'm no good at making new things. I only help finance them."

"Deborah's a good woman, but she doesn't always get things right. In fact, sometimes she gets things very wrong." He paused. "You're a good man, Chase. Honest. I hope you prize grace and mercy as highly as you prize honesty."

Chase took a long draw on the cigar, tasting the earthy flavor on his tongue. Arthur wouldn't understand, but what had happened between him and Elena—it went far beyond grace. He could forgive Elena, eventually at least, but his heart desired much more than that. He'd wanted to marry her, but he couldn't marry a woman he didn't trust.

Hopefully, he could trust her father.

He tapped the cigar on the arm of his chair and ashes sailed to the ground. "Father says you have a factory in Chicago."

Arthur shook his head. "The bank is closing it down on Monday."

"But you still own it?"

"For four more days."

"What if you had guaranteed work?"

The older man sighed. "There is no work. After the World's Fair and then the economic panic, no one in Chicago wants to invest in a new industry right now."

"It seems to me that a bank would reconsider if you could pay back the loan."

Arthur took another draw on his cigar, contemplating his words. "They might."

Chase held out the cigar in his hand, pointing to the blue sky. "Do you like stars?"

"I suppose I appreciate them, but not like my daughter does. She loves everything about the night sky."

"Did she tell you about my telescope?"

The man's eyes widened. "Is that what you're working on?"

Chase leaned toward him, placing the cigar at his side. "I need you to be honest with me, sir. Did Elena tell you about the telescope?"

He shook his head. "She never told me anything about you…or what you were working on."

Chase sat back in his chair. He wanted to believe the man, desperately. He wasn't sure what to do with the information, though. Elena might have kept his secret, but she had still deceived him.

He took another draw of the cigar, looking out at the trees. "I have a proposition for you."

Chapter Twenty-Eight

Nell delivered a fresh pot of English tea and hot scones with lemon custard to the drawing room, and Mrs. Darrington poured a cup of tea for each of them. The older woman didn't rush the discussion, like Mama would have, but allowed silence to bridge the awkward gulf between them.

Elena's hands trembled as she reached for her cup, spilling the tea on her shirtwaist. The brown liquid pooled across the navy stripes.

Chase's mother must think she was a simpleton.

She sipped the tea, though she didn't taste it. She tried to put the cup down with grace, but it clattered on the saucer.

The curtain was up on her life this morning. She was supposed to be smiling and pretending that all was well on the stage, a skill she'd mastered long ago, but even though her audience was watching her, she couldn't seem to pretend anymore.

"Elena." Mrs. Darrington reached forward, taking her hands again. Instead of pity, compassion weighed heavy in her eyes and her voice. "I can't tell you how sorry I am."

"Sorry?" Elena asked, watching her face. "I thought—I thought you would be angry with me."

The compassion in Mrs. Darrington's eyes turned to surprise. "Why should I be angry with you?"

"Edward—they put him in jail. And then he left Sarah."

"According to the lieutenant, you did nothing wrong."

"I was walking in the woods alone."

"Well, there is certainly no crime in that." She released Elena's hands and took a sip of her tea. "The lieutenant said he got to you in time, that Edward didn't hurt you."

Elena grimaced. "Only my pride."

Mrs. Darrington took a scone from the tray. "Will you be all right?"

"Eventually."

"Very good." She took a bite of the scone. "Do you remember when I was here before, how I mentioned that Chase was courting someone?"

"I do." Her voice shook.

"It seems that I was wrong."

"You were?"

"That's what I get for meddling," she said with a shrug. "A mother should never meddle."

Elena swallowed the laughter that bubbled in her throat, knowing that Mrs. Darrington was meddling at this very moment. And the woman seemed quite aware of what she was doing.

"My son, though—he needs a good wife. A woman he can trust." She dipped a piece of scone into her teacup and ate it. "Someone who knows how to forgive."

"Does your son need forgiveness?"

"We all need forgiveness, my dear. That's why the Lord sent His Son."

"And you and Sarah—I suppose you have to forgive, as well."

"It will take us awhile to work all that out," she replied. "But, yes, we must forgive Edward."

Mrs. Darrington poured them both another cup of tea. "Have you been drawing?"

She shook her head. "Not recently."

"You mustn't stop, you know. My son said you were a fine artist."

"Chase exaggerates."

One of Mrs. Darrington's eyebrows slid up, and Elena realized her mistake, the familiarity of using his nickname. "Chester. I mean, Mr. Darrington."

Curses. She would never get it right.

"I've never known my son to exaggerate."

"That's because I don't exaggerate," he said from the doorway.

Elena looked at him, and his handsome face seemed worn without the easy smile that had slipped across his lips when they were alone at the lighthouse.

It was true; they were both very different people away from that world. Perhaps it was impossible to merge their real lives with the moments they shared, what seemed like a lifetime ago.

"We must go, Mother."

Mrs. Darrington stood and Elena sat up straighter, controlling her voice but not daring to stand. "May I speak with you a moment, Mr. Darrington?"

He hesitated before he replied. "Certainly."

"There is no rush," his mother called as she bustled out into the hallway.

He didn't come into the drawing room. "What is it, Miss Bissette?"

She hated the way her name sounded on his lips, all formal and stuffy, like they'd never gazed up at the stars together, never laughed together or shared their secrets. Oh, for him to call her "Andy" one more time. To smile at her with admiration and joy instead of disdain.

To say that he loved her.

But it was all business for him, and she would oblige.

"Claude—our manservant," she stumbled, "I discovered his grandfather." Oh, she was getting it all wrong. "I didn't discover his grandfather. I discovered his name. It's Nickolas Westmount from Magdelaine's journal."

Chase shook his head. "I don't understand."

"Claude would like to read Magdelaine's journal."

He shook his head. "I left it in Chicago."

"Perhaps when you return—"

He backed quickly away, shoving his hat on his head like there was urgent business he must attend to. "I'll send it back with your father."

"My father?"

He tipped his hat. "I'm glad to see you are quite recovered."

She collapsed back on the couch when she heard the *click* of their front door.

She hadn't recovered at all.

* * * * *

"An apology, that's all I asked for." His mother reprimanded him from across the seat on the carriage ride back to the Grand. "Instead, you were perfectly awful to her. Again."

He felt like a twelve-year-old, getting scolded by his mother. But she didn't know what Elena had done to him. If she did, she would be just as rude.

"Elena is my friend, Chase."

"But she's not mine."

His mother huffed. "What is wrong with you?"

"You saw her, Mother. She was entertaining that Randolph fellow when we arrived."

"What of it?" she asked, her hand swiping through the muggy air. "Elena's one of the prettiest girls on all of Mackinac, if not *the* prettiest. That doesn't mean we're rude to her."

He cringed at the thought of Elena courting any man, just as the thought haunted him of what Edward had tried to do to her in the forest. Part of him wanted to protect her from future harm, but she had parents who cared well for her. She didn't need him.

And he couldn't allow himself to need her.

"You have to do something," she insisted.

He looked out the window. "You're meddling, Mother."

"If you were fifteen years younger, I'd put you over my knee and spank you with a willow switch."

"It didn't hurt then—"

"You want to marry Elena," she blurted. "You know it, and so do I."

He shook his head. "I'm not ready to marry."

"You most certainly are," his mother murmured. "You're just being pigheaded."

"I am not."

"Years ago, you told me you wanted to marry a woman who spoke her mind."

He glanced back at her. "I don't think that any longer."

His mother muttered something else, but he didn't ask her to repeat her words.

* * * * *

Claude and Nell left the dining room table cluttered with dishes after Papa asked them to give the family a few moments to discuss a private matter. He spent the first fifteen minutes telling Mama the grim facts. How the bank was about to foreclose on both the factory and the house in Chicago. How all his investments were being held captive in a bank vault until he repaid his loans, but that most of them were worthless anyway until Chicagoans began buying and selling real estate once again.

And then he told them that he'd never liked producing farm equipment. He'd always wanted to be part of developing something innovative, something that no one else was producing en masse. Elena knew that men like the Darringtons were part of a small group of financiers who actually made money on innovation. To her knowledge, her father didn't have anything new to produce.

But as he spoke, life returned to her father's face and to his voice.

"He said what?" Mama exclaimed.

Elena blinked. She'd missed something.

"He is looking for a place to manufacture several items in Chicago, and he remembered that I have a factory."

"Who remembered?" Elena asked.

He glanced at her. "Chase Darrington."

"But what—what is he planning to produce?"

"Something for a fishing rod." He winked at her. "And something I'm not at liberty to speak about while the patent is pending."

He was going to use Papa's factory to make his telescope?

"How could you consider working for him, after what he did to us?" Mama persisted. "After what his brother-in-law did to Elena?"

Papa sighed. "Mr. Darrington isn't responsible for his brother-in-law's behavior, and I don't believe Mr. Darrington meant to hurt Elena. I don't have much of a choice. Not if we want to keep our home in Chicago."

"What of this place?" Mama asked.

He shook his head. "We'll still have to sell it at summer's end. The factory work will keep us afloat for now, but it won't pay all our obligations."

Elena tilted a spoon and watched the light from the chandelier reflect in the silver. Then she looked up. "I think you should do it, Papa."

Mama looked at her with surprise. "Are you certain?"

Elena nodded.

"Mr. Darrington won't be there," Papa said. "He'll leave the work for me while he returns to Detroit."

"See, Mama." Elena attempted a smile. "We'll probably never see him or his family again."

Papa pushed his plate away. "I'll have to leave with him in the morning."

Silence filled the room. Papa was the steady calm to Mama's chaos. Even though Mama never seemed to acknowledge it, she didn't operate well when he was gone.

"Perhaps we should all go with you," Mama finally said. "It will only take a few days to pack up our house."

"We don't have days. Mr. Darrington wants to start production right away." His voice slowed. "Besides, you and Elena should stay here and enjoy the last weeks of the summer."

Their last summer on Mackinac.

Chapter Twenty-Nine

The first officer from the *Manitou* stood on the stern of the boat, his arm raised. As the second hand ticked toward the hour of nine, he dropped his arm and the gangplank was drawn aboard for the ship's departure.

With tears in her eyes, Elena waved good-bye to Papa from the pier as the steamer left the port. She hadn't seen Chase in the crowd, and she was glad of it. With God's help, she was trying to forgive him as Mrs. Darrington suggested, but she knew that one day she would need to ask him to forgive her as well. She'd never tried to deceive him, at least not in the way he believed. Perhaps they had both been wrong. She never should have hidden her identity from him.

She heard a dog bark in the crowd behind her, and she turned to see Galileo pushing toward her. She crouched beside him, laughing as he licked her face. Her chest lurched for a moment; she was afraid to look up and see his owner. When she did, Mrs. Darrington was in front of her, smiling down.

Elena stood up, trying to hide her disappointment. "Good morning, Mrs. Darrington."

"You must start calling me Lydia." She grasped Elena's elbow gently, leading her away from the boat. "Is your mother here?"

Elena shook her head. "She hates to say good-bye in public."

Galileo barked, and she rubbed his head again.

"Chase says that this dog is an excellent judge of character."

"I must have him fooled." She petted him again. "Where is Sarah?"

Lydia nodded at the water. "She's at the hotel, preparing to leave for Detroit next week."

"I'm sorry she has to go."

They reached the end of the pier and stepped onto the sidewalk. "Elena—do you happen to know how to play lawn tennis?"

Elena glanced at her, wondering at the odd question. "I do not."

"Neither do I." Lydia's laugh was as light as the breeze. "But they've built two courts up at the Grand, and I have to admit, I'm a bit intrigued by the sport. I've been in the audience, watching men and women play, for the past two days."

Elena thought back to her house, looming large up on the bluff. There was nothing for her to do there. "Would you like to learn how to play?" she asked.

"Oh, I do, but I need a partner." Lydia slowed, turning to her. "You wouldn't want to learn as well, would you?"

"I suppose I could try."

"Oh, splendid." She clapped her gloved hands together. "Now we need to find two more ladies."

"For what?"

She laughed again. "To play against."

Elena thought of Mrs. Grunier and Trudy, but she couldn't imagine either woman playing a sport.

Mrs. Frederick wouldn't have a partner with Gracie off with—

Lydia interrupted her thoughts. "I believe I might be able to convince Sarah to play, at least for a game or two."

Elena smiled back at her. "I have an idea."

"I thought you might."

"I need to go home first."

Lydia scooted her forward. "Take your time."

Elena found her mother in the drawing room, stitching another needlepoint for the wall. As her mother worked, she proposed her plan. Mama eyed her like she'd lost her mind. "I can't play tennis."

"It's simple, Mama." She leaned back, trying to demonstrate with her arm. "All you do is hit a ball, back and forth, over a net."

Mama shook her head. "I can't even hit a croquet ball on the lawn with a wide hammer."

"We'll all take lessons. The instructor will show us exactly what to do."

Mama set her needlepoint on her lap. "Who else is going to play this game?"

"Mrs. Darrington asked me to be her partner, so you and her daughter will be partners."

"The ladies will think it's ridiculous."

Elena smiled. "Who cares what they think?"

* * * * *

"Not only are you miserable," Richard said as he plopped down on the chair in front of Chase's desk, "but you're miserable to be with."

Chase didn't look up from the papers in front of him. "A good morning to you too."

"Since you won't bother to tell me what happened out on that island, I can only assume that you met a girl and that this same girl did something to wreck your heart. And I can also assume—and I'm only guessing here—that she might be known by the name of Andy."

"She didn't wreck my heart."

Richard leaned forward. "Then what happened to you?"

"I don't know what happened, not exactly." Chase glanced up at his assistant. "I met a young woman and enjoyed her company for a while, as I have other ladies. And just like the others, I found out that she was someone different than I had thought."

"You don't think you're an inventor, Chase, but you are."

"I am not—"

"And an artist at that."

Chase shook his head. "What are you talking about?"

Richard leaned back against the chair, crossing his arms. "I'd venture to guess that you've created a masterpiece in your mind, your own invention of who you wanted this girl to be."

Chase dipped the end of his quill in the ink and drew a line on the bottom of the paper. "You don't know what you're talking about."

"And then when your invention didn't work out, you bailed."

"She's not an invention," he insisted.

"There is no perfect woman out there."

"I don't want perfect." His blood—it felt like it was boiling. "I want trustworthy."

Richard laughed. "Perhaps you should get a horse."

Chase pushed away the papers, preparing to stand. "This is going nowhere—"

"Of course you have to trust her, Chase. And you have to love her too."

The door opened, and Arthur Bissette stepped inside, his cane tapping on the floor. He hesitated, glancing between the two men. "I don't want to interrupt."

Richard waved him over. "Perhaps you should join us. We're talking about Chase's miserable luck with women."

"Arthur doesn't want to hear about that."

Instead of responding, Arthur nodded toward Chase. "May I speak with you in private?"

Richard stood up, setting his hat on his head. "Don't worry about me. I'm needed at the bank."

After Richard walked out the door, Arthur sat across from Chase, resting his cane across his legs. Chase hadn't asked the man to work with him because of Elena. He'd hired him because of his solid reputation for quality work and secrecy when necessary.

And because they needed a factory in Chicago.

"You've done so much for me already," Arthur said, twisting his hat in his hands.

"Actually, I believe you're the one who's done quite a bit for me."

Arthur glanced at the papers on the desk and then looked back at him. "I have one more favor to ask of you."

Chase crossed his hands on the desk. "What is it?"

"The bank is asking for another signature to continue my loan for our house. Someone who has the income to pay for it if necessary."

"You're asking me to sign for your loan?"

"I'm going to sell the house on Mackinac, but I'm not ready to—if I default, you can sell the house in Chicago."

Chase considered the man's words. He didn't like getting involved with personal affairs such as this, and his father probably wouldn't approve, but he couldn't in good conscience allow this man to lose his home. He hated dabbling in real estate, but if Arthur defaulted, he could find someone to sell the house and regain his money. "I'll sign for you," he finally said.

"Thank you," Arthur breathed. "I'll do everything within my power to pay this loan…or pay you back."

Chase nodded. He might not be able to trust Elena, but he'd begun to trust her father.

* * * * *

The four society ladies giggled like girls as they whisked their rackets through the air. Every time they missed the ball they laughed, again and again. Elena had no skill for the game—none of them did—but she was having more fun than she'd had in a very long time.

The instructor was a patient man named Leonard, a native of Great Britain. He told the ladies that his colleagues had warned him about the women he'd find in the United States—that they would be far more prone to silliness than their counterparts on the other side of the Atlantic. The Darrington and Bissette ladies had proved his colleagues right, but none of them cared.

His newest students had played for three days straight now, and they rarely hit the ball over the net. When they did make it over, by sheer luck, it usually continued over the heads of their opponents, landing among the umbrellas of their spectators. But every time they hit the ball, no matter where it landed, they cheered for each other. The small audience that gathered around the courts each time they played cheered for them as well.

Elena's mother swung her racket once again, sending the ball over Elena's head and into the bushes in a most ungraceful manner. Her mother propped the racket over her shoulder, waving at the small audience like she was the victor.

Leonard sighed as one of the Grand's youngest employees ran to retrieve the ball. "Mrs. Bissette, you are supposed to hit the ball inside the white lines."

She turned to him, waving her racket toward the crowd. "Whatever for?"

"So your opponent has the opportunity to return it to you in a timely manner."

She pointed her racket at Elena. "That's not my opponent. That's my daughter."

"But in this game," Leonard attempted to explain patiently, "she is your opponent."

"It's a silly rule."

The ladies laughed, and poor Leonard laughed along with them.

"Let's break for lunch," Lydia announced.

Leonard concurred. "That is a fabulous idea."

"But we'll return, after we've eaten."

He gave a slight bow. "And I shall be waiting for you."

If given the choice, he probably would have taken the next train from Mackinaw to New York City and then a boat on to England, but Elena admired him greatly for his endurance.

The women ate chicken salad and fresh fruit on the porch as the orchestra played behind them. For dessert, cherry sorbet was served in chilled silver bowls and garnished with cinnamon sticks.

The first day they played tennis, Sarah didn't speak to Elena, but by the second day, her coldness began to thaw. Sarah often came with red eyes to their game, but instead of crying on the court, the women laughed together. And in their laughter they began to heal. They never spoke of Edward, but perhaps Sarah began to feel a common bond with Elena. Edward had hurt them both, in very different ways.

Somehow Lydia seemed to have known this, bringing the women together to play a game like tennis. All their men were gone, the senior Mr. Darrington having traveled to Detroit on business. Even if none of them spoke the words, they needed each other's company.

Elena's loneliness had been swept away in the company of the women. She never would have guessed that her mother would socialize with Sarah Powell, or Lydia for that matter, but Mama respected both women on and off the clay court.

Sarah was finally leaving in the morning to return to Detroit, and Elena would miss her. She'd thought Lydia would return home with her daughter, but she had decided to stay another week—to enjoy the remnants of her summer vacation, she said.

Sarah twirled a cinnamon stick in her sorbet. "I believe we are better entertainment than the orchestra."

Elena lifted her glass of bubbly mineral water in a salute. "We're certainly having more fun."

Mama and Lydia laughed.

"They will have to start charging an admission fee to watch us play," Mama said.

"I need to finish packing." Sarah took her last bite of sorbet and pushed back her chair, glancing at Mama and then Elena. "I'm going to miss all of you."

The tears in Sarah's eyes surprised Elena. How they could be friends, after all that had happened between them, was yet another miracle.

As Sarah walked toward the lobby, Elena scanned the patio and saw the Frederick family, Mr. and Mrs. Frederick dining with their two sons. Mrs. Frederick's arms were like spindly tree limbs growing through the billowing sleeves of her canary-yellow dress.

When had she lost so much weight?

"Mama," Elena said, elbowing her mother.

Her mother turned to see Mrs. Frederick, and Lydia's gaze followed. Mama looked back at Lydia. "She looks terrible."

Lydia lifted her iced tea and took a long drink, as if she were teetering between forgiveness and clinging to her bitterness. "Perhaps she should join us for dessert."

"Thank you," Mama said as she scooted back her chair.

In that moment, Elena had never been prouder of her mother.

The news of Gracie Frederick's running off with Edward had trumped the gossip about what he had tried to do to Elena, but she hadn't heard Mama talk ill about what Gracie had done, not even once. And now instead of gossiping about the Fredericks, she had gone to talk with Mrs. Frederick. Perhaps if any good were to come out of what happened with Edward, it would unite people—like her and Sarah—who might otherwise have remained divided.

Except for Chase. He chose to separate himself.

Mama pulled out a chair for Mrs. Frederick, and the woman placed her glass of wine on the table before she sat. Long shadows dipped under her eyes.

"My husband and boys—" she began. "He is taking them fishing for the afternoon."

Elena nodded. "I'm glad you can join us."

"Have you heard from your daughter?" Lydia asked.

Mrs. Frederick stared at the red liquid in her glass. "I received a letter from her yesterday."

Lydia set down her tea. "Oh?"

"She said they are in Toronto."

She didn't mentioned Edward's name, perhaps out of respect for Lydia or perhaps out of respect for her daughter. They all knew she'd left with him; they didn't need to know anything else.

Lydia turned the glass. "I hope she is well."

"As well as to be expected, I suppose." Mrs. Frederick managed a tight smile. "She said they would summer here with us, next year."

The moment the words came from her mouth, Mrs. Frederick looked mortified. "I'm so sorry," she blurted as she stood up, looking as though she might run. "He's still married, to your dau—"

Lydia stopped her. "Sit down, Elizabeth."

Mrs. Frederick sat faster than Galileo at the command of his master.

Lydia's eyes softened. "I'm glad your daughter is safe."

"I hope she is."

"Sarah will get the divorce if Edward doesn't."

Mrs. Frederick smoothed back her hair, as if the straightening of her appearance would somehow repair the mess inside of her. "It's a terrible state of affairs."

"Elizabeth." Lydia leaned forward. "I have a very important question for you."

Mrs. Frederick looked terrified. "What is it?"

"Do you know how to play lawn tennis?"

Chapter Thirty

Lovers promenaded hand in hand on the walk around Lake Michigan's shore. People rode their bicycles, and children licked all manner of flavored ice cream from cones.

Chase maneuvered around a couple laughing quietly together, trying to clear his mind with a walk, but Elena seemed to haunt him wherever he went. Another couple embraced near the railing, and he looked away. Other people found love in their lifetime. Why couldn't he?

Someday, perhaps, he would meet a woman he longed to be with as much as he wanted to be with Elena. A woman who wanted to be with him as well. If only Elena had been a governess or even a housemaid. If only she hadn't known who he was...

Elena would be back in Chicago in four weeks, her father said—but Chase would be gone, back to Detroit, by then. He would begin working on a new project while Arthur oversaw the production of the telescopes. Richard had a list of things he wanted Chase to test, a number of people to meet, but Chase seemed to have lost his enthusiasm for his work. Another financier had won the bid to invest in the dish-washing machine that had once intrigued him, but he didn't even care.

Richard was right. He felt miserable, and it was rubbing off on all those around him.

He wandered down the walk until he arrived at a restaurant near the pier. Aunt Lottie was waiting inside, her lips rosy with salve. She was ten years his mother's senior, but she never seemed to age.

He kissed her cheek before he sat across from her at the table.

"You look tired," she informed him before she took a bite of her peach pie.

He raked his hands through his hair. "I've been busy working."

She tsked. "You and your father are just alike, always working. How long have you been in Chicago?"

"Almost three weeks now." Not including his trip back to Mackinac.

"And in three weeks you couldn't find the time to come see me?" She stirred cream into her coffee. "Did you meet my friends on Mackinac, the Bissette family?"

"You know everyone in Chicago, Aunt Lottie."

The steward poured coffee into a cup for him. "But I wanted you to meet the Bissettes in particular."

He sighed. "I made their acquaintance."

"They're a fine family. The daughter is quite the belle of Chicago."

"I can see why."

"I like Miss Bissette." Lottie sipped her coffee. "I admit, I was hoping you'd like her too."

He choked on the coffee and put it down.

"There, there," she said. "I didn't mean to upset you."

"I'm not upset. Just took too big of a sip." He wiped his mouth with the napkin. This was the exact reason he hadn't scheduled a visit with Aunt Lottie before now. He thought he was ready to talk about Elena, but apparently he wasn't.

"I was actually hoping you might help me find someone."

She sipped her coffee again. "Who is it you're trying to find?"

"I found an old diary on Mackinac. It's a story without an ending."

"Fascinating," she said, before she took another bite of her pie.

"I want to track down the writer of the diary and her descendants, to see what happened to them."

Aunt Lottie looked at him like he'd lost his mind.

"For a friend," he clarified.

"I have a close friend whose husband owns a detective agency." She picked up another piece of pie with her fork. "He might be able to help."

"Thank you, Aunt Lottie."

He leaned back on the chair, hoping he could do this one last thing for Elena...and for Claude. She wouldn't even have to know who instigated it.

*****

A four-year-old girl spun a top back and forth across the room while Elena played blocks on the floor with a little boy. Four mattresses were propped up against the wall with two more children bouncing on a fifth mattress as Jillian fed the baby her bottle. The general and his wife had escaped to dinner in the village for the evening, and they had allowed Elena to come and help her for an hour.

Jillian laughed as Elena told her about their lawn tennis games—how ridiculous the women had looked on the court and yet the fun they'd had. Their game had ended abruptly with a swollen ankle for Lydia and a bruised pinky for Mama when Lydia ran to hit a ball and tripped. That was the exact reason, Mama had informed Leonard, that a lady must never return a ball. The hotel boys were there to return the balls for them.

Still, there was talk of playing again next year, if the Bissettes returned to the island.

"Are you happy here?" Elena asked her friend.

Jillian looked at the baby in her arms and wiggled one of her toes. "For now."

Elena set another block on the tower and it toppled down. She thought the boy might cry, but he cheered instead. "Again!" he demanded.

As she helped the child build the tower once more, she marveled. Not only did God create the majesty in the skies, but every single day, He created on the earth, forming children like this one in their mother's womb. Each of the children in this family looked different. Each was a unique creation of His.

She set down another block. "Has Parker been back to visit you?"

Jillian shook her head.

"I'm sorry."

Jillian lifted the baby to her chest to burp her. "It's all right, Elena. I'm content."

"But still—"

Jillian interrupted. "Have you heard from Mr. Darrington?"

"I won't hear anything from him."

"I don't understand," Jillian said. "He loved you, Elena. It was as plain as the stars in the sky."

If only she and Chase could go back in time. If only they could keep pretending that her name was Andy and that he was a soldier at Fort Mackinac. But her secrets—and his obstinance—had ruined it.

"You can't always see the stars as clearly as you'd like, not with the clouds in the way."

"He was kind to both Silas and me, and he made sure I found a good position."

Someone knocked on the door, and the sound relieved Elena. She didn't want to hear about Chase's kindness.

"Could you get that?" Jillian asked.

Silas blushed when Elena opened the door, a bouquet of flowers in his hand.

"I brought these for Jillian," he explained, handing them to her.

"Would you like to say hello to her? She's right—"

He shook his head as he backed down the steps. Then he was gone.

*****

It was almost the end of August before Aunt Lottie sent Chase a letter about Jonah Seymour, and he read her response quickly. Part of him wished he could tell Elena the news in person, but he didn't want to see her again—or her and Parker again. Perhaps her father could deliver the letter. Or he could leave it here for whenever she returned to Chicago.

He stood up from his desk and walked over to the window, looking out at the steamers crossing the lake.

The door opened behind him, and he turned. Richard walked inside, eyeing Chase's stance by the window along with the tall stack of papers on his desk. Then Richard sat down. "You're thinking about her again, aren't you?"

Chase shrugged. "It doesn't matter."

"This woman—she's haunting you, Chase." Richard scooted the chair closer to the desk. "Are you going to tell me about her?"

Chase thought for a moment. Richard was the best friend he had. Perhaps Richard could help him sort through all the warring feelings he'd had, help him rid himself of them so he could return to the contented state he'd enjoyed before he visited that lighthouse. "She's a woman I met on Mackinac. A woman who loves the stars."

"Why do you call her Andy?"

He sat on the chair. "It's kind of a joke."

Richard raised his eyebrows. "You don't joke, Chase."

He shrugged. "She said she liked the name of the nebula Andromeda. So I called her Andy."

"She said she liked Andromeda?"

Chase nodded.

Richard leaned back in his chair. "Fascinating."

"Why is that so fascinating?"

"Because Andromeda was named after a chained princess."

"A chained princess?"

Richard shook his head. "Haven't you read Greek mythology?"

"Very little."

Richard folded his arms across his chest and propped his feet on Chase's desk. "It's a Greek myth about a princess who was chained to a rock as a punishment for her mother's boasting."

"Her mother's boasting?"

Richard nodded. "She was going to be sacrificed, to a sea monster or something, but was rescued."

Chase tapped his fingers on the desk before looking back at Richard. *"I understand her."* That's what Elena had said about Andromeda. Was it the chains she understood…or the sacrifice?

"Who rescued her?" he asked.

"Per—something," Richard said. "He rescued the princess and married her."

Chase swiveled his chair, looking back out at the water. He supposed it was possible Elena didn't know who he was at the lighthouse, but it didn't change the fact that she'd set her mind to marrying him. Or at least, her mother had decided it for her. Perhaps she felt that she was chained, that she couldn't marry for love. That she had to sacrifice herself for others.

Perhaps she did need someone to rescue her. Not from poverty, but from the other chains that bound her.

His heart raced within him. Could he still love her, after all that had happened? And more importantly, could she love him?

"Chase?"

Chase turned his chair back, raking his hands through his hair. "That—it explains a lot."

"Andy's chained to a rock?"

"Practically."

"And is there a sea monster?"

"No, but there's a mother." He turned to his friend. "What time does the next steamer leave?"

"For heaven's sake, Chase, you'll have to wait until the morning if you take the steamer."

Waiting until morning… Suddenly that felt like forever.

Richard grinned. "Go rescue her on your own boat."

July 4, 1813

It's Independence Day for our country, but we can't celebrate on Mackinac since we're no longer independent.

It's been almost a year now of waiting. Waiting for Jonah, waiting for our country to take back this island. But the British aren't leaving, and Jonah hasn't returned.

There is plenty of food for our summer—squirrels, rabbits, wild strawberries, nuts.... But the children and I, we don't have enough wood or food to survive another winter.

For Thomas and Molly, I must find out what happened to Jonah. And for me.

If he is in prison, I will figure out a way for us to wait for him. If he is dead, the children and I will sneak onto a fishing boat to get off the island, though I don't know where we will go. When Nickolas was last here, he said the British have control of the entire Michigan territory and all the ports along the Great Lakes.

Last week, when I was picking strawberries, I saw a British soldier in the woods. He didn't speak to me, nor I to him. I thought he might question my allegiance, but he didn't, perhaps because of the Chippewa in my skin, a gift from my mother.

If it weren't for the sake of my children, I would be quite willing to die for my country.

Who would take care of them if something happened to me?

I will beg the Westmounts to care for the children while I search for Jonah. It will be the first time they've been out of our house for almost a year.

I pray I find him at the fort. And I pray we find a way to bring my dear husband home.

Chapter Thirty-One

The Bissette household was aflutter again, preparing for the final ball of Mackinac's summer season. Jillian came back to the Bissette house for the evening to help the ladies prepare. Mama asked Jillian if she would return to Chicago with them, but she said she wanted to remain on the island until the general left with his family, the first of next year.

When Mama left the room, Elena whispered, "Does this have something to do with a certain lieutenant at the fort?"

Jillian's smile emerged. "He's been coming to call."

Elena grinned. She was disappointed for Parker, sad that it wasn't going to work for him and Jillian to marry, but Silas Hull was one of the finest men she'd ever met. He would be a good catch for any woman.

"No one else knows," Jillian whispered.

"He'll take good care of you."

She glanced down at the floor. "It's not as if he's proposed."

"But he will." Elena hugged her friend. "And you will be the wife of a lieutenant."

She shook her head. "I don't know how long he will be in the army. Mr. Darrington is investing in his fishing rod, you know."

Elena didn't know.

"If enough people order the rod, we may be able to buy ourselves a house."

Elena hugged her again. "I'm so happy for you."

At least one of them would be marrying a man who cared for her.

"We have to get you ready." Jillian turned Elena back toward the mirror. "Who are you planning to dance with tonight?"

"I don't care to dance with anyone."

Jillian pinned a headdress of mauve-and-ivory rosettes on Elena's hair and then helped her fasten her sleeveless mauve evening gown. A satin bow gathered the long skirt at her hip, ivory ruffles cascading to the floor as her matching gloves climbed up past her elbow.

"It's too bad Mr. Darrington won't see you tonight."

Elena waved her hand. "He wouldn't care."

Jillian clasped the chain of Elena's heart locket behind her neck. "I wouldn't be so sure of that."

*****

Chase surveyed the elegant ballroom in the Grand Hotel. The crowd had thinned over the summer, the dance floor now almost vacant. He'd come straight from his family's yacht, not even stopping to knock on his mother's door. He had to see Elena before the night was over, to ask her forgiveness for not trusting her. She'd been living in the chains of expectation and loyalty to her family, but he'd been living in chains as well. He'd believed she was like all the other women who'd tried to deceive him, and it had crushed him.

Because he loved her.

"Mr. Darrington?" The Grunier young lady, the one with rosy cheeks, smiled at him, but she didn't reach for his arm to confide in him, as she'd done at the masquerade party. Instead, Parker came up beside her with a glass of orange punch.

Parker smiled when he saw him. "Are you here to see Lanie?"

"Who?"

"Elena—have you seen her?"

"Not yet."

Parker nodded toward the porch. "Last time I saw her, she was standing out there."

Trudy drained her glass of punch, setting it on a tray. "Come, Parker," she said, tugging on his arm.

Parker patted her hand, the slightest smile on his face as he looked back at Chase. "My fiancée loves to dance."

Fiancée?

Trudy giggled as Parker swept her toward the dance floor. Chase watched them dance for a moment, and then he rushed outside.

He didn't find Elena on the porch, but his mother was sitting on a wicker chair, drinking a demitasse of coffee. Her face lit up when she saw him. She stood and hugged him. "I didn't know you were coming back."

"It was a last-minute decision."

"I see." She couldn't seem to help her smile. "If you are looking for the Bissette family, I believe they went home."

"Already?"

"It's after midnight."

A dog barked above them, and his mother laughed. "Galileo's been missing you too."

"You mind if I go get him?"

"He's your dog, Chase."

His mother kissed his cheek, promising to meet him for a late breakfast in the morning.

* * * * *

Green light rippled across the sky, and Elena watched as the flickering swarm of stars chased the clouds away. Purple strands fluttered across the horizon like fireworks, exploding in the night. Yellow threads weaved through the curtain of color.

In all her years on Mackinac Island, she'd never seen anything like it.

The aurora borealis, that's what Claude called it. Lights from the north that danced in the sky whenever their Creator saw fit. Their majesty was unrivaled.

There was only one more day before she and Mama returned to Chicago. She was excited to see Papa and be in their home for as long as the bank allowed it, but she couldn't help the sadness that filled her as well. This would be her last night at the lighthouse for the summer—perhaps for her lifetime. If they returned to Mackinac, their cottage would belong to another family.

Orange light dripped over the blackness above her, but even with the beauty around her, there was a void in her heart. She knew God would fill it in time, but right now, it still ached.

She was trying—and failing—to capture the display in her sketchbook when she heard the sound of a dog barking. Her heart leaped.

"Galileo?" she called down from the tower.

"It's Galileo," a voice called back. "And his owner."

Her reply caught in her throat.

"We wondered if we could come up and watch these lights."

"I—I don't know," she replied so quietly that she thought he hadn't heard.

"Edward once called me a fool," he said.

A grin sprang to her lips. "Were you being one?"

"I believe I've been one for the past two months."

Slowly she walked down the steps. The door to the lighthouse had a keyhole, but there was no key to lock it. Even so, Chase remained outside.

She cracked open the door, and he slid an envelope through to her. "I brought this for you...and for Claude."

She took the envelope. "What is it?"

"The rest of the story."

She swallowed. "Thank you, Chase."

Galileo barked again as she closed the door. She wished she could let him in along with his master, but she wanted so much more from Chase than a letter.

She slid it into her pocket and waited.

*****

Chase shivered in the cool weather, his ear pressed against the door. He wished he could see her eyes, to know if she was smiling or crying or still angry with him.

"I know now that your father didn't send you to check on my work," he said to the door.

She was slow to reply. "You thought I tricked you."

"I was being ridiculous." He waited. "You didn't try to steal my telescope just like you didn't try to steal Sarah's husband."

"Most certainly not!"

"Someone told me you wanted to marry me for my money."

This time she cracked open the door. "I'm sorry for deceiving you."

He took a deep breath, needing to ask one more time. All he wanted was the truth. "Did you know who I was that first night, after the masquerade ball?"

She shook her head. "My mother wanted me to marry you, but the you she had in mind was Chester Darrington, not the man I knew here in the lighthouse. I didn't think Chase had any money."

His voice was sad. "You wouldn't have married me if I wasn't wealthy."

"My heart wanted to marry Chase, but my parents were hoping I'd marry Chester."

"A man you thought you'd never met."

"You don't understand what it's like, Chase, not only to be a daughter but also an only child." She took a deep breath. "Our family's finances were in ruin, and I had no way to support my parents except to marry well. Marry a man like Lottie Ingram's nephew. It wasn't what I wanted, but I felt I had no choice."

"And now?"

"With the factory...with your help"—she swallowed—"Papa said there will be no more talk of marriage in our house until I'm ready."

Chase paused, fingering the simple ring in his pocket, a diamond molded into a golden heart to match her locket. "I wonder if you might be ready now."

This time she pulled the door completely open. "What?"

He drank in the sight of her, the ringlets in her hair and the worn calico dress that had fascinated him.... Her eyes sparkled in the light, and he was certain he'd never seen anyone lovelier in his entire life.

He cleared his throat. "I wanted to rescue you, like I did with Galileo here." *Like Sarah had done with Jillian.* "I wanted to be your hero, until I realized you didn't need a hero after all...at least not the kind I was envisioning."

"I did need you."

"You needed my money, not me."

"No, Chase," she whispered. "I needed—I need you."

"I hurt you—"

"At the masquerade party, you told Mrs. Grunier that you didn't want to meet me because of my reputation."

He swallowed, remembering well the night. Not because of what he'd said about Elena, but because he'd met Andy. "I never should have said that."

"Why my reputation?"

"Mrs. Frederick said you were trying to marry me."

She sighed. "She was right."

"I didn't want you to care for me because of my money."

"I'm so sorry, Chase. At the time, I *was* hoping to marry you for your money. I didn't know—"

"It would have been all wrong, wouldn't it? If we'd met someplace other than here."

She nodded. "We might never have stepped off the stage."

"I don't want you to pretend with me, Elena. Ever."

"Come." She reached for his hand, tugging him toward the steps. "You're missing the show."

Upstairs, green-and-white sparks flashed across the night, more beautiful than any firework display he'd ever seen.

When he put his arm around her, she nestled into his suit jacket like she'd belonged there all along. "I want to trust you, Chase, as Magdelaine did Jonah. Never once did she suspect that he'd deserted her. But trust—it takes time to build."

"We have time, don't we?" He kissed the top of her silky hair. "I found some answers about Magdelaine in Chicago."

"You were looking for answers?"

He laughed. "They're all written in that letter for Claude, but I wanted you to know first."

"What happened?"

"According to Thomas Seymour's grandson, Nickolas Westmount was a hero."

She stepped back. "He was?"

He nodded. "Apparently when Magdelaine went to find Jonah, there was a fire at the fort. Nickolas and his wife assumed they were dead."

She nodded. "Magdelaine died in 1813."

"That's what she wanted the British to believe, but she didn't die until the 1840s. She and Jonah hid on the island until they could retrieve their children from the Westmounts in 1815, the day the United States regained control. Then they stowed away on a boat to Cleveland. They lived together as a family until Thomas became a lighthouse keeper on the mainland."

Elena was silent, a small smile on her lips. "I wonder why Claude is so ashamed of his granddaddy," she said finally.

"Perhaps he only knows the part about Nickolas being a traitor."

"Not everything is as it seems."

He wrapped his arm tighter around her.

"Chase?" she whispered.

"Mmm."

"I don't want to run away anymore."

"I'm glad," he whispered. Ever so gently he tipped back her head, and the warmth of her kiss splayed through his skin like the lights.

She nestled against his chest, whispering to him, "I don't want to run, and I don't want to pretend."

He held her away from him, her face glowing in the lights as he examined it. "Are you pretending to love me?"

She smiled. "I've been trying to pretend that I don't."

He pulled her close, smoothing his hands over her hair, before he tilted her chin again. "No more pretending, Elena."

In her kiss, he knew. God was here, with him and Elena, and this time Chase could almost hear Him whisper.

"It is good."

Epilogue

June 1895

Henry and his team drove Chase up the hill, to the pathway that led to the back door of Castle Pines. Galileo stayed behind with Henry as Chase snuck between Mrs. Bissette's budding gardens and around the reflecting pool. Snagging a small stone, he crept around the side of the house and hoisted it over his head to toss at Elena's window.

Before he threw it, a window on the first floor shot up. Mrs. Bissette crossed her arms on the other side of the frame. "Go home, Chase."

He dropped the rock.

"She doesn't want to see you." Mrs. Bissette checked the time on the chatelaine that hung from her dress. She was no longer the lady of Castle Pines, but she continued to act like she owned the cottage. "Not for three more hours."

He eyed the partially opened window above him in the room where Elena was staying. "Can't I ask her a question?"

Her eyes narrowed slightly. "I suppose."

He stepped back, shouting, "Andy—will you marry me?"

His question was met with silence, and Mrs. Bissette nodded to him before she shut the window of the drawing room.

He called back to the upper window. "You're not going to change your mind, are you?"

Jillian peeked out. "Elena says this is a good exercise in patience."

"Patience? I asked her to marry me ten months ago!"

"Then you can surely wait until four o'clock."

Four o'clock seemed like an eternity to him, just like the length of their engagement. He'd honored Arthur and Mrs. Bissette's request to wait for marriage, needing to win back Mrs. Bissette's affections in particular before she allowed him to marry her daughter. Her affections remained prickly, but at least she'd finally approved.

He took another step back, peering into the dark window above him, hoping for just a glimpse of Elena's smile. He didn't see her, but he heard the beautiful sound of her laughter.

"You're still here, aren't you?" she called.

"I just saw the minister, and he said he could marry us right away."

"Chase!"

"You're still going to marry me, aren't you?"

"Of course I am. At four."

"I'm afraid you'll change your mind." He plucked a tulip out of her mother's garden and twirled it in his fingers. "I can't wait to marry you, darling."

She hushed him. "The whole bluff can hear you."

He cupped his hands around his mouth and shouted, "I love Elena Bissette!"

She laughed again.

"I can shout even louder if you'd like."

"It's not necessary." He caught just a glimpse of her beautiful profile, her hair swept up with flowers. It was all he could do to keep himself from bolting through the door and sprinting up the steps to steal her away…like Perseus had done with Andromeda.

"Mr. Darrington," Claude whispered from the bushes.

He turned away from the window, sighing. "You're supposed to call me Chase."

Claude held up an envelope. "I got it."

Chase stole a glimpse at the contents of the envelope and then put his hand on Claude's shoulder. "You're a good friend."

As Claude snuck away, Chase looked back at the window. “I still love you,” he called.

Her voice softened. “I love you too.”

He whistled as he started back up the path. Then he stopped and laughed when he saw Silas crouched by the reflecting pool.

After the booming sales of his fishing rods during the spring, Silas could purchase a house much larger than Castle Pines, but he’d chosen this one for Jillian. After he was discharged from the army, he could fish all summer on Mackinac Island and then ice fish in the winter.

Chase nodded toward the back door. “That woman is a better guard than your fellow soldiers ever were.”

Silas didn’t stand, eyeing the house instead. “I think I can sneak past her.”

Chase grinned at the determined look on his friend’s face. “You do realize that you can go into the house any time now.”

The younger man shook his head. “Jillian would be mortified if Mrs. Bissette found out I was here.”

Chase laughed. “You own the place!”

Silas sighed. “I don’t think anyone told Elena’s mother that the papers she signed were to sell the house.”

“After the ceremony, we’ll remind her that she’s sleeping at the Grand tonight.” As gracious as Jillian had been to the former lady of Castle Pines, even she wouldn’t want Mrs. Bissette in the house when Silas joined her.

Chase clutched the envelope in his hands. He and Elena wouldn’t be spending the night at either the Grand Hotel or Castle Pines. He’d made other arrangements for their first night together.

“How’d it go?” Henry asked as he climbed into the back of the buggy. Galileo was waiting on the seat for him, wagging his tail.

“Mrs. Bissette wouldn’t let me see her.”

“Of course not,” Henry replied as he urged the horses forward.

He smiled. “But she’s still going to marry me.”

“You’re the only one worried about that.”

* * * * **

Thankfully Elena didn't change her mind that warm afternoon. Three hours later, he held her hand on the lawn of the Grand, with hundreds of friends and family members sitting in rows behind them. Rays of sunlight rippled across the green lake in front of the gazebo, and a light breeze ruffled feathers and ribbons alike.

Their parents were in attendance. Sarah. Aunt Lottie. Richard. Nelson Reese. Even the Fredericks and Gruniers, though there was no sign of Edward Powell or his mistress. Elena didn't think the Randolphs would come since Silas and Jillian were marrying alongside them, but Mrs. Randolph sat beside her new daughter-in-law, Trudy. Parker was on her other side.

As the orchestra played, Chase pressed the key from the envelope into Elena's hand.

She wrapped her fingers around it, whispering to him. "What is it?"

"I thought you might want to look at the stars tonight."

"We don't need a key to get inside the lighthouse."

"No." He grinned. "But we need one to lock the door behind us."

The smile she gave him melted his core. He understood how Adam must have felt, looking at Eve for the first time. He wouldn't be able to take his eyes off Elena tonight, not even to look at the stars.

"How did you borrow it?"

"I didn't borrow it...I bought it."

Her eyebrows climbed. "You bought it?"

"Claude managed to get it for me—from Thomas Seymour's grandson."

When the music stopped, Chase vowed to love the woman before him in both sickness and in health, whether they were rich or poor. And she vowed the same. The wealth of the world could pass away, but he would still have Elena's love and the love of their Savior.

After Silas and Jillian repeated their vows, while the guests were still dancing and dining and toasting both brides and grooms, Henry whisked

Mr. and Mrs. Chester Darrington away. When Henry stopped the carriage, Chase asked him to retrieve them late in the morning.

For a moment, he thought Elena might refuse to climb the trail in her wedding gown, but she picked up her skirts and began to hike over the rocks. She slipped on the moss, but before she fell, he caught her arm.

She smiled at him. "I can't blame the wind this time."

"I'm here, Andy, to catch you."

Together they laughed in the breeze.

When they got to the door, he scooped her up and carried her over the threshold. She gasped when she saw the transformation inside. There were new lace curtains on the windows, a goose-down mattress on the bed with fine sheets, and a quilt. The mice were gone, along with the dust and dirt that had coated the old furniture and floors. Bouquets of flowers decorated the clean surfaces, their fragrance drifting through the rooms. There was a bottle of wine near the bed, fresh water in a basin, and a basket with food on the dresser.

"I wanted the lighthouse to be a place of joy again."

She wrapped herself in his arms, and he rested his cheek on her soft hair. "It's beautiful," she said.

"Our mothers worked together to help me clean it."

She stepped back, questioning him with her eyes. "Mama climbed up here?"

"I was going to ask for Jillian's help, but your mother insisted."

He took her hand, leading her to the steps. "Come upstairs."

The lamp room was filled with dozens of candles, but instead of lighting them, he and Elena stood by the window in each other's arms, watching the colors of the sunset radiate across the island—the work of the Master Artist. He wished he could stay here forever, watching the sky with Elena in his arms.

As night fell, she motioned to the candles. "Shall we light them?"

He patted his pockets and then laughed. "I forgot the matches."

She joined in his laughter, her fingers running up his lapel.

"Perhaps we won't need matches after all."

He kissed the top of her head and then lifted her lips to his. When he stepped back, the heat from her lips almost overwhelmed him, his throat gruff when he spoke again. "Did I mention that I love you?"

"I believe you did."

"And that I'll never stop loving you?"

She gently traced the cleft of his chin, and then she took off the simple locket from around her neck, handing it to him. "My heart is yours, Chase."

In the hours that followed, Chase loved Elena Bissette Darrington like he had no other woman, with the sweet passion of a husband. And in those late night hours, when darkness folded over the island, he entrusted to her as well all that he'd kept in his heart.

Author's Note

Due to a gale coming off Lake Michigan, my arrival on Mackinac Island wasn't much different than Elena's. Because of the autumn storm, it was a long journey from my home in Oregon to the island in Michigan—three plane rides, an unscheduled landing in Saginaw due to wind and fog, a 180-mile midnight bus ride to the Pellston airport, a 3 a.m. car ride with a new friend (thank you, Vickie!) to Mackinaw City, and finally a bumpy ferry ride across the Straits of Mackinac.

The sun finally emerged the next afternoon, the winds calmed, and I savored the beauty of this island in all its glory. I explored the island by carriage, enjoyed a five-course dinner at the elegant Grand Hotel, biked the eight miles around the island, and spent hours roaming through the quiet forest, the narrow lanes between the summer cottages, and the buildings in Fort Mackinac. Growing up in Ohio, I always wanted to visit this island where there are no cars, where I could freely walk and bike and explore. Researching and then writing this novel was truly a dream come true for me.

Standing on Mackinac Island during the late-night hours, gazing at the thousands of stars flickering in the sky, I reveled in the majesty of the Milky Way far from the village lights. I'd never seen the splendor of our galaxy—the masterpiece of our Creator—so clearly in my life.

While the current Mackinac lighthouse was built in 1895, this story was inspired in part by an intriguing note on my tourist map, a note about an old light station on the eastern bluffs. I mapped out my bike ride to find the site of this old station. I asked locals and a lighthouse expert about the location. I climbed the bluffs searching for it. No one seemed to know about the station, and even though I found some old buildings and ruins on the east side of the island, I never found the site for this old light.

When I returned to Mackinaw City, I toured a historic lighthouse that looks out into the Straits of Mackinac. And I wondered, what if…? What if there had once been an old lighthouse high above the eastern shore? And what if the lighthouse keeper disappeared?

The British took control of the island in 1812, saying it was a "fortress built by nature herself." Americans who remained on the island had to swear allegiance to King George III. Those who didn't change their allegiance were arrested and sent away, some of the men leaving behind their wives and children. The Americans returned in 1815 after the signing of the Treaty of Ghent.

While I try to remain as historically accurate as possible in my novels, I've taken license with a few facts in this story. The mansion for Michigan's governor wasn't built until 1902, initially as a private residence. Instead of Silas Hull, George Varney of Poughkeepsie, New York, filed for patent for his fishing rod joint in June 1894.

It wasn't until the 1920s that astronomers determined that Andromeda was actually a separate galaxy instead of a spiral nebula within the Milky Way. While the exact number is unknown, scientists now believe there are at least one hundred billion galaxies in our universe. For some incredible images of these galaxies, check out the Top 100 on www.spacetelescope.org.

And the Grand Hotel did hold a dog race in the late 1800s, the village dogs running amok. The hotel never held a dog race again.

As with all my novels, parts of this story reflect my own journey. In the midst of writing it, I joined eighteen other women for a life-changing week outside Port-au-Prince, Haiti. Each of us was asked to speak about one of God's many names, and I spoke about our mighty Creator. The beauty of God's creation was reflected in the eyes of my Haitian sisters, His Spirit clearly moving among them as they spoke of miracle after miracle. In the midst of incredible devastation, God continues to work through each of them and their families in miraculous ways.

Thank you to Diane Comer and Jodi Hughes for inspiring me to learn about the many names of God and love my sisters in Haiti. My American "sistas"—Jodi S., Ann, Caryn, Vicki, Beth, Orlena, Amanda, Liz, Whitney, Allie, Jenna, Kay, Penny, Julie, Mary Kay, and Kathleen. I loved studying God's names and loved even more sharing these names alongside you.

Writing a novel truly takes a village, and I'm grateful to every person who has journeyed with me in the writing of this book. A special thank-you to:

Rachel Meisel, for her enthusiasm for this story. I love working with you, Jason Rovenstine, Ellen Tarver, Connie Troyer, and the entire Summerside team.

Jim Beroth, my amazing dad and expert fisherman, who is not only a huge encouragement to me but who flew out to Oregon multiple times in the past year to play with his granddaughters while I wrote, had surgery, and spent a week in Haiti. We're pretty sure Pop Pop might have helped hang the moon!

Michele Heath, Leslie Gould, Nicole Miller, Dawn Shipman, and Kelly Chang, the best of friends and critique partners, for their insight and ideas. My stories would not be the same without your enthusiasm, direction, and honesty when something is just not right.

Bob Tagatz, the historian at the Grand Hotel, for sharing so many fascinating stories from the hotel's past. Mary McGuire Slevin, from Mackinac Island's Tourism Bureau, for checking my facts about Mackinac today. Anne St. Onge at the Mackinac Island Public Library, for her gracious assistance in locating a mound of resources. I've tried to get my facts straight, but I'm all too aware that I make mistakes. Any errors in this story are my responsibility.

Thank you to my earthly angels—Sarah Wilmot for helping me carry my load. Sandra Bishop for her friendship and insight. Vickie Texada and her father for giving this stranger a ride in the middle of the night.

My dear readers, for your e-mails and letters. Not only do I treasure every one of your notes, I love hearing your stories.

Jon, Karly, and Kiki—the delight of my life. God wove our four hearts together, and your love, prayers, and many hugs overflow my heart daily. I am so blessed....

Words can't express my gratefulness to the mighty Creator for His many gifts. As I linger under the night skies, savoring the work of the Master, I marvel at His infinite creativity both in the heavens and on this earth.

With joy, Melanie

About the Author

Melanie Dobson is the award-winning author of ten novels, five of them historical romances for Summerside Press, including *Love Finds You in Nazareth, Pennsylvania* and *Love Finds You in Amana, Iowa.* In 2010, Melanie won ACFW Carol Awards for *Love Finds You in Homestead, Iowa* and *The Silent Order.* Also in 2010, *Love Finds You in Liberty, Indiana* was chosen as the Best Book of Indiana (fiction). Melanie's next historical romance, *Where the Trail Ends,* will be published in October of 2012.

Melanie is the former corporate publicity manager at Focus on the Family, and she worked in public relations for fifteen years before she began writing fiction full-time. Born and raised in the Midwest, she has lived all over America and now resides with her husband and two daughters near Portland, Oregon.

WWW.MELANIEDOBSON.COM

**Want a peek into local American life—past and present?
The *Love Finds You*™ series published by Summerside Press
features real towns and combines travel, romance,
and faith in one irresistible package!**

The novels in the series—uniquely titled after American towns with romantic or intriguing names—inspire romance and fun. Each fictional story draws on the compelling history or the unique character of a real place. Stories center on romances kindled in small towns, old loves lost and found again on the high plains, and new loves discovered at exciting vacation getaways. Summerside Press plans to publish at least one novel set in each of the fifty states. Be sure to catch them all!

Now Available

Love Finds You in Miracle, Kentucky
by Andrea Boeshaar
ISBN: 978-1-934770-37-5

Love Finds You in Snowball, Arkansas
by Sandra D. Bricker
ISBN: 978-1-934770-45-0

Love Finds You in Romeo, Colorado
by Gwen Ford Faulkenberry
ISBN: 978-1-934770-46-7

Love Finds You in Valentine, Nebraska
by Irene Brand
ISBN: 978-1-934770-38-2

Love Finds You in Humble, Texas
by Anita Higman
ISBN: 978-1-934770-61-0

Love Finds You in Last Chance, California
by Miralee Ferrell
ISBN: 978-1-934770-39-9

Love Finds You in Maiden, North Carolina
by Tamela Hancock Murray
ISBN: 978-1-934770-65-8

Love Finds You in Paradise, Pennsylvania
by Loree Lough
ISBN: 978-1-934770-66-5

Love Finds You in Treasure Island, Florida
by Debby Mayne
ISBN: 978-1-934770-80-1

Love Finds You in Liberty, Indiana
by Melanie Dobson
ISBN: 978-1-934770-74-0

Love Finds You in Revenge, Ohio
by Lisa Harris
ISBN: 978-1-934770-81-8

Love Finds You in Poetry, Texas
by Janice Hanna
ISBN: 978-1-935416-16-6

Love Finds You in Sisters, Oregon
by Melody Carlson
ISBN: 978-1-935416-18-0

Love Finds You in Charm, Ohio
by Annalisa Daughety
ISBN: 978-1-935416-17-3

Love Finds You in Bethlehem, New Hampshire
by Lauralee Bliss
ISBN: 978-1-935416-20-3

Love Finds You in North Pole, Alaska
by Loree Lough
ISBN: 978-1-935416-19-7

Love Finds You in Holiday, Florida
by Sandra D. Bricker
ISBN: 978-1-935416-25-8

Love Finds You in Lonesome Prairie, Montana
by Tricia Goyer and Ocieanna Fleiss
ISBN: 978-1-935416-29-6

Love Finds You in Bridal Veil, Oregon
by Miralee Ferrell
ISBN: 978-1-935416-63-0

Love Finds You in Hershey, Pennsylvania
by Cerella D. Sechrist
ISBN: 978-1-935416-64-7

Love Finds You in Homestead, Iowa
by Melanie Dobson
ISBN: 978-1-935416-66-1

Love Finds You in Pendleton, Oregon
by Melody Carlson
ISBN: 978-1-935416-84-5

Love Finds You in Golden, New Mexico
by Lena Nelson Dooley
ISBN: 978-1-935416-74-6

Love Finds You in Lahaina, Hawaii
by Bodie Thoene
ISBN: 978-1-935416-78-4

Love Finds You in Victory Heights, Washington
by Tricia Goyer and Ocieanna Fleiss
ISBN: 978-1-60936-000-9

Love Finds You in Calico, California
by Elizabeth Ludwig
ISBN: 978-1-60936-001-6

Love Finds You in Sugarcreek, Ohio
by Serena B. Miller
ISBN: 978-1-60936-002-3

Love Finds You in Deadwood, South Dakota
by Tracey Cross
ISBN: 978-1-60936-003-0

Love Finds You in Silver City, Idaho
by Janelle Mowery
ISBN: 978-1-60936-005-4

Love Finds You in Carmel-by-the-Sea, California
by Sandra D. Bricker
ISBN: 978-1-60936-027-6

Love Finds You Under the Mistletoe
by Irene Brand and Anita Higman
ISBN: 978-1-60936-004-7

Love Finds You in Hope, Kansas
by Pamela Griffin
ISBN: 978-1-60936-007-8

Love Finds You in Sun Valley, Idaho
by Angela Ruth
ISBN: 978-1-60936-008-5

Love Finds You in Camelot, Tennessee
by Janice Hanna
ISBN: 978-1-935416-65-4

Love Finds You in Tombstone, Arizona
by Miralee Ferrell
ISBN: 978-1-60936-104-4

Love Finds You in
Martha's Vineyard, Massachusetts
by Melody Carlson
ISBN: 978-1-60936-110-5

Love Finds You in
Prince Edward Island, Canada
by Susan Page Davis
ISBN: 978-1-60936-109-9

Love Finds You in Groom, Texas
by Janice Hanna
ISBN: 978-1-60936-006-1

Love Finds You in Amana, Iowa
by Melanie Dobson
ISBN: 978-1-60936-135-8

Love Finds You in
Lancaster County, Pennsylvania
by Annalisa Daughety
ISBN: 97-8-160936-212-6

Love Finds You in Branson, Missouri
by Gwen Ford Faulkenberry
ISBN: 978-1-60936-191-4

Love Finds You in Sundance, Wyoming
by Miralee Ferrell
ISBN: 978-1-60936-277-5

Love Finds You on Christmas Morning
by Debby Mayne and Trish Perry
ISBN: 978-1-60936-193-8

Love Finds You in Sunset Beach, Hawaii
by Robin Jones Gunn
ISBN: 978-1-60936-028-3

Love Finds You in
Nazareth, Pennsylvania
by Melanie Dobson
ISBN: 97-8-160936-194-5

Love Finds You in Annapolis, Maryland
by Roseanna M. White
ISBN: 978-1-60936-313-0

Love Finds You in
Folly Beach, South Carolina
by Loree Lough
ISBN: 97-8-160936-214-0

Love Finds You in
New Orleans, Louisiana
by Christa Allan
ISBN: 978-1-60936-591-2

Love Finds You in
Wildrose, North Dakota
by Tracey Bateman
ISBN: 978-1-60936-592-9

Love Finds You in Daisy, Oklahoma
by Janice Hanna
ISBN: 978-1-60936-593-6

Love Finds You in Sunflower, Kansas
by Pamela Tracy
ISBN: 978-1-60936-594-3

Coming Soon

Love Finds You
at Home for Christmas
by Annalisa Daughety and
Gwen Ford Faulkenberry
ISBN: 978-1-60936-687-2

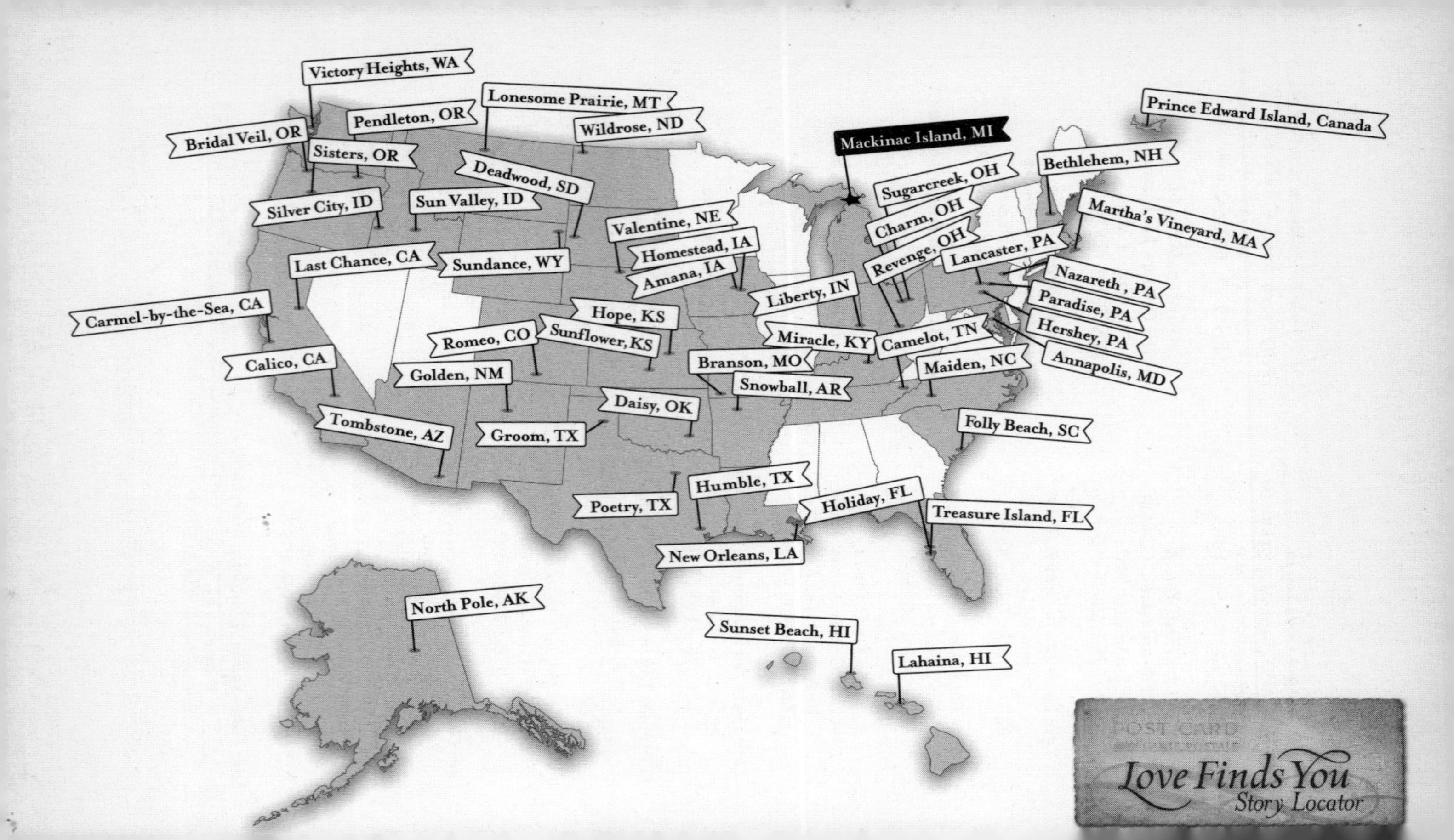
Victory Heights, WA
Lonesome Prairie, MT
Pendleton, OR
Wildrose, ND
Bridal Veil, OR
Sisters, OR
Deadwood, SD
Silver City, ID
Sun Valley, ID
Valentine, NE
Homestead, IA
Last Chance, CA
Sundance, WY
Amana, IA
Carmel-by-the-Sea, CA
Hope, KS
Romeo, CO
Sunflower, KS
Calico, CA
Golden, NM
Daisy, OK
Tombstone, AZ
Groom, TX
Poetry, TX
Humble, TX
New Orleans, LA
North Pole, AK
Sunset Beach, HI
Lahaina, HI
Prince Edward Island, Canada
Mackinac Island, MI
Bethlehem, NH
Sugarcreek, OH
Charm, OH
Martha's Vineyard, MA
Revenge, OH
Lancaster, PA
Liberty, IN
Nazareth , PA
Paradise, PA
Miracle, KY
Camelot, TN
Hershey, PA
Branson, MO
Maiden, NC
Annapolis, MD
Snowball, AR
Folly Beach, SC
Holiday, FL
Treasure Island, FL
POST CARD
Love Finds You
Story Locator